PRAISE FOR MADDIE DAWSON

SNAP OUT OF IT

"*Snap Out of It* is a laugh-out-lo[ ]th characters that are drawn with [ ]to human nature. My heart is full, [ ]ely loved this book."

—Annabel Monaghan, author of *Nora Goes Off Script*

"Maddie Dawson has a rare ability to craft quirky, offbeat characters that are also utterly believable. Dawson is at the top of her game with *Snap Out of It*, a magical, wise, tender, joyously relatable read. From the moment Billie the Heartbreak Bunny stepped onto the page, I felt as though I'd met a soulmate. There is only a handful of authors whose name on the cover elicits from me an automatic buy; Maddie Dawson is one of them."

—Marie Bostwick, *New York Times* and *USA Today* bestselling author of *The Restoration of Celia Fairchild*

"Maddie Dawson's *Snap Out of It* is as delightful as it is original. Protagonist Billie Slate is on a one-woman mission to rid the world of unnecessary heartbreak—while dressed in a bunny suit. The consequences are both messy and magical. Dawson has given us an utterly charming story that manages to be both light and profound; it is a clear-eyed and sometimes laugh-out-loud look at the complications of grown-up love with an important lesson at its heart: healing is always possible when we keep our heart open to the possibilities of love."

—Barbara Davis, bestselling author of *The Keeper of Happy Endings*

"*Snap Out of It* is a wise, funny, heartfelt novel filled with complex relationships and whimsical surprises—a book that leaves you better than it found you. Love it."

—Kerry Anne King, bestselling author of *Improbably Yours*

THE MAGIC OF FOUND OBJECTS

"Readers may have the impression that they're enjoying a typical rom-com, but unexpected decisions open the way for a welcome twist we didn't even know we needed."

—*Booklist*

"*The Magic of Found Objects* is wonderful fun! Maddie Dawson is such an engaging and charming writer."

—Robyn Carr, #1 *New York Times* bestselling author

"With humor, tenderness, and some of the strongest female characters to ever grace a page, Maddie Dawson delivers with *The Magic of Found Objects*."

—Karen Hawkins, *New York Times* and *USA Today* bestselling author of *The Book Charmer*

"Written with loads of humor and heart, *The Magic of Found Objects* is a delightful, feel-good tale of friendship and marriage, motherhood and sacrifice, disillusionment and hope. Dawson takes the reader on a quest for the perfect life partner. Is it the kind, comfortable friend right in front of you, or does the universe have something more exciting in store? Maddie Dawson at her finest!"

—Amy Poeppel, author of *Musical Chairs*

"Maddie Dawson has hit another one out of the park with this charming tale about what happens when your head tells you to settle but your heart keeps whispering something else. Funny, poignant, and beautifully clear-eyed, *The Magic of Found Objects* is a delightfully grown-up coming-of-age story, peopled with quirky, real-life characters who remind us that sometimes before we can open the door to the future, we must first open our hearts to the past."

—Barbara Davis, bestselling author of *The Last of the Moon Girls*

A HAPPY CATASTROPHE

"Dawson has created a truly quirky story, filled with a little bit of magic (think unicorn glitter and sparkles) and a lot of love . . . An optimistic, feel-good story that celebrates love, community, goodness, and the creation of family, however it might appear."

—*Kirkus Reviews*

"Alive with action, compelling and evolving characters, and screwball comedy, Dawson's latest will appeal to readers looking for a story that is both pleasurable and substantial. Personal growth is achieved by overcoming obstacles, and the ending is honest and satisfying."

—*Booklist*

"An inherently engaging and entertaining novel from cover to cover, *A Happy Catastrophe* by Maddie Dawson will prove to be an immediate and enduringly popular addition to community library Contemporary General Fiction collections."

—*Midwest Book Review*

MATCHMAKING FOR BEGINNERS

"A charming read . . . For fans of Liane Moriarty's *What Alice Forgot* or Aimee Bender's *The Particular Sadness of Lemon Cake*."

—*Library Journal*

"A delightful, light-as-air romance that successfully straddles the line between sweet and smart without ever being silly . . . The novel is simply captivating from beginning to end."

—Associated Press

"*Matchmaking for Beginners* is lovely from the inside out."

—HelloGiggles

"Infused with the kind of magic so frequently lost as we become adults, this one-of-a-kind novel pushes the boundaries of coincidence and connection by asking us to believe in fate and, possibly, magic once again. The characters jump off the page with their quirky habits and capture hearts with their meaningful development and interactions, leading to moments that will bring readers to tears one minute and [have] them laughing out loud the next."

—RT Book Reviews (Top Rated)

Let's Pretend
This Will
Work

ALSO BY MADDIE DAWSON

Let's Pretend This Will Work

A NOVEL

MADDIE DAWSON

LAKE UNION
PUBLISHING

Text copyright © 2024 by Maddie Dawson
All rights reserved.

No part of this book may be reproduced, or stored in a retrieval system, or transmitted in any form or by any means, electronic, mechanical, photocopying, recording, or otherwise, without express written permission of the publisher.

Published by Lake Union Publishing, Seattle

www.apub.com

Amazon, the Amazon logo, and Lake Union Publishing are trademarks of Amazon.com, Inc., or its affiliates.

ISBN-13: 9781662515484 (paperback)
ISBN-13: 9781662515477 (digital)

Cover design by Alicia Tatone
Cover image: © CSA Images, © AskinTulayOver / Getty; © Eladora / Shutterstock

Printed in the United States of America

To Jim, for all the light and love

CHAPTER ONE

March 19, 1982

Ren and I are standing in the back of the darkened auditorium watching our Piedmont Academy students rehearse *Guys and Dolls*—they're right then mangling the number about betting on horses—when he leans over and whispers the words I didn't ever expect to hear. From any- one in the whole wide world, if I'm being honest—and definitely not from a guy who makes Robert Redford look like he should try harder.

"Mimi," he whispers, "what do you say we make this crazy thing between us official . . . and get ourselves married? You want to?"

There's a silence, during which I believe it's technically my turn to say something. I look up into his tanned, gorgeous face, feel myself tip over into his melting liquid brown eyes, and when I open my mouth to speak, what comes out is a high-pitched "Yeah, right."

Not my finest moment, really, but I haven't had much practice with marriage proposals, you see, especially ones that come sailing in on an ordinary Friday afternoon without warning. It doesn't help that I almost can't look directly at Ren for more than five seconds; it's like looking into the sun. Besides all that, he's the head drama teacher at Piedmont, and I'm just a newly hired English teacher—and yes, okay, so we've been ducking into supply closets for make-out sessions for a few months now, and I've met his friends, and I see him every weekend for fabulous sex—but I'm certainly not at his level, if you know what I mean. If he's a ten, I'm probably a seven on my very best day, and even then only if my straight iron doesn't cause a fuse to blow.

"No, I mean it," he says. "I want us to get married. Why are you so surprised?"

My mouth has gone dry. "I-I guess I've been under the impression that we're just doing this for fun." *And maybe I'm surprised because I'm thirty-two years old and not one man in the history of my dating life have I so much as introduced as a boyfriend without him correcting me by saying something along the lines of "Well, actually, we're just hanging out with each other every now and then."*

"That's how you know it's real, you crazy girl. Because it's fun. Why not make *fun* official? Besides, I'm in love with you," he says, and he takes my hand. There's a long pause, and then he whispers in a voice gruff with feeling, "I'm coming over tonight, and I'm going to get down on one knee and ask you to marry me with a proper proposal, and I'm bringing two dozen roses and my mother's engagement ring. If that's all right with you."

"Okay," I barely manage to say. My heart has started galloping in my chest, and defibrillators may be required if this goes on much longer.

Fortunately, something happens onstage just then, and he has to excuse himself. One of the senior girls—Samantha Donovan, who is playing the part of the missionary Sarah Brown—has suddenly dissolved into tears, and Ren murmurs to me, *"Awww,* my goodness. We'll continue this later," and then he strides quickly up the aisle, nimbly leaps up onto the stage, and goes over to her and puts his head next to hers, listening.

The other actors mill around, looking morose. We all know the problem. Samantha's mother died two months ago, and she's having a tough time. A lot of directors probably would have replaced her under those circumstances, but not Ren. He's too caring for that. Not only did he encourage her to stay in the role, but he comforts her when she's having a hard time, like now. This is why he's the entire school's favorite human. As my teacher friend Ruth Benson says, you rarely find such kindness and gorgeousness in one package.

A few minutes later, Samantha is back to saying her lines with sparkle and confidence, and he slips in next to me once again and holds my hand in the darkness. I can feel him smiling.

"So is there a father or someone whose permission I need to ask for your hand in marriage?" he whispers. He runs his fingers through his dark brown hair and squints those gorgeous eyes at me.

"It's 1982," I say. "If you asked anyone for permission to marry me, I'd have to give up my subscription to *Ms. Magazine.*"

"That's what *I* thought," he says. "Glad to hear I'm marrying me a feminist."

"You sure are," I say. He nuzzles my neck, and a few of the sound-crew boys, standing nearby, swivel their heads over to us. I can feel them smiling knowingly and elbowing each other in the ribs. *Mr. Yardley and Ms. Perkins are about to go at it again.*

Sure enough, Ren pulls me into the A/V closet that's conveniently located nearby. We kiss and kiss until we hear the cue that means that the scene is over, and then we readjust our clothing and wipe the grins off our faces and go out and turn into teachers again.

My knees are actually wobbling.

$\sim$

Perhaps you, like me, are wondering how we got here.

It wasn't anything I did, believe me. My psychic says it was some kind of magic that I just happened to walk into.

And yes, I do have a psychic. I see her once a week for a spiritual tune-up, and I recommend everyone get themselves one, especially if you're open to being encouraged all the time and hearing about how you're made of stardust. My psychic is called La Starla, and she's a wiry-haired grandmother type who lives in Brooklyn, the most down-to-earth person you could imagine except for the fact that she has relationships with spirit guides and knows how to read star charts. She also gives me recipes for beef brisket and points out when my hair needs cutting. But most importantly, she tells me that I'm in line for a big, happy life that's going to zigzag in directions I never would have dreamed of, as long as I stay open to it. Love, she says, is my natural state—and I am going to be fabulous and creative, and love will bloom all around me.

Really. Who doesn't need that said to them once a week?

As for how Ren happened, La Starla says that the universe is flowing me good luck through a skirt I bought for two dollars at a thrift shop a year or so ago. This love-inspiring skirt is not what you're thinking: it's the least sexy garment I've ever seen, something an ordinary housewife in the 1950s might have worn to hang out her washing—knee-length, light blue cotton, with some limp little ruffles trimmed with pastel-colored ribbons. Believe me, you wouldn't look twice at this skirt. When I wore it to one of my appointments with La Starla, her eyes widened and she came over and touched the hem of it with reverence, as though I'd shown up with the Holy Grail of clothing. I was stunned. I think I actually laughed when she told me the skirt had powers. "This old thing?" I said.

But, I have to admit, it has proven itself over time.

As it turns out, I was wearing it the day I got the job at Piedmont Academy, which is a private school in Manhattan that prides itself on the fact that it is the alma mater of three US presidents, sixteen senators, and untold numbers of judges and corporate executives. I came across Piedmont's ad for an English teacher just by chance, on the subway, and somehow I got hired right on the spot, even though all I'd ever done was work as a sub in a junior high. (The skirt, obviously.)

I was also wearing it when I got the lease on my apartment in the West Village, being chosen over several richer potential tenants. This skirt even runs interference for me when I'm in line at a bodega and manage to score the last poppy seed bagel, even though there are five people in front of me who have loudly contemplated buying it for themselves.

And . . . I was wearing it on the day last September when, two weeks after being hired, I locked myself out of my classroom, and Ren came along and helped me break in with a credit card. He whispered that one should never underestimate how handy some basic criminal skills are in this day and age. He advised that I look into crime as a possible auxiliary career, as he had.

He kept telling crime jokes, and we were both laughing by the time we got into my classroom. Then he hung around for quite a while, beaming his famous crinkly smile in my direction, walking around and admiring my bulletin boards in a way that made it clear we weren't talking about bulletin boards at all. And then pretty soon we were lounging against the desks and he was telling me funny stories about his disasters in teaching. He mentioned how hard it is to get high school kids to appreciate Shakespeare, and that's when I might have said, "I just read them all the obsessive parts between Hamlet and Ophelia and in *Romeo and Juliet*, and then we talked about obsessive love for the whole rest of the period. I don't know. They seemed to love it."

He nearly fell off the desk. "*What?* Good God, woman! Am I going to need to defend you when the Piedmont Morality Police show up and toss you out into the street?" he said. "You do know that we have *trustees* here who have never heard of human emotion and would be shocked if they found out mere *children* know about it."

I lifted up my chin and said, "Ha! I have news for you. The students had *quite* a few interesting stories about things they'd done in the name of obsession. Some of their stories would have curled the trustees' hair."

Well. His dreamy brown eyes looked directly into the soul of me, and then he said in a low, smoldering voice, "You know something? I think you're going to be the great love of my life."

Bam.

By the time he suggested dinner, I was a goner. We wandered over to a nearby diner, where we laughed and effortlessly flirted, and I was having the time of my life, blooming like a little flower in the hothouse lights, like I was someone else entirely.

And then the manager came over and asked Ren about his kids. Kids?

That's when I might have noticed the charming little glints of silver right around his temples, and that he had actual smile lines around his eyes. All of which only made him look more distinguished and attractive. He was a man who had experience.

He ducked his head charmingly and smiled and told me he was forty-five and that he'd been divorced for four years, and he had two daughters, Jenna and Parker, who were twenty-two and nineteen and were always on the verge of moving into their own places but so far still lived with him.

In fact, he said, glancing at his watch, he needed to stop at the market before he went home. So after dinner, we went into a bodega and bought milk, bread, and oatmeal for their breakfast the next day. Then, on our way to the subway, he asked if I minded if he stopped to call home. I listened as he asked Parker how her freshman comp exam had gone. He grinned at me while he talked. Then he asked a question about Jenna's boyfriend—had he gotten his promotion? Yes? Ah, that was great news. He grabbed my hand and held it in the air, sharing the triumph.

"I don't like to show up at home not knowing the news," he said to me when he hung up. "I need to prepare either my Consoling Father face or my Thrilled Father face."

He walked me to my subway and said that he'd see me at school the next morning.

There was no kiss, no melting gaze, no lascivious look. He was suddenly just a colleague of mine, a divorced father wise in the ways of the world of groceries and the art of consoling daughters—and he'd welcomed me to the school and taken me to dinner, and probably didn't even remember saying that bit about me being the great love of his life.

All hyperbole. He was clearly one of those older guys who's nice to everybody.

I yelled at myself all the way home on the subway for thinking that he was even interested in me for one tiny second. My reflection in the smeared subway window told the whole story: I was just a girl with unruly brown hair, hazel eyes, and a routine figure, looking like some kind of naive, wide-eyed little chicken, disheveled and discombobulated and alone. Certainly I was nobody's idea of a great love.

⌒୭

But then four days later, as we walked down the hallway together, he took my hand and kissed it and gazed into my eyes, and within minutes we found ourselves ducking into a supply closet off the school's main hallway and ripping at each other's clothing like we'd just heard the end of the world was coming and it was up to us to populate the planet before we got incinerated.

Coincidentally, that was the day I also learned how loud it is when five boxes of wide-ruled filler paper, a carton of Sharpie highlighters, and four cases of manila folders all crash to the floor at once.

As luck would have it, the janitor happened to be walking by, and, hearing some untoward noises, he threw open the closet door and discovered us in a profound state of *dishabille*. Within thirty minutes we had become a minor scandal. Not that what we did was illegal or anything—Ren is not my supervisor, and neither of us is married— but somehow the grapevine considered the evidence and decided that *I* was a lawless temptress who had somehow snagged the only eligible man in the whole school and put him under some kind of spell.

Within thirty-six hours, I went from being seen as a mostly unre- markable woman in her early thirties to a femme fatale. It was actually kind of wonderful. I carried myself differently. The other teachers at Piedmont took to smiling at me in the hall and inviting me to their happy hours. Cabbies stopped for me. Men whistled at me on the street. And according to La Starla, I had tapped into my wealth of magic, and I was headed for a big, beautiful life designed just for me.

I couldn't resist calling my mother to tell her that the man-catching example she had set for me finally paid off and also it seemed that I might have developed at least one feminine wile that I had put to good use.

The call didn't go all that well. My mother, who likes to refer to herself as a "marriage maven" since she has tied the knot *five* times now, said I should never encourage a man who is more than five years older than me. I believe her exact words were "In no time at all, you'll be spoon-feeding him Yankee bean soup out of a strainer while your youth drains away!" And when I mentioned that he had daughters, she said I should get out while I still could. It would only lead to misery, trying to be a stepmom to people of the female persuasion.

So I called my best friend, Eleanor, my old college roommate, who is happily married to a very nice man with perfect posture and a good job in the banking industry. She said, "Mimi, try to remember. This is *your mother* talking. Nothing she says about you has ever been remotely accurate. You need to just have fun."

Fun, she said. Just have fun while it lasts.

No one—especially me—seemed to think it would last very long.

As soon as the rehearsal is over, I do the only rational thing: I go straight to a phone booth and call up Eleanor to tell her about the engagement and for another pep talk.

She's at work at the United American Equitable Life Insurance Company, so we have to yell to be heard above the stampede of IBM Selectrics in the background. We both know that Eleanor technically doesn't have to work because her husband Ira makes a ton of money, but one of her core beliefs, after reading Betty Friedan and Gloria Steinem, is that women shouldn't depend on a man's income even if it means that they have to type all day and come home and cook and do housework all night.

As soon as I tell her Ren's coming over to propose, she makes a high-pitched screeching noise. "Oh my God! *Ohhh!* My! God! I was praying this was going to happen!"

This is true. She's a huge Ren fan. She and Ira came to New York just after Christmas, and Ren and I took them out for dinner. I was a nervous wreck the whole time, worried that they wouldn't like each other, but Eleanor and Ira thought he was great. I think they were shocked that I was going out with a real grown-up, and a charming one at that. Eleanor said he reminded her of Tom Selleck, only possibly more handsome. And, to my surprise, he seemed to find them interesting, too.

Anyway, after she stops shrieking with joy, she gets right to the point. "So what are you going to wear?"

"I was thinking something in, ah, white lace. Perhaps with a veil. You might know the sort of thing I mean."

She sighs. "I mean, what are you going to wear for the *proposal*, you nutcase?"

I adjust the phone to my other ear while I think about this. It seems there is no end to the things I don't know about adult life. "*Ummm*, I kind of thought we'd be in bed when it happens."

"For when he answers the door, Mimi. You want to look amazing for that, don't you?"

"Do I? I think I'll just wear what I'm wearing now. My lucky skirt. Which, *just so you know*, Ms. Skeptic, I was wearing today when he told me he was going to propose, so I'd say this skirt has now proven beyond a shadow of a doubt that it's got some serious magic to it."

"Uh-huh," she says. Eleanor is a practical person who doesn't believe in lucky clothing, magic, coincidences, signs from the universe, or psychics. She says it's cute the way I rely on New Age theories instead of going to therapy like normal people do when they're trying to get over their childhood.

"So what do his kids think about you and him getting married?" She wants to know.

"I have no idea if they even know yet," I say after a long moment, during which my heart starts its slow slide down into my stomach.

"Oh, Mimi," she says. "Oh, *honey.*"

"They're *old*, Eleanor. They're not going to be living with us. They'll be fine."

It occurs to me right then that they will not be fine.

She's silent for two beats. Then she says in her enthusiastic, camp-counselor voice that she uses with me when I'm about to fall into a hole: "Of course! Anyway, you're charming, and you'll win them over even if they don't already love you."

She knows they don't already love me. *Everybody* knows they don't already love me, even Ren, who claims that they *will someday* adore me once they know how important I am to him. He is unwaveringly optimistic on this point. The times that I've been along on some neutral family outing with them, showing up as merely their dad's colleague from school, they have been cool and dismissive toward me, and I'm ashamed to say that I tried too hard and was cut down with icy, stealthy precision, as I deserved to be. Trying too hard never works with young people. They need to be treated like hostile, dangerous jungle cats who will slash you if you so much as make uninvited eye contact.

"The point is that your whole life is just about to get so much better," Eleanor chirps. "And now that you're going to be a wife, you probably won't need your psychic anymore. What does Ren think about *her*, by the way?"

"Well . . . he doesn't really know about her," I say.

"Oh, Mimi, for heaven's sake." She actually roars with laughter. "You never told him you see a *psychic*?"

"It hasn't come up yet," I say.

"You're scared he won't love you anymore if he finds this out, aren't you?"

"Well, I wasn't until you said that." (Full disclosure: I have been terrified of it since the day I fell for him.)

"Listen, Mimi," she says. "This is very, very important. Don't get married to someone who requires that you act quote, unquote, 'normal' in order to please him, okay? You don't have to be anybody's idea of normal. You're wonderful and you're an *acquired taste*, not just some generic woman who might be a match for just any old random guy. Remember that, and let him see the whole wonderful you. Psychic appointments and all. Just do it before the wedding, rather than after, maybe."

Eleanor doesn't have any oddities. She goes about the world intact, gravitating to the center of things in the most carefree way possible. While I—well, I might have arrived on earth already a little broken, a little overemotional, and without the wiring necessary to make small talk. Eleanor was probably elected the Baby Most Likely to Succeed right there in the hospital nursery.

Thank goodness something happens just then on her end of the phone that means she has to hang up. I hear a bunch of beeping noises and commotion behind her, and she says, "Gotta run. The fire alarm went off again. Third time this week, but we have to evacuate. I'll call you tomorrow!"

And she's gone.

Which is a good thing, because Eleanor, I'm sorry to say, perhaps doesn't remember how, when you're in the first flush of love, you are 90 percent of the time having sex, and the other 10 percent you're thinking about having sex, and it's hard to work in a conversation about your belief in psychic phenomena when you're busy being ravished. At some point should I have said, "Could you kindly stop licking my earlobe for a moment so we can share whether or not we believe that there are people who can predict the future?"

No.

Lots of other things haven't come up either. Like I've never mentioned the last four of my mother's marriages, my colorful history of 4,378,542 first dates, my tendency to hide in my apartment taking three-hour baths on Saturday afternoons (with books and candles stacked on the side of the tub), my alarming lack of cooking skills, or the fact that I'm phobic about spiders, thunderstorms, all rodents, snakes, bank statements, little kids, and being the center of attention.

I think my best plan is to hope he's already aware of these things through osmosis, and then, if I have to, roll out details slowly, over time.

Because I've just realized something huge: I can't blow my chance to marry this wonderful, kind, lovely, hot, attentive, handsome man who, for reasons I'll never understand, happened to fall in love with me.

He makes me feel special in a way no one else ever has.

Let's face it: for the very first time in my life, I'm besotted.

I call my mom to tell her about the proposal, which is strictly a formality. These days we are on a postcard-only basis, mostly consisting of her sending random messages to me from her various ports of call. She's perpetually on cruises, which is how she's met many of her husbands. The later ones, at least—not the uncaring ones that supposedly were going to help her raise me but who threw up their hands and disappeared instead.

Anyway, she's hard to reach, and I'm not sure she'll be all that happy about my news to begin with. But I still think a mom should be informed when her offspring has just received a preproposal, so I dial her number. Of course I get her answering machine.

"Darlings!" she trills to the public. "I'm away on a cruise—you can leave a message if you want, but better to maybe drink a martini and toast to me! I'll be at the captain's table, and I'll call you back when I'm a landlubber again!"

I think this is her standard message, even if she's between trips. But now I remember that I did get a postcard from her just last week, from Miami.

In it, she wrote:

Mimi! Are you over 30? Oh my God, you are, aren't you, darling?!?! Just thought of something I meant to tell you long ago: Preparation H is the surefire cure for bags under your eyes! This is a beauty tip from your sweet old ma. I'll call you soon! Headed for Bermuda! Kisses and hugs!

CHAPTER TWO

As soon as I hang up the phone, I head out to the market to buy food for tonight. I know only one dish that I can make when there's not much time. A friend gave me the recipe. She said all you have to do is smash a bunch of tomatoes and garlic and white beans together, throw them in a frying pan with some olive oil, and wait while they coalesce into something otherworldly and delicious. Then you put some globs of cheese on it and pour the whole thing on top of pasta, and *voilà*, you might as well be Julia Child.

After I get everything put together in the pan, I leave messages for La Starla ("He's asking me to marry him tonight—everything you said about my life is coming true!") and Ruth Benson ("Ren is proposing tonight—oh my God, oh my God, oh my God!").

So there I am, cooking and dancing to "You Can't Hurry Love" by the Supremes and laughing at the great irony of this song. Apparently you *can* hurry love! And when you do, it leads to getting married and moving out of your teeny-tiny apartment and moving into larger quarters with the person you adore.

Not that I don't love my apartment, but I live in a space so small that I actually have to store my vacuum cleaner next to the toilet. I stand on a chair to access my clothing, which is stacked on a piece of plywood, loft-style, above the mattress. Worst of all, I must cook on a hot plate, which is a mere eight inches from the front door, and my refrigerator is a dorm-sized contraption that's jammed in right next to the hot plate.

I store my coffee mug, three plates, four forks, four spoons, and four knives on top of it.

Ren, however, being a grown-up, lives in a people-sized apartment on the Upper West Side, which has a legitimate kitchen, three bedrooms, closets galore, high ceilings, an actual *hallway*, a balcony, and a doorman. That is where I will turn into the person I want to be: the kind of woman who can have more than two people over at a time, with everybody permitted to sit down on something furniture-y rather than each other's laps. I'll make more of an effort to appear intelligent and classy with his friends, some of whom I've met when we've attended their avant-garde plays, the kind of shows that Ren says are very, very important to his future career as a playwright, but that often only involve a person sitting in a chair in a black box pontificating about ennui. Ren agrees with me that these are often boring as hell, but nevertheless, we always have to lead the standing ovations and clap harder than we ever have in our lives. I've felt a little bit like the Awkward Younger Girlfriend, as if I'm a child trying to make conversation with the adults who clearly aren't interested in me.

But now all that will change. I'll be Ren's Wife, and we'll have his friends over for dinner, and I'll learn to cook something besides smashed tomatoes and white beans or that brisket recipe I got from La Starla. It will be so nice to spread out, to have a dining room with windows overlooking the park, plates that match, beige carpeting that's deep enough to hide your baby toes in. And by the time we marry, I definitely think that his daughters won't be living with him anymore. He always says they're just about to move out. I wonder if he's going to want to have his ex-wife, Judith, come for a visit, and if that would be the weirdest thing ever. But I'm getting ahead of myself.

I actually don't know all that much about his former marriage, because he doesn't talk much about Judith, which I respect—so many men I've dated just go on nonstop about their exes. You'd think it was their favorite topic. I've had to glean most of my information about Ren's twenty-year marriage from the other teachers, primarily Ruth

Benson, who also knew Judith from long ago when Ren first came to Piedmont.

According to Ruth's account of things, Ren and Judith are polar opposites in nearly every way. They're both affable, lovely people, she said, but how they ever got together just proves that opposites attract and then go on to hate each other. Judith is capable, organized, brilliant, and knows her way around corporate boardrooms; she can fire off an interoffice memo that mobilizes a staff of thousands. She could run the world.

As for Ren—well, everyone knows he's a dreamy, impractical type who writes plays and poems, and couldn't run the world unless what the world needed was a sonnet—scrawled impulsively on the back of an envelope and then lost in his glove compartment. Ren said once that he learned everything he knew about life from lolling about in hammocks reading novels at his childhood summer home in the Hamptons, and Judith, who never found a novel she was patient enough to finish, learned everything she knew about life from spreadsheets. Ruth said that they fought all the time and yet they were both committed to their two girls—and so their split, when it happened, was one of those modern, confusing, we're-not-really-breaking-up-we-just-don't-live-together kinds of things, the type of muddled mess that people mistakenly think is easier for kids to handle.

And it was all due to Piedmont. Ren had been unhappily teaching English at an inner-city school in New Haven and writing plays on the side when he was invited to teach drama at Piedmont. It had been his dream to teach at an independent school that valued the arts and had a faculty committed to helping each and every student achieve excellence. It didn't hurt that Piedmont was in Manhattan, where plays are actually produced, and that, in addition, the school represented everything he aspired to. It has an upper and lower school, a squash team, several national debating team championships, and a theater program—but what made it an offer he really couldn't refuse was that it included scholarships for his kids. Jenna was in fifth grade, and little Parker in second. How could he say no to this great opportunity for them?

Judith, however, was perfectly capable of saying no. She had a big job as an administrator at Yale New Haven Hospital, and she was furious when he accepted a job in New York, so furious that she refused to go along with the rest of the family. At first, according to Ruth, she said she was staying behind to finish up some work projects she was committed to, and that she'd join him and the children when everything was settled. But then, when months passed, she changed her mind and said she was making a feminist point for their daughters—that she wanted to make it clear that her work was as important as Ren's. Basically, months turned into years, and it turned out that Judith pretty much saw the family only on weekends and holidays and, of course, for family summer vacations in the Hamptons.

"That must have been so hard for Ren," I exclaimed when Ruth told me that part. And she laughed and said that Ren didn't seem to mind one bit. He loved being a single dad in Manhattan, he loved his colleagues at Piedmont (who adored him and were always inviting him and the children over for dinner), and he even loved ferrying his kids to lessons and museums, cooking dinner, supervising homework. Meanwhile, he wrote plays that got produced, and between that and being charming to everyone he met, he saw his incandescently angry wife as little as possible. Her own career soared, as she was practically a unicorn in her field: a fast, efficient, unencumbered woman genius who could put in eighty-hour workweeks without having to arrange for childcare.

"So it was a win-win," Ruth said. Then, four years ago, when the children were fifteen and eighteen, Ren and Judith made the split official and called in the lawyers. All very amicable. Everybody stayed civil. The Piedmont faculty even sent flowers to Judith. And from what Ruth told me on the sly, several of the unattached women on the faculty (and one very attached one) made it rather plain that they would like to be considered for the position of Ren's second wife, or at least his bed partner. But he didn't seem to notice.

In time, she said, they all watched as he seemed to slowly become more somber, less excited about life.

"He was waiting to meet someone like you," she told me with a wink. She said he'd never seemed happier, that the black cloud that hovered over him dissipated as soon as we got involved.

"He lights up when he sees you," she told me. "You're not like anybody else here."

Well, that's certainly true. They're all so put-together and classy, with their expensive tweed suits and their stockings and their shoulder pads. It's hard to believe he's attracted to me instead of one of them. Is it that he feels sorry for me, for the way I get flustered and blush easily? Or how I'm often frazzled and confused, searching through my pockets and book bags, chasing down the keys to my classroom, my subway tokens, money for the vending machines, and scrunchies to keep my hair out of my face? I can't seem to help myself. Chaos follows me around. I stammer at meetings. I laugh too loudly. When I try to make small talk, I tell jokes that no one thinks are funny. None of those qualities seem desirable in any way. But for some reason he chose me.

He, on the other hand, is the kindest person I know. He weeps over movies with dead dogs or hurt children. He tears up when he hears violin concertos, honest to God. And the man has never yet missed an opportunity to check in with one of his kids. It's like dating Clark Kent, patiently waiting while he ducks into phone booths, just to make sure nobody needs him at the moment.

I love how he speaks so glowingly of his girls. Jenna graduated from Columbia last May and is a grant writer, and according to Ren, she's hyperorganized like her mother, and also slightly neurotic, with a tendency, he says, toward denying any and all feelings. Also, like her mother, she maintains that the trouble in the world is caused by people who let their hearts run amok without paying proper respect to the practical things in life, like spreadsheets and experts. She has a semiserious boyfriend who lives in DC, and they see each other mostly on weekends.

And then there's Parker. Little Parker. (Insert Ren's sigh here because he always sighs when he speaks of her.) She's nineteen and flunked several classes in her first semester at NYU and is now only taking freshman comp, which means that she has way too much free time. She's taken to the party scene rather heavily—which he sees as mostly her subconscious effort to punish her mother for not moving to the city with the family. He claims she's running through the gamut of bad behavior almost as if she had a checklist: bad men, smoking, drugs, alcohol, unemployment, refusal to eat vegetables, staying out all night at clubs, inappropriate footwear, and one bold Celtic knot tattoo on her shoulder.

He feels guilty about all of it.

This is why we can't spend the night together. His girls still live with him, and he's determined to set a very good moral example for them.

Ruth said that's actually a good thing. "This is the kind of loyal man you're getting involved with," she said kindly. "When he and Judith were splitting up, he drove himself crazy trying to make sure that the kids stayed well above the fray and that nobody suffered for even one second. And he's got enough love and enough energy to see it through, bless his heart."

～

At exactly 6:59, my buzzer rings. I dry my hands on my skirt, fluff up my hair, and open the door. My heart is doing its best impression of a jackhammer.

There he is, all six feet of him down on one knee on the filthy hall carpet, grinning and holding a bouquet of so many red roses, I can't even begin to count them all.

"Oh my," I say. I feel like I might cry.

"Mimi Perkins, will you—wait, is Mimi your given name or just a nickname?"

"Nickname. It's short for Miriam."

"Oh. Nice. Say, did you ever wonder about Ren? It's short for Reynolds. Which was my mother's maiden name. So Miriam and Reynolds. Huh. That has a nice ring to it, don't you think?"

"I do." I laugh. "And I'm so glad we've gotten this out of the way at last," I say. "Now won't you come in?"

"After I ask you to marry me."

"Oh. Right. Sure."

He closes his eyes. Oh God. This will be a soliloquy. How will I keep from bursting into tears? "Mimi," he begins, "I never knew that life could be this much fun or hold so much promise. You are my lifeline, baby, my getaway car, the smoky fires in my soul. I love how you've enhanced my life with your sunshine and your moondust and your starlight. Every day I'm so grateful to have found you." He opens his eyes and holds out his arms to me, roses and all. "For your beauty and the goofy, bold way you teach Shakespeare, and for a million other things about you that make me laugh and smile, *you* are the subatomic particle of which my bones are made. And now that Judith is leaving for Chicago, it's the perfect, convenient time, so will you make me the happiest man alive, and agree to be my wife?"

I had been all set to say something along the lines of *Yes! Yes! I will! I will!* But instead, something horrible is happening with my heart, which has completely slid out of its usual spot, and a sound like a sob escapes from deep inside me. My hands drop to my sides.

He looks at me in alarm. We're both shocked. Am I *crying*?

"What?" he says.

"I don't know," I say, because at first I really *don't* know what has stopped me in my tracks. It's just that everything feels so sad and spoiled. Then it hits me: How the hell did *Judith* show up in the proposal?

He struggles up from his kneeling position, looking confused. "Are you mad because I called you goofy?"

"Ren," I say, "Reynolds." I wipe my eyes, which are now leaking. "You are *the* most sensitive, caring man I've ever known—but I-I just wish you hadn't mentioned your ex-wife's name when you proposed to me. It sort of makes more of a point of that second-wife thing. You know?"

His eyes are blank. "I didn't mention her."

"You did. You said her name. And I know I shouldn't mind, because she's important, and you were married to her for such a long time, but this is the only marriage proposal I'll ever get, and I have to say, while we're at it, I also never expected the word *convenient* either. I don't know. I'm just . . . I don't know."

Oh my goodness. I'm the stupidest person in the world. I can't believe I'm being proposed to, and I'm finding fault with the wording. Where do I get off, being so picky? Something in my head points out that I'm lucky he even *wants* to marry me.

"Oh God," he says. "I did say that. Why did I say that? I'm kicking myself. Let's rewind and have a do-over. Go back inside and close the door . . ."

Still, I can't stop my eyes from filling up.

"No, stay here," I say. "You've got to tell me the truth. Do you really still love Judith in some corner of your heart that we're just now shining a light on?"

"No!" he says. His face is ashen.

"And the kids don't have some need to think of you guys as an intact family anymore?"

"God, no. It's been years."

"Well, why do you think you said that, then?"

"Sweetie, do we *have* to analyze this? Really? I was mentioning that she's leaving. It's a good thing. She put the house on the market in New Haven, and she's gone to take a job in Chicago, and I'm feeling younger and freer than I've felt in quite a long time, and by all that is holy and good in this world, I want to marry you, so can we just forgive me for being such an ass and move on from this?"

21

I look down at the too-many roses he's dropped on the dirty hall rug. "I have to warn you, I can't take it if you're misguided on this get-ting married business. If you're still in love with your old wife, I will fall apart in a very serious mental-health kind of way, and since I'll be on your insurance, it'll cost you piles of money in copays, and you'll have to visit me in the asylum, and they probably won't let us have sex there."

"I know." He takes both my hands and smiles at me. "So, will you marry me, for fuck's sake, and let's put this behind us?"

"Only because you used the word 'fuck' in your do-over proposal," I say. "That is the only reason."

"I thought that might work. And now, if it please the court, could we *for God's sake* not let my ex contaminate any more of our evening? I'll tell you anything you need to know some other time, but right now I have other, more pressing matters on my mind. Here, let's leave Judith in the hallway and lock the door. Good-bye, old life."

He mimes picking up a huge heavy box and setting it down outside the door, and then stepping inside my apartment and locking the door and tossing away a pretend key as far away as he can throw it.

I pull him into the apartment, kissing him as we go, kicking the door shut and leaving his old life in the hall with the roses scattered everywhere; it looks like there's been a massacre out there. He begins peeling off my clothes, and I get to work peeling off his, both of us breathing hard now and bumping into the front door and the wall. We make our way to the bedroom, squeezing past the dinner bubbling in the frying pan, and scrunching ourselves past the coffee table and my pair of winter boots, which have somehow escaped from their home under the couch.

Into my room we go, my crazy little cell of a room, where we fall onto the bed, careful not to get concussions from the wooden loft over the mattress. And oh God. If I appreciate how he excels at spontaneous supply-closet sex, let me just tell you that when we actually have a few hours together and a bed and no worries about his children needing phone calls, it is astonishing. At Eleanor's suggestion, I have studied

The Joy of Sex in preparation for this relationship, and therefore, I know what good sex consists of. He stares into my eyes, he caresses my face and drops luxuriant little kisses on my neck and eyelids and cheekbones and collarbone and then down my rib cage to my stomach. He is especially good at the techniques on pages 151 and 207, and the underrated earlobe work on page 112.

∽

"I think the dinner has burned," I say once we're finished and we're lying there spent, staring at the ceiling.

"Maybe the pan, too. It smells like burned metal in here," he says drowsily. "Do we care?"

"I do love that old pan," I say. "I found it at a thrift store in Brooklyn."

"We'll order in. And I'll buy you a new pan. Brand new." He rolls over and kisses both of my shoulders and pays some more close attention to my collarbone, which he says was feeling neglected, and then he says, "So let's make plans. When do you want to get married?"

"I'll be right back." I leave the bed and go turn off the stove. The dinner has indeed turned black and bubbled away, and the pan is certainly ruined. I grab two dish towels and set it outside on the carpet in the hallway, next to the imaginary box containing his family complications atop the rose petals that look like a bloodbath. Tomatoes spill onto the carpet, but I am naked and can't stop to pick them up just now. I close the door before anyone can see me.

When I get back, Ren has turned on the bedside light, the one with the fringed shade, and he's sitting up, propped against the wall, with my two pink silk pillows behind his head. He holds out his arms, and I crawl in next to him. "We could do any kind of wedding you want—church, garden, beach . . ."

"Something quiet," I say. "Maybe on a beach somewhere is a good idea . . ." I don't add that I would love it extra much if only he and I are in attendance. Maybe Eleanor if she insists.

"Okay. *Near* a beach, perhaps in a country club," he says. "Now. How many bridesmaids and ushers should we have? A minister?" He kisses my jawline, five hundred little kisses.

"If it has to be at a country club, let's ask Penelope Harrington to be a bridesmaid," I murmur.

He laughs. Penelope Harrington is the very proper, formidable assistant to the headmaster at Piedmont, the one who is always chastising me for what she calls "inappropriate public canoodling." She, of course, adores Ren and finds nothing amiss in *his* behavior.

"I'll insist that she wear an ugly pale yellow dress, and it'll have a huge butt bow," I say.

He has moved away from my jawline and is now working his way to my breasts, via the collarbone. "*Mmm.* I love this vindictive side of you."

"What are your kids going to say?" I ask. Bravely.

"Whatever people say when they're happy," he murmurs. He's heading down my torso with his kisses.

"You do know that stepmothers aren't highly regarded in the culture," I say. I hesitate a moment before adding, "And surely you know that they don't really like me yet. It probably doesn't help that I'm only ten years older than Jenna."

"*Yet* is the operative word here," he says, stopping at my belly button for a rest. "I'll bet Jenna and you will end up being best friends. Trust me: they'll be thrilled. In fact, I say we call them right now and tell them!"

"Right now?"

"Right now!" He sits up.

"Really? Because what if they're not thrilled? Won't the evening be spoiled?" I say.

"There's no spoiling this evening. I tell you, it's all going to be wonderful. And then after that, we'll call your mother," he says. "And anyone else who'll be so happy for us. Think of a list of people."

"If you think so," I say. "I don't really have a family. My dad died when I was five, and my mom's on a cruise. She's on cruises pretty much all the time. It's sort of her thing. Cruising."

It strikes me that Eleanor is right; I've told him so little about my life. That's because his life is so much more interesting than mine, and besides that, the facts of my upbringing make me seem so pathetic, so needy. Which I do not want to be. Ever.

He gets a tragic look on his face, and I'm afraid we'll have to right now go through the sympathy bit about my dad being gone and all the stepfathers. But he moves on quickly. "Okay, sweetie. We'll start with Jenna. She's going to be the happiest."

I bring the phone over, which isn't hard because it has a twenty-five-foot-long cord that pretty much covers the whole apartment, and then I settle down in the bed next to him. He squeezes my hand and kisses my hair, and says to me, "Are you happy?"

"I am very happy," I tell him.

"Oh, I should get the ring out of my pants pocket," he says. "How could I have forgotten that part of things?"

"We can get it later," I tell him.

"Okay," he says. "First I'm going to give you a million kisses, and then I'm going to dial Jenna. And then I'll get the ring. And then a million more kisses, and then we'll call Parker. Anybody else we should call, for you?"

"Well, there's Eleanor."

"Sure." He smooches me all along my hairline, my nose, my jaw, my face, ending with my lips.

And then, smiling, he dials Jenna's number. She picks up right away. I can hear her screaming bloody murder right through the phone.

Screaming and screaming and screaming.

Like she will never, ever stop.

CHAPTER THREE

I go rigid with fear. My best guess is that both her legs have been cut off in a serious chain saw accident, and she's waiting for the ambulance. That's what kind of screaming this is.

At last I can make out words, her voice squawking out from the receiver between gasps and sobs, that it's about Judith. A car. Something something something. He asks questions, and then he puts his hand over the receiver and whispers to me, "Judith was driving to Chicago, and she was in a car accident, and she's been taken to the hospital. The doctors don't know anything yet. A lot of blood."

He says all the right things to Jenna: It's terrible news, but it might not be serious; maybe they're checking her out at the hospital just to be safe, and why don't we wait until we know for sure before we push the panic button. "People get patched up," he says. "Let's hold the good thought. She'll most likely be good as new. Even if she has to be late starting her new job, they'll wait for her. It's going to be okay," he says. "When can we talk to the doctors?"

"Where *are* you?" I hear her say.

"I'm with Mimi," he tells her. He says a whole bunch of reassuring things, and then, mystifyingly, he hands the phone to me as if I should right now start being someone Jenna wants to talk to. I swallow hard and say reassuring things, too. I say I'm sending her good energy.

Jenna is silent while I'm speaking and then she says, "Put my dad back on the phone, please."

He takes the phone and walks into the living room, but I can still hear little snippets of her voice, outraged little bleeps like you might hear in a *Peanuts* cartoon when Charlie Brown's teacher is talking, and then he says, "All right. No, I get it. Yes, I'll come to New Haven. Yes. I'll leave now."

He comes back into the bedroom and very carefully places the receiver back in its cradle and looks at me. "I have to go to New Haven," he says. He puts on his underwear and pants, and then his shirt. He buttons it up wrong, and that's when I notice his hands are shaking.

"Of course," I say. I swallow hard. There's a cold wind blowing through me. "This sounds really serious."

He's staring at his buttons like they don't make sense to him anymore. "Yeah. Well, who knows?"

"So, New Haven. Are you going to have to stay there, do you think?"

"Yeah. Seems like it. I'll stay in our house," he says. *Our house.* The house he hasn't lived in for the past twelve years. The house that he gave to Judith in the divorce settlement, according to the report from Ruth. At least he's figured out the shirt buttons, though.

"I thought she sold it," I say.

He shrugs. He's now putting on his jacket, stepping over my clothes on his way to the door. "I don't know. I mean, it didn't sell. I guess."

"Well, that's good. You'll have a place."

"She's falling apart. Jenna is."

"Yes," I say. "It sounds awful."

"Not the strongest person."

"It's scary as hell."

"I need to go see," he says. "Hold everybody up. See what's what."

"Of course you do," I say. "Will you call me?"

We can't seem to string more than four words together at any one time. Should I offer to go with him? No, that would only make things worse. I realize I am not in the picture at all. This has nothing to do with me. I'm an outsider here.

He pats his pockets for his keys and wallet. His eyes are smoky. When he looks in my direction, I'm not sure he sees me.

"Call me," I say, and kiss him.

He leans over and gives me a peck on the cheek and mumbles that he'll call when he knows something.

"And anyway you'll be back tomorrow," I say. "I bet."

⁓

He is not *back tomorrow*.

He doesn't even manage to call *tomorrow*. I mope around all morning, unwilling to leave home or even to eat. I have realized two things: he did not give me the engagement ring, and also, for some reason, the universe now requires me to stare at the phone and *will* it to ring if I ever expect to hear from him. I bring it onto the bed and dust the little spaces between the buttons to encourage its cooperation. I polish the receiver to a lovely gleam. That is how faithful and good I am to this phone.

It does not care.

Late that afternoon, after hours of staring and beseeching, I punish the phone for not ringing by going out for a walk around the block. I have to step over the flower petals and the burned pan and pieces of tomato all over the hall carpet. When I come home, I realize this phone knows how to play hardball. There is not one message on the answering machine.

"Okay," I say. This is enough. Surely he knows *something* by now.

I stick my tongue out at the phone, and it sticks its tongue out at me, too.

This is war.

At five in the afternoon, I remember that I haven't eaten anything in probably twenty-four hours, and the wavy feeling in my stomach probably means I'm in an advanced stage of starvation. I go rummaging through the cabinets. There's a can of olives, and it takes me ten minutes to open it and then twenty-five seconds to eat every single olive.

By six thirty, I am lying in a heap on the bedcovers on the floor when the phone comes back to life. I feel like I've been under water. I pounce on it.

It's Eleanor. She squeals, "So how did it go? Did he ask you?"

"He did." I rub my head.

"Well? And did you say yes?"

"I did."

We're silent.

"For heaven's sake, Mimi, tell me the details! So you're engaged? You don't sound very happy. Is he . . . still there? You can't talk, is that it?"

I wrap my fingers around the phone cord until it hurts. "No. He's gone." I take a deep breath. "His ex was in a car accident, and he's gone to New Haven."

"*What?* Is she okay?"

"I don't know. He hasn't called me."

"Well," she says. "Well." She takes on the voice she uses when she is trying to manage my feelings. "He's probably not sure what's what yet. They've no doubt been meeting with doctors. And such."

"Which is why I need to get off the phone in case he's trying to call right now."

"Okay. Yes. I suppose you should. Just tell me this to tide me over: Was it romantic?"

"Was what romantic?"

"The proposal, idiot."

"Not really. Maybe. I suppose. He mentioned his ex-wife's name when he was proposing." Before the words are even out of my mouth, I regret it.

Sure enough, she runs with it. Eleanor has decided that she loves Ren, and she'll defend him to the death. "Oh, gosh! Sweetie, on the bright side, at least he didn't call you by her name, right? That happens sometimes, more often than you'd think."

"No, he didn't do that. And he was sorry."

"Well," she says. "Maybe you should call your psychic. There might be something you're overlooking that happened in his head, like Mercury going into lemonade or something. Isn't that what happens to Mercury sometimes?"

"Retrograde. Mercury goes into retrograde. Please don't try to be funny right now."

"Yeah. Okay, baby. Sorry. Well. Hang in there. You've got this. Keep me posted."

"Okay."

"And Mimi?"

"Yes?"

"It's going to be fine. I promise."

From the moment I met her on the first day of freshman year, Eleanor was my savior. I showed up at Trinity College at age eighteen as a bit of a mess: shy, overemotional, and wearing black socks with sandals. I even had a unibrow and hair that was so wild and stuck out so much that it almost had its own zip code. Eleanor had tons of friends, great clothes, and almost *too* many loving family members, and right away she knew instinctively it was her duty to introduce me to parties, hair straighteners, and depilatories. She could also see that I was hopeless in wardrobe management, and had no background in rock and roll appreciation, and, worse, I was in desperate need of full-time remedial education in how to handle boys—the good ones *and* the bad ones. And she was just the woman for the job. We'd sit up late into the night, analyzing my life.

I offered up plenty of possible reasons for my inadequate preparation for life. My father's untimely death had left me with no male role model. And also, because I was an only child, I had never learned how to be super close to other people. She nodded. Yep, that was hard. And my mother had married four times since my father's death. Also very, very hard.

But it wasn't until I happened to mention that my mother was the 1960s Tupperware queen for six counties in the state of New Jersey that Eleanor stood up and raised her arms over her head in triumph. "Eureka!" she screamed. "That's it! Oh my God! You're a Tupperware orphan!"

It was true. Between traveling across the state running Tupperware parties and working to line up new husbands, which required an excruciating amount of dating, Angelina Perkins Smith Taylor Harrison Robertson didn't have a lot of time for me. She was brilliant, but she had no aptitude for mothering. It's possible that when she gave birth to me, the hospital didn't fully explain that I would now be her child forever and ever. It wasn't that she was mean or abusive; it was as if no one ever spelled out for her the level of care and attention offspring require. I think I might have been a child who cried a lot. And if I had to guess, I think my dad must have ensured my survival through the first five years. And fortunately, by the time of his untimely exit, I pretty much knew how to get what I needed for myself.

Thank goodness I was able to hang out with kindly neighbors in our apartment building. Mrs. Schneider next door had four kids and didn't seem to mind having one more showing up at the dinner table. Down the hall was Mrs. Hancock, who gave me hand-me-downs from her granddaughters. It seemed I moved through life with people always showing up to provide me with what I needed. Mrs. Schneider fed me, helped me with my homework, drilled me on Spanish verbs, taught me how to drive a stick shift, and gave me detailed instructions on how to use a tampon. Her son, at age fifteen, one memorable evening, taught me very gently how to French kiss. Mrs. Johnson at the high school helped me with college applications, and when I was accepted to Trinity, she drove me there and dropped me off.

And that's when Eleanor took over, showing up just in time to teach me how to stop being a loner and how to maybe trust people, and how to date guys, and how to be proud of being what she called an *acquired taste*.

Now I just wish she still lived in the same room with me so I could look over at her and say, *Is this guy ever going to come back to me?* and she could tell me over and over again what she said right before we hung up: "It's going to be fine."

Later I go out and bring in the burned pot and try to pick up some of the rose petals and pieces of tomato skin. There is a big hole in the rug where the pot scorched it. I'm not surprised. The whole world feels like it has a big hole in it, and that we're all living in the aftermath of a horrible accident. I throw the pan away and scrub at the tomatoes as best I can, which isn't very effective.

Ren finally calls me late that night when I'm lying awake in the dark, wondering if I should get up and eat a box of Cheez-Its or just lie quietly and starve myself to death. Even now he says he can't really talk, but he wants me to know it's very serious with Judith. They think she possibly had a stroke that caused the auto accident, and she's still in the ICU and the kids are a mess. The doctors have induced a coma so that Judith's brain won't swell too much.

I can't hear news about possible brain swelling without coming close to fainting myself, so I sit on the floor with my head between my knees, holding the phone as far away from my own brain as I can, so it won't get any ideas. I ask about Parker and Jenna. He says they're wrecks. Oh yes, I realize he had just told me that a minute ago. The three of them, he and the girls, are mostly staying at the hospital, eating cafeteria food, crying, and either sitting beside Judith's bed or, when the nurses kick them out, standing in the hallway and waiting for news.

I hear some commotion and he says, "Okay, right," to someone else, and then he says, "Listen, the doctor is here with the results of her tests, and I have to go. I'll call you again when I can. It's hard getting to a phone around here."

"Okay," I say in my new voice, which feels very thin to my own ears. "I'm so sorry."

"Oh, one more thing. Darling, I hate to do this, but I'm taking a leave of absence. There's no way I can come back right now. So, as much as I hate to miss doing the play, I do feel it's in good hands with you. You need to finish it up."

"But—"

"No buts. You gotta do it for me, okay? We've worked too hard on this thing to just give up on it."

"But I think the kids need *you*. They hardly listen to me."

"You can do it. I need you to do it." Then he says, "I've gotta go. The doctor is waiting. I love you." And he hangs up, just like that. Possible stroke, induced coma, brain swelling, do the musical, it'll be great, do it for me, I love you.

"I miss you," I say to the dial tone.

The dial tone doesn't miss me.

CHAPTER FOUR

The next morning is Sunday, not my usual appointment day with La Starla, but I get on the subway and go to see her anyway. It's an emergency. I'm in need of triage.

She lives off the L train, near McCarren Park in Brooklyn, on a street lined with aluminum-sided row houses, all run down, with cracked concrete stoops, where people are usually hanging out and conducting their social lives at full volume. Most stoops are adorned with artificial flowers and have crucifixes in the windows; La Starla's stoop features Tibetan prayer flags as well as a statue of some nondescript but pious-looking person in a tunic, with his arms outstretched.

I ring the doorbell, and it takes her forever to answer. When she opens the door, she's not wearing her usual turban and black dress. She's got on bright yellow bell-bottoms like someone would have worn in 1966, and a man's blue denim work shirt that goes almost to her knees. Her gray hair is sticking up in little tufts.

I should have called first. I may have misjudged whether or not I'm her favorite client.

"What in the world are *you* doing here?" she says. And then: "Aren't you getting engaged?" And then: "Oh my God. What's happened?"

You might think that, of all people, *she* would know what's happened, being psychic and all—but as she's explained to me, psychics can't know absolutely everything going on in the whole world. How would they manage to even make it through their morning cup of coffee with all that information flooding in? No, they keep blockers up. They have to.

All the words come pouring out of me. I tell her about the prepro-posal at school, then the real proposal, the phone call, the stroke, the coma . . . and by the time I'm at the part about Ren taking a leave of absence from school, I'm fully in tears.

About halfway into my story, she takes my arm. "Come in, come in," she says with a sigh. She leads me back through a dark hallway filled with bookshelves, and we go to where her husband is sitting at the blue Formica table in their sunny, old-fashioned kitchen, reading the *New York Post*. He looks up and grins.

"No, it's not good, Gary," she says. "There's been something of a tragedy for our Mimi. We have to be very quiet while this settles so I can get a read on it."

She fixes me a cup of coffee and Gary hands me a cinnamon bun. I can hardly deal with either of these things. I just sit there, blinking in the early spring sunlight streaming through the windows; occasionally I nibble at the bun. La Starla bustles around, washing up the cups in the sink, wiping down the counters, and then bringing her dishrag over to the table, where she sweeps cinnamon bun crumbs into her hand and then swipes at the table with the rag. Her eyes are unfocused, but every now and then she stops and gazes into space.

"I'm thinking," she says. "This is how I think when I don't have my turban on."

"Do you want me to get your turban, dear?" says Gary.

"I do not. Sometimes the spirit guides talk to me better when I'm doing active things."

Gary leans over to me. "You're in good hands," he says in a low voice. "I don't know what's going on in her head, but I can see that something is."

"*Shhh*," she tells him. "My guides are talking to me right this minute."

Gary and I wait. I take a sip of the strong Italian roast coffee that I suspect runs through La Starla's veins night and day. My stomach rumbles. I know this look of hers when she's getting information. Her spirit guides, whoever they are, *wherever* they are, are always interrupting her conversations to impart some info we earthlings have been waiting for. Sometimes it's mundane, maybe because it's filtered through the sensibilities of a Brooklyn grandmother: don't eat so much before bedtime, separate your laundry, floss your teeth, make up your bed first thing in the morning and you'll have at least accomplished something. But sometimes it's blinding news of your future. *You will get married sooner than you think.*

Soon she comes and sits down and takes my hands in her rough, craggy ones.

"The news is not what you want to hear," she says.

"Oh God. Tell me." I start to cry.

"No, no. It's just temporarily not what you want to hear. The spirit guides know that you were expecting some kind of happily-ever-after, and you will get it, just not the way you think. Right now, for a while, they say you've got some shit to go through."

"Is that the technical term?" I say. "Did they actually say 'shit'?"

"They might have. I'm not sure. They use other things than words. You wouldn't understand, which is why you come to me. But yes. They want me to tell you that you're basically fine, but now is not the auspicious time you thought it was. It's not all going to be beer and Skittles for a while, sweetie pie."

"Oh my God, oh my God," I say. "Tell me this: Is his ex-wife going to make it?"

"We don't know. You are on a journey . . ."

"I hate the word 'journey.' I don't want to be on a *journey*. I want to be planning a small, two-person wedding that no one attends, and then moving in with Ren and having great sex every night for the rest of my life."

"Well," she says. "It ain't going to go according to your plan, not yet. But look at it this way. The spirit guides say you're on the personal quest of your life, and you've got some twists and turns ahead of you, a bit of a detour. They see tears and laughter and . . . hmm . . . lots of children."

"Children?" I say. *"Children?"*

"But it ultimately all works out, like life has a way of doing."

"Ask them this," I say, and I suddenly feel a surge of what could almost be called fury if I had any energy in me whatsoever. "Is Ren Yardley going to marry me, or not?"

She gets a funny look on her face, exactly like she's hearing the news that he is *not* going to marry me, after all these months of the guides saying he was madly in love with me due to my magic skirt. Then she says, maddeningly, "That's not the point. Who cares if he does? The important thing is that either way, you're going to have a big, wonderful life."

"I don't *want* a big, wonderful life," I say. "I *want* Ren."

"Do you hear yourself?" she says. "If he's not going to bring you a big, wonderful life, then you don't need him."

"I want both! I want everything!" I say.

"Finish the cinnamon bun, darling," says La Starla. "I think your blood sugar is low."

CHAPTER FIVE

Monday morning I get called first thing into Penelope Harrington's very elegant office, the place where it all happens, where the parents of the future leaders of America are told that their little darlings must work harder or else be expelled from Piedmont Academy. Penelope is the executive assistant to the headmaster, Francis X. Flannigan, although I suspect she really runs the place. He's a bit of an empty suit, there just to smile in photographs.

She's one of those chic society women with good skin, and she wears wool suits and thick stockings, and she doesn't like me, and I don't like her. Usually when I'm called into her office, it's because some parent heard that I kissed Ren in public or let a student who doesn't happen to be their child have more time on a test, which for some reason upsets the balance of nature. But today I sit in the big Hitchcock chair across from her mahogany desk, dabbing at my eyes and expecting to get some sympathy.

That is not what happens, however.

She folds her hands and glares as she tells me that no one in the whole school thinks I can get the musical organized in one week, but that Ren, mystifyingly, is insisting I can. The only saving grace, she says, is that without him around to "distract" me from proper adult behavior, maybe I will do a bit better in my career there. She tells me that my unorthodox teaching methods have not gone unnoticed by the administration, and that everyone sees that I've behaved very much like an adolescent in heat.

"I'm frankly not sure how it is you got this job in the first place," she says. "Did someone recommend you? I believe I was out the day you got hired."

I'm not going to give her the satisfaction of an answer, but I do often wonder if my hiring wasn't a fluke. I was working as a part-time aide in a middle school library, which was the only job my degree in library studies had managed to get me, when I came across that want ad for an English teacher at Piedmont. It was already late September, the semester had already started, and apparently a longtime Piedmont teacher who had been on maternity leave had decided to be a stay-at-home mom.

I went for an interview, met Francis X. Flannigan, and because I could start that very week, he hired me on the spot.

Penelope and I sit there, glowering at each other. Then she says, with a sigh, "You're dismissed. Try not to turn this play into a disaster."

In the afternoon, still shaky, I gather the students into a group and tell them that Mr. Yardley was called away and that we need to put on the play without him. They're sitting on the floor, very still, looking at me with blank eyes. Then two boys start a slap fight, a girl blows a bubble with her gum, and someone wants to know if she can have a different part in the play now that Mr. Yardley isn't there.

I see what I'm up against. I clap my hands, and then I take a very deep breath and point out that we are all on the same team and that we are equal partners and also that we are indomitably cool together. I can tell by the way they look at me that no one is buying one thing I'm saying. I swallow hard and say, "Ren is insisting that we do this for him. And we have one week to prove to him we can do it." (I will never refer to him as Mr. Yardley again, I think.) Then I go around and do fist bumps with everyone. I may even tell them I love them, because I'm that desperate.

Later, while I listen to them run through their lines, I come up with a plan. I'll bribe them with doughnuts and chocolate bars. I'll compliment even their smallest efforts and fuss over them and give them subway fare, hugs, and Cokes. That first afternoon, I let Samantha use the phone in my office to call her boyfriend at college. I tell Schuyler Bassett, who is playing Sky Masterson, that he's the best thing in the play and that if he could just woo Samantha a little more insistently, then the audience will swoon. I say the same thing to Dirk Connors, who is rather listlessly playing Nathan Detroit opposite Adelaide. At one point, I get up onstage and grab his lapels and hug him to show him just how flamboyantly he needs to move his body. Then I make Tina Janssen practice Adelaide's Bronx accent by telling her she must speak that way for the next five days—every single conversation she has, even at lunchtime, even in my Shakespeare class, even at home. I must be having an out-of-body experience when I get up onstage and do a pseudo-sexy rendition of the Hot Box dancers' main number just to show them how it should look. I teach Samantha how to sound drunk when she has the Bacardí.

I am a woman on fire, operating quite outside of anything that might be called a comfort zone. I can't even see my comfort zone in the rearview mirror.

◦◦

Ren calls me that night and tells me everything he's already told me.

"It was a stroke," he says in a heavy voice. "They induced a coma to let her brain heal."

I say the things I said before, too: how awful, how are the girls, I hope things will get better.

He says, "Apparently she's had high blood pressure for years, all that job stress. And then the move. It must have pushed her over the edge." His voice trails off.

We're silent for what anyone would know is too long a time. Finally, I tell him about the musical and the kids, and the mean things Penelope Harrington said to me, and then comfort him by reassuring him that I can do the play, and it's going to be great.

"I love you," he says. "But I'm not a quitter. I'm having to be the strong one here, holding everyone up, and I am so sorry to be away from you. But I'm not a quitter. I'm not."

"No," I say softly. "Of course you're not. How long is your leave of absence, do you think?"

He says, "No idea. Oh! The doctor is going in to meet with us now. I've got to go. I love you. Bye."

On Friday we have the worst dress rehearsal in the history of dress rehearsals. Samantha, who forgot to look drunk through the entire Bacardí scene, looks like she might start crying. Two of the Hot Box Girls have stopped speaking to each other, the gangsters think their hats are "stupid," and the lighting guys can't seem to understand that the point is to illuminate the actor actually talking, not the one you think is cute. It's so damned bad that afterward I have to walk outside and take deep breaths of the spring evening air. Cars are honking all around me, and I watch three changes of traffic lights—green, yellow, red.

Finally I gather enough of my sad little self to go back inside the Piedmont auditorium, where I can hear the kids arguing in the back. I decide that radical action is necessary. I go into the office and call Antonio's Pizza Palace and order five large cheese pizzas and fifteen Cokes to be delivered as soon as possible. And then I square my shoulders and tell all the actors to meet me onstage. We sit in a circle on the dusty floor, and I tell them that there's an old adage among theater people—that a horrible dress rehearsal means that opening night is going to be fabulous.

And then I tell them about the magic skirt. I pull it out of my backpack and start cutting the bottom ruffle into little squares, which I hand out to them.

"Theater is all magic, really," I say. "And here is a little piece of magic for you to carry with you while you're doing the show. How do you think drama works anyway? It's all smoke and mirrors and magic in the first place."

I look around at their glum faces and feel suddenly filled with a crazy zigzagging hope.

"Not sure magic is really, you know, scientifically *real*," says some future naysayer who will definitely be in Congress someday, killing the funding for school lunches.

"You may be too educated already to believe in magic," I say, "but I think you might want to keep an open mind. I happen to believe in magical properties, and this skirt is proof to me that it works. I was wearing this skirt when I got this job and when I met Ren, who is the love of my life. And now we're engaged. And this skirt will make this play work, too. Carry it onstage, tuck it in your costume. Believe me, this is going to work."

We eat the pizza. We do half of a run-through that maybe does not suck so badly. I clap and cheer for them. We all walk together to the subway afterward, linking arms and singing. I love these children.

And as soon as I think that, it hits me then that maybe these are the children that La Starla was referring to, the ones who are going to surround me in my life. Which maybe means that eventually Ren is going to come back and be the love of my life once again. This makes me so happy that I actually spin around in the street in front of my apartment, with my arms outstretched. I love the whole world.

～

The play, magically, goes off without a hitch. Perfectly! Not only are the cast members carrying the pieces of the skirt inside their costumes, but we've hung the skirt itself up near the makeup mirrors so that it can be inspiring while they get themselves painted. And it works. They all remember their lines. The lighting guys get the cues right. Adelaide speaks in a perfect accent, and Samantha can be heard all the way to the back of the auditorium. Sky and Nathan woo these girls to within an inch of their lives. Backstage, we're all swooning.

After it's over, the audience rises to its feet and applauds and applauds and applauds.

But then something weird happens. The applause is just dying down when Schuyler comes lurching back out onto the stage, holding his arms high in the air. He starts chanting "Mee-mee! Mee-mee!" and suddenly the Hot Box Girls pull me, blinking, into the spotlight.

His eyes are wild. Too wild, I think, but I have no time to run back into hiding.

"I have to thank the *most amazing* director there ever was!" he says, and he swings his arm around my shoulder. "Ms. Perkins went to a level that *no* other teacher at Piedmont has ever gone! She told us all about magic and theater—*and—and—*" Here he cuts his eyes over to me, and I feel the first alarm bells going off in my head, so I try to shush him, but he's too full of emotion to stop. "*And s*he told us all about this magic skirt she has, which got her the job here, and also how it got our drama teacher, Mr. Yardley, to fall in love with her! I mean, we've all seen them all year, passing notes and sometimes *making out—*" I drop dead at this, and the audience roars with laughter. "Well, you were, and you know you were," he says, "and anyway it's all fine because now she told us they're *getting married—*"

Then he has to stop talking because Penelope Harrington has come roaring onto the stage and rushed at him like she's from the New York Giants and he's a New England Patriot who's got possession of the football. He's laughing and protesting and making the most of his exit, while the audience laughs and gets to its feet, clapping and cheering. The orchestra starts to play the overture to *Guys and Dolls* once more, even louder than before.

And . . . the curtain comes down.

❧

On Monday morning I get fired.

Penelope Harrington pushes some papers toward me across the desk and says in a flat voice: "You need to sign these separation papers and then gather your things immediately."

I sink down in the chair and give her a blank look. "But the play was a *triumph!*"

"Sign where I've put the little arrows, please."

"May I know why?"

"You are seriously asking me why? After everything that's happened?"

"But the play—"

She heaves herself up and crosses her arms. "Where do I even begin? Insubordination. Public displays of affection. Failure to follow the school regulations. Being inappropriate with the students."

"Wait a minute. I'm not—"

"Cut your losses, Ms. Perkins, why don't you? You were never the type of person we needed in this position. Frankly, if it hadn't been for Mr. Yardley, you'd have been let go months ago. Sign these papers and collect your severance check and go. And maybe in your next job, you'll remember that no one appreciates seeing somebody acting out with no self-control. You have been *shameless.*"

"May I talk to Mr. Flannigan?"

"He's not available. Anyway, the board made this decision late last night," she says. "Sign the papers."

We stare at each other for what feels like forever, and then there doesn't seem to be anything to do except to sign the papers, which I do with a shaky hand. But then when I stand up, something deep down inside me starts growling to get released, and I hear myself say to her, "Here's what I want to know, Ms. Harrington. Were you ever madly, passionately in love with anyone? Did you ever, even once in your life, get pulled into an A/V closet and kissed until you couldn't stand up anymore? Do you even *know* what love is?"

Her mouth twitches. "Get out," she says. *"Now. "*

There is nothing to do but go.

I glide across the room and slam the door *hard*. I hope one of the stuffy old paintings falls off the wall and breaks all her toes.

CHAPTER SIX

When I get home, I find my landlord, Henryk Jablonski, who is approximately 170 years old, on his hands and knees, with a bucket and a scrub brush, outside my door, groaning as he attempts to clean up the hopeless mess that the carpet has become. All that tomato sauce and the ground-in rose petals and the scorched rug where I set the burning pot.

"Oh no!" I say, rushing over to him. "Please! I'm so sorry, Mr. Jablonski. Let me do this! I left a pot outside with tomato sauce—"

"Is blood," he says.

"No, no. Is not blood. Really. I was cooking, and the pot burned. So I put it outside."

"You burn hole in rug."

"I'm sorry."

"And blood too."

"No, not blood. I swear. Tomato sauce."

"I no can have this," he says, straightening up and looking at me through his old rheumy eyes that make me feel even worse. "I'm old man now. You make noise, fine. You pay rent two days late, okay. I no like it, but I say okay. And now this. Blood. What? You kill somebody out here?"

"Not blood, tomato," I say. "I'm sorry. I—I'll pay for cleaning. Here, you get up, and I hire somebody. I promise."

"No," he says. "I want you out of here. You are rug killer. You cannot stay here."

There doesn't seem to be any point in arguing with him. I don't have a job anyway, so how will I keep paying the rent? I stand there helplessly while he keeps scrubbing at the rug.

"How long do I have?" I ask with a sigh.

"How long?" He peers at me, considering. "I want to say you have one hour, but law says thirty days."

∽

The next morning the phone rings early. I now sleep with the phone—it even has its own pillow—so I roll over and answer it before I'm even fully awake.

It's Ren.

"Sweetie, I just got off the phone with Penelope. What the actual hell? She's a vindictive, horrible person, and I can't believe she fired you."

"I know," I say and start to cry. "She said I was shameless."

He actually laughs. "I love that about you. It's my favorite thing."

"Yeah, well, she said if it hadn't been for you, I would have been let go a long time ago."

"She's wretched, sweetheart. They don't deserve you. I tried to tell her what a mistake she was making, and that you're a wonderful teacher." He laughs a little and lowers his voice. "I even told her that some, if not all, of your so-called *shamelessness* was at my instigation. She wasn't having it."

"Well," I say. "Thank you."

"And you know what? After this family stuff cools down and I'm back at school, I'm going to sit down with Francis X. and get him to take you back."

"I'm afraid my situation is even worse than that, if you can believe it."

"Oh no," he says. "What?"

So then I tell him about Mr. Jablonski throwing me out of my apartment because we ruined the rug. "So now I don't have a job, *and*

I've got no place to live. So I don't mind telling you that I'm slightly freaking out."

I hear Ren suck in his breath. A few beats of silence pass and then he says, "I know what we can do. Come to New Haven. Be here with me."

I roll the phone cord around my fingers. "Come to be . . . with you? But how would *that* work? Aren't you staying at . . . *Judith's* house?"

He laughs again, easily. "Well, yes, of course. You can't stay *here* at the house. I didn't mean that. By *here*, I just meant New Haven."

"Are you sure?"

"Hell, yes, I'm sure. It's the perfect solution. In fact, Parker was telling me the other day that she has a friend who needs to leave his apartment before the lease is up, and he's looking for someone to sublet it. Let me see if it's still available. If it is . . . well, it's right in my neighborhood. So that would be pretty great."

"Move to . . . New Haven," I say. I feel a little faint. "I've never been to New Haven."

"You'll love it. And this way, at least we can see each other—well, not like before, of course, because there's all this horrible hospital stuff going on. But we can be together when I can get away. I miss you. And this would make things so much easier."

"But I-I can't possibly do first and last month's rent *and* a security deposit."

"There won't be any security deposit or last month's rent because you're taking over someone else's lease, you little goose. And I'll pay the rent until you find a job."

"Really?" I say. "Oh. Wow. But this—this seems like a lot to ask."

"Mimi, of course I could do that. You're going to be my wife. Remember?"

"Yes," I say. The blood is beating loudly in my ears. "And maybe now I can get to know your family. I can even help out."

He says stuff about how he's at the hospital a lot of the time, he won't be able to see me much, but that there's amazing progress with

Judith. She's out of the coma, and he says she'll most likely be discharged soon, probably to a rehab facility, but no one knows for sure, and the kids are still a mess, and he's negotiating between them.

I start to work up a rosy fantasy in my head: getting to know his daughters up close, being a person they can count on. I can—oh, I don't know—give them rides to places and help out with errands and have deep conversations, comfort them. Jenna, after all, is so close to me in age that we could start in being good friends. Obviously *these* are the *children* that the spirit guides said were in my future.

He says, "Well, I gotta admit, it's high-level hysterics and drama around here." He sighs. "Parker is trying to overcompensate for her life as a juvenile delinquent, I think, by insisting that we all honor Judith by taking care of her ourselves at home, and Jenna, the more practical one, thinks we should turn everything over to the doctors and experts, and have Judith go to rehab. Which Parker won't hear of. So we're treading water here." He laughs shortly. "You sure you want to come be a part of all this?"

"Yes. Yes, of course I want to come."

CHAPTER SEVEN

Three days later, Parker Yardley meets me at the train station in New Haven. I had hoped so hard that it might be Ren who would come meet me, but he had warned me on the phone that he probably wouldn't be able to get away. Hospital stuff, doctors to meet with.

I've only seen Parker in person a few times before—a couple of brunches in Manhattan with her and Jenna, and then at a few opening nights of Ren's friends' plays. He did not once mention to them that we were dating, at least within my earshot, but even so, I worked so hard to be likable around them that my cheeks ached later from all the fake smiling I did.

And now there's no mistaking her here in the train station. She's the only woman wearing a cowboy hat and a purple feather boa that floats over her tight dark blue jeans and pink paisley midriff shirt. Peeking out from underneath the cowboy hat is shoulder-length blonde hair, fried to within an inch of its life.

I square my shoulders and walk over to her. "Hi, Parker," I say. I shift my bag to my other arm.

"Yeah, and you're Mimi, I guess," she says, like she doesn't know perfectly well who I am. She looks me over, flicking her eyes, taking in my trying-too-hard navy-blue cardigan with the padded shoulders and my creased jeans and clogs, and I believe she might be actually sneering. In the face of such coolness, I am back in seventh grade with my corkscrew curls and my oily skin, and the cool kids are whispering about me behind my back. I have to remind myself that I'm an adult, and her father is in love with me, and I have every right to be here.

But here's what I don't know: Is she contractually obligated to hate me for not being her mother? Probably. Too bad I don't have a piece of a magic skirt to offer up to her, like a pork chop to a snarling dog. Or maybe I could wave it in front of her, like a matador with a bull.

Which reminds me: *Where* is *that magic skirt? Did I leave it at the school?* There is, however, no time to think about that. Parker rummages through her huge tapestry carpetbag and pulls out a cigarette and lights up. "Want one?" she says.

"No thanks. And by the way, thank you for coming to pick me up," I say. "And—and for the lead on the apartment. Also, I'm so sorry to hear about your mom."

"Right," she says. "Thanks." She dives once again into her bag and emerges this time with car keys, and without saying another word to me, she heads for the double doors that lead out of the station. She has an impressive saunter, swinging her hips like they're on swivel mode. I hurry along behind her. We get to her car, which, to my surprise, is an old brown sagging Plymouth Duster with a black piece of material dragging on the ground from the trunk. I slide into the passenger seat, which is covered with a navy-blue nylon slipcover that has suspicious-looking stains on it. The car smells like old, rusted metal and cigarettes, and the windows are coated with a kind of yellowish film.

She sees my face. "This is my friend Barney's car. He doesn't do upkeep. We'll be lucky if we don't have to buy a couple of quarts of oil on the way home."

"Is Barney the guy with the apartment?"

She turns the key in the ignition, and the car roars to life, smelling like smoke. "The apartment? Ha! I can't imagine what it would look like if Barney had lived in it. Barney moved to Vermont to join a commune. Left his car parked in front of my mom's house and took the key with him. Which she did not appreciate because she's Judith the Queen of Neat, and also she was trying to sell the house at the time, and there was this piece of junk out there that nobody had the key for. And then just before she was going to have it towed, Barney came through and mailed us the key." She jerks the steering wheel and plunges us into traffic, narrowly missing a police cruiser parked at the curb. "Anyway, now that she's half dead and *her* car is destroyed, I get to drive it. Lucky me."

The words "half dead" sit there between us on the blue nylon slipcover. I know this type, the kind who trades in shock value. She twists her mouth around.

I murmur, "So tragic what happened. How's she doing?"

Parker's face suddenly closes. "Who knows? The medical people talk about her like she's a piece of cabbage just because for a week she couldn't talk. And now that she's started talking, they still act like she's not going to get better. I hate all of them."

"Wow! Talking!" I say. "That seems like progress."

"Yep. Today she said two words."

"Oh, what did she say?"

She looks at me as if that is the stupidest question ever. "Who knows? She probably said some syllables that meant *get me the hell out of here*."

We're zooming past a brick housing development, populated by old men standing on the sidewalk, drinking from cans in paper bags. The light turns red, Parker slams us to a halt, and my bag is flung on the floor.

I might have screamed a little bit in my throat.

"I'm a New Yorker," she says. "We don't drive."

I pick up my bag. "No, I get it," I say. "But hey, if you'd like me to drive, I'm happy to. You could navigate."

"And *you're* an expert on driving?"

"Well, sorta. I had a car in high school. Dent-free for four years."

"Well, good for you, but I hardly think that makes you some kind of expert."

"Okay, true. But I have noticed that in most cases, if you don't slam your foot down on the brake pedal, things go more smoothly. You arrive places with all your teeth still in." I laugh, to show that I mean this as a fun-loving joke—something we'll bond over later, perhaps, if we ever get to that point.

She responds by jerking the steering wheel, and the car slides around a corner, possibly on two wheels. Two pedestrians dash out of the way.

"Could you just, maybe, slow down a little bit? Maybe two notches?"

She sighs loudly, but I notice she does reduce the velocity. Somewhat.

After a moment, when I recover the power of speech, I say, "Are you—I mean, your mom's home now, right? So are you guys . . . able to take care of her?"

"Able?" She laughs and presses on the gas, roaring forward once again. "As you know, I'm not the one in the family who is considered *able* to do anything. At least, according to my mom, who doesn't get a vote right now, but you know she will. She's not the most maternal human there ever was. My dad is the one who raised me and Jenna."

"Yes," I say. I knew that part.

"We're a *team*," she says. "That's what he calls us. The Yardley Team."

"Yep," I say. I get her message exactly.

"It's like I belong to my dad, and Jenna belongs to our mom. Jenna is the golden child, which is why it's just so crazy ironic that it's the *golden child* who wants to put her in rehab! I mean, she has brain damage from the stroke—and you can't tell me that when your brain is trying to come back to life, you need to be in some locked ward! You need your family around you."

"*Mmm,*" I say. "I'm not sure rehab consists of locked wards."

She ignores this. "She and my mom are like carbon copies, all about work and statistics and degrees. It's me and my dad who are about the *humanities*. The arts. Things with feelings. I was thinking I'd write a memoir about my family, and that's what I'm going to call it. *Things with Feelings.*"

"Interesting," I say.

I've decided she must be high, talking this much. Now she slumps down in the seat, chewing on her fingernail, making me question whether the road is figuring into her consciousness at all, if she can even see over the steering wheel. I stare straight ahead, as if I can use the force of my will to keep the car in its lane.

I'm already exhausted.

"So." I take a wobbly breath. "Tell me about the apartment."

"Yeah. So, the apartment," she says. "My dad says you want to stay here for the summer because you got fired?"

"*Yeeeesssss . . .*"

"And you don't have anywhere else to go, he said."

"Just for the record, we're also engaged," I say quietly. Might as well make this clear from the beginning, although it makes my teeth ache to have to say it. "You knew that, right?"

"Well, sure. Of course. I knew that." I see her glance at my hand. "What's with him not giving you a ring? Aren't you supposed to be wearing some rock to scare all the other men off and announce that you're somebody's property?"

I feel myself blinking too much. "Well," I say. "Actually. Funny story about that. He was about to give me the ring, but then he found out about your mom, and he accidentally left with it still in his pocket."

"Uh-huh," she says. "Kind of a worlds-colliding moment."

"What do you mean?"

"Well, there you are, thinking he's starting a whole new life, and the old life calls him back in, and he forgets to give you the one symbol that would make it like it's a reality. That must have been hard on you, having nothing you could flash around."

"It was the least of my worries," I say quietly. "Don't put that in your memoir, if you please. It would be inaccurate."

"I'm not sure how far my memoir is going to extend. You might not even be in it."

Touché, I think. I almost want to laugh. This girl is no pushover. We've turned off a main road onto a residential street now, with a dizzying number of turns, and then we pass a high school and a park, with paths and park benches and a playground.

She swings the steering wheel, making an abrupt left turn, and says, "*We* live here," pointing to a pink two-story colonial. I crane my neck so I can see. It's stately and neat, with white shutters and an asphalt driveway, a trimmed lawn, and shrubs shaped like ice cream scoops. It's the kind of home you'd see in a *House Beautiful* spread and just know that it's quite well-appointed inside. How wonderful it would be to see Ren there, standing on the steps above the sloping lawn, perhaps waving and smiling. Welcoming me.

Parker is watching my face. "He's not there. He's taken Judith and Jenna to see the doctor. I should be there, too, but he told me to come get you. Said to tell you he'd catch you later."

"Oh," I say. "Thanks. Sorry you had to miss the meeting."

"They don't want me there. I'm the pain in the ass that the medical experts don't want around. Nobody but my dad wants to hear anything I have to say." She shrugs and drives a few more blocks and then turns the corner onto a street lined with smaller, skinny three-story houses. Wedged in between is a little mom-and-pop store with a metal sign that's flapping and banging against a pole. The sign says **EMBASSY MARKET**. A knot of high school students is hanging out by a dumpster filled with cardboard boxes. Parker pulls over in her inimitable fashion, which means I have to grab for the door handle. The car jumps with a growl of protest. She turns off the ignition, and the Duster shudders.

"So, this is it. Jason's apartment is on the second floor."

I lean down and peer up through the car window. She points to a brown-and-white three-story building. It has aluminum siding and a wooden porch, with two front doors. One has a wreath made of Popsicle sticks. All in all, not bad looking. The large, porch-facing first-floor windows have colored construction paper flowers taped to the glass. Upstairs, in the windows of the apartment that will contain my new life, the shades are closed. A third-floor window looks like it might be in an attic.

She says listlessly, "So if you take the place, obviously you won't have a car. You'll be stuck just going to places you can walk to, unless you want to ride the bus. Which *I* wouldn't, but you might have to."

"So . . . why is Jason moving, if I may ask?"

"There's a daycare downstairs, he says. He's an artist, so he needs quiet."

"A daycare? An entire daycare?"

"Yep. A million kids and parents. A lot of crying and whining and people coming and going. Kids screaming in the backyard, fighting over toys." She shifts her cowboy hat on her head and looks at me with something like satisfaction on her face. "Wow. My dad should have probably mentioned that, huh? This could be a dealbreaker for you."

"No . . . ," I say. Compared to living on the street in New York, or moving into the YWCA, living above a daycare seems pretty good.

To my surprise, Parker laughs. "You should see your face. Hope you like little kids!"

"I don't know any little kids, now that I think of it."

"Ha! Your face says you don't *want* to know any little kids."

"Actually I find them terrifying."

"Interesting," she says. "Well, maybe this isn't the place for you."

As if to prove her point, one of the front doors opens, and four toddlers come zooming across the porch and barreling down the steps, followed by a concerned-looking man who's holding another small person on his hip and attempting, with his other hand, to unfold an umbrella stroller by beating it against the floor of the porch. It does not open. Even I know that thrashing a stroller against the floor probably isn't going to make it magically open up.

"Stop! Wait!" he says. He's got a mop of unruly dark hair. "Please, kiddos. Don't go any further than the grass! We talked about this!"

He might as well be talking to wild animals. I mean, he *is* talking to wild animals. One little girl with dark hair, in a tiara and a net skirt, laughs and twirls around on the grass until she falls down, knocking into another kid, who falls on top of her. This leads to pummeling, as it would, of course.

He calls back over his shoulder, "Katherine? You coming?" He's triumphed somehow over the umbrella stroller, which has blossomed into an actual thing in which a kid might ride. He doesn't put the baby in it, though, because he has to suddenly sprint over to the two kids who look as though they might run into the road. He uses one hand to steer them back to the patch of dirt, and one kid goes limp and pretends to slump to the ground. "Here, stand up, Davy!" I hear him say. "Let's get in a line, okay? Remember how fun it is to be in a *line*?" I note the desperation in his voice. A woman comes out onto the porch with another child, shades her eyes, and then darts back inside because someone is yelling that Toby has to poop. One kid starts dancing too close to the sidewalk and the man attempts to call him back.

I hide my eyes. "Oh my God, I can't look."

"*I* just wonder if you're going to be all that happy here," Parker says.

I don't want to tell her that I have no choice. I don't want to tell her that I love her father more than anything and that I would do whatever it takes to stay near him and that, therefore, I am casting my net to catch her in it, too. I take a deep breath and say, "No, I'm fine. Okay. Let's go look inside."

The woman, possibly Katherine, has now reappeared, and she and the man have somehow corralled everybody and started on a trip along the sidewalk. I see them making their way in their perilous pilgrimage, dancing and dipping as they go. I shudder and head across the porch and then upstairs to the second floor.

∽

The apartment is fine, even glorious in its way. It has more than double the space of my New York place, for one thing. Maybe triple! It has a living room, hardwood floors, big windows, an actual dining room with built-in shelves, and a kitchen in the back with a stove and a loud-motored refrigerator containing two open cans of beer and something that looks like it might have once been a tomato. Sunlight streams into every window. There's a pink-tiled bathroom with a tub, and two bedrooms with actual closets—and suddenly I feel delirious from the effects of light and space.

So what that there's a daycare downstairs? Piffle! It might be wild during the day, but at least it won't be noisy at night, like my former apartment was, what with people trooping up and down the stairs at all hours. No buses rounding the corner and screeching their brakes. No long walks to the subway. No panhandlers on the corner. And best of all, Ren is here. My heart is here.

Parker, who is lying down on a brown corduroy couch, has pulled her cowboy hat over her eyes.

I go back into the living room. "Is it my imagination, or does that couch smell like beer?" I say.

She lifts up the edge of the hat and looks at me. "Jason has beer flowing in his veins, pretty much, so probably," she says. "This whole place stinks a bit, if you ask me."

"Nah," I say. I look around. "It's all right. It needs some TLC, but I like it. I'm going to take it."

"Really."

"Yep, I'm taking it."

"Daycare and all."

"Daycare and all."

She gets up off the couch. "Okay. Suit yourself." She hesitates a moment and then gives me a long look. "If I may say something: I just hope you're doing this for the right reasons." Her eyes narrow at me. "Because my dad isn't going to be free anytime soon to whisk you back to New York. He's definitely not going to go as long as Jenna and I need him. Just so you know."

"That's fine," I tell her. And then, because I don't have the good sense to hold on to even the slightest bit of my heart, I smile at her winningly and say, "In the meantime, you're the only person I know here, besides your dad, so if you ever want to do something, I'd like that. You know, maybe you could show me around New Haven a little bit. If you're ever . . . you know . . . free."

"I doubt that very much," she says. "Maybe you somehow missed the message that my mother is in critical condition just now, and I'm doing everything I can to keep her alive, and so that's taking a lot of my *leisure time*."

We don't speak on the way back to the train station. She turns the radio up and beats her hand on the steering wheel to some punk rock music that's beyond human understanding. I go back home to New York, tell La Starla that my new life is beginning and that I won't be seeing her in person for a while, and then a week later I pack up my clothes and arrange for two guys with a truck to come and move my couch, my bed, my stereo and speakers, my dresser, my coffee mug, my three plates, four forks, four spoons, and four knives to New Haven.

The afternoon I arrive, I find a vase of daisies sitting on a folding table on the porch, along with a note from Ren.

My love—welcome home! Hiring nurses for J, so life crazy just now. Sorry I'm not here to welcome you in person. Soon! XOXOXXOXO R

So there's that. He won't be coming over to see me.

I didn't expect how sad it would feel to move into a bare, gigantic apartment with my paltry pieces of furniture looking like deserted little islands in the great sea of floor space, and no one to welcome me. I didn't think how much it would feel like I had been plopped down onto a different planet. I don't even have electricity or a phone because I haven't had time or transportation yet to go and sign up for these things.

I walk around the apartment, making a list of things I need in order to create a nest here: phone service certainly, but also curtains, lamps, maybe a coffee table, a kitchen table and chairs, a rug or two, some artwork. I'll make it homey and lovely. Bring in plants. Paint the walls, which are now a disheartening clay color.

First, though, before it gets dark, I *have* to rid myself of this beer-soaked couch. I push and drag it out through the dining room and kitchen and shove it into the little hallway that leads to the back stairs and the first floor. With just a little heave-ho, I could throw it down to the bottom and then drag it out to the curb.

But . . . well, it gets stuck in the stairwell just at the place where the stairs turn the corner, and no matter how much I kick and swear at it, it won't move.

So I go back inside and lock the door. This will need to be solved another day.

I fall asleep on the first night of my new life with the streetlight shining in my front window, sending a big blank rectangle of empty whiteness across my bed.

CHAPTER EIGHT

The next day, I walk downtown and sign up for electricity and phone service, just like a real grown-up woman who knows how to move to a new city. Then I march myself into the high-ceilinged, cool New Haven Free Public Library and fill out an employment application. After that, I walk across the Green, a rambling, spacious public park, bordered by old-looking churches and big, brown, official-looking buildings that must be Yale, and I head back down Church Street toward home.

I'm not proud of this, but before going home, I walk past Judith's house. I keep my head down, in case someone is looking out the window. The worst thing would be to have somebody see how desperately I love the man inside, how strongly I feel that he should be outside here with me. Then, because this isn't pitiful enough, I go across the street to East Rock Park and stand behind a tree for a long time, surveilling the house from afar. It's not until an older woman comes over and asks me if I'm okay that I truly see how pathetic I am, and I slink home.

Late in the afternoon, I'm sitting on my front porch when a pregnant woman comes out of the daycare, trying to lock the front door with one hand while holding on to a small tow-headed boy who is laughing maniacally and trying to wiggle himself out of her grip. She's too busy concentrating to notice me, and no wonder. I don't know much about small boys except what I learned when I was a child having to cope with them on the playground: they are dangerous rascals who are always attempting death-defying feats like walking on porch railings, leaping from top steps onto cement sidewalks, and chasing balls into streets. And this one is no different.

He succeeds finally in getting away from the woman I assume is his mother while she's working on the door and swearing, and as he leaps down the porch steps, I hear her tell him that he better not run into the street again because she doesn't know if she can catch him anymore, and what if a big truck is coming. He'd get smushed is what.

He dances backward and yells to her that if there's a big truck, he'll just scoot down low, and the truck can just drive over him because he'll be between the wheels. "Ta-*dah*!" he says.

This is where I come in. I know from chasing dogs that it's better not to rush toward him, but I do walk down the steps and clap my hands and get him to look at me. He stops dancing and stands there with his fingers in his mouth. "Who are you?" he says.

"I'm Mimi," I say.

"Oh, Toby, come back over here," his mom says. She nods at me and goes down the front steps, steering her hundred-month-pregnant belly, which is covered in denim overalls with a black scoop-neck T-shirt underneath. She has glossy, curly brown hair—the way mine could be if it would only behave—and she smiles at me peacefully. "Sorry," she says. "He's always a bit over the top when we're leaving. And by the way, just so you know, he wasn't really going to run into the street. He makes that joke every day, about the truck." She rolls her eyes. "Three-year-olds! Am I right?"

"Well," I say. "Just in case, I was ready to save him if necessary. Flag down the truck. You know. Whatever it took."

She smiles and I smile back at her. She is so beautiful, I think—just a walking, glowing billboard for love and . . . belonging to someone. It's funny how I've never seen pregnant women quite this way before; I've always looked at them on the subway with sympathy, as they sighed and shifted their weight and closed their eyes. But this one is different—the small-city version. Coping. Relatively calm. Even though she's got a kid who jokes about possible instant death at the hands of a large motor vehicle, she seems very Zen.

"I'm Nicole," she says. "Are you the person who moved in upstairs?"

"Yes. I'm Mimi." I aim one of my biggest smiles in her direction. It feels a little fake, like I'm something of a ghost.

"Welcome." She looks at the formerly prancing boy, who is now glued to her side, staring at me and sucking his thumb. "Toby, say hi to Mimi."

"Hi, Toby," I say.

He takes his thumb out of his mouth and buries his face in his mother's overalls.

"Oh well," she says. And then she remembers something and smacks her forehead. "Oh no! I've got to go back inside and get my bowls. It was my food week, and I left everything inside. Come on, Toby Moorehead, we're goin' back in!"

"Can I get them for you?" I say.

"Well, you won't know which ones—well, yes, actually, could you? Thank you. They're sitting on the countertop in the kitchen, a red mixing bowl and a CorningWare white thing. Here's the key. Thank you." She rubs her enormous belly, like she's a Buddha and this belly-rubbing will bring her luck.

I go inside and am instantly floored by the . . . daycare-ness of the place. The layout is just like my apartment, but this living room doesn't even pretend to need furniture. It's all decorated with big pillows and wooden bookcases filled with toys. I make my way through the living room and back to the kitchen, where there are little toddler-sized tables and chairs set up. The place has the smell that I can only think of as a little-kid smell—sweat and milk and perhaps a diaper or two. Sure enough, I find two bowls on the counter, and I take them outside. My mom had that same CorningWare roasting dish, white with little blue flowers on the side. For a moment, I wonder if my mother ever was maternal. Ever? I can't imagine her ever being pregnant with me, gently rubbing her stomach while I rocked around inside.

When I get back outside, Nicole is putting Toby into a car seat in an old beige Datsun station wagon parked near the curb. She straightens up and takes the bowls out of my hands and thanks me.

"Come down and visit us sometime. I hope we don't run you off like we did the former tenant. We try to behave, but we do specialize in chaos."

"Chaos is cool," I say, ridiculously. Then I don't know what to say. I just want to stand there soaking up her life, which is weird, so I say, "Looks like your baby is coming soon!" And she shrugs and says, "Yeah, well, you'd think so, from the size of me. But actually I have probably four more months to go."

"Four more months? I know nothing about pregnancy, but you look ready to pop."

I'm immediately sorry for saying something so personal and perhaps rude, but she leans back and places her hands on her belly and smiles at me. "Yeah. Second babies—you know. No muscle tone anymore to hold 'em in, so you look gargantuan. I'm at the stage now where I'm being pummeled from the inside pretty much ninety percent of the time, and my back hurts, and I have to pee four times during the night. Do you have kids?"

"I don't."

"I forget that people don't go around talking about how often they get up to pee. You're just lucky I didn't mention stuff like varicose veins and mucus plugs." She hands the bowls to Toby, who is reaching for them from his car seat.

"Seriously . . . there's such a thing as mucus plugs?"

"Forget it. Mucus plugs are just a . . . thing . . . and when it comes out, you know the baby is coming somewhat soon. But you still don't know when. Sorry."

"No, no. It's fine. I did ask. By the way, I'm sorry about that couch stuck on the back stairs. I'm trying to work on getting it unstuck."

"No problem," she says. "It doesn't interfere with the daycare."

She gets Toby to wave to me, which he does by waving the red bowl, and then she laughs and closes the car door and walks around to the driver's side and gets in, a Madonna in overalls with shiny hair and bright eyes. I see the way she arranges herself so that her stomach will fit behind the wheel, and I wave to her and watch as she pulls away.

∽

The next three days drag by. And there is still no sign of Ren. I remember Parker's warning that he won't ever see me as long as anybody over there needs him. Apparently this means that he won't *ever* see me.

I pace around the apartment, and then I decide to phone La Starla. "I was an idiot to move here!" I say as soon as she answers. "Why didn't you stop me? I followed my intuition, like you said, and now I'm completely alone in a strange city with nobody to talk to, and I never see Ren because he has no time for me. The universe has reduced me to spying on his house from behind a tree in the park."

La Starla roars with laughter. When she can pull herself together again, she says, "Darling, the universe is not responsible for your need to spy! Why don't you just call him up?"

"How would *I* have Judith's number?"

"Mimi. Really?" she says. "Call directory assistance. Ask for the number, write it down on a piece of paper, and then punch it into—"

"I know that part," I say. "But what if one of his daughters answers?"

She sighs. "Well, *then* you say, 'May I speak to your father, please?'"

"And what if they want to know who's calling? I suppose you think I should just say my name!"

"I think that would be a good next move. And by the way, the spirit guides say you're not an idiot for following your intuition and moving there. All of this is information you need for your life. No matter which way it turns out. Stay open."

After we hang up, I call directory assistance and am informed that Judith's number is unlisted. I call La Starla back immediately and tell her this new problem.

She says gently, "Mimi, it's time you realized you're a person in his life. Go over to his house, honey, and ring the bell. Smile. Say hello. Maybe take some brownies."

"Oh," I say.

∽

On day five, I go across the street and buy coffee and eggs and bread at the Embassy Market, and a woman there tells me about the cheap antique shops—which are really junk shops with tons of discarded furniture for sale—on State Street, so I walk the few blocks over and find myself in a haven of old tables, lamps, rugs, and artwork, all crammed along the walls, stacked up into piles, or else hanging from the ceiling, all presided over by a rickety old man named Arnie. It's actually quite wonderful. If I can't have Ren, at least I can make a home for myself. I don't have to sit in a depressing apartment by myself. I buy a coffee table for five dollars, an eight-by-twelve Turkish rug for ten, a pole lamp and two table lamps for four dollars each.

There is, of course, no way to get them home, so I tell Arnie that I'll just make multiple trips and carry them myself. "You could rent a truck, you know," he says. "Or you could hire somebody."

"Nope. I'll just walk some of them home every day," I tell him. He looks at me and shrugs. But what I can't explain to him is that in walking my new possessions home, I realize I'm walking myself home, too. Peering into shops, little restaurants, being open to life. There's a bakery across the street called Marjolaine's, and I buy a bag filled with croissants and almond pastries, and then there's no way to make it home except to carry the bag in my mouth while I struggle with getting the rug back to my apartment. After I manage to get the rug forced up the stairs by pushing on it from below and bumping it up all thirteen stairs,

I unroll it in the living room and then sit back and admire how it brings the room together.

Tomorrow I'll go back for the rest.

After that, I take a bubble bath in the big claw-foot tub, and when I get out, I put on my nicest pair of jeans and a lavender top that does not look like it's trying too hard, and I take my bag of pastries and walk straight over to Judith's house.

I am quite surprised at myself.

But I can do this because I am in action mode now. No more hiding behind a tree! I have made up my mind that I will take things into my own hands. I will give him my phone number. I want to see his face. I want to see his daughters. I want to peek inside his new life, and then, with my smile, remind him that this life he's in right now is temporary, and that I'm the future and I love him.

I look in the mirror, fluff up my hair, tell the universe that I'm being brave and that it had better reward me for this huge amount of courage, and off I go.

❧

"Oh my God." That's what he says when he opens the door.

He looks behind him like he's hoping not to be seen, and then he slips out onto the porch and closes the door behind him. I stop breathing.

"What are you *doing* here?" he says. Then he takes me by the elbow, and not in a very gentle way either.

I feel my smile freeze on my face. "I wanted to see you," I say, and my voice cracks. "I thought I'd bring over some treats for your family."

"That's very nice of you, but I can't really talk here. Come on. Let's walk over to the park." He's looking behind him, rushing me down the porch steps and then across the street.

There is nothing about this moment that is okay.

"Wait a second," I say. I stop walking. Everything is a little blurry. "Was this a mistake? Me moving to New Haven? You don't want me here?"

He grips my arm and steers me into the park, where the trees can hide us. I know because they've hidden me in the last few days.

"Of course I want you in New Haven! I'm glad to see you!" He sees my face. "*Ohhh, noooo.* Don't be upset. Please. I shouldn't have reacted that way. I'm delighted to see you. I miss you something terrible." He pulls me to him now that we're hidden from the house.

"I-I've been here for over four days, and I haven't heard from you."

"You didn't get my note? And the flowers?"

"I did."

"Well then, that's hearing from me! Oh, sweetie. What did you think, that I was just going to be able to come hang out anytime I want? Look, I'm going through hell here, trying to get my family in some kind of position where life seems even halfway possible. You can understand that. It's hard on me, too." He kisses the top of my head, and then takes my hand and starts us walking again. Apparently we are in a spy movie, and we have to keep moving.

We walk along the path for a minute or so. I can't look at him, so I just stare at the ground and at my kitten heels, the ones he'd liked so much in New York, which are not meant for walking on a dirt path in a park. I stop and pull a rock out of my left one. He groans.

"Where are we going?" I say. "In fact, what's going on?"

When he speaks, his voice is a little softer. He takes my hand. "I'm sorry. I'm just trying to get us away from the house. Maybe you perhaps didn't understand the direness of the situation here. Judith is home, but she's pretty sick still, and I'm hiring caregivers, and trying to negotiate between Jenna and Parker, who have opposing viewpoints on just about *everything*. And nobody's getting any sleep or anything they need, and it's awful. I don't even want to go into it all because you're just going to think you can help, and you can't."

"So what you're saying is that I'm the last thing you need showing up," I say.

"Well . . ." He runs his hands through his hair. "Yeah. I think that's exactly right." Then he hears himself and adds, "It's not that I'm *not* glad to see you. I mean, I am. You're a sight for sore eyes, you are, but you're from a part of my life that isn't exactly . . . operational . . . just now. We're at the worst of it, but it's going to get easier, baby, I swear it."

I refuse to walk anymore. It's taking all my concentration to keep myself from bursting into tears. "I came over because I wanted to see you and Jenna and Parker, and also I wanted to give you my phone number. But you're acting like I'm the *other woman* or something, you know, when that is not the kind of person I am! This is not what we're all about."

"I know, I know," he says. "Listen . . . Give me your phone number, and also . . . well, maybe I can slip out some nights after everybody's settled down, and I could come and visit you. How would that be?"

"Visit me?"

"Yeah. Like I'd come to your apartment and we could . . . you know . . . shake the sheets." He grins.

I stare at the ground. My fingertips are throbbing with the need for him. He reaches over and pulls my knit hat down over my ears and strokes my cheek.

"It won't always be this way. I love you, you rapscallion hothead of a human. But now I really, really have to get back. All right?"

"Well. What choice do I have? All right."

"We okay?"

"I suppose."

"I promise I'll come over soon. Be strong." He brushes his lips against the top of my head and does the thing he used to do back in the days of supply-closet sex, which is kiss me up and down both sides of my neck and then say a thing we heard some clueless kid saying to his girlfriend in the hallway that used to always crack us up: "I love you so much! You're my dime a dozen!"

We don't leave the park together. He goes first, walking rapidly, and he tells me to wait a few minutes before I follow and go back to my apartment.

I think I hate this.

◈

That evening the doorbell rings, and I have a mad moment of thinking maybe it's Ren coming to see me after all, realizing his mistake and wanting to apologize. But no. It's the landlord, John, and he is so apoplectic that the veins are popping out in his neck, bulging above the collar of his business suit. Apparently I have this effect on landlords.

This one I have only met one other time, for five seconds, on the day I moved in, when he showed up to pick up the rent check and shake my hand, and already I have him looking at me with murder in his eyes.

"What is the *meaning* of that couch in the stairwell?" he says. He looks like he's dressed for a formal dinner, with slicked-back black hair, a suit, and pointy shoes. "What are you thinking, putting that there? That is not okay. Have you not read the lease?"

"Oh! I'm so sorry, but it's not my couch," I say, smiling at him in my most reassuring way. "It was Jason's old couch, but he left it, and I didn't want it."

"You didn't want it, so you . . . *threw* it there?"

I smile again. More sweetly. "I tried to get it outside by myself, but I didn't have anyone to help me. Jason should have to come and get it. Right?"

"So you just *threw it*?" he says. His eyes are bugging out.

"I shouldn't have done that? Okay. I'm sorry."

"You are allowed to put exactly nothing in the stairwell. Nothing, you hear? Public spaces are not for your junk. Bulk trash day is coming soon. Get it to the curb. Immediately."

"It wasn't my junk," I say. "It was *Jason's.*" But he's already gone down the front steps, shaking his head in disgust, and he gets into a fancy Cadillac, driven by a woman with mile-high hair. They pull away from the curb.

I go inside and lie down on the rug and think dark thoughts about how I don't have a partner in life. This is when it would be so nice to have someone who can lift half a couch and bring it gently down the stairs and out to the curb, and then walk with me back upstairs and say something like *shall we have tacos tonight or chicken masala, which do you feel like,* and *or whaddaya say we just go to bed and read our books and make love and turn in early*—and then as years go by, the talk would be *and did you pick up the new bassinet because the one we used for Julia looks like it has a little mildew on it, and oh yes, I told the babysitter to be here at seven.*

I hit myself, hard, on the top of my head. What the hell are babysitters and bassinets doing showing up in my daydream? It's got to be the daycare vibes, curling up the stairs from below. Very dangerous place.

Oh my God, I am so lonely. And I have no idea what to do with that couch.

CHAPTER NINE

Another week goes by, and I learn what you do while you are waiting for your lover, alternately loving and hating him.

You make a nest. You decorate your apartment, forcing yourself to revel in the vastness, the sheer number of walls. You ignore the couch lodged in the stairwell and distract yourself by drawing stencils of flowers on the wall in the bathroom. You paint the living room and dining room walls a shade called porcelain peach, and then you hang paintings of the sea with plenty of clouds and birds, paintings you found leaning near a trash can outside a huge colonial. You scrub the old tub of rust stains and you buy candles and place them everywhere, on every surface.

During the weekdays, you stand at the kitchen window, holding a cup of coffee and watching the children in the yard, nearly all of them dressed in corduroy overalls and long-sleeved shirts. It's officially spring now, but still cold outside. They run around in dizzy circles.

After that's done, you lie on your old used couch with the ten blue throw pillows you bought and read the books you brought from your old life—*Jane Eyre* and *Fear of Flying*, as well as ten issues of *Cosmo* magazine. You learn seventeen tips to make him feel like the only man in the world—all doable only when he's present, I notice.

You apply for jobs at two bookstores and at the Hall-Benedict pharmacy, which is only two blocks away. While at the pharmacy, you buy some moisturizer, some foundation called Tan-I-Am, a tube of mascara, and some Kiss Me Pink lipstick. When you go home, you paint yourself up just for fun and use the kitchen shears to cut exactly one-eighth of an inch off your split ends. Then you wash your face and go to bed and stare at the streetlight out the window, shining through the yellowed, aging shades that probably have been there half a century or so.

When the landlord contacts you and says that if that couch isn't freaking gone within twenty-four hours, he's taking drastic measures, you bake some brownies and then go outside at five o'clock and wait for some unsuspecting young daycare father to show up. You will offer brownies, babysitting, whatever he wishes. But the couch must go.

Then I see him, my unsuspecting victim—the man I last saw fighting with an umbrella stroller while managing the lives and safety of several out-of-their-minds toddlers. He's coming out of the daycare, obviously leaving for the day, and he has the adorable little dark-haired girl with him, the one who was wearing a tiara and who has serious, smoky eyes that look like she's been alive a lot longer than however many years daycare kids have been alive. I have no real idea. Two? Four?

She says to me, "Hi, upstairs lady."

"Hi, downstairs lady," I say lightly.

I am looking at the man, who has a perpetually worried expression on his face every time he looks over at his daughter. He slides his eyes away from her long enough to smile at me, a rushed, nervous smile. He is thin and anxious, with hair that looks like it's yet another detail that he hasn't gotten to just yet.

I recognize immediately that he is not the one to burden with my couch.

But "bulk trash day" is coming, and I don't have much choice. He's the only one currently available. Up and down the street, tables, old TV sets, boxes, kitchen appliances, and chairs are starting to appear with some regularity.

So I smile at him. "Hi, I'm Mimi. I've moved in upstairs. I think I saw you a while back, helping a whole bunch of kids while you were heroically fighting with a stroller."

He smiles weakly. "I'm Jamie," he says, "and this is Alice. And yeah, I'm the number one enemy of umbrella strollers everywhere. They fear me."

"I hate to bother you, but I'm in a bit of trouble with the landlord already, and—"

"Oh, the couch on the back stairs? We noticed that," he says.

"Yeah. I'm so sorry. It's stuck, and I'm wondering if you and I together might be able to dislodge it and drag it out to the street. I'd hate to be evicted before I've even settled in."

"Well," he says. He looks over at his little girl. "Alice, honey, would you like it if we helped Mimi?"

"Mimi, Mommy, Mimi, Mommy." She twirls around, arms stretched out.

I see him physically startle at this.

"Mimi Mommy, Mimi Mommy. That's what I call her."

"You just met her," he says. "How do you call her anything yet?"

"I know her," she says smugly. "She's upstairs."

"Well," he says. I look over at him, which I'm free to do for as long as I want, because he's intently watching his daughter. He's handsome in a kind of anxious, distracted way, but my God, he's wearing glasses that are so smeared that I can't believe he can see out of them. And that hair! Longish and curly, flying everywhere. He's wearing a rumpled blue button-down shirt and khaki pants—an attempt at normal office wear, from the looks of it. He kneels down next to his daughter and holds her arms and gazes searchingly into her face. "Shall we help Mimi, Alice? Do you want to be a helper with Daddy?"

We are both breathlessly awaiting her answer. I'm ready to throw in all the brownies and a cookie and perhaps the promise of a pony to be delivered later if she will just okay this transaction.

"One thing," she says, and her big brown eyes settle on me with a direct stare. "First tell me. How your name is Mimi?"

I look at him for guidance, but he's looking down at her. "My mommy gave it to me," I say. "Just like your name. Your mommy and your daddy gave you your name."

"*My* mommy—"

He clears his throat and scoops her up into his arms. "We'll be glad to help you, won't we, Alice?"

"Yes," she says, perturbed at the interruption, and determined to get back to her sentence. "*My* mommy is in the ground now, so we can't see her anymore. Did you know her?"

Jamie swallows so hard I see his Adam's apple go up and down. He smiles sadly, like this is something he deals with all the time, and he kisses her cheek. Then he says, "Alice, honey, let's go help Mimi with the couch. Want to? And then we'll go get some food and maybe some ice cream."

"What food?" She crosses her arms. "And what kind of ice cream?"

"You can pick," he says miserably. "Any kind you say."

"Um, I have brownies I baked for you," I say.

"I don't like brownies," she says and squirms out of his arms and starts twirling on the grass.

"So what about us being helpers? Did you decide?" Jamie asks her.

She considers. My possible eviction hangs in the balance. I hope I don't have to explain that to her. After a moment she stops twirling and meets my eyes and says, "Can I call you Mimi Mommy?"

"Sure. You can call me that if you want to," I say.

"Please," says Jamie in a low voice. "I'm sorry about this. She's . . . well, she just turned four. We deal with . . . stuff."

"It's fine," I say. "In fact, don't worry about this. If the couch thing is too much, I'll figure something else out."

"No!" says Alice. "We do the couch!"

"Great! Thank you, Alice. This is very sweet of you," Jamie says. And the three of us trudge to the back door, and then we go up six stairs, to where the couch is angled impossibly tightly against the wall. Jamie says, "Hmm," the hopeless way I've seen men do when faced with inanimate objects misbehaving, and then he goes into masculine planning mode, and after a few moments of frowning and sighing, he says I should go upstairs and push from there, and he'll pull from below.

"Great," I say.

Alice says she's coming with me. She puts her little hand in mine, and we walk together around the house to my front door, and when we get inside, she says I have too many stairs, and how many are there, and because I don't exactly know, she says we have to count them while we climb up, one at a time. This takes forever, but I do it, mostly because I'm in awe of this terrifying little girl who knows the secrets of loss and life and death and also is apparently the authority in her household, ruling over mealtime and treat time and all social interaction.

After Alice and I get to the kitchen and open the door to the back hall, Jamie and I manage to push and tug the couch all the way down the stairs, huffing and puffing, and he calls up to me that he's gotten a contact beer buzz just from being in that stairwell, and no wonder it had to go. "I'd have to be taking ibuprofen every day just for the hangover," he says. I like a man who can make jokes even when he's obviously lost his mind. His daughter is now behind me, spinning in circles and yelling, "MimiMommyMimiMommyMimiMommy" over and over again.

"Got it!" he calls as the couch gives way and suddenly slides to the bottom of the stairs. I offer my hand to Alice, and she and I go downstairs together, and sure enough, there is the couch, lying on its side out in the daycare yard. It has not crushed her father on its ride down, I'm pleased to see.

"Okay, let's take it to the curb." He changes back to his father voice, soft and appealing. "Alice, would you like to ride on the couch while we take it to the street?"

"Yes!" she says.

"Don't fall off," says Jamie. "Hold as tight as you ever have in your whole life."

I'm alarmed by this development, but she rides like a princess on a parade float. We get it in place on the curb, and then she wants us to take her down the street on it, and I'm scared he's going to say yes, and we'll break our backs doing that, so I jump in and say, "Hey! I'm making tacos tonight. Would you two like to come upstairs and have some?"

"Hmm," says Jamie. "Alice, would you like to eat at Mimi's house tonight?"

She considers with her index finger on her chin. Then she says, "Yes! I want to eat with Mimi Mommy!"

"Great," I say.

"And you'll eat on Mimi's plates?"

"*Ummm* . . . yes!"

"And sit at Mimi's table?"

"Yes!"

"Will you eat with Mimi's forks and spoons?"

What the actual hell?

But he is not done. He's still looking at her with a solicitous look on his face. "Shall we get your baby doll from the car and she will go upstairs with you, too?"

"No baby doll," she says, spinning around.

"Okay, if you're sure. Are you ready to go upstairs?"

"Um. Two minutes!" she says.

We wait at least two minutes, during which we admire the placement of the couch on the curb, and I thank him again, and then finally Alice says it's okay to go upstairs for tacos, and so we head up the back stairs, and into my kitchen, and I offer him a glass of wine, which makes him look so excruciatingly uncomfortable that I wonder if his wife might have died from alcoholism, but then he says yes, but in a drawn-out, hesitating way that might mean he doesn't really think he should. This guy!

"Are you sure?" I say. "We don't have to."

"No. Yeah. I mean, I just have some work to do tonight after she's gone to bed, so usually I like to be somewhat sober, but what the hell? I'm already drunk from the fumes of the couch, so what's a little more?"

"That's what I think," I say. I stand on tiptoe and reach up to the second shelf over the sink to get my wineglasses, which I just bought at the junk shop today, and I say, "So what kind of work do you have to do?"

"Ugh," he says. "I'm in grad school. Business. I've been taking classes but now it turns out I need to do a capstone project, so I'm researching that little problem."

"My daddy goes to school," says Alice in a very serious voice. "My grandpa makes him."

Jamie looks embarrassed and smiles. "Alice! That's not really true—honey, I like going to school!"

"You said that he makes you, Daddy. You did. I heard you say it on the phone."

"Okay, well. I was joking." He looks at me and says in a low voice, "Mostly. I used to be a furniture designer and a carpenter before this grad school thing came along."

"Not that I'm going to know what you're talking about," I say, "but what is your father making you study?" I pour the wine into the two glasses.

"Not my father. My, uh, wife's father. He's the CEO of a company that makes and sells machines for printing textbooks, and—and, well, he's paying for my grad school in the hopes that I'll come and take over his company at some point. I mean, we both hope that."

"*I* hope that," says Alice. "Also, I would like a drink, please."

"Oh! Of course you would!" I say. "I'm so sorry. I didn't offer you a thing!"

"It's okay," she says. "You forgot me."

"Wait! Hold on, hold on!" says her dad. "No one forgets you, pumpkin. Who could *ever* forget you for even one second?"

"Mommy forgot me." She says this matter-of-factly, without a trace of sadness. Just reporting the facts.

He had been leaning against the counter, but now he drops down onto the floor in front of her and puts his hands on her arms. "Sweetie, Mommy never forgot you. She loves you very much, so much more than she loved anything else in her life."

"Does she remember me from in the ground?" She pokes out her lower lip.

"Yes. Yes, she does." He swallows hard.

To my surprise, she laughs. "I know that, Daddy-o-Daddy! She didn't forget me." She thumps him on the chest and winds herself into his arms. "Daddy-o-Daddy, you're too worried."

I look at the two of them. She's laughing, but she has a kind of sad look back deep in her eyes, and he—well, he's just a wreck. How could he *not* be? I tell her that I have milk, orange juice, and water, and she comes over and looks in my refrigerator and says she'd like the pickle juice from my jar of pickles, if she could. And then she laughs uproariously when I say, "How about milk?"

"How about . . . soy sauce?" she says and spins herself around.

"Milk will be fine," says Jamie. I pour her a glass of milk, but she wants a wineglass, and he has to negotiate with her to accept a plastic cup, and then, leaving it untouched, she dances away, off to see the rest of the apartment and do whatever four-year-olds do when they get out from under adult supervision. I'm a little nervous, frankly, but not so nervous that I want to stop her. Instead, I take out the hamburger meat and start frying it up in the pan. And then I remember that I'd asked him what his capstone project is about, and so I ask him again, and he says, "Oh yes. The relationship of financial incentives to worker retention in midsized corporations, and how to enhance employee participation in work-improvement programs."

"Ah. Kind of like you pay higher salaries, and more people stay?"

"Something like that. A couple thousand more unknown, boring details thrown in."

Alice comes back into the room and announces that there are not enough toys in my apartment. So the two of them go down to the daycare and bring up a riding toy car, which Alice then thunders around on, through the kitchen, dining room, and living room, turning right at the little hallway and into my bedroom and then into the bathroom. I hear her yelling, "Beep! Beep!" There's an occasional crash into a wall, which makes him sit up straighter and crane his neck, but we can hear her laughing. It's fun, crashing. I'll put everything back together later, I tell him.

I put my Bonnie Raitt album on the stereo and get out the tomatoes and lettuce and cheese and start grating the cheese. He wanders around with his glass of wine. I keep stealing little glances over at him. I've never met a young guy who's endured such a tragedy, and I want to see how it sits on his shoulders. I bet he doesn't sleep much. I bet every noise in the night wakes him up. And I can't even imagine what the mornings are like, in negotiations with Alice for getting dressed, eating breakfast, and finally getting out the door.

But mainly it's the death that I'm fixated on.

I'm fighting myself from saying something ridiculously inappropriate and nosy like "How and when did it happen?" when he clears his throat and says, "We had no idea that the guy upstairs was leaving. What a pain he was, always leaving mean little notes saying we had to clean up the yard and stop making so much noise." To my surprise, his face breaks out in a big smile. "One day he wrote that we were, and I quote, 'horrible people with no respect for human life.' We all got a big laugh out of that."

"Ha."

"Anyway, I just wanted to say that I certainly hope whoever subletted you this place explained in advance how horrible we are so you won't be shocked."

I'm starting to say that I'm not shocked at all when Alice pipes up. She's back, sitting on the riding toy, looking like Dale Evans relaxing on horseback. "Why we horrible?" she says.

"Because we make a lot of noise, I guess," says Jamie.

"Why?"

"Because? We're a daycare? With lots of kids? Having fun, maybe?" he says.

"Why?"

"Fun makes noise," I say.

She turns to me. "Do you have a kid?" She squints and looks up at me. "Where your kid is?"

"I don't have any kids," I tell her.

"Why?"

"I don't know. I just—"

"It's okay," says Jamie to me and shakes his head. He may have identified me already as someone who is quite willing to explain my unfortunate dating history to a four-year-old just because I can't think of how to get out of it. "Alice says 'why' four hundred thousand times a day lately. And once you start answering, you can get into this thing where you can't stop, and thirty questions later, you end up having to explain all your life choices."

"This is why I'd never be good at being a parent," I say. "I can't explain why I've ever chosen anything."

"No. Nor can I."

Our eyes meet, and she gives us both an exasperated look and then climbs on him and kisses his cheek over and over again, and then she jumps down and heads back to crash some more objects with the riding toy.

"So tell me more about this horrible daycare," I say lightly. I start chopping up lettuce, and he jumps up to help, but I figure he cooks enough dinners, so I motion him back down to his chair. Someone should wait on him for a change. "I'm fine. You want some more wine?"

"No, no, I shouldn't even have this much wine," he says.

Alice is back, twirling around, barely balancing on one foot.

He watches her, looking concerned, and clears his throat. "Well, *I* don't think we're *horrible* horrible. It's just that it's a co-op, you see, so we all work there, taking turns. We mean well, at least. We're just loud because we have eight to ten kids all going at once, so it gets chaotic. If you're a student or trying to work from home, it could get . . . bad, I think. What do you do? For work, I mean?"

"I just moved here from New York. And as weird as it is to admit, I'm . . . not doing anything. First time in my life I'm just a slacker. I was a teacher, but things happened, and now I'm going to have to look for a job."

"Oh," he says. "What brought you to New Haven?"

"Love. My fiancé has an ex-wife who lives in this neighborhood—and well, it's complicated."

"It so often is." He smiles. "Especially when *fiancé* and *ex-wife* show up in the same sentence. Never mind in the same neighborhood."

"Yeah, she was literally driving to Chicago to move away for good, and she had a stroke and got in an accident and was in a coma, so he moved back to help his kids figure out how to help her, and on and on and on like that, and on the day of the accident, we had just coincidentally decided to get married, and so he wanted me to move nearby, and even as I'm saying this to you, it all sounds kind of crazy, because he suddenly doesn't have any time for me at all, and I'm just kind of in the way. His daughters don't like me, and why would they? I mean, I didn't break up their parents' marriage or anything, so please don't think that, because I am not that kind of person, but it's like the whole family is now all back together again three streets away, and I don't belong."

He's looking at me with his eyebrows in the surprised position. "Isn't it awful when you have to tell complete strangers that you're not the kind of person who breaks up people's marriages?"

I shrug. "Sorry," I say. "I can't seem to tell a condensed version of anything lately."

I would like to take back at least half of what I just said, especially the part about the accident. Maybe Jamie's wife died in an accident. Also, I sound rather pitiful and spiteful, talking about not seeing Ren, when he's got plenty of other serious things to think about.

Jamie drains his wine. "So he's living back in the house with her?"

"He is. That sounds bad, doesn't it?"

"Well. It sounds hard. On everybody."

"Yeah. You have no idea what a wuss I am. The other day I took over some pastries, thinking I could be, you know, somebody everyone in the family actually knows about, but he says I can't go back over. It's not *the right time.* And I'm so pathetic that sometimes I just go over to the park that's facing their house and I just stand behind a tree and stare at their living room windows, like a spy or something. And now I can't imagine why I'm telling you all this, because you are clearly going to think I'm a psychopath, and I'm really not."

He does smile at that. "I don't know. It kinda makes sense to do that, *I* think. Maybe he'd look out and see you and come running out screaming about how he's free at last!"

"Yep. Well, so far it's not working out that way." We're silent for a minute, while I turn down the ground beef and rake it around with the spatula as it sizzles. "So . . . this daycare is a co-op? That sounds cool."

"It is cool. Sort of fly-by-night-cool. No rules, no regulations. Just us and the kids. We all take turns working there. Four hours a week, no matter what else your life holds or how little you know about parenting, which in my case is quite a lot."

"Ah, yes. I met Nicole the other day. She mentioned something called food weeks?"

"*Ohh,* food weeks," he says and smacks his forehead. "Yeah. Those can bring a person to their knees."

"You have to feed *everybody* for a whole week?"

"Yep. And maybe I have special trouble with it because—well, I never really knew how to cook until . . . well, Lauren . . ." He stops for a moment and watches Alice, and then skips the last half of the sentence. "Anyway. Now I am mostly proficient at noodles with butter and grilled cheese and chicken nuggets and . . . broccoli . . . and oh, yes, macaroni and cheese! We have lots of macaroni and cheese, don't we, sweetheart? But lots of people in this daycare seem like *chefs* compared to what I do."

Alice suddenly pipes up and says, apropos of nothing I can see, "I wanna go home, Daddoo." She starts pulling on his jacket sleeve.

"That sounds like a big learning curve," I say, wanting to keep him talking.

"I wanna go*ooo,*" she says.

He stops what he was about to say and looks down at her. "Can we eat first?"

"No. I want to go now." She's starting to cry.

He kneels down next to her and strokes her hair. "But, Alice, sweetie, Mimi has made all this food just for us."

"I don't care. I want to go! Take me *hoooome*!" It's like a switch has been flipped, and she's suddenly in full meltdown. I am a little bit in awe. We could have used this kind of emotional talent in the Piedmont drama department.

"Did you really want to try some of that pickle juice?" I say, hoping to make her laugh, but she's too clever for my tactics. She gives me a sad look and then wails louder than ever.

"Okay, honey," says Jamie quickly. "Let's get you ready, and then we'll go put you in your car seat." He gets up and turns to me, his face drawn. "We should go. I'm sorry. It's been this way since . . . well, you know." He mouths the name "Lauren."

He picks her up and then we both notice that she's not wearing her shoes.

"I'll find them," I say. I'm still shocked. Is this just the way little kids are, or did something happen to make her want to go right this minute? Should I offer to run over and get some ice cream at the Embassy Market, bribe her to stay? Get down on the floor and offer to play with the toy car? I look at Jamie for help, but he's not looking at me.

"No, no, it's okay. I'll get them. Alice, sweetie, where did you leave your shoes?"

She's starting to cry in earnest now. "I . . . don't . . . *know*."

"Are they in the bedroom?" he says and looks to me. "Is it okay if . . ." And when I nod at him, they head off in that direction, with her leaning against him whimpering.

While they're gone, I pack up taco stuff for them and put it in some plastic bowls I found in one of the cabinets. My hands are shaking.

"Here," I say when he comes back. Alice has her shoes on now and is wiping her eyes. "You can heat this up at home."

He gives me a long look and says, "Thank you. I'm sorry. This isn't personal. It's the way . . ."

"I know," I say, although I don't. I don't know anything, in fact. I've lived a life that can't compare to what he's gone through.

He carries Alice to the stairs and then turns and looks at me. "You know, if you ever wanted, I don't know, to just come down and say hello to everyone in the daycare, we'd like that. We're a friendly bunch, just disorganized and a little—well, as I said—loud. Frantic. Out of our minds possibly."

"*Ooh*, tempting," I say.

"*Daddoooooo!* Come *onnnnn!* Go! Go! Go!"

At the moment when I should simply close the door behind them, I don't. Instead, I walk out with them, crossing the porch. The bottom step wobbles a bit when I step on it, but I manage to keep from tripping.

"Hey, look, the couch is already gone," he says. "That's the story of bulk trash. It drifts back and forth through neighborhoods. Comes and goes."

I'm silent a moment, picturing the beery old couch floating through the neighborhood, up and down the streets, visiting homes for a little while and then getting put back on the curb due to its smell.

"I hope this couch doesn't come back here when people figure out it could pretty much function as a brewery," I tell him.

"That could be its greatest selling point," he says.

I stand and watch while he squats down next to the back seat of his car, trying to talk Alice into getting into her car seat. I can hear him saying things like "Will you sit in the car seat if I sing 'The Wheels on the Bus'?" There's a silence and then he says, "Okay. What about 'Twinkle, Twinkle, Little Star'? Okay, then let's just sit here for a minute and close our eyes and think about happy things, and when we get home, we'll play Candy Land before your bath." I hear him sigh. "Okay, now if you put on the seat belt, then you don't have to take a bath tonight."

She's crying in earnest now, overtired and filled with grief she must press down every single day, and I think of how any typical parent would have simply placed her into the car seat, buckled her in, said *stop your crying*. Any typical parent might have even insisted she stay upstairs and eat her taco.

But I get it now.

I get all the ways he's punishing himself. For some reason, this brings me to the brink of tears.

As I walk back up to my porch after they've pulled away, I can't help but think about my own father. I don't remember much about losing him. I was a bit older than Alice is now. I have a slight memory of a whiskery cheek, the sound of his deep voice rumbling in his chest when he'd hold me, and a difficult memory about a time we colored together. I was nearly five at the time, and for some reason, I only wanted to use the yellow crayon, and he said my picture could be so much nicer if I used my other nice crayons. He kept picking up the other colors and holding them out to me, urging me to use them. And I wouldn't. I remember taking that yellow crayon and breaking it into about four pieces in front of him, and then I went to my room and slammed the door, and after a while my mother came in and said I had hurt my daddy's feelings and that he was very, very sad, and I should say I was sorry.

I wouldn't do it. I was embarrassed that he was telling me how much nicer my picture would be with other colors, and also that I had broken my favorite crayon. And then soon after that, he was in a hardware store, buying something mundane like a screwdriver or a hammer, and a gunman came in and shot him dead right up there at the counter, for no reason that the police could ever figure out.

I didn't know until I was much older what had happened to him. I only knew that my daddy didn't ever come back home, and I was sure it was my fault. The yellow-crayon incident had made him go away. It gave me a stomachache every single time I thought of it.

I sit down on the porch steps now and trace my finger in the dirt on the splintery, wobbly one.

I wish I could call Lauren up in whatever afterlife there might be. I'd tell her that I know she didn't want to leave them, but that Jamie's doing a freakishly good job at this parenting stuff. Sure, he asks Alice permission for things that most of us would just never think to ask about—but maybe that's what being attuned to all her needs looks like just now. Maybe this is what love looks like to a wounded, grieving child.

If love can get people through—and I think that it's the only thing that can—he and Alice are going to be okay.

If I were Lauren, I would probably like to know that.

After that, I'm always hoping to see Jamie and Alice when I'm watching out the kitchen window, although I've now made up stories about everyone I see down there. This parenting-with-other-people thing looks more complicated than I ever thought. People are always in intense discussions with each other, laughing and gesturing, chasing kids, or struggling to carry them and buckle them in and out of car seats. No one ever looks put together in the slightest. Kids show up at daycare wearing one set of clothes, and leave wearing different outfits that look like they were thrown together by accident.

These are nothing like the New York parents that I used to see in the park. Toddlers dressed in matching outfits, wheeled about in strollers that cost as much as my first used car. I'm fascinated by this new iteration of parenthood.

Once when I saw Jamie and Alice arriving, I knocked on the window and waved, and he looked up and waved, too. I thought I saw Alice's mouth making the sound of "Mimi Mommy," but I couldn't be sure because the window was closed.

CHAPTER TEN

The next night, Ren shows up. It is *twelve days* since I've moved in, and a full week since the day I went to his house with croissants. I would be nearly hysterical by now and making plans to start a new life without him, except that the three times I've talked to Eleanor on the phone, she's reminded me that the path to true love hardly ever runs smoothly, especially when there's a car accident, a stroke, and stepchildren involved.

"Also, don't be like your mother—always ready to walk away when there's the slightest bit of trouble," she says. And she's right. A person doesn't get married five times by being patient in the face of adversity. "Maybe it's time you waited something out without pushing the panic button."

Still, twelve days *is* twelve days. It's not nothing.

When the doorbell rings at ten thirty on a Thursday night, I'm painting the wall next to the stove. So I put down the paintbrush and go clattering downstairs, wiping my hands on my sweatpants, daring to hope it might be him, but holding my breath against that hope, and then there he is, standing on the porch under the weak beam of yellow light above my door. I can't breathe for a moment. He's got his hands jammed in his pockets, and he's looking down at the floor of the porch, and when I open the door, he looks up slowly and gives me a sad, surprised smile, as if I were the last person he expected to see.

Oh my God, he is so gorgeous that it's like getting an electric shock just to see him. Why is that always so surprising?

"Sorry," I say to him. "Nobody in this apartment remembers who you are."

He does his best imitation of a guilty smile. "I know, I'm sorry," he says.

I do the worst possible thing then, which is that I start to cry. He comes inside and we stand in the hallway, smooshed together, and he dries my tears and makes little crooning noises, and kisses me over and over again. He keeps saying that he's sorry, he loves me, he missed me so much. He smells like wet wool and soap and maybe salad dressing and some vestige of the Piedmont auditorium that must have just been his scent all along, not the school's. When we pull apart, he stands looking at me with sad eyes and touches my face. "I can't stay here long," he says in a whisper, as though his family might hear him from three streets away.

I take his hand and we go upstairs, past the little square window with its colored glass that sits in the stairwell. I'm quiet, almost shy and nervous.

He doesn't look around the apartment. He seizes me in his arms like I might be thinking of running away, and then he carries me to the bedroom.

We tear off our clothes quickly, without saying anything. I shiver as he kisses my collarbone, then my hair, tucking it behind my ears before kissing them, too. He nudges me down onto the bed, and there we are, falling down on top of the comforter. He says my name over and over again, which makes me for some reason remember Alice, little Alice, saying "Mimi Mommy," and I have a fleeting moment of wanting to tell him about that.

But he is on fire. There's no waiting for a conversation to bloom. He masterfully steers us right back into our old life: hugs and kisses and sex, and I am consumed with him.

He just moves across my body, touching all the best parts, frowning in concentration, like he might be working from a checklist. I touch him and kiss him all over and feel his breath and his warmth, and I settle down into the familiarity of love.

"I've missed this," he says after it's over. He's lying on his back, looking at the ceiling, but with his hand tracing my thigh. "It's been horrible without you. I can't bear this."

"It's been so long," I tell him, a complaint.

"Too long," he says. "We knew it would be this way, but somehow it doesn't help."

He doesn't mention Judith or his daughters. He closes his eyes and for a moment, I swear he's actually fallen asleep. We just lie there holding each other until my arm cramps up, and I have to move it. Sure enough, he stirs, having remembered where he's supposed to be. I feel his body tense, and I know he's going to sit up and say he has to get back. If only I hadn't had to move my arm, maybe he would have fallen asleep, and then he would have stayed, and I would still have him in the morning. We'd smile into each other's faces when we woke up. He'd be shocked that he stayed, but he'd say it had been wonderful, and then we'd talk about getting married and how we'd soon spend every single night together, and maybe he'd say, *Hey, well, why not just start now? Why don't I live HERE and just go visit Judith for a few hours every day and see how she and the kids are doing and then come back?*

He doesn't say any of those things. He sits up, shakes his head like he can remove the sleepiness. I love him this way, when his hair is all messed up from my hands, and his whiskers are growing in along that perfect jawline of his.

"How are you?" I say, to stall him. "And by that I mean, how are you *really*?"

"*Ohhh*, Mimi, I don't even know how to tell you. Listen, baby, I'm so sorry, but I have to get back."

He reaches to the floor for his shirt.

"Now? You already have to leave? I thought we could have tea—or a glass of wine . . ."

"Please," he says. "Don't . . ."

"No, no. I understand you have to go. Just tell me . . . How is Judith?"

"Oh." He waves his hand in the air, like he could bat everything away. "She sleeps a lot, and she's having trouble with mobility and speech. She can't come up with words when she wants to. But she's *docile*, for lack of a better word. Like a tiny, obedient, scared child."

"Ohhh," I say because there's not much else to say.

He stops and looks up at the ceiling. "It actually breaks my heart to see her this way. She was so feisty, so opinionated, such a brilliant hard-ass." He looks grim. "We used to fight about everything. And now she talks in odd little snippets, and she's just a placid, mostly vacant, sweet stranger who is living in my wife's body. Smiling at me. Being grateful."

Wife, he said.

Sweet, he said. *Grateful.*

Then he turns and looks at me while he buttons up his shirt, squeezes off an impersonation of a smile. "So new subject. Quick, tell me in thirty seconds about the play."

"Yeah." I try to shift gears. "It was exhilarating," I say. "Seeing those kids—seeing how they pulled together and actually made it work!"

"Yes," he says vaguely. "There are those transcendent moments in teaching. I'm glad you got to have that."

"Sky Masterson actually wooed Sarah Brown. You would have loved to see the transformation."

"And Adelaide?"

"Perfect. Her accent was sublime. I had her speak in a Bronx accent for the whole week. When I'd pass her in the hall, I'd make her say something in Bronx-ese."

"That's fantastic," he says, but he's not really here anymore. He's probably thinking about Judith and how heartbreaking her condition is, now that she's not a *brilliant hard-ass* anymore.

"Yeah, well. She came through."

"That's great. You're the one who came through." He gives me a long look, and then he pulls on his pants, zipping up the fly and buckling his belt. "Listen. I can get away for a bit some nights, I think. After she's been put to bed, I'll say I'm going out for a walk, to get some air. And I'll come to you."

"But why can't you just tell the girls that you're coming here? They know I live in New Haven!"

He frowns. "Please. Don't do this. It's too soon. It would be like throwing gasoline on a fire. Trust me on this. I'll know when the time is right."

I don't say anything.

"Look, I know it's not enough, it's not nearly enough," he says. "But maybe it can sustain us until certain . . . harder decisions get made."

"I feel like I'm in one of those old movies about an affair," I say. "This is not what we're doing! I'm not having an affair with a married man."

He laughs a little and leans over and kisses me. "Don't get up. I'll let myself out. This is how I want to remember you, lying here naked on the bed in your new apartment." He pats my ankle, which is sticking out from under the covers.

And then he's gone, and he's taken the glow right out with him.

CHAPTER ELEVEN

One day, hanging out talking to Arnie in the junk shop during my daily trek to town, I discover the cookbooks section, and suddenly I am enchanted. I sit on a wobbly old cane chair and thumb through them.

That first day, I buy an armload and take them home and read them as though they're novels. The next day I go back and get four more. My favorites are the old ones with their pages stained and thin, sometimes with notes crawling around the margins: *"Made this for the Hendersons! Will make again!"*

And then one day I buy an apron and start in on deciphering the recipes, like they're foreign languages I need to understand: chicken thighs in wine sauce, mashed potatoes au gratin, asparagus with lemon butter. Chili. Lasagna. Chicken piccata.

These words are so much better than the other words that have had full access to my head, words I've now ushered to the back room of my brain, locking them in a quiet little closet: *Judith, stroke, daughters, illness, future. Ex-wife.*

Uncertainty.

There is comfort to be found in spicy dipping sauces and in floury, buttery shortbread cookies, in creamy custard baked in ramekins, and the gleaming crispiness of a roasting chicken just out of the oven, its skin crackling when you touch it.

Best, though, is baking bread.

I'm addicted to the hard labor of kneading dough, which is followed so reliably by the reward of soft, warm loaves, lined up on the counter, glistening from an egg wash. I am alone with this aroma, and I love how it fills all the spaces of the room, even up in the corners of the high ceiling, even the cracks in the floorboards, the jagged pipes by the radiator. How to explain how much I treasure pulling the loaves apart with my bare hands or becoming mesmerized by the simple way the butter slides, molding itself into every nook and cranny.

I should be out following up on applications I've put in at the public library, at Hall-Benedict, at the bookstores on Chapel Street and the restaurants along Whitney Avenue. I even applied to be a receptionist at a dentist's office, imagining myself in a crisp white uniform saying, *Mrs. Smith, Dr. Hamilton will see you now.*

No one has called me back.

Which is fine. I love the dependability of cooking; it's way better than depending on human beings. Oven temperatures don't lie about when they're going to show up. Ingredients abound in every neighborhood market. You can just pick them up in your hands, put them in a paper bag, and after you pay for them, you can bring them home to stay.

One day I take three loaves of warm bread I've baked and put them on a plastic table outside the daycare with a note:

From Mimi, upstairs. XOXO.

Evenings now, I wait, perfumed and decorated, for Ren to come by, which he does most nights. It's a pleasure to have him there, a crusher when he doesn't show. I should have never let myself get to this state of dependence, and when I tell Eleanor about how passive I feel, she says, "Oh, sweetie. I think it's just a matter of waiting this out. Don't panic and throw everything away when you're so close to the finish line."

Easy for her to say. In her relationship with Ira, the finish line was right there at the starting gate.

It's ridiculous how my heart races whenever I hear the doorbell ring, and how when I let him in, I want to show him the tasty morsels I'm making. I display my creations on a lovely white platter: orange cranberry muffins, biscuits with honey, deviled eggs. He gives a perfunctory nod in the direction of these delectables, and then practically sweeps the platter to the floor in his passion to get to me. Off to bed we go, his strong hands at the small of my back, his eyes shiny and moist in the darkness of my room, lit only by candlelight.

The sex is still mind-blowing, although, to be honest, after he leaves, when I'm thinking it over and analyzing our time together, I see that it's not so much the sex that I'm craving these days as much as reassurance and information. The questions I ask are all designed to ferret out any forward motion in his life. Anything. I would like to change the ratio of sex to talking, from ninety-nine to one . . . to perhaps fifty to fifty.

But he's uncomfortable talking. "You're my respite from all that," he says. At my insistence, he squeezes off a few facts, recycling them from the night before and the night before that. Judith sleeps a lot, and blah blah blah; when she's awake, she's sweet and placid. She needs help with everything. It's hard to know which symptoms are the result of her stroke, and which are because of the accident.

I picture a queen, propped on satin pillows while her family brings her hot tea and crumpets.

"The house," he says, "is filled with occupational therapists and physical therapists, all evaluating her and working with her. There's some progress, but no one knows for sure just how much she'll recover." There's no more talk of putting her in rehab. Parker seems to have won that battle.

"It's a waiting game," he says.

"It's pretty much a waiting game over here, too," I tell him.

He winces and gives me fourteen hundred kisses all along my breasts. "Not for much longer," he says. "Please hang on. I love you more than I've ever loved anyone. I'm yours. Here, I wrote you a poem. You can read it when I'm gone."

Roses are red, violets are blue.

I can't wait until I can marry YOU.

I tape it to the bathroom mirror. That's how bad off I am.

⁂

I tell La Starla: "I am now the kind of person who has quick sex three nights a week with a man who doesn't talk, and coincidentally, I now am a person who owns a Dutch oven and a griddle. Is this seriously the kind of progress that the spirit guides saw for me?"

"Oh, for heaven's sake, Mimi, you are on a *journey*," she says. "The end result is something you can't see yet, but the spirit guides are united in their feeling it's going to be exactly where you need to be."

"Please don't use the word *journey*. Just tell me this: Am I going to get married to Ren?" I say.

"Who knows? Who cares?"

"*Who cares?* What kind of psychic are you, anyway?" I say. "When I first saw your flyer on that subway platform, it had zero evidence that you would ever answer a client's question by saying *who knows* and *who cares*."

"I save those answers for my very favorite clients," she says.

⁂

One morning at daycare drop-off time—my favorite time of day—I'm looking out the front window, holding my cup of tea, and I see a man and woman get out of separate cars with their kids and greet each other on the street. He's holding a baby, and she has a little boy who's tumbling and skipping around like a puppy, and the woman has to repeatedly set him back on course. I can hear their feet stamping on the porch beneath me, hear the boy's high voice and the woman's lilting laugh, followed by the man's deep, resonant voice. The front door opens and slams. After a few minutes, during which I'm still standing with my cup of tea, brooding, I see the same man and woman come out. I really look at them then, these busy parents, obviously close friends. She has on cowboy boots and a hippie-like sundress, and he has a gray beard and long hair in a ponytail and baggy khaki pants and a faded red T-shirt— and as soon as they get to the street, they stand talking beside the cars. They're so animated and alive, gesturing toward each other, laughing.

And then suddenly everything changes around them, as though the air itself has shifted. They lean toward each other; she reaches for his face and keeps her hand there, lightly, on his cheek, dragging her fingers through his beard. They glance over at the daycare, almost furtively, it seems, and then they hug, for far too long—it's like a movie hug—and I feel my stomach drop. I'm obviously watching something so private yet unprotected, two people wrapped up in each other. When they draw apart, looking around them a little guiltily and laughing, I see him tilt his head, and point to his car, and she goes over to it and gets in. Just like that.

Love just showed up, right there on the curb on a Tuesday morning. The feeling slams into me.

They ride off together, leaving the car she arrived in.

I don't know why this is yet another thing that brings me nearly to tears, but it does.

Standing there at the window . . . all I can think of is, What the actual hell is my life about? Am I really going to just live here in New Haven, alone with cooking projects, waiting to be employed? Am I going to always be looking out the window at other people having real lives, real love?

Why the hell am I living in thrall to a man who runs in and does a quick, jiffy rendition of sex, and then runs back to his family?

"I'm heading back into the night," he said to me one evening, "like a reluctant, dutiful soldier going off to the wars, while you get to luxuriate here on your own, doing what you please."

Something occurs to me now, just a little unwelcome twinge poking itself up in my brain. Ren isn't really a soldier going off to the wars.

Really, Ren is going back home.

CHAPTER TWELVE

Two days later, I'm cooking quiche lorraine, like everyone else in America seems to be doing lately, when I happen to glance outside my kitchen window and see a little boy, seemingly drifting all alone in the backyard, using both hands to push a truck through some weeds right up against the fence.

I crane my neck to see if there's an adult nearby, but I can't see one from my vantage point.

He stops and puts his hands on his hips, looking around like he's studying the situation, and then he pushes another truck over and stacks it right on top of the first truck, balancing it perfectly. And then—oh my God—he stands up on these two trucks. He puts one leg up against the boards, like he's going to climb the fence. He actually might climb this fence! Or the trucks might roll away in opposite directions, and he could fall on his head.

I watch him for a couple of seconds, and then, without even thinking, I run like hell through my apartment and down the front stairs, slamming the door, and I tear across the porch and down the steps, almost tripping on the loose one at the bottom, and I run around the side yard to the gate to the backyard. He's still there, puzzling out his climbing plan. I run over and stand beside him.

"Hey there, are you Mimi from upstairs? The bread lady?" It's a woman's voice, coming from the back door. "Hey, William, honey, maybe don't stand on that truck, okay?"

"I can stand on it! I won't fall!" he calls to her. "Anyway, I have two trucks!"

"Let's not test out your relationship with gravity today, okay, honey?" she says. "You and gravity aren't always friends."

I feel soggy with relief and look at the woman standing on the back steps. I've seen her during my surveillance activities, herding kids, serving snacks at little plastic tables in the yard. I look closely. I do not think she was the one kissing the man. She's tall, with long dark hair that's parted in the middle and big brown eyes. She's smiling, even though she's balancing a child's potty chair in one hand and clutching the arm of a naked boy with the other. I think it must take a special kind of person to smile and hold a conversation while balancing a potty chair and a needing-to-poop boy, so I mumble something about being sorry, I was just concerned when I looked out my window, please go on with your day, I'm so sorry, really sorry. I thought he was going to escape . . .

She laughs and plunks down the potty chair right there on the back steps. "Here, Toby, do your business here." He sits right down like going to the bathroom outside on a plastic potty chair makes as much sense as anything else in life and puts his chin in his hands. Then he says, "My poop needs a story to read. It won't come out without a story."

Without even blinking, she says she'll get the poop a story in a minute, that first she needs to finally meet the lady upstairs. She tells me her name is Joyous, and I say I'm Mimi and what an interesting name Joyous is, and she says, well, it was really Joyce, but her grandmother from the old country always pronounced it Joyous, so when she went to college, she started calling herself that and it stuck, and it's fine with her because sometimes she doesn't feel so joyous, but her name makes people treat her nicely anyway.

"So welcome to the Children's Cooperative Madhouse Daycare," she says.

"Is *that* what it's called?" I say.

"No. But it should be. It's actually the Children's Daycare Cooperative. Or is it the Kids' Co-Op Daycare? I don't know. I never can remember what we decided on." She laughs and puts her hand on Toby's head because he's twisting all over the place, jumping up from the potty seat to peer into its emptiness and then sitting down again. "Jamie said he met you and said that you were nice and probably weren't the type of person who would spend all your spare time complaining to the landlord about us."

"Ah, yes, Jamie," I say. "What a sweet guy he is!"

"Isn't he the best?" she says. "He and Alice—we're so lucky they found us."

More than anything, I want her to tell me everything she knows about Jamie and Alice. I have a list of questions: When did his wife die? Were they in daycare already when it happened? What did she die of? And mostly, Are they going to be okay, in her professional, fellow-daycare-person opinion?

Instead, I point to Toby and then to William. "Life and death and poop here. The elements of life. Along with trucks."

"And gravity," she says and laughs. "The gross, raw materials of life—that's what we deal in here. Although I do want to assure you that William would not have been allowed to escape."

I'm a bit embarrassed. "No, no, I knew he wouldn't," I say. "I think I just needed an excuse to finally come say hello."

She smiles.

"Which one is yours?" I say.

She says, "Oh, mine is Lily, who's still napping inside with the rest of them. You'll see her when she comes out, because she's going to want to ride around on my hip the whole time. She won't want other kids to come near me. Always happens when a parent is on the turn."

Toby is fidgeting on the potty, wiggling around. "Joyoyoyoyoyous! Listen, listen, listen to me! The poop says it is *not going to come out* until it gets a story!"

"Well, Mimi," she says, "your first task as the upstairs bystander, if you choose to accept it: Will you keep an eye on Toby and William here for a sec while I go inside and get a story for the poop?"

"Yes. Sure," I say. "I can't wait to see what a poop story might be. A whole new subset of children's literature."

While she's gone, Toby sits back down on the portable potty seat and hums a little song while he examines his toes, holding them up in the air as though they need extra scrutiny.

"Is Alice here?" I ask him in a low voice.

He says, "Now I am going to talk like a robot." He moves his arms in the air, stiffly, turning his head from side to side. "Where. Is. My. Poop. Story."

William comes ambling over holding a truck in his two hands. I crane to peek inside the daycare.

"Um, is Alice here?" I try again, with William.

He shields his eyes with one hand so he can look up at me. He stares at me for a disconcertingly long time, and then he shrugs. "I. Am. Not. The. Boss. Of. Alice," he says, also in a robot voice. "I'm the boss of this truck and it says it wants to run over your foot."

Possibly this is how kids tell you how inappropriate you are, which is exactly why I find them terrifying. I don't know exactly *what* children know, but it's possible they know everything, that they see into the heart of us, just how we all are bumbling around looking foolish while pretending we know what we're doing.

"Stick out your foot," he commands me. And so I do. The truck bumps into me again and again.

⌒

Later, after I've gone back upstairs, I see Jamie parking his car, then heading up the walk to the front door. And a few minutes later, he shows up again on the front lawn, holding Alice and her bag of stuff in his arms. They start to get into their car, but then they look as though they've changed their minds, and they sit down on the grass. They just sit there, talking.

She's crying, and he's comforting her. She sits on his lap and puts her head on his shoulder. He rocks her back and forth. I see his hand on her back, patting and patting and patting and patting.

And then, in a move that threatens to undo me once and for all, her little hand reaches up and she starts patting his back, too.

Two little warriors/survivors.

CHAPTER THIRTEEN

The next day I wander downstairs to the daycare yard during playtime again.

Jamie and Alice are way, way too much in my thoughts. If I went to a therapist instead of a psychic, maybe I'd be told that I'm overrelating here due to my father's death. Lately I'm wondering if Jamie asks her permission for *every* single thing they do in the morning, or if some activities are covered by previous permissions she's given. It could get sort of tedious—and also comically crazy—that kind of fearful attention. Does he say, "Can we put on your right sock? Now can we put on your *left* sock? Can we walk to the kitchen? Can we take a spoon out of the drawer?"

He's like one big mushy cake filled with pudding—kindness and worry and fear and love all smushed in together, stirred up with the grief. What's going to happen when he cracks open, I wonder. Who is there to comfort *him*?

There is full-on, month-of-May gorgeousness now, and the morning is filled with flowering plants and big puffy white clouds that later might create a ruckus and usher in a thunderstorm, and there's something so lovely about this tremulous air before all that happens, and the sounds of little children playing in the sandbox and chasing each other through a patch of clover, when no one is about to die from any cause whatsoever that anyone can see. All the parents and children seem to be breathing. And yet, all I can think about is death.

After my father died, no one said anything more about him. My grandmother came to visit us, but then she left, too. I asked where Daddy was, and my mother cried, so I didn't ask her again. It was because of the yellow crayon, I knew, and she probably hated me for that. It was as though he vanished into thin air, and we couldn't speak of him again.

But here I am. It's twenty-seven years later, and I walk out into the backyard, into this daycare moment, of trees and children and clouds and flowers.

Two of the moms—named Maya and Katherine, they tell me—are stretched out on the grass, watching the kids play and looking pleasantly maternal and also like they had once maybe been hippies and smoked their share of dope and they know things about peace and love and also how to deal with bedlam when it breaks out. They're wearing jeans and T-shirts and sandals, and they both have hair that proudly does what it wants. They don't even have on lipstick or mascara. They'd be drummed out of Piedmont in their first five minutes.

I smile and say hi and ask if I can sit down, and they say, "Sure, come on and join us. Pull up a spot of grass." Maya introduces me to her sweet, black-haired baby, Gabriela, sitting on her lap, and Katherine grimly holds up a project she's working on: trying to stitch up the filling on a wild-eyed, wrecked-looking baby doll, something anyone in their right mind would have thrown out long ago.

The sun is shining on my face, and we talk about how peaceful the kids are this morning, and soon little Toby plops down next to me and asks me very solemnly if I have a baby in my belly because his mommy does. I'm delighted when Alice, holding a baby doll in her hands, comes over and sits down a little distance away and smiles at me shyly. I smile back at her and motion her over, but she shakes her head.

"DO YOU HAVE A BABY IN YOUR BELLY?" says Toby. I feel like he and I are old friends from the day I thought I might have to save his life when his pregnant mom was leaving daycare with him and he was threatening to run into the street. And then, of course, I waited with him while Joyous retrieved a poop story for him. We have history now, Toby and me.

"I do not have a baby in my belly," I tell him. I didn't answer right away because I was stunned, wondering if this question was evidence that I needed to go on a diet, or work on my abdominals, or if children even judge these things. I'm almost tempted to ask him.

"She doesn't have any babies at all," says Alice with a kind of satisfaction I've noticed in women before. "I've been to her house." She is in the know. I motion to her again and pat my lap invitingly. She grins and ducks her head but doesn't come to me.

"Why you went to her house?" Toby wants to know. He looks impressed.

"I helped her move the couch," she says. "And she gave me a taco."

Everyone looks at me. Maya and Katherine smile. "So that's where the couch went," says Maya. "Alice moved it."

"She's a lot stronger than she looks," I say.

Toby is clearly unhappy with the hijacking of the previous conversation, the one about my belly. "Well," he says to me, "did you know that mans can't have babies in their bellies? Not ever?"

"I did hear something about that," I tell him.

"I came from my mommy's belly," he says, leaning over to whisper like this is sacred news, which I suppose it is.

"Yes, you did," Katherine says. "And now there's a new baby in there, too. Right where you used to be."

There's a moment as he copes with that fact, and it's unclear whether he finds that to be an amazing coincidence or a tragedy that needs to be corrected immediately.

"I came from my mommy's belly, too!" says Alice, and then she starts pulling up tufts of grass and throwing them in the air. "But then she died and she went in the ground. And we can't see her anymore, but she still loves us."

I feel my heart skip, but Katherine says smoothly, "That's right, Alice. Want to come over here, sweetheart, and sit next to me? Your baby doll is almost back together. What do you think? Will you take care of her when I get her all fixed up?"

Alice sticks her fingers in her mouth, and then she sidles over and, to my surprise, backs herself up onto *my* lap. Just all casual-like. Katherine raises her eyebrows and gives me a little smile.

Toby leans forward and whispers, "Well, tonight, you know what I'm gonna do? I'm gonna go *back in my mommy's belly again*, and I'm gonna say hello to the baby." He licks his lips and leans back with satisfaction, like this is the best plan ever.

I nod, unsure what I'm supposed to say to that, if I should burst his little bubble with some scientific facts, and then he adds, putting his hand up to shield his words from the others: "And when I'm in there, I'm gonna fight him! Fight, fight, fight!" He stands up to demonstrate some rather convincing punching moves.

I look to Katherine for help, and say loudly enough so she'll hear in case there is some educational protocol that needs to be adhered to: "Fight him—why?"

But Katherine keeps her eyes on the doll she's working on.

"I will tell that baby, 'You *get out*, baby! This is *my* mommy!'" Then, having delivered this plan, he slumps against me, nearly knocking Alice and me over.

Maya hides a smile and murmurs something about the fun times ahead at Nate and Nicole's house, and Katherine says with a philosophical sigh, "Boy, if that isn't the story of life. We all just want to be the only one, forever and ever."

Maya is married, she tells me, to Jerome, who was a member of the daycare before, with his first wife and daughter. And now he and Maya have Gabriela together, who is fourteen months old. She's the baby I might see being trundled around in the umbrella stroller sometimes. Jerome is a big bear of a guy, a journalist who worked in Washington, DC, for a while, and was proudly on Nixon's enemies list long before Maya met him.

Katherine says she's not married, never has been, and her kid is Sanborn, who is two and a half. They tell me all kinds of things about how the daycare got started, and why they love it so much. Mostly it seems that they love taking care of each other's kids themselves, not with paid teachers. In fact, an ad they placed in the Yale Co-Op has a line drawing of a bunch of little kids looking like flowers blooming in a garden, and underneath it says: **"WE GROW OUR OWN KIDS."**

It's a very important point, they tell me, to realize that experts don't have all the knowledge about your own dear child.

❧

"Oh, by the way," Maya says to Katherine later. She has stood up, declaring that she's going to head for the kitchen to start getting lunch ready. "Did you hear that the State called Nate again? Now they're poking around, talking about our license."

I had been watching Alice making rock soup in the sandbox, but my ears stand straight up.

"Oh man," says Katherine, stretching her legs out and wiggling her toes. "We can't seem to shake 'em, can we? What do they think—that we're eating children here?"

"They just like to see us as incompetent, but Nate will take care of them," Maya says. "He's so diplomatic."

"Except he's having a baby," Katherine says. "With our luck they'll show up one day and shut us down and nobody will have the slightest idea what to do because Nate's off trying to get a newborn to sleep."

"Let's just hope they don't show up when Jerome is here," says Maya, and they both laugh. "Mr. Enemies List will eat them alive." She starts walking to the door.

"Oh God," says Katherine. "He'll chew them up and spit them out in the dumpster and have them carted away."

I look over at Katherine and it suddenly hits me. She was the woman I saw the other day, the one kissing a man in front of the daycare.

And the man. I feel a piece of knowledge fly into my head and click there, locked down tight the way it happens sometimes. One minute you don't know something, and then somehow you just have a new fact that is part of you.

The man was Jerome. And the child he was carrying into daycare was Gabriela.

Katherine smiles at me. "It's a fun place," she says.

∽

After those first visits, I go down often. I feel like I've got to get to the bottom of everything having to do with these humans and their crazy stories. In ways I can't quite explain, I *need* these people.

Sometimes I show up in the morning after I get up, then stay for snack, and then for some reason I'm still hanging out at lunchtime. I can't seem to leave is why. Waiting for me on my kitchen table are several new employment applications I should drop off—one is for a health food store and another is the *second* one for Hall-Benedict. *They* lost the first one, and I figure I am at least competent enough to simply take people's prescriptions and then walk them over to the pharmacist, who works three steps above in a fortress with shelves full of pills all around him. Could there possibly be a more boring job? I could do it in my sleep.

Not that I want to. I don't want to work there, I realize. Not there and also not at the grocery store, putting price tags on produce. Not really. I want to work somewhere where I can be part of things.

Maybe that's why for now I'm happy to be a daycare groupie.

Will change diapers in exchange for human companionship and gossip.

∽

One of my great needs lately is watching Alice drift through her day. I tell myself that's why I need to go down to the daycare. I'm watching her for Jamie. I'm watching her for her mom who would have probably loved to know somebody besides Jamie was going to keep track of her. I wonder what her position was on his possibly falling in love again. If she had thoughts, that is. What would a young woman dying of something want to say to her young husband who has probably fifty or so years left to live? I can't imagine it, that's all.

So why do I think about it, like, all the damn time?

My father was shot in the head. He was young. He had probably never thought of how he felt about my mother remarrying. I wonder what he would say if he somehow could have known she would marry four additional times, making marriage look like it was just another routine change of address. Was this how she mourned him, always looking for someone to replace him and never quite finding the right person?

I hadn't really thought of it that way before.

Sometimes Alice sits in the "house" corner, where there's a little pretend stove and refrigerator and some dress-up clothes, and she rocks the now fixed-up baby doll (whom she's named "Fixie") and puts her in the cradle again and again. If she sees me watching her, she smiles, almost flirtatiously, casting her eyes downward when I look her way. I notice that she never cries, even when she doesn't get the coveted red bowl at lunchtime, even when she falls down. She just holds herself together, a sturdy little person making her way through a hard day. I almost can't believe she's the same child who fell apart so dramatically in my kitchen.

Maya told me that kids who hold themselves together in school and daycare need a place they can let go, can cry and have tantrums and still feel safe. Does that mean she felt safe in my kitchen?

Mostly she doesn't ask for anything, but then one day she starts pushing a tricycle across the yard, and the grass and rocks make it hard. When she's just quietly out of her mind with frustration, she looks at me and says in an evenly controlled voice, "Mimi Mommy, will you help me ride this?"

I feel like I've just received the presidential Medal of Honor. Or been invited to dinner with the queen.

I help her climb onto the seat and place her feet with their little blue sandals onto the pedals. "Do you know how to pedal?" I say, and she shakes her head. It's as though her glossy dark hair is giving off sparkles in the sun. My fingertips are pulsing with the need to pick her up and hug her and carry her to somewhere safe, where her mother didn't die, where the world is not a scary place, a place that can take from you the one thing you counted on. I can't believe I'm acting this way. I'm honestly about to break into tears.

"Okay, then I'll just push you," I say, and my throat is clogged. "Try to keep your feet on the pedals."

It doesn't work very well, and she frowns as we work—*I* work—our way across the grassy tufts and dirt, going in fits and starts, over to the sandbox. She takes her feet off the pedals and lets them stick straight out.

"Whee!" I say. "Is this fun?"

She laughs. She actually laughs, so I push her faster over the grass, running alongside, and she squeals in happiness.

It's the best sound I've ever heard in my whole life.

That afternoon I watch from my upstairs window when Jamie arrives. I watch him park his VW Rabbit on the street, expertly pulling into a parking spot right in front. And then he checks his teeth in the rearview mirror, turns off the car, and ambles out. There's something sexy about the way he walks. I mean, sure, he's still a guy consumed with grief, but his walk makes me think that he's deep down still himself. He's been through hell, he's *still* going through hell, and he's trying to get a graduate degree at Yale in addition to all his other daily hells, but . . . I don't know, there's this way he has of moving like he belongs in the world. Lauren didn't take him down into the ground with her.

I stand there, so transfixed by the look of him, by the way the sun shines in his brown hair—that I'm startled when he suddenly swings his eyes upward and sees me there, watching him.

I want to jump back behind the curtain. But it's too late. He's waving.

I wave back. He does a little soft-shoe step. Totally out of character. He smiles.

And then he's gone, up on the porch, where I can't see him.

I fight myself from going downstairs and accosting him. I stop myself because I wouldn't be able to stop myself from saying to him, "Guess what! I made Alice laugh today, and my life may just be complete."

CHAPTER FOURTEEN

Ren comes over that night, and I'm so full of daycare life that I make him talk to me. "This is what I've managed to learn about the daycare," I tell him. I use my most suspenseful, storytelling voice, so that he'll be transported out of the story running through his head—the story of daughters, strokes, ex-wife, and misery—and can hear my story.

"Can't we just be swoony together?" he asks plaintively. "You used to be so hot for me all the time."

"I'm *still* hot for you," I tell him, letting my fingers trail along his perfect jawline, "but sometimes I need to tell you stuff."

We're lying on my living room floor, surrounded by pillows and glasses of sherry. I've put Miles Davis on the stereo for him (not Motown, which I had been dancing to before he came) because Ren says that appreciation for jazz is the sign of sophisticated taste, and lord knows I'm not sophisticated, but every so often I check to see if any sophisticationary tendencies are blooming in my head yet. So far I can listen to Miles Davis quite happily, but back in the months when we lived in New York, Ren would take me to jazz clubs where the smoke was thick and the music wove around my head in ways that often made me sleepy but sometimes made me want to jump up and start screaming. I told him one time that jazz sounded to me like ducks were being slaughtered onstage.

That did not make me sound very sophisticated.

It takes some doing to get him interested in the daycare life. He's tired, but God bless him, he tries to look interested.

"Here," I say, starting over for the third time, after two previous interruptions, "is what I've learned about this daycare cooperative. It's very sociologically interesting, which you, as an educator, might want to think about."

"I don't give a fuck about sociologically interesting things," he murmurs as he's nuzzling my neck. "Have you forgotten who I am, woman?"

"No, no, it's fascinating. It got started back in 1972, when a group of countercultural parents decided that families needed full-time childcare so women could work, and they wanted to form a co-op, where they'd take turns watching each other's kids. *No* state regulations, no licensing. Just friends taking care of friends' kids."

"Ah. Hippies," says Ren with a sigh. He caresses my right breast. "Gotta love the hippies."

"Sure, okay," I say. I press on, putting excitement into my voice, hoping to get him truly interested. "All parents have to do four-hour turns each week; nobody can get out of it by claiming special status, like being really important or having a penis."

At the mention of the word *penis*, he groans. "I love the way you put things."

"Yeah, men have to do the childcare, too. Every single one of them."

"Radical," he says.

I pull farther away, smiling at him, and run my fingers along his inner arm. "One parent is responsible for the meals each week: two snacks and a hot lunch every day, and the food-week person has to make sure the food is there on time and can be easily prepared by the people on the turn. And it has to be something kids will eat—no fancy-schmancy eggplant casseroles or spiced deviled eggs—and it has to be healthy," I say.

He closes his eyes. "Why don't they each just bring in their own kid's food? Wouldn't that be easier?"

"Who knows? Maybe because they don't want some kids to have preservatives and hot dogs or that macaroni and cheese junk that comes in a box with orange powder. And sometimes making the food can be a kid project."

"Huh," he says. "My kids lived on that orange powder stuff. Didn't do them any harm. Really, parents today make it so much harder than it has to be."

"Also," I tell him, knowing this will blow his mind but kind of wanting to get some sort of reaction out of him, "the daycare is *not* a school. They're not here to teach toddlers the alphabet or make them feel like they're being tested. That's why this daycare got started in the first place. People here think that little kids get all the learning they need just by playing and being read to and figuring out how to get along with each other. Also, there's no punishment stronger than a time-out and a hug. They don't want to shame kids. If someone is hitting or biting, the way they see it, that child needs comforting and understanding just as much as the kid who was hurt."

He rolls his eyes, just like I knew he would. "When their kids grow up and hate them, they can point out, 'Well, darling, at least we didn't try to teach you the alphabet!'"

"Well, maybe," I say, submitting to his unbuttoning of my blouse. "But my impression is that it's like a huge, wonderful, dysfunctional family. There's a guy named Jerome who was there back at the beginning with his first wife and their kid, and now Jerome is remarried and has a new kid, so he's back, and he's like the granddaddy of the place, always grousing about how people aren't as countercultural and committed as they used to be. I heard that when he was in the daycare the first time, they actually debated whether it should be open on weekends since some parents have to work then, too, and it was discriminating against them to be closed. Jerome himself thought it should be open on *Christmas*."

He kisses my hair. "Good God. What have you gotten yourself into? Is this some kind of cult?"

"I find it delightful. Oh! And way back then, two sets of parents switched partners—just decided they didn't love their spouses anymore, and the husbands switched residences. All hell broke loose when a guy would come in to pick up his new girlfriend's kid and leave his own kid behind. And when they were naming the place, somebody wanted to call it Uncle Ho's Children. After Ho Chi Minh. Isn't that funny?"

"Please. This is hurting my brain. Why are you telling me this?"

"Why am I telling you this? Because it's so interesting! Why *aren't* you telling me about the things in your life? Don't you think it hurts my feelings that you tell me nothing about your days at home with your ex?"

He kisses me behind my ear, which gives me the shivers in spite of myself. "Believe me, you don't want to know."

"But I do want to."

"No, you really don't. You're the secret ingredient to my life, the cherry on the top of the sundae."

"Am I still the subatomic particle?"

"That, and so much more. You're the *quick* in my quicksilver, the *tilt* in my Tilt-A-Whirl, the *cheese* in my cheeseburger . . ."

"Will you *stop*?"

"I'll never stop. You'll always be the subatomic particle and the Tilt-A-Whirl, and without those, I'm toast."

Then he rubs against my face with his scratchy beard and tickles me just under my ribs, which makes me laugh and almost makes me pee, and that makes him laugh, and pretty soon he's carted me off to my room, with me kicking my legs in the air and licking his neck, and we fall on the bed, and it's better than ever between us.

Wondrous. That's the word he says.

Afterward, we're lying close together, and I'm tracing my finger along his ribs, and I suddenly feel so playful and expansive, so I say to him, "Do you know how I got the play to work?"

"Yes," he says sleepily. "Hard work . . . lots of rehearsals . . ."

"Not really. I performed magic." I run my fingers through his sparse chest hair and smile at him.

"You performed magic."

"Yes."

"At Piedmont."

"I did!" I laugh.

He sighs. "And what might that have entailed? Did you do magic spells? Get a cauldron? And eyes of newts?" He's running his hand along my thigh, like that's the most important thing, not my story.

"I had a magic skirt."

"A magic skirt, huh?" He squints at the ceiling and then reaches for his watch, which he had taken off because it was scratching me. "Could I ask you something?" he says.

"Sure." I think he's going to want to hear about how I got the skirt and exactly what I did that was magic.

Instead he says, "Could you turn out *not* to be crazy? Please?"

I look away. I can't stand to meet his eyes. My own eyes feel hot. "I'm actually not sure this is crazy," I say.

"Just for the time being, let's assume this falls into the crazy category," he tells me. His eyes are lit up like he's teasing me. "Don't worry. I'm not asking for a whole lifetime commitment to noncrazy or anything like that. It's just that while I'm dealing with all this Judith stuff, maybe you could tamp down the wacky factor. Just a tad."

"That skirt," I say, "just so you know, it's how I met you, as a matter of fact."

"Uh-huh. Jesus, Mimi. I don't think that's what made you and me meet, and it certainly didn't make the show work. What made the show work was the hours and hours of rehearsals you put in. And they put in."

"*Wellllll,*" I say. "You weren't really there, so I'd say it's all kind of debatable what part was rehearsal and what part was magic skirt."

Then he yawns and stretches and sits up. He looks down at me lying there. "You're very funny and very adorable," he says and kisses me on top of the head. "But maybe you're spending too much time alone. In related news, how are those applications coming?"

I go quiet. So quiet.

What I don't say, because my throat is too clogged and I don't trust it to form words: I miss sharing a life with him that we can talk about. I want to bring him my little anecdotes that we can analyze and laugh over like in the days of long ago. It's been, what, three months? I feel like it's another century. Did we have cars back then? Radios? Did women have the right to vote?

"Never mind," he says. "The last thing I want is to fight with you. Let's stop this right now. I'm sorry. I'm just overtired."

He hauls himself out of bed and puts on his clothes, while I lie there under the sheet watching him. What did I expect—that he'd think this was important? That it would feel real to him?

The air shifts around him as all his molecules get recombined into being the other, official Ren. Just like that, with the buttoning of his shirt, the pulling on of his trousers and socks, there he is, completely rewound back into being Ren the Father, Ren the Ex-Husband Who Is Caring and Perfect in Every Way.

By the time he gets to the front door, he'll be entirely reconstituted.

Every time he arrives at my apartment, he's hard-nosed and grim and wrapped up tight—and then it's my job to soften him, jazz him up, feed him food and sherry and loving. I unwind him from the straitjacket of his daughters and his ex-wife and his responsibilities and paperwork, and I am light and airy and never demand anything. Until now. Now I have asked him to think about the world in a playful way.

Hell, I don't even know if I totally believe that the skirt is magic. I mean, I like thinking about it—but is it real? I don't know.

He comes over and sits on the edge of the bed and chucks me under the chin. "Hey, cheer up, squooshie. It's not going to stay this way. God knows there'll probably come a time when I'm going to be begging you to fire up your magic—what was it?—oh, magic skirt and change around the whole world and get one of my plays produced, but right now . . . right now, there's just not much left of me, I'm afraid. My whimsy is all depleted."

"You need to lighten up," I say, scooting out from underneath his hand.

"What I *need*," he says, "is for the woman I'm in love with to understand that sometimes whimsy isn't the thing that's needed and to dial it back. Just a small request, please."

I stick out my tongue at him, and he pretends to grab for it.

"Come on," he says. "I love you more than life itself. You're my future. You're my dime a dozen."

CHAPTER FIFTEEN

One day I'm outside with about four kids, including Alice, who now consistently calls me Mimi Mommy, which seems to make the daycare parents nervous. I know how much she must be missing Lauren. Also, as I keep explaining to them, it's not that I've *asked* her to call me this.

"It's the alliteration," I say. "All those fun *mmmm*s."

They nod when I say this, but I have the feeling that because I'm not a parent myself, my expertise about alliteration as it affects children's grief might be suspect.

It's the subject of a daycare meeting one night.

The Alice Situation was on the agenda, put there by Joyous, who says that the air needs to be cleared on this topic. I am invited to the meeting, which is being held in Nate and Nicole's apartment, located on Orange Street, not far away.

We discuss whether or not Alice really thinks I am somehow her mother—which no one, not even Joyous, really thinks is true. Is she then playing some kind of elaborate pretend game? Is she not facing reality? Should she be corrected?

Or has she simply gotten me confused with her mother? Do I, in fact, look like Lauren? Jamie gazes at me and reports that no, I do not look like his deceased wife. Still, I can feel a question hovering around the group: What am I doing there anyway? I'm not a mole from the State, am I, here to rat them out on possible violations?

"I just . . . well, I just *like* you all," I tell them shyly. "But if you'd rather I didn't hang out—I mean, I completely understand."

"You're not dangerous or anything, are you?" says Suki, the mother of William. She's smiling when she says it. "You're not on some mission to recruit every kid to call you Mommy, like a modern-day pied piper?"

They all laugh.

Jamie looks uncomfortable. And solemnly adorable. He leans forward and smiles worriedly at me as he insists that he is not in the least concerned about Alice calling me Mimi Mommy, because he thinks it's a four-year-old's idea of a joke.

"It always gets a reaction," he says. "And, as you can imagine, it got *quite* a reaction when she did it in front of Lauren's family. She told them with a big smile on her face that *Mommy* comes to daycare sometimes. Which of course caused Lauren's mom to try to explain once again that we can't *see* Mommy anymore because she *passed away*, and that made Alice explain that she didn't mean *Mommy*, she meant *Mimi Mommy*." He gives me a smile. "That didn't go over much better."

I think I want to go over and take off his glasses and clean them for him, and then, much to my surprise, I realize that—well, then I might want to kiss him.

"So later they took me aside and said it was of paramount importance that I keep Alice grounded in the truth," he says. "But I think she knows her mommy isn't coming back. So then I had to explain to her the entire way home what *passed away* meant. She kept saying, 'Passed away where?' Then she settled down in the back seat and chanted, 'passed away, passed away, passed away' for the rest of the way home."

"Oh, that's fun," says Joyous.

"Well," says Emily, who is Davy's mother. "What she says at daycare is that her mommy is in the ground but still loves her very much, and, what do I know, but that seems very healthy to me. For now, at least." She's curled up on the couch.

Nicole is lying on her side on the floor with her eyes closed and her head on a paisley pillow, her hands on her enormous pregnant belly, while Nate sits next to her, absently stroking her arm. The rest of us have dragged in mismatched kitchen chairs to sit in or are leaning against the wall, sipping wine out of red Solo cups. The furniture is all sixties boards-and-bricks vintage, a typical grad-student apartment with beanbag chairs and meditation posters and kids' art hung haphazardly all over the stucco walls.

"Do you talk about Lauren much at home, Jamie? I imagine it's very hard . . . ," Joyous says.

Jamie looks pained. "Of course! I talk to her about Lauren all the time, as much as she'll let me. But whenever I do it, she turns it all onto me. She gets this sad look on her face and strokes my face and says I have to be a big boy now, and she'll take care of me. She says, 'Don't worry, Daddy-o-Daddy. You're safe.'"

We're all silent. I stare at my hands, suddenly busy twisting my rings around and around. I'm wearing a bunch of silver rings with nonprecious stones in them, but of course, still no engagement ring. Ren never did remember to give that to me—or at least that's what I guess happened. It never comes up anymore. And why am I thinking about this *now*?

After a few minutes, Jerome clears his throat. He seems to be in command of all knowledge about children, grief, snack foods, daycare policies, and anything else he cares to think about, and now he gruffly says that children experience life irrationally just as the rest of us do, and there's no need to correct Alice and make her feel wrong for saying what she says.

"Hell," he says, "if she wants to call us all freaking Bozo the Clown right now, what's it to us? This is a child who's obviously missing her mother, and I'm sorry, but that deep, primal grief is a heavy feeling, and it takes all kinds of forms. Just let it go, for God's sake. Why do we have to analyze every little thing and pathologize it? I don't see why we even had to have a meeting about this."

Everybody stops talking.

Katherine, sitting next to him, leans over suddenly and pushes his gray ponytail into place and says, "Jerome is absolutely right. I think that Alice's grief is like a garden sprite, leaping around and figuring out how to express itself. She *knows* full well that Mimi isn't her mother—Mimi isn't even a daycare mom, for heaven's sake—but Alice is expressing something important to her. Maybe it's only that she wants somebody to call Mommy, too, like the other kiddos. Or maybe it's that she just needs to try out saying the word."

"That's right," says Jerome. "There you go. So all we have to do is love her. Not show her legal documentation of her parentage. For God's sake." He gets to his feet and pushes back his ponytail which Katherine had flipped over his shoulder. For a moment, they look at each other, and the air around them goes a little bit funny. Staticky. Maya is not in attendance; she's at home with Gabriela, and he is here.

"Well, thank you. I don't have it in me right now to be worried about this," says Jamie, sounding uncomfortable. "My life is just a matter of getting through each day. Getting Alice up in the morning, getting her dressed for daycare, trying to talk her into eating something, then getting her to agree to get in the car seat, answering a million questions, reassuring her about monsters and spiders and the stairs to the basement . . . and by the time I get to work I feel like I've already put in a full day."

"And then there's work, and then you come pick her up, and then you have a whole night to get through," says Nicole, sitting up and holding on to her stomach. Her face looks flushed with just the effort. I do not see how pregnant women operate in the world.

Jamie is looking at his hands. "We're doing fine. But I need to work more than I have been. The pressure is on, and they've all been patient with me because I'm, you know, a grieving single father, but I can't get my research done. So there's that. I always need more time."

"Jamie," I hear myself say. "Why don't I bring Alice up to my apartment after daycare when you need to stay at work late? I can feed her and play with her until you can come get her."

The group goes silent, and with everyone looking at him, he suddenly seems both grateful and embarrassed. *Maybe I should have made this offer privately.* "Well," he says, "that would be sort of great. I've been thinking I should hire a sitter, but—after a day already spent away from me, well, she'd hate that."

"Let me do it," I say. "Really. I'm there every day. I would love it."

His eyes meet mine, and he raises his eyebrows in a question. *Really?* I nod so vigorously I'm in danger of losing my balance.

"That would be wonderful," he says.

"Okay, then!" says Jerome. "Daycare comes through once again in our usual intuitive, nonpressure, inimitable, can't-be-explained, miraculous style! And now, could we possibly adjourn this meeting so some pregnant folks could get some sleep? Katherine, come on. I'll drive you home."

Everybody gets to their feet. Some are yawning. Jamie smiles at me and says we can talk tomorrow and figure out if I really mean it. And I say I do mean it. We decide that she'll stay with me on Mondays and Tuesdays. Alice is asleep in the back bedroom with Toby, and Jamie tiptoes back to get her, and then carries her out in his arms.

"She's such a sweetie," Nicole whispers to him. "We're lucky to have you two here."

His eyes look shiny as he thanks her. "She loves being here." And then he gives me a grateful look and he's gone.

Emily and Nicole are in the kitchen when I bring in some cups. Emily is saying, laughing a little bit, "Well, that escalated fast."

At first I think she means Jamie and me.

But then Nicole says, "Come on. It's just the way he is and he's always been. He believes in free love. Why should he limit his magnanimous sexual self when the rest of womankind is so obviously in need of his greatness?"

It takes me a moment to realize they're talking about Jerome. And Katherine.

"You know what he told me?" Joyous says, laughing. She goes into a singsong voice and waves her hand in the air like she's in a ballet. "That love is a butterfly, and when it lands in your hand, you can't squeeze it . . . or . . ."

"It flies away, and it's lost forever," finishes Emily. "Oh God. I am so sick of that analogy." She wipes off the counter. "Does anybody know how Maya is doing with this latest?"

I feel like I shouldn't be hearing any of this. I think of how it felt with Maya and Katherine on a daycare turn together a few weeks ago. They seemed fine to me. They were even laughing about it being a good thing Jerome didn't hear that the State was concerned about our daycare.

Listen to me: *our daycare.*

"She says the usual, that everybody gets crushes, and it's no big deal," says Nicole. "Which I sincerely hope is not true. If Nate falls for another woman, I'm heading out."

"With kids or without?" says Emily.

"Depends on which way would make him the most miserable," Nicole says.

Joyous says, "Maya is a second wife, and maybe second wives have a wisdom to them. They saw how things went down the first time."

Nicole says, "Maybe because they were the *cause* of it the first time."

And then Emily looks over at me and says nervously, "We're scaring Mimi. Who knew parental life was this hideously interesting, right?" She looks at me, smiling. "I don't know about you, but I thought life was supposed to be that you finished up with all that dating crap and you got married, had a kid, and then the rest of your life was just going through all the boring stages of raising children, going to work, and vacuuming the living room on your day off, until you retired from your job and got old and died. And then it turns out it's nothing like that."

"I haven't even gotten to the first stage yet, the getting married part," I say.

Joyous laughs. "Yeah, well, that part *is* wonderful. It's the rest of it that can turn your hair gray and make you gain thirty-five pounds and start to think of feeding your husband to the squirrels."

"No, no, no. It's all wonderful," says Emily. "Or at least wonderfully interesting. So what's your story?" She's looking at me kindly. "I hear there's a guy . . ."

"Well, it's complicated."

"Isn't it always!" she says.

"Well, yeah. I'm here because my fiancé is here. He and I were living and working in New York, and then his ex-wife had a stroke. She lives here in New Haven, and they have two daughters who are mostly grown, but not quite, so he came back."

They're staring at me, so I swallow and go on. "Yeah, he's a bit older than I am. And blah blah blah, we were teaching at a private high school and were just about to start planning our wedding that minute when we got the news that she'd been in a car accident and had a stroke and was in a coma, not completely expected to live. But she did live, and he's moved back into the house, and . . . well, he moved me here to be near him, but somehow it seems like they're all a family again." As I hear myself say this, it hits me that it really is true. They *are* a family again, and I'm just being strung along.

They're still looking at me expectantly. Nicole says, "And it would be in very bad taste of you to mind for one single second, I'm sure."

I'm afraid I'm going to choke up when I say, "Terribly bad taste. My job is to not mind anything, and to stay on the sidelines, and to be available at night in case he comes over late, after he's gotten his ex put to bed."

"Good God!" says Joyous. "That's the only time you see him?"

"Well . . . yeah," I say.

"What does he say is going to happen?" This from Nicole. "Like, what is he, in fact, *doing* at his ex-wife's house?"

I swallow. "He says we're still going to get married and that it's going to be wonderful. He says that this is just a detour until his daughters can cope and take over the responsibility for their mom's future. *Aaaaand* that he's showing his loyalty and his kindness, and that I should be grateful to see what kind of man I'm marrying."

"And providing sex every night," says Emily. "Sure."

Nicole says, "Now, Emily. I'm sure he's a wonderful man, and we shouldn't be saying those things. He's in a terrible position—with kids, and the stroke . . . and all . . ." She looks at me. "Do *you* feel like the marriage is still going to happen?"

"I do," I say slowly. "I just think it's going to take him a while to figure out what's going to happen with his ex. And the daughter duo. They're pretty powerful."

Nicole says, "It's hard to picture what kind of marriage you'll have, isn't it? No matter what happens with the wife, if she recovers from the stroke or not, the trajectory of your marriage to him has been forever changed."

Joyous says, "Way to be negative, Nicole," and fills up the sink with water and squirts some green soap in there.

Emily looks pensive. "I don't know anybody who has exactly the marriage they expected, do you? You know, Michael has an ex-wife, and for a long time after we got together, it seemed like she was always over, always needing something from him, always trying to be my best friend. I was afraid that she was going to lure him into leaving me and going back to her. And then—well, it was like it all kind of blew away. She got over it, I stopped worrying about her, he didn't feed the flames—who knows what happened? I haven't heard from her in years."

"It helped that she finally left town," says Nicole. "How much did you have to pay to get that to happen, by the way? You've never said."

Emily snaps her with the dish towel but she's laughing. "Plenty! I also had to promise Michael blow jobs every night for the rest of our lives."

Nicole suddenly gets a funny look on her face. She has her hand on her abdomen. "Wow! Feel this! This little one is really starting some dance moves," she says. "Here, look. Here's a knee going across my belly."

She lifts her shirt and they all put their hands on her smooth pink skin.

"Never gets old," says Emily. "Makes me want to have another one."

"May I?" I say shyly.

I don't know the first thing about pregnant bellies, nor do I expect I'll ever get to have one, but I go over and place my hands on her abdomen, which feels warm and alive to my touch. Nicole smiles at me. "Did you feel that?"

I feel a little bit speechless, so I just nod and go back to the sink and plunge my hands down into the soapy water and wash every plate and cup and then the frying pan on the stove, and I wipe off the table, too.

Because I can. Because I am here. Because somehow this feels so sacred, these women, this kitchen, this baby on the inside, this warm sudsy water.

༄

Later that night, when Ren comes over at eleven thirty and walks in the front door and immediately takes off his pants and his shirt and his shoes and leads me to my bed, I tell him that there's a little girl at daycare who calls me Mimi Mommy and that we had a meeting about it that night, and I think I'm becoming an honorary member of the daycare.

"What?" he says, and laughs. I'm lying next to him, and he's kissing my neck. "Why does she call you Mimi Mommy?"

"Because her mommy's dead. And she likes me. So I'm going to start keeping her a couple of afternoons per week because her dad has to work on his grad school project."

"For pay?"

I draw back and stare at him. "No, *not* for pay! Are you kidding me? I wouldn't charge him!"

"Hey, don't get mad at me. I just thought maybe you were looking for babysitting jobs now. Now can we please get to the new-business section of our meeting, do you think? Because I've got to get up early in the morning and meet with the occupational therapist."

I look at him. "Are you really going to wear black socks while we make love?"

"Mimi." He takes his hands off of me and lies back on the pillow. "What's going on?"

"Nothing. I just think wearing socks while we're having sex is gross."

"That's not what this is about."

I stare at the ceiling. We're both lying side by side staring at the ceiling.

"You don't have time to hear it," I tell him. "And I'm not in the mood to complain and have you tell me that nothing can be done. Forget it. It doesn't matter anyway. You have to do what you have to do, and I have to put up with it. And so that's just the way it is. Sometimes . . . I need more."

"I know you need more. And I'm working on it."

"Actually, you're pulling away. I can feel it."

"Maybe you're the one pulling away. All you want is to talk about these daycare people. And what things you've learned to cook."

"And all you want is to have sex with no talking."

"Baby, I'm talked out. Can't you see that? I spend my whole day talking to Judith and talking to my kids and then talking to the doctors and therapists! I'm *swamped* with talking! I just need a place to be myself. To have some peace and quiet, and now I come over here and there's more talking that needs to happen."

I feel myself ready to cry.

"I'm sorry, I'm sorry," he says. "God, what is wrong with me? Of course you need talking. Please! Forgive me! Let's start the evening over."

"I don't want to."

"Please," he says. "Please. Forgive me for being an asshole."

"I'm tired."

"Here," he says. "I'll take off my socks. Does that help? Would it help if I remind you that you're the subatomic particle of my bones? And if I admit that I am a selfish, horrible bastard who is trying his best but falls short every single day, and you are the one thing in my life that makes sense?"

And so we make love, but it's not really like starting over, and we both know it. When he leaves finally, thirty minutes later, I'm relieved as I close the front door. And I think he's probably just as relieved to be free, going back into the night.

CHAPTER SIXTEEN

I start taking care of Alice twice a week after daycare ends, and Jamie joins us at about seven, after he's finished at school.

She's happy to come with me and trots up the stairs, leading the way. I was worried that I didn't have enough stuff in my apartment to keep her interested, but she loves going through my jewelry box, such as it is, trying on bracelets and necklaces and telling me she's now a grand lady. Sometimes we do the Jane Fonda workout tape. Often we sit on the floor next to the fan, and she plays with my hair, which she tries to put in a braid. Then I braid her hair, and after that, we go to the park, and at her request, we look for little feathers to stick in our braids. Sometimes we walk down to the river and launch little leaves and sticks to float downstream.

I love these lazy days, like summers should be.

After we walk back home, I start getting dinner ready. I'm hoping that, with my newfound cooking skills, I can get Jamie to stay each evening when he comes to pick her up—tempt him with the aromas of dinner cooking. Mostly he agrees but sometimes he's too harried and acts like he might be worried he's putting me out. "It's fine, it's fine," I say to him. "Really, you're doing me a favor, helping me eat up all this food. I'm only one person!"

The truth is—it feels homey having him and Alice sitting at my kitchen table, all of us chatting away like we've known each other forever.

Dangerously homey, I know. Believe me, I know. I'm not happy about it either. It's just something I have to do for these two people.

∽

So it's no wonder that on a July day that's too humid and too blazing hot, I lose my mind.

It starts on a Saturday when I'm making my usual rounds through the neighborhood, always circling past Judith's house because I'm probably a crazy person and I have to see what's going on, and I stop in disbelief when I see so many cars parked outside. Like, seven of them, four in the driveway, wedged there, and one on the lawn, and two others on the street in front.

At first I think that something terrible has happened. Like—what if maybe Judith died, and Ren hasn't been able to get away to tell me? Or maybe all the medical authorities are there to evaluate her condition, and she's about to be transferred to a facility, like Jenna supposedly wants.

But then—well, I watch as a young woman in a sundress comes out the front door and walks over to one of the cars parked in the driveway and reaches in and brings out a present and some pink foil balloons that say **GET WELL SOON** and **HAPPY BIRTHDAY**. A man comes out and joins her and lights a cigarette, and the two of them sit on the steps with their heads together.

I'm sorry, but these are not medical people about to transfer a woman to a nursing home.

This is company! The Yardley family is having freaking company. I smell hamburgers! And when I crane my neck, I can see a barbecue grill and some streamers. Streamers!

Honestly, it had never occurred to me that they would have company. Parties. A regular life.

News flash: *Mimi, you are not part of his family in any way.*

I stand there in the park, idiot that I am, and I realize again that I'm just the secret woman, hidden around the corner, waiting for his morsels of attention. Lying beside him late at night when he comes over to make love. And aching for more. Always that ache.

∽

When he comes to see me again—he has to miss a few nights—I meet him at the door with a preternatural calm. If he were a more tuned-in man, he would know just from the look of me that things in his life are about to change.

But, ha, he doesn't seem to get it. He goes on with his usual sighing and claiming how tough life is over at the house, how grueling the whole mess is, how maddening that there's progress some days and then back to zero.

I tell him that I noticed he had a party the other day.

A beat goes by. "Yes," he says, "and it was such a hassle. It was Judith's *birthday*, and her parents and old friends all stopped by."

"Did your mother come, too?"

He blinks. "Yes."

"And do all of these parents know that you and Judith are divorced?"

Now he pulls himself up, suspecting a trap. "Of course they do."

"And do any of them—any one of the three of them—know that you're engaged to be married to someone else?"

"Mimi," he says.

"Your Honor," I say cheerfully, "I ask the court's permission to treat the witness as hostile."

"Do not even pretend that you wish you were included in that little festival," he says. "I get it that you feel left out, but believe you me, that party was nothing to be desired. I would have given anything not to have to be there."

"I'm sure you do feel that way," I say, "but I have a difference of opinion. Things are going to change. I'm coming over to your house, and I'm bringing a goddamned roast chicken and some mashed potatoes and a salad. Maybe a loaf of homemade bread, too. And I'm telling Jenna and Parker that I love their dad and I want to love them, too, and I think it's amazing what they're doing, but they deserve a break from this. I'm going to tell Parker she can take a day off and go to New York if she wants to—"

"She won't."

"—I don't care if she does or not—and then I'm telling Jenna that she can take a whole goddamned week and go to DC to see her boyfriend, because I'm going to show up and be there. I can take Judith for walks in her wheelchair, and I can read her stories, and I can play music, and I can hold her hand and sit with her when it's needed."

"I'm not sure this is a good idea," he says.

"Well, I predict that you'll come to see that it's a fine idea."

"It's not. I beg you not to do it. I need more time."

"You don't need more time," I say. I'm not even mad anymore. I go over and chuck him under the chin and smile at him. "You poor man. It's like you've never seen even *one* romantic movie about love. You don't have any idea how regular people become each other's families."

I wake up the next morning and get busy assembling ingredients, before I've even brushed my teeth, before the sun is even quite over the roofs of the houses, before the trucks bringing dairy products and vegetables to the Embassy Market have swung around the corner and backed up to the delivery entrance in the rear. I throw my whole self into kneading dough and then tucking it lovingly into a large blue bowl I found at the junk shop.

I rub butter on the skin of a roasting chicken and put four sprigs of rosemary inside. I want the skin to be golden and crispy, and the chicken inside to be moist and juicy, just like the recipe said. I'm singing as I slide it into the oven, and I watch gleefully while it pops and sizzles in the roasting pan.

I look down at the daycare, children playing in the sun, chasing each other, and throwing a ball. It's Jamie's turn today, and I can see Alice holding on to his leg as he tries to push kids on the swings. He keeps having to stop and pick her up and pretend to gobble her under the chin until she laughs hysterically.

I boil and mash up some potatoes with plenty of butter and chives, and at precisely 3:30 p.m., I put on a blue skirt and a pink shirt with pearl buttons, and I put on some lipstick and a little mascara and put a headband on my unruly hair, and then I put the chicken on a platter and the rest of the food into two large shopping bags, and I march myself over to Ren's ex-wife's house.

I have to take a deep cleansing breath when I get there, for courage, and I head up the front walk and ring the doorbell.

White light, white light, white light. La Starla taught me that.

Then I have to ring it again.

More white light.

The third time I ring it, I hear somebody say, "I'm *coming*, for Christ's sake!" And then the door flies open, and Jenna stands there. She stares at me in a way that makes clear she knows who I am. Her arms fall to her sides, and the light goes out of her green eyes. This is fine. I know I have a lot of work to do with this family.

She's slim and tall and imposing, and her long blonde hair is all pinned up in a bun, and she's got on a pair of tan shorts and a short-sleeved blue shirt that looks like it has little boat flags on it. And loafers.

"Hi, Jenna," I say and smile at her. "I brought you over some dinner, and—"

She's looking at me with dead eyes. "I'm sorry. And you are . . . ?"

White freaking light.

"Oh!" I smile so wide my face feels like it might crack open. "So sorry! You don't recognize me! It's been so long—I'm Mimi Perkins. Your dad's fiancée?" I wasn't entirely sure if I should throw my official relationship out there like that—What if he's denying everything these days, in the interest of maintaining family harmony? But then I decided *What the hell, Ren? You can't keep living a double life, buddy—not with me in the picture, you can't.*

"Oh," she says. "Right."

Before she can say anything, I keep going. "Anyway, I've taken the liberty of bringing your family over some dinner. I've made, let's see, a roasted chicken and some homemade bread and mashed potatoes and green beans."

She still looks blank, so I add some culinary facts to help things along. "I put butter on the potatoes, and the chicken is made with rosemary and a special glaze I found in the market."

Nothing from this girl. I keep going.

"I'm so sorry that I haven't come around before now to tell you how deeply saddened I am to hear of your mother's accident. I should have brought food by much sooner than this. But here I am, better late than never. I hope."

She just looks at me, blinking. And then she says, "All right. Well. Thank you."

I hold my breath. This is a delicate part. She might just take the food and close the door, and that will delay the formation of our deep friendship bond.

So, to stop this from happening, I say, "Here, honey, I'll just take these to the kitchen for you," and I start to move forward, through the doorway—and really, what can she do but step aside. And then I am in. In!

I follow her to the kitchen, looking around a little, but trying not to be too obvious about it. I am just one big wadded-up ball of curiosity, wanting to soak up every single detail. It's a house that is very grand—high ceilings, ornate fixtures around the fireplace, and once it was probably all lovely and fantastic in here, but now it looks a little bereft. Of course, Judith was in the process of selling it and moving away, so it's no wonder.

The kitchen is bright and airy, with long windows and a white tile floor and white-white cabinets with glass fronts. It looks like it was once elegant, with new shiny appliances, but now the butcher-block countertops are crammed with stacked-up dirty dishes and piles of mail, pill bottles, and an overturned bottle of seltzer. There's a fuzzy blue bedroom slipper on the floor next to the sink, and a maroon sweatshirt flung onto a round breakfast nook table, next to a plate of unfinished scrambled eggs that look as though they might have been there since yesterday. I put the bags down on the kitchen island.

Jenna has good manners and is also probably too weary to figure out how to get rid of me, so she offers tea. "I don't want to cause any trouble," I say. "You must be busy with all the care you're giving your mother. Tell me: How *is* your mother?"

She says that it's not going particularly well. And that it's no trouble to make tea. She was just about to make a cup for herself. Her mother is upstairs napping. Parker is with her. "None of us are medical people, so we're just making sure she's never alone. That's the important thing, don't let her be alone," she says, without emotion. "Other than that, other than following the advice of doctors and therapists and nurses, we don't quite know what we're doing. We keep hiring and losing night nurses. So it's not great. We've pretty much decided that it's up to us to keep her alive."

She is very, very, very, very tired.

"It's so hard," I murmur. "Something so sudden like this. I'm so very sorry. The mind can't adjust."

She looks a little bit like Parker, only more worried, less flamboyant, a little bit more beaten down by life. I suppose this is to be expected. She's the older daughter, after all, and she's the one not getting her way, according to Ren. He said both girls have complicated, twisty feelings about Judith, because of the fact that she wasn't around for so much of their childhoods. And mothers are complicated just by being mothers.

Jenna is rummaging in the cabinet for some tea bags, so I go over to the sink and fill up the teakettle and go turn on the burner. She says,

"Earl Grey, lavender mint, English breakfast . . . or something called gunpowder tea?"

"Earl Grey, please." I laugh a little bit. "It would have to be a pretty bad day for gunpowder tea."

"This one comes close," she says under her breath, and then she yells, "Fuck! There aren't any clean teacups! Can *no one* in this house ever manage to run the damned dishwasher? Even *once*? Ever?"

"Here," I say. I pick up two dirty cups I see on the counter and go over to the sink and start washing them. She looks as though she wants to protest that, but I shake my head. "It's fine. Let me do this for you."

After that, I put away the chicken and mashed potatoes in the refrigerator, which is another place that seems to have been marauded by wild bears. A bottle of syrup is canoodling with a bottle of ketchup, both splattered with the other's drips.

"You two are not a good match," I tell them. "Syrup, you belong with the butter, if anything." I move it away and put the ketchup by the mayonnaise.

"Please tell me you're not talking to the refrigerator," she says.

"No. Sorry. Just to the syrup and the ketchup bottles," I say. "They were spilling on each other. Getting too familiar." When she looks blank, I say, "Never mind."

We sit down to tea, and I try to make conversation, get her to talk about her work or her boyfriend or her former life or her hairstyle, anything, just so we can start being friends. I'd love her to tell me where Ren is, without my having to ask. Maybe she'll tell me if indeed her mother is now sweet and docile and lovely, or if this is just a fantasy of his, and of course I would like to know if everybody is in agreement that she's going to recover.

Instead, she's the one who has questions for me. The first one is "Why are you here?"

"Here?" I say, smiling. "Here, in your kitchen? Here, in New Haven?"

"I guess here in New Haven. I thought you lived in New York. Didn't you and my dad teach together?"

"Really?" I say. "You didn't know I was in New Haven? You do know that your father and I—"

"Oh yes. I've been told *that*," she says. "But—when did you come?"

"Well, actually, I've been here for a few months." I try to hide my irritation. Does this family truly not communicate *anything*? What I come around to, after a few seconds of deep despair, is that this is precisely why they need a friend like me to help them. They're like satellites floating about in the outer space of this airless existence they've been thrust into. I feel myself soften. "And, actually, I'd like to help out, if I can be of any use."

We sit there for a moment, with her looking sad and withdrawn, and I'm tempted to start babbling about her mom, so I'm kind of relieved when the phone rings, and she goes off to the dining room to answer it. I pop up and very helpfully wash all the dishes, throw out the day-old scrambled eggs, wipe down the counters, organize the mail, and position the medications with the labels all facing front. I am polishing the dials on the stove when Ren comes in the back door, sees me, and stops dead in his tracks.

He has a frozen smile on his face and he's holding a bag from the Hall-Benedict pharmacy, which he finally drops onto the kitchen table.

"Oh my God. *What?*" he says, and he looks quite miffed, I'm sorry to report. "*What* are you doing here?" he whispers. "You *didn't*. You didn't do the thing, did you?"

I square my shoulders. "I certainly did. I told you: I'm going to help out here. And I've been sitting here talking to Jenna, who's on the phone now, so I also did the dishes." I go back to scrubbing the knobs on the stove.

"Don't you see, it just makes things so much harder . . ." He's still whispering furiously. "They're not ready for this."

"It'll be what it is," I say. "I'm not worried. I really think this is the right move. Toward love, family, connection. And that's what we're here for, isn't it?"

"What we're *here for* is to get things settled down."

"But don't *you* get it that things are never going to be *settled down*, as you call it? You have a family. You have responsibilities, and you're always going to have them. When you marry me, that means that I'm officially a part of your life. That's pretty much the basic definition of marriage, becoming a participant in the other person's life."

"But you simply can't snap your fingers and have that happen," he says, and just then Jenna comes back in the kitchen, and Ren turns and says to her in an altogether different voice, "*Honey!* How are things? Parker upstairs with Mom?"

She says something, but I suddenly can't hear anything because a really weird, strange thing is happening. I can't hear anything but buzzing, and my vision isn't so great either, and my heart seems to be galloping off, moving my chest up and down. It is possible that I can't remember how to breathe.

I am obviously having a heart attack even though I'm young and I haven't even lived yet, really, never had a family, never fixed things with my mom, and I couldn't even put on a play without the educational authorities firing me, even though I think the kids did like me and that's worth something, although nothing you could put on an epitaph if this is *it, the end,* and what if I die right here in Judith's kitchen, wouldn't that be the worst kind of melodramatic scene anyone could ever think of? And maybe it would serve him right, him with his hissing and his guarding everybody against me, which is what he's doing, whether he sees it or not. A possibly dying ex-wife upstairs and a definitely dying fiancée in the kitchen. What a Hallmark movie this would be!

I don't want to die, but I'd love to see the look on his face when it happens.

"I think you need to call an ambulance," I say to him in a low voice and stagger over to a chair.

～∾

It turns out that it's a panic attack, that's all. I'm not dying after all.

Even though it did feel like the black death coming for me, I'm recovering and will be fine. No ambulances are called. Jenna gets me a glass of water, and Ren has me sit down and put my head between my knees and take deep breaths. When Parker comes downstairs, rubbing her eyes and looking exhausted, I'm breathing into a brown paper bag that someone handed me.

"What is *she* doing here?" she says, and Jenna says, "Maybe go upstairs and get the blood pressure cuff, why don't you, and the oximeter."

"But what is she *doing* here?" Parker says again. "Dad?"

Ren puts his hand on my arm. "Are you okay now?" he says, which is the first thing someone has said that has the slightest tinge of kindness to it.

After that, they turn on each other, the way I've heard families can get away with doing. Not in my mother's house, we couldn't. An argument, a complaint, a harsh word—any of these would get you sent to your room. *Be polite. If you can't say anything nice, don't say anything at all. He's your stepfather. And now be nice to your* new *stepfather. Oh, and this other new one, too. He deserves your respect. All stepfathers deserve your respect.*

I take deep breaths that blow up the paper bag and then deflate it again. Over and over. But I am keeping track of their conversation. Looking at them over the top of the bag, I discern that Jenna is mad that no one told her I was living in New Haven. Parker is mad because Jenna didn't come upstairs to take her shift with Judith. Apparently it's true that someone needs to sit next to her bed at all times—to keep her from trying to get out of it, to listen for words she might say, needs she might have, or to make sure she keeps breathing.

"You didn't tell me . . . that Mimi . . . ?" I hear Jenna say, her voice coming through only in fits and starts like there's still some static hovering about the room.

"Didn't . . . think . . ."

"No matter," says Ren. Then he says something unintelligible. And after that, they're all livid, and he says, "No! I'm . . . not going . . . anywhere . . ."

I press the paper bag harder against my face, squeeze my eyes closed. Jenna yells, "Dad! This is how you always are!"

Parker says something, something, something. I hear the words *apartment* and *so what's it to you.*

Over the edge of the paper bag, I see it play across his face, the back-and-forthness of him regretting that I'm there and then realizing that forces are beyond his control, and finally seeing that he must man up and *say something.*

And so he does.

He turns and faces them. I put the bag down so I can hear it all. "So, my darling daughters, I need to tell you something. I love you two. And I love this woman blowing into a paper bag here. And there is a way in which I still love your mother, and what I want to say is: there's enough love in life for everybody, no matter what form it takes. And we have to take care of each other." This is not exactly an award-winning Hallmark movie speech. But he's trying. He swallows and his Adam's apple goes up and down. Nobody moves, so he presses on. "And by that I mean, we're *going* to take care of each other. Mistakes and all. Life is what you make it. Grab on to a life preserver, because we are each other's life preservers. You know what I'm saying?" His eyes look too shiny all of a sudden, and I think, *Oh my God he's going to cry or maybe he's now having a stroke.* He pauses, looks down, and then he goes on: "And we have to be positive, move forward, go into the future with bravery . . . life is what happens when you don't know what you're really doing, so this is what we're doing now . . . the way it's going to be, and Mimi is here in New Haven, and we are all going to live our lives, difficult as that may be . . ."

He probably would have said a hundred more clichés because we can all see that he's lost his mind, and nothing he says has made one bit of sense, but then Parker cuts him off by going over to him and putting her hands on his forearms and saying, "Dad, stop. Please. For the love of all that is holy in this world, you've gotta stop talking. Here, I think you need to eat. The glucose has obviously forsaken you and you don't have any brain cells functioning."

He says weakly, "Well, I mean it. I may not be putting it in the right words."

"You're making zero sense," says Jenna. "You're exhausted, Popsy. Give it up."

Popsy?

I'm shocked, seeing her go over and put her arm around the two of them, after she'd just been yelling. They're a family unit, these three, closing ranks so effortlessly. I can't seem to stop myself from looking at them because I want this so much. I want exactly what they're having.

Parker pulls away and growls, "Hey, who cleaned up this kitchen, and—wait, is this what I think it is, a loaf of bread on the counter? How did this get here?" She looks at her dad, who tilts his head toward me.

My insides are still wobbling, but I manage to put the bag down and say, "Is anybody hungry? We could heat up the chicken and the mashed potatoes."

"Oh," says Parker. "Well, maybe." She turns to Jenna. "What time is the visiting nurse coming tomorrow? Did you change the schedule like I asked you to?"

Jenna sighs loudly. "No. She'll be here at noon."

"Damn it, I told you we have to take Mom to the neurologist at one, and that's not enough time! Why is it up to me to do all the scheduling stuff?"

"I don't know. Because you're turning into a control-freak asshole?"

"No. Because *you* have decided that your work here is done and all you want is to go back to your precious life no matter that our mother needs you, and so you've decided to just take a hands-off approach and be a failure at calendar and clocks and leave it to me to be the adult here."

"Listen to you! Fresh from the party life in New York City, telling the rest of us how to be an adult."

"*Fresh from*? Is that what you said? For your information, I've been here every single day for nearly four months!"

"Girls," says Ren. He cuts his eyes over toward me, almost apologetically, but I nod at him. I cannot possibly express how much I love that I get to be here, even in the midst of this exchange.

"I just hope to God the nurse tells you in a way you can finally hear it that the current setup is untenable. We need to move her downstairs, and we need a hospital bed, one with rails. She's going to fall out and break something now that she's moving around more," says Jenna. "And while we're at it, we need to find a decent night nurse so that we don't have to worry all the time."

"I know, but even with rails, she could try to get out," says Parker. "And you think a nurse is going to solve everything? You think the hospital bed is going to make it possible for you to go back to DC? People break their hips all the time going around the rails of a hospital bed. It's not going to mean *we* don't still have to watch her. You still have to take your shift."

"I never said I'm not going to take my shift!"

"She's moving around?" I say.

"She's moving around," says Jenna.

"Is she talking?"

"She talks sometimes. This morning I was bathing her, and she said the wind was pink with butter sausage."

"It's like poetry," I say.

"Butter *sausage*?" says Parker to me. "That's poetry?"

"It's kind of lovely," I say. "She's thinking about food. Food poetry." I get up and take the chicken out of the refrigerator. "Is anybody hungry?"

"Yes," says Parker. "Starving."

"I'll heat this up. Ren, could you turn the oven on to 350, please?"

Nobody smiles at me, nobody says thank you, but they also don't kick me out. So there's that. Ren turns on the oven, and later he puts his arm around me when Jenna goes upstairs to take her turn watching her mother. And I somehow know I'm in. I'll have a probationary period, of course. Nobody gets by without a probationary period. I wouldn't respect them if they didn't put me through some stuff.

But I'm in.

Later, while I'm doing the dinner dishes, I see him looking at me and shaking his head, smiling. "You're something, you know that?"

I have never loved him more.

⌒⊙

The next day I bring over some cinnamon rolls and Jenna actually squeezes off a tiny smile when I tell her about how crazy my mother is and how she thinks she won the life sweepstakes because she's been married five times now and keeps getting upgrades to her housing and cars with every divorce settlement.

Today, in fact, when I come over with an apple pie, she takes me upstairs to where Judith is. Judith is in her gray-blue bedroom, lying on her back on her newly delivered hospital bed, supported by pillows. She has Nancy Reagan–style blonde hair that's combed off her face, obviously due to some daughterly effort at grooming her. Her eyes are closed, and her lips look chapped. There's a blank paleness to her expression, and to the way her hands just lie there, still, on her abdomen. She looks like she could be dead. I have never seen her in person before.

I sit next to her bed, feeling a mix of emotions. Sympathy, horror, lurid fascination. I sit there thinking how weird it is that this is the way I first meet my rival—and then I am horrified that, even in my head, I'm thinking of her as a "rival," since she is decidedly *not* in any way, shape, or form my *rival*.

She wakes and her unfocused eyes swim around the room. Her mouth moves.

She says, "The air dirge."

"Yep, she's talking," I say.

"Come on," says Jenna to me. "Let's not disturb her anymore. She needs to sleep."

Just then Judith's hand jerks out from under the covers, and she grabs my hand and holds on to it. For just a moment, her eyes lock onto mine. She looks like somebody who's just resting there on the bed, who maybe just woke up from a bad dream. She says, "Weezy!"

"Come on," says Jenna.

I pat Judith's hand and stand up.

In the hallway Jenna says to me, "Can you let yourself out? I should go back and sit with her, make sure she doesn't suddenly spring to life and try to bolt out of that bed. Wouldn't do to have that happen on my watch, you know."

"It's a good sign that she's moving and talking, though, right?"

"Yeah, sure. I guess so. They don't really know how much damage was done."

"How do you bear this?"

She says, "How do I bear it? I don't. My hair is starting to fall out. I'm not sleeping. I fight with Parker all the time. My boyfriend thinks I don't love him anymore, and my boss says my leave can't last forever. Add to that the fact that my mother might never be able to make sense again, and you've pretty much got what my life is now."

I reach out and touch her arm. "I can come over more often," I say, barely above a whisper. "I can take a turn."

I wait for her to say, "Don't bother," or "Who do you think you are? You're not family!" But she doesn't. She just shrugs. Maybe she's even too weary to reject me.

"You really love my dad, don't you?"

"I do. And—and I want to be helpful here. For you and Parker. I'm not the enemy, you know."

She smiles.

∽

I go over a few times in the next couple of weeks, on the afternoons when I don't take care of Alice, and I sit with Judith.

I play music for her—Simon & Garfunkel, Carly Simon, the Rolling Stones. She seems to like it. I see her tapping her fingers to the beat on the coverlet of her bed.

One day she says, clear as a bell, "Do you have my guest book? I have twenty thousand signatures today."

I sit back in the chair. "Wow. That's remarkable."

"Somebody should give it back."

"They probably should," I say. "Would you like a sip of water?"

She nods.

I hold the cup up to her mouth. She closes her eyes when she drinks, the way a child might. Her eyelids are crescent-shaped and nearly transparent, like little shells. And her eyelashes rest against her smooth cheek so delicately, as if she's completely new and reborn. She opens her eyes and smiles at me.

"Weezy, you came," she says.

Nothing in my heart works as it should anymore.

⁓

That night La Starla calls me.

"I'm getting a new vibe when I think about you," she says.

"So what's the vibe?" I say to her.

"Love," she says. "Capital *L* love. From out of nowhere."

"See? I knew it! It's Ren," I tell her triumphantly. "I'm now taking meals over to him and his family. Things are moving along."

"Sweetie baby, I'm pretty sure I'm talking about something else altogether than this Ren love. I'm talking about real, *real* love, the kind that moves into your heart and won't let you go. The only kind of love that's worth having, if you ask me."

"My love for Ren is *very* real, La Starla, and now that I've pretty much been accepted by his daughters, I can see that these are clearly the children the spirit guides have been directing me toward. So everything is going along just swimmingly. I even sit with his wife some afternoons now. I'm becoming part of their family, which is something I never thought could happen. You should tell the spirit guides."

She laughs. "I still think you're delusional," she says. "But I love you anyway."

"Just tell me this," I say. "I need to know. Are you ever wrong?"

There's a long, long silence. "I have been wrong," she says, "but not about this."

∽

I start going to see Judith a few times a week. I take her brownies and ice cream, and we sit outside on her deck underneath the maple trees, and I read her stories, recipes, and articles from *Reader's Digest*. Unlike my time at daycare or even my times with Alice, these afternoons feel languid and soft.

Sometimes when I'm there with her, I am Weezy, her dear friend from childhood, and it's as if we are just two old friends sitting around talking, and sometimes she holds my hand and smiles into my eyes, and it's as if my life with Ren has somehow been erased, and *my* life connected to her is in full Technicolor all around me.

She dozes off sometimes, and at other times she tells me things, haltingly, looking intently into my eyes while she talks. Sometimes she just strings together nonsense words, about horses and guest books and sea captains. No matter. I write everything down.

And then sometimes she says something so profound that I think she might be the wisest one in her family.

She says, "I may have missed some of the warning signs about love and children."

She says, "Weezy! Weezy! I need someone to hold my hands during scary movies, or when there are bagpipes around."

And don't we all need protection during scary movies and when there are bagpipes threatening? Judith and I—we are not so different.

CHAPTER SEVENTEEN

One early August afternoon I make chicken and dumplings with Alice, even though it's a million degrees outside, because she tells me she's never had that, and also she's always thought *dumpling* was a "beautiful word."

"I think I want my name to be Dumpling when I'm a baby getting borned one more time," she says.

"Huh," I say. "That sounds like a very amazing plan. Getting born one more time."

"I *am* amazing," she tells me. "I'm going to get borned over and over again, and one time when I am a mommy, *my* mommy will be the baby, and she won't have to get dead."

Often I don't have the faintest idea what I should say.

I set her up in the kitchen standing on the footstool and let her mash up the biscuit dough while I cut up the chicken and carrots and onions. After that, she rolls the dumplings into balls and declares that they are so cute and that we should name them.

"I am Alice Dumpling, their mother," she says. "And this is Mimi Dumpling and Daddy Dumpling and Daycare Dumpling."

After we get some cookies in the oven and the chicken bubbling away in the pot, we put in my Jane Fonda tape and start our workout in the living room, stretching and kicking and jumping around.

"I want those things she wears on her legs," she says.

"Leg warmers? I want some, too, but it seems kind of hot outside for leg warmers," I tell her.

"Let's tell Daddy to buy us some," she says. "We have to do this right."

Instead we go into my room and get some knee socks from my drawer and cut the feet out of them and pull them up over our legs.

When the dinner is on the stove, she rummages through my drawers, which is her usual favorite thing to do at my house. She needs to know where I keep everything. She brings in a tube of lipstick and wants me to put some on her, which I do—just lightly. It probably wouldn't be great if Jamie came home and found I'd tarted up his daughter.

When Jamie arrives, she runs to greet him, and he swings her around. She insists that we have to demonstrate our leg warmers and the workouts we do, although I'm a bit shy about doing all the kicking and jumping while he watches, so I stop after thirty seconds and declare that he must be thirsty.

"Daddy, we made chicken dumplings for you!" she squeals. "So we have to stay and eat with Mimi Mommy. And now I'm going to be Alice Dumpling, and everybody will call me that. And you have to tell Grandma and Grandpa that that's my new name."

"Okay," he says. He looks helpless in the face of all this.

"A beer?" I say, meeting his eyes over the top of her head.

"Please," he says. He and I head to the kitchen, and Alice bounces off to pillage more of my possessions.

"Aren't you worried about what she's doing?" he says.

"No. She likes to play with my jewelry," I say.

"And you let her? Are you out of your mind?"

"It's not that kind of jewelry. Just fun stuff."

"Let's go make sure," he says. And there she is, sitting on the floor in my room, going through my jewelry box.

"Oh!" I say. "You look very fancy!" She's got necklaces around her neck and has rings and bracelets spread out around her, and she's dangling three pairs of earrings off her fingers. Horrifyingly enough, sitting on the floor next to her is a bright green package of condoms that had been in the drawer, and when I reach for it, she says, "Oh, that. Those looks like candy, but they're not."

"No, they're not," I say. "Let me take them out of your way."

"*Okay,*" says Jamie. "I think we should go back into the living room, shall we?" He looks at me and mouths, "Sorry."

"It's okay. You can leave me here," says Alice. "I'm not going to eat them, Daddy."

"I know you won't, sweetie, but maybe we shouldn't be going through Mimi's stuff."

I say to him that it's really fine, she can play with the jewelry, and he shrugs and says okay then, though I do swoop down and pick up the box of condoms and put it away, across the room in a top drawer, before she starts taking them all apart and handing them out to us as dinner favors.

He and I go back to the living room.

"Well," he says, rolling his eyes. "*That* went well." He sits down on the couch and looks at me. Something has changed in his eyes. I don't know where to look, exactly, or what to say. I'm a grown woman, and surely not embarrassed by *condoms*. Why can't I look up?

Luckily he starts talking in a calm, boring voice about two grad students he works with. At first it seems to be a routine story about work, how everyone works so hard, and people don't have much time to socialize, and he doesn't really, really fit in—he's the only parent in the program, much less the only *single* parent, and even *less* the only widower. (*Widower,* he says, and the word just rolls off his tongue like he's accustomed to it by now, the feel of it in his mouth.)

But then he takes a deep breath and says, "So can I talk to you about a vibe I have?"

I'm afraid for a moment he means me. But I nod.

"This is weird, and you're probably going to think I'm making a mountain out of a molehill, but one of the grad students I work with keeps inviting me to go to the movies with her. And now I think I need some advice on just what I'm supposed to say."

"Well, that would depend on one thing. Do you *want* to go to the movies with her?"

"Not on a date, I don't. But I'm not sure if what she's proposing is, you know, actually a *date* date, or is it just a casual everybody-go-to-the-movies thing? I don't know how to read signals anymore. This is why I need a relationship guru. And that might have to be you."

He's mentioning this because of the condoms. I can just tell. We're now going to be people who discuss our love lives, or lack thereof. Which is fine, I guess.

"Well. Not sure I qualify as a guru, but a good rule of thumb is: if other people aren't coming, too, then she is asking you out," I say with more certainty than I have any right to. "So if you don't want to go out with her, then you could maybe say you're not quite ready for that or you're too busy with your kid or . . . ?"

He thinks about it, and then he says, "But what if I'm wrong and she's just trying to be nice and it's not romantic at all? She probably sees that I'm a horrible mess and just wants to be friendly. Also, on the other hand, I mean, it's flattering that this woman wants to see me, right? Or would be if I cared. But I don't care about any of that stuff."

"Don't overthink it. Just say thank you, you're flattered, but you can't go."

"You gotta admit, it's weird to say that."

"No, it isn't."

"I wasn't ever that great at dating in the first place, and I'm certainly not good at it now. Lauren just kind of came along and plucked me out of the pack, and that was that. And now I don't ever want to do it again."

"No one does," I say. "I wasn't ever good at it either. Awful!"

"Did you also get plucked out of the pack by your fiancé? Sorry. I don't know his name. But how's it going? Do you guys have a date set?"

I shrug, feeling embarrassed all of a sudden. "Oh hell, I don't even know if it's going to happen. The time isn't ever right, and I don't think it's ever going to *be* right."

"Why not?"

Once again, I can't look at him. "Oh, I don't know. He's completely involved with his family. They own all his time, and I don't see that he's ever going to get over this. And maybe he *shouldn't* ever get over it. It's huge, what happened to his wife. I mean, his ex-wife."

He nods.

"Last month I got so fed up with the situation that I told him I was going to take dinner over to his family and make friends with his daughters and *help out*. And he *begged* me not to, said it was too soon, it wouldn't work. But I did it anyway, and I think I won over the kids. I cooked them dinner, I cleaned up the kitchen, and then I went back the next day and did it all again."

"What? Why?"

"Why? Because I want to be part of things!"

"You want to be part of things, when he's not offering you any encouragement?"

"Well . . . yeah."

"Hmm." He gets a mock-serious look on his face, with a twitch of his mouth like he might burst out laughing. "So then . . . do you think this might be a case of mental illness?"

"It's cowardice is what I think it is."

"No!" he says, and he falls over laughing. "I mean *you*!"

"What? Me? I'm the only normal one here! Although, come to think of it, I did have a fairly significant panic attack when I was over there."

"Of course you did. Come to your senses, woman. Why do you stand for this?"

"What choice do I have?"

"Oh man, I can't believe *I* have to be the relationship guru now. Listen to me. You can't be this guy's doormat. Geez, I don't know anything about love or dating or reasonable timetables, but he's totally taking you for granted. One hundred percent." He takes a swig of his beer and wipes his mouth. "Tell me. How long has it been?"

"Since I moved here? Um. Over four months."

"Four months is a pretty long time for no movement, I'd say. I don't know, I probably am not the right guy to consult on this kind of thing, but this frankly doesn't sound like much of an engagement to me."

"Yeah. I don't even know for sure if we *are* engaged anymore," I say. "In his version of things, he only wants to see me at night."

"To enjoy those things that are *not* candies." He lifts his eyebrows.

"Yep. And then he runs back home. I don't see how we get from that to being married and living in the same house. He won't even spend the whole night here."

Just then the timer dings, which means that the chicken and dumplings are done, and thank God he goes off to retrieve Alice, and I have a minute to recover myself while I put the food in the bowls. He's probably right; this love has made me seriously unbalanced, and he can see it. Probably everyone can see it. We sit down to eat, and Alice is laughing and smiling and pulling the dumplings out of her bowl and waving them around. She says she won't answer to any name except Alice Dumpling from now on.

After dinner, just to keep them a little longer, I put on the music she and I had been dancing to in the afternoon. Alice pulls him into dancing to "I Love Rock 'n' Roll," jumping around and waving our hands in the air. He's reluctant at first, but then it turns out the guy has some serious moves. I turn the music up louder because one of the best things about living above a daycare is that at night, you don't have to worry about disturbing anyone at all.

We've moved on to "Twist and Shout" when the doorbell rings.

"What time is it?" I say. The room has gotten steadily darker, lit only by the light coming from the dining room, but I never thought how late it must be. "Wow, oh my goodness, I think that's Ren." I crash back to earth.

"We should get out of here and let you have your evening. Get on with the noncandy portion of your night."

The doorbell rings again.

"Please," I say. "It's totally fine. I'm just gonna go down and let him in before he starts leaning on the bell."

"No, no. I'm getting her stuff. Come on, Alice. We can go out the back."

"Go out the back? You don't have to sneak out! Stay up here, and he'll come in and you can meet him."

"I don't know . . . this doesn't seem like a great idea."

"Come on. Please. He won't bite."

I run downstairs and open the door, and sure enough, there is Ren.

"How are you?" he says, leaning in for a kiss. "I really should get my own key, you know. Then I wouldn't have to stand out here like a fool, ringing the doorbell four hundred times. The neighbors are going to talk."

"I know. Sorry. Come on up. A friend from daycare is here. A single dad, with his daughter, Alice. Come and meet them."

"Ah!" he says, and his face is wreathed in smiles by the time we get upstairs. Jamie is still sitting on the couch, trying to buckle Alice's sandals while she sits on his lap. I introduce them, and Ren says, "An honest-to-god daycare dad person! So nice to meet you! Someday I want to know all about this crazy daycare of yours. As a father who raised his kids pretty much alone—although I'm not permitted to mention any of that now, under the new rewriting of history that's going on at my house—may I just say I *know* what you're going through!"

Jamie smiles and says something polite before sliding Alice off his lap, and she holds out her hand to Ren, who shakes it.

"My name is really Alice Dumpling," says Alice, and Ren takes this news in with great aplomb. He shakes her hand again and says he often goes by the name Biscuit Gravy, and they should get together.

Then he stands there, beaming at his own cleverness, smelling good and looking all-American handsome, like a smoldering Paul

Newman—all picture-of-health and competent-in-the-world—and then he leans over Alice and grasps Jamie's hand and says, "I'm actually so glad you're here because I'm a theater guy, and I was going to do this thing I've been meaning to do, and it'll be even more meaningful with friends here. Will you help me, Dumpling?" he says, and she beams at him.

"Ren, they really have to go," I say.

"No, it'll just be a minute. Bear with me." He takes a ring box out of his pocket and winks at me. Then he bends down and says to Alice, "Honey, do you want to open this for Mimi?"

She reaches out her hand, and Ren leans down to help her open the box, keeping up a patter with her in a low voice. "I was supposed to give this to Mimi months ago, but I lost it, and now I see that was a good thing because *you're* here to help me. I was waiting for *you*. Do you know what this is, sweetheart?"

When I glance over at Jamie, I see he's staring at me, and his eyes are wide and his mouth has gone into an exaggerated O shape. He pantomimes putting on a ring, and then a simpering smile with his hands under his chin. I think that is supposed to be me. I give him a grim look.

"Okay, here goes," says Ren. He's looking down in concentration and now he puts his arm around Alice and says confidentially, "I got down on one knee last time, so I don't have to do that this time." He straightens himself up, smiles at me, and clears his throat. "Mimi Perkins, will you make me the happiest man in the world and marry me?" He says to Alice, in a loud whisper, "I actually already know the answer because I asked her before and she said yes already, so I don't think she needs to say yes again, do you?"

"No," says Alice. "She already said it."

"Wait. Let me put the ring on her," says Ren. "We have to do this up right. None of this slap-dash stuff anymore. I suppose you may have heard that after my last proposal to her, all hell broke loose, and life turned into a disaster. Which it still is, technically speaking, but now at least we have a ring. Signaling my intentions. Right, Mimi?"

He puts the ring on my finger and kisses me, much to my embarrassment. But Jamie and Alice Dumpling clap their hands, and the ring fits, and actually, this is probably a lovely moment if I could just relax and enjoy it. After I'd been complaining that I didn't know if the engagement was still on, Ren comes through with a ring. Jamie is smiling at me.

Ren says, "Do we have champagne?"

"I don't think so," I say, and Jamie says, quickly, "Sorry, but we've got to get moving anyway."

He stands up, says it was nice to meet Ren, and then he mumbles something about *oh yes Mimi I put your earrings on the table* and *thank you for the dinner* and *sorry we stayed so late.* And I say things like *it was so much fun* and *have a good sleep, little Alice, I mean Alice Dumpling,* and *I'll see you both on Monday, right?*

And then they're gone, and Ren stands there and shakes his head.

"Those days—alone with a kid—I remember it so well. Look at that guy. He's just one big throbbing well of loneliness. Come here, you, and let's celebrate engagement try number two. How about we actually go downtown and have a drink together?"

"In public?" I say.

"Of course. Why not? Let's take that ring for a test drive."

And so we do. And it's nice, like old times, sitting with him in a darkened bar, drinking gin and tonics, listening to a jazz quartet, and smiling into each other's eyes.

I don't tell him about daycare, and he doesn't tell me about his home life. And even more surprising, he spends the night at my apartment. This means he has to call home a couple of times just to make sure everything's okay and that somebody is sleeping in the bed next to Judith.

I try not to mind. I just love stretching out next to him in bed, hearing his soft snoring through the night. I wake up several times just to check and make sure he's still there.

And he is.

CHAPTER EIGHTEEN

One morning, I'm awakened by the doorbell, and when I go downstairs, I find Maya and Toby standing on the porch, looking intently at me, like they're bursting with news.

She says, "Oh! Oh my goodness! Sorry to wake you. But I was wondering if you might be available to come downstairs and help me. Nicole has gone into labor, and Nate was supposed to be on the turn, but obviously he's gone, so—can you come down?" She holds up Toby's hand. "This is a big day! Toby's going to be a big brother today!"

"Wow, sure!" I say. I'm still wearing the T-shirt and shorts I slept in, but when I look down, I decide they seem pretty acceptable for a daycare turn on a hot August day.

I look down at Toby, and he smiles shyly and bites his lip.

"Let me just brush my teeth and put on a bra and I'll be right there."

Two minutes later, I'm following the two of them across the porch through the daycare's front door. I tousle Toby's hair. "Look at you, big guy!" I say to him. "You're getting a new baby at your house!"

"Yeth. And I making airpoit for the baby," he says solemnly as we walk across the porch. He tucks his little hand in mine.

"An airport?"

He gives me an angelic smile. "Yeth. For the baby to fly away. See?"

He runs over to a LEGO structure in the middle of the room, where there's a haphazard stack of red and green and yellow LEGO bricks. "It's the tower," he explains. "The baby goes in the tower."

Maya gives me a meaningful look. "Good times ahead," she says.

I'm pleased when Jamie and Alice show up. He grins at me and waggles his eyebrows as he's putting Alice's stuff in her cubby.

"What are you doing down here so early in the morning?"

"I'm actually doing a turn today. Nicole's in labor, so Nate can't do his turn."

I look down to see Gabriela toddling toward me. She has just perfected her walking skills and is heading, single-mindedly, for some blue play dough that's stuck to the floor. I swoop over and pick her up, just in time to see Maya barreling out of the kitchen, boiling with outrage.

"You are simply *not* going to believe this!" she says to Jamie. "The lunch today is clam chowder."

He wrinkles his nose. "Well, *that* sounds like something no kid is going to eat."

Her eyes are blazing. "*And* it's simply a bag of unshucked clams, a couple of raw potatoes, and a gallon of milk. **KID PROJECT.** That's what it says in huge red letters. And then **HAVE FUN.**" She holds up a piece of paper and waves it. "*Have fun*! It says that right here!" And then she barks out a laugh.

He scratches his head. "Oh no! Whose week is it?"

Maya heaves a huge, exasperated sigh. "It's Katherine. Wouldn't you know? All right. I'm going to call her right now and tell her to get her ass down here with something else for lunch and get it here pronto. This is untenable. I've just about had it with that woman! Do you know that last week, she—"

I anxiously wait to hear what sin she's going to tell us about. I just hope it doesn't have anything to do with Katherine sleeping with Jerome. I don't want to be here when that little drama gets unpacked, especially during a daycare turn.

But then suddenly she just stops talking. Her eyes narrow and her mouth clamps shut, and the look on her face is like things have dialed up from bad to end-of-the-world bad. I'm almost scared to turn around and see what she's staring at across the room. When I do, I see a strange man and woman standing just inside the front door, looking around. They've obviously just knocked and now have taken the liberty of coming right in. Who the hell are they? They're highly conspicuous, wearing official-looking suits, and the woman has her hair scraped away from her face and tied back, and she's looking aghast at everything she's seeing. The man is ageless and silent, as though he's a Secret Service agent who finds himself in the wrong movie.

Toby has sauntered over and is talking to them in a friendly, just-making-conversation voice, as if he's a guy at the office water cooler asking about any weekend plans. "Do you have a uterus? My mommy has a uterus," he says with a smile. (We've all—male and female—had to divulge our uterus-ownership status to him lately, practically every day in fact.) From the looks of the two, one of them most likely does have a uterus, and I'm curious if she'll eventually cop to it. These two suit-wearers, however, do not look the type to discuss their reproductive organs with a three-year-old.

I rush over to intervene, when from the other side of the room, Sanborn, who is two and a half and is being potty trained, starts yelling, "I have a poop! I have a poop coming *right now!*" And, because when hell starts to break loose, it so often breaks loose *everywhere*, William suddenly feels the need to run across the room in his excitement over an impending poop situation, but he trips on a wooden block and falls flat on his face, hitting his chin on the floor.

And he bleeds. And howls.

"Oh my God," says Jamie, barely above a whisper. He was supposed to be leaving for work, but he has no choice but to spring into action, picking up William, while I leave Toby to his anatomy questions and run to the kitchen for ice. Maya dashes to scoop up Sanborn, who is squatting down now and has his eyes closed in concentration—and she runs with him under one arm and Gabriela under the other, to the bathroom. There's no time to wonder how these grown-ups from the real world are dealing with the uterus conversation.

When I turn around after getting the ice pack out of the freezer—thanking God there was an ice pack in there, which seemed highly unlikely—there they are, standing behind me, looking around the kitchen like they're mentally composing a twelve-page report. The man is actually writing something down.

"We would like to talk to you," the woman says.

"Fine. I've gotta get this ice over to that busted lip in the living room first!"

"Then come right back," she says. "We have a few questions." She has a name tag and a clipboard, I see. I hate clipboards.

I speed away. "So those two scary strangers are now in the kitchen, and they seem to be taking notes," I whisper to Jamie as I'm handing him the ice.

He has William on his lap, and he places the ice gently next to his lip. "Here, buddy, this is going to help." Then he whispers to me, "I think they're from the State. They're inspecting us. We failed last time, so I bet they're here to see if we did what we were supposed to."

"Did we?"

"Who knows? Knowing us, I'm guessing not."

"Oh, great. Are we even licensed?" I ask. I suddenly remember someone talking about the State coming around.

"God knows. I mean, of course we are. Sure. We'd have to be, wouldn't we?"

"I hope so. What should I tell them?" I say. "They say they want to talk to *me*."

"Tell them . . . tell them . . . that you were just hired as the new director here and that you are systematically working your way through their previous list of violations, and you'll be in touch. You're new, so you haven't gotten everything squared away yet. But you're continuing to observe and reconnoiter. Be sure you use the word *reconnoiter*. It will impress them."

I can feel my eyebrows lifting up so much, they're in danger of leaving my forehead altogether. "Do you know what the violations were? Are we running a dangerous organization here?"

"Shhh." He laughs softly. "Just some minor things. We talked about them at a daycare meeting a month or so ago. Seriously. Just say that you're currently reconnoitering about them."

"No deaths or disfigurements, then?"

"No. But they did want us to hire a director, so you can say that's you." His eyes are dancing.

"Should I really say that?"

He smiles at me. "Sure, why not? I think you pretty much have to. Otherwise, they might close us down right this minute, and I have to get to work."

I look into his eyes to see if he's kidding, but he just looks back at me, placidly smiling. His glasses need cleaning, but this might not be the time to mention that.

I go back to the two inspectors and find them peering inside the bag of sandy clams, and then at the two potatoes and the unrefrigerated gallon of milk. From their frowns I can tell that no doubt they've already written loads of things on their clipboard: likely mentioning the play dough on the floor and the sippy cup I now see tipped over under the table.

I try to straighten myself up and offer a pleasant smile. But this whole thing takes me right back to being in Penelope Harrington's office. My hands are sweating.

"Is this some kind of a joke—this bag of clams?" the woman says. I now see that her name tag says she's Millicent Hamilton. "For lunch for these children?"

"Actually, someone dropped that bag off for *me*," I say. "I have company in town this weekend, and she had gone clamming. Lunch is—ah, lunch is macaroni and cheese. And carrot sticks. And milk."

She looks around. "I thought I heard someone say this was lunch for the children. But you say it's not."

"It's not. Children don't like clam chowder! Who would give them that?" I laugh. "That's why they're absolutely not for the children. They're mine."

She scratches something off the clipboard and purses her lips. "All right, then. Where's the macaroni?"

Ah yes. The macaroni. Where the hell is that macaroni?

"The man who is bringing it isn't here yet. It's coming."

She eyes me. "You are *quite* sure these clams are *not* for the children, then?"

"Of course not. Little kids won't eat clams."

She looks around. The man is opening drawers and looking into the refrigerator, which seems forward and rude, and I wonder if he has any right to do this. Doesn't he need a search warrant? Probably not, since he's not a cop. And anyway, who's going to argue with him? Certainly not me.

"All right, then," the man says, turning to me. "Did a director ever get hired? Is anyone in charge at all?"

"That would be me," I say, and I can tell by the expressions on their faces that they actually believe me.

And why not? I kind of believe it myself. I say the part about how I'm recently hired and that, yes, I'm reconnoitering and I'm going through the list of violations. We're all working quite hard to come up to code.

They hesitate, look over their notes, put their heads together, and then the woman says grudgingly that they're willing to give us some extra time since I'm new. They'll come back for a reinspection. They'll be back sometime within the next six weeks, and they expect that all the violations will have been dealt with, or this time there will be consequences. We'll get a letter in the mail.

I take the piece of paper they hand me, with all its red checkmarks and scrawled complaints.

"We're not fooling around about this," says Millicent Hamilton, as William and Sanborn and Alice come charging through the kitchen, pretending to be part of the fire department. All three of them have decided to impersonate the siren, and they sound quite legitimate, decibel-wise.

"I'm glad this facility finally got a director," Millicent Hamilton yells. "It was *abhorrent,* the way they'd let things slide around here. You let everybody know that we're not putting up with violations anymore. The State is cracking down."

Abhorrent? Cracking down? My eyes start to blink extra fast.

"I will," I say. "I will definitely do that."

And I will. Right after I explain to the members that I've somehow become their new director.

⁓

It requires a meeting, of course. You don't just get to be the director/coordinator/leader of the Children's Sometimes Cooperative Daycare (or whatever the hell the name is; no one seems to really know) without having to show up and explain that you're a good person and that you love everything about the daycare and that you're sorry you couldn't consult anyone first, but you were on the spot. If it doesn't work out, I'm totally explaining that Jamie thought it was a great idea. They love Jamie.

They're grateful, as it turns out. It's probably just as well that Jerome didn't attend this meeting, because he's the one who probably would find some objection with the daycare simply capitulating to "the man," Joyous tells me with a laugh. But he is not here—he's away on business in New York. ("What? Is there something going on in the rabble-rousing business?" whispers Emily.) Coincidentally Katherine is also away, but I am *not* noticing that tonight.

As for the rest of them, they've known for some time they had to hire somebody; they were just procrastinating while they half-heartedly searched for the right person. And it seems that I am that right person, sent from who knows where.

"You even have experience teaching," says Emily. "And best of all, you live upstairs, so you'll never be late."

"No, best of all is that I adore all of you," I tell her. "As far as my teaching experience—um, I was teaching teenagers about Shakespeare and how to put on a play when no one knew their lines. So not that many incidents of biting. And hardly anyone ever needed their mommy."

"I'm sure they did, but they couldn't admit it," Jamie says with a smile. "Don't we all need our mommies?"

"I think it's probably best if around here, we don't call you *the director*," says Michael. "It sounds kind of authoritarian."

"Right. For goodness' sake, I won't be *directing* anybody," I say.

They go back and forth. Should I be known as the leader? The coordinator? The grand pooh-bah? Maybe the queen? I tell them, shyly, that I have always wanted to be the queen of something.

But then Emily says, "How about she gets to be the octopus. They're smart, they're cute, and they have eight arms, which is just about the right amount for this job."

So that's it. I'm officially the daycare octopus.

It is agreed that I will work six hours a day, five days a week—from the opening at nine a.m. until three—and I'll be paid enough to cover my rent and buy food, and with luck, I can pay the utilities most months.

As we're all packing up to leave, I say the thing I should have mentioned in the first place. "We still do need to do those things the State wants, or else they're going to shut us down. Just hiring an octopus isn't going to keep them quiet."

No one hears me. They're already gathering themselves to go out into the night. Joyous comes over and hugs me, and Michael gives me a peck on the cheek. "It's great you're doing this," says Emily.

Joyous says, "We're so relieved!"

"You're our fearless leader," says Suki. "We're so lucky to have you!"

No one, I point out to Jamie as we're walking out, has said anything remotely practical about bringing things up to code.

"Welcome," he says, "to daycare."

⁓

"You're not going to believe this, but I have a job," I tell Ren when he comes over that night.

"Let me guess. Hall-Benedict finally hired you."

"No."

"Marjolaine's wants you to come make pastry."

I frown. "Did I ever want to make pastry professionally?"

"You could do anything you set your mind to. Look what you did with the Piedmont students."

"Well, that," I say. *That was when I was helped by magic. Something I don't think he wants to hear about again.*

"Maybe you'd better just tell me what your new job is," he says. He's unbuttoning my shirt as he talks. He's smiling but ready to move on from the conversation portion of our evening to what he considers the real thing. After all, he hasn't seen me since five thirty when I hurried to his house with a sheet pan of beef burritos. He was busy then, tending to Judith, so we only had a moment to say hello.

"I'm going to be the—well, I'm the person in charge at the daycare."

He stops his unbuttoning, and his eyes search my face. "A person in charge, huh? Would that be like the director?"

So I explain about how this daycare operates, that terms like "director" denote governments and bosses and are a turnoff. Somebody used the term "coordinator," but even that had an officialness to it that could be off-putting. "One of the women said I'm the daycare octopus. So that's how I'm seeing my role."

"The daycare octopus, I see." He smiles at me. "How is it, my dear, that you move somewhere completely new and yet you find people just as . . . eccentric . . . as you are?"

"I don't know," I say. "But I love them."

"And I love you," he says, and off we go to bed.

Afterward, while he's getting dressed, I tell him about the inspectors showing up and the fact that we're going to need to bring the place up to code. There are some minor violations, I try to explain. I have a piece of paper with the list of them.

He shakes his head, smiling at me fondly, already distracted by needing to go back home. "Ah, my little love. What in the world have you gotten yourself involved in? Is this a cult?"

"If it is, it's wonderful," I say.

"It's wonderful until it isn't," he tells me. He tips up my chin and kisses me on the lips. "Just keep in mind that you don't *have* to solve this random daycare's problems with the State. This job is just a little side trip, not your real life."

"But what is my real life?" I say to him.

"What is your real life? Are you serious?" He stops kissing me and touches my cheek. "Your real life is the life we're going to make together. It just got detained temporarily; don't forget that part. You even have a ring now. In fact, let me see it. Did anyone mention it?"

I hold out my left hand, where the ring glints in the candlelight. He kisses that, too.

"Did they say anything about that rock on your finger? Your day-care people?"

"Well, no."

"See? They're not your people. I'm your people." He gets back up, finishes buttoning his shirt. "You know, in a crazy kind of way, this accident may have been helpful to our relationship. It's given us some time to slow down and reflect, and for me to really get to know my family as helpers and adults before I move on. I think they're going to understand me more. And accept *you*."

"Please do not say this accident was a good thing."

"No, no! I mean, I wish it hadn't happened. Of course I do. Judith is forever changed. Not that that is a totally bad thing either; she's softer toward me somehow. But in terms of us—just from a selfish perspective—I've gotten to step back and look at my life in a whole different way. I get to spend time with my daughters that's more meaningful than anything we did in New York. And I get to see you like this—in bed, every single night. Almost."

"Ren, I think if I played you a recording of this conversation, you would hate yourself for every word you've said."

He winks at me. "Possibly. I may be a bit of a bad apple. Be careful."

And then he's gone into the night.

CHAPTER NINETEEN

A couple of days later, when Jamie comes by to pick up Alice, it's still plenty light outside, so I pack us a picnic supper and we walk over to the park. I bring hard-boiled eggs and watermelon and cold barbecued chicken that Jamie says Alice will never ever eat, but which I happen to know that Alice likes.

The park is filled with couples walking along the river and kids sliding on the sliding board in the playground area, or running around in crazy circles, playing tag by touching all the trees. One little boy has made it his mission to gather up every rock he can possibly locate and put them in a pile.

I'm feeling drowsy and relaxed after we eat. I wish I'd brought the two beers I have in the fridge, but maybe, I think, we'll have them when we get back. We just have to make sure we're finished with everything before Ren arrives. I don't want to go through that kind of scene again. It makes my stomach hurt, seeing the two guys together.

"We need to plan a daycare workday," I say, but I yawn as I say it, which might take away a little bit of the immediacy of the problem.

"Gotcha," says Jamie, and he yawns, too.

Alice gets bored with us and goes over to help with the rock-collection project, and Jamie scoots over closer to me on the blanket.

He pulls up a piece of grass and examines it and then says, heavily, "I really do care about this daycare workday. But I may need some more help from the relationship guru. Can you help with one more?"

"Not *another* woman dilemma!"

"Worse. It's family."

"Hmm. My duties seem to have expanded here. Let's see, I'm now Alice's minder, *and* a person who agrees to take whatever daycare job you make me take, as well as the provider of the only barbecued chicken that Alice will eat, and apparently now I'm a *full-time* relationship guru for you."

"Don't forget that in return, I'm the guy who will remove all couches from stairwells for you. And listen to men propose marriage to you."

"Okay. Still seems a little unbalanced, but . . . here, let me get on my relationship guru uniform." I mime pulling something on over my head, sticking my arms into it. "Okay. Go ahead."

"So you know how I take Alice to see my in-laws most weekends?"

"Right."

"Well, they seem to have decided that I'm not doing all that well. And I find myself having to ward off a friendly takeover."

"A friendly takeover of what?"

He points to Alice, who is piling rocks ten feet away and chattering to the little boy, who is listening intently. It seems she has to educate him on the proper way to stack rocks.

"Our . . . *Alice?*" I say in a stage whisper. "They can't take her over."

He nods. "That's what I think, but my father-in-law talked to my professor and found out that he doesn't exactly love my capstone project, and so my mother-in-law says I obviously need more time to study and work and so why don't they take Alice to live with them in West Hartford until I get everything sorted out?"

"What? But you're doing fine!"

"Well. They've discovered that I'm depending on you two evenings a week, so that's not me doing *fine*, in their book."

"But did you tell them I don't mind keeping her? That I love it, in fact?"

He gives me a sad smile. "I don't think you understand what we're up against here. *You* might just be the threat that they fear the most."

"What? Me?" I say.

"Yeah, ever since they heard that Alice calls you Mimi Mommy, they've been on high alert. And also, well, I'm afraid that historically they don't approve of the daycare. Not one bit."

"What's wrong with the daycare?"

He laughs. "It's a den of hippies," he whispers. "Did you know? And it doesn't fit with their rather conservative view of early-childhood education." He sits cross-legged on the blanket, his eyes serious, turning a little twig around and around in his hands. "Also, there's a bit of history here you don't know about."

"Please," I say. "Tell me everything."

He's speaking in a low voice so Alice won't overhear. "Well, when Lauren first was diagnosed with lymphoma, she underwent treatments here in New Haven, and all the doctors were saying that it was probably curable. But after a few months—well, the cancer just started spinning out of control, and then one day the doctors sat us down and told us there was nothing more they could do—"

"*Ohhh*, no," I say.

"All-hands-on-deck time." His voice skips a little bit. He looks over to check on Alice, who is busily supervising her new friend. He says in a low voice, "So we moved in with her parents. Her younger sister, Mandy, left college to come back home to help out. It was awful. Alice was nearly two, and she was having a really tough time, and I was trying to be there full-time for Lauren, who was trying *so* hard to be brave for everyone else, and meanwhile Lauren's mom, Denise, was freaking out—"

"Of course," I say.

"Yeah," he says, seeing my face. "Yeah. Family drama to the nth degree. And then—well, months later, when the end finally came, and those last days were so much worse than we'd ever anticipated—we were all just devastated. I never knew before how grief drives people apart. Everybody in their own private suffering. I wanted to go back to my life, but Denise said that Alice had just lost her mom, and she shouldn't be uprooted and lose her grandparents, too. And besides, *they* needed us! I felt like I had to repay them, in some kind of weird way, so I agreed to stay. So months went by. Then my boss at my old job called me and said he really needed me to come back to fill a lot of orders for custom furniture, so I decided to move back to New Haven and hire a babysitter for Alice. But when Denise heard my plan, she said I couldn't possibly take Alice away from them and have some *stranger* looking after her while I worked. So, out of guilt, I gave up the job and stayed longer. Longer than I probably should have." He looks away, overcome for a moment.

Alice is sitting in the dirt, collecting little pebbles into a pile.

"I'm sounding ungrateful, and that's bad," he says after a moment. "This family—Lauren's family—is so nice. They're so *loving*. I was *not* their first choice for son-in-law—I mean, come on, from their point of view, I was a *carpenter* with no real prospects—and yet they still wanted me to be in their family."

"Incredibly open-minded of them."

"So then, Otto, Lauren's dad, came up with a plan. I could get my business degree at Yale grad school, and he'd pay for it. Then—*voilà*—when I'm done, I can work with him and eventually take over his business. I'm the son he never had, he said. And I've got a good head for business, and this way he'll make sure Alice is taken care of. So they proposed that we continue to live with them and I commute to Yale to classes."

"Jamie, that sounds awful."

"Yeah. It was brutal. Over an hour drive each way. Every day. And then homework." He looks down at his hands. "We did it for four months, and then I'd had it. The driving, the studying time, the never getting to be with Alice, who was acting out like crazy by then. And so one day I was in the Yale Co-Op and I saw the flyer for the daycare, and then I found an apartment. Serendipity, right?"

"Definitely," I say.

"And so that night I told Denise and Otto I was leaving, which maybe I didn't do in the most wonderful way possible, and they freaked the hell out. Denise said that *everyone* knows daycare is bad for kids, it's only for poor children who don't have relatives to help, and how could I do this to my own child—and *then* when I said I *was* doing it, she said *she* would commute to New Haven and look after Alice while I was in school. Only her idea of commuting was that she would stay over in *my* apartment for five days a week and sleep on a foldout couch in my office and go home on weekends."

"Jesus, Jamie. That's the kind of nice that can kill you if you're not careful."

"Thank you. Yes. You get it. After a while, I couldn't . . . I needed my own life back. So I sat them down and said I'd raise Alice *my* way, using daycare, *and* as a compromise, I'd take her up to see them every single weekend. And so that's what we do. Otto still wants me to take over his company when I graduate, which probably means I'll have to move up there, but we'll cross that bridge when we come to it. I've got over a year to go."

"The only thing their plan leaves out is that what you *really* want is to make furniture. Are you the person who's made all the great bookshelves in the daycare?"

He looks at me with eyes that suddenly seem luminous. "Well, yes."

"And the toys?"

"Yeah."

"Jamie, they're beautiful."

"Well, thank you."

"So why aren't you just doing that, which is what you want to be doing?"

"I think Lauren would have wanted her parents to be in Alice's life."

"I get it," I say.

He looks down at his hands. "So anyway, last weekend I got the speech. The speech that says that even *I* don't know how bad off I am, and also now that Alice is four, she should be in nursery school instead of daycare. She needs to be in a place where she can learn to read and write and, I don't know, start earning a living doing people's taxes or something."

"Ugh."

He gives me a mock stern look. "Also, young lady, they would like you to know that this daycare has not taught Alice to read or do arithmetic yet. All she does is play all day. As the octopus, you have a lot to answer for."

"We octopuses do let children play all day."

"Octo*pi*."

"Whatever. So they want to take her to West Hartford and put her in nursery school?"

"That's what they want."

"And you are not going to let that happen."

"*No*, but I'm just so tired of fighting them. These are people who have our best interests at heart, or believe they do."

He stretches out his legs and puts his hands behind his head. He has long, hairy legs, and he's probably unaware that his feet look so gorgeous they could be in a photo shoot. I can't quite take my eyes off these feet. He's waiting for me to respond.

"Sorry," I say. "I was mesmerized by your feet for a moment."

"My feet?" He looks down. "Are there ants coming for them or something?"

"No. No, they're just lying there, being feet. Nice sandals. In Manhattan, we don't see guys so much with the sandals."

"Is that so?"

"Yeah. More your pointy-toed boots and shiny loafer things. These are suburban summer feet."

"Oh. Sure. Yeah, I've got that going for me, two feet and sandals. That actually match. Unlike any kids' socks at daycare. Ever."

"Matching socks are not required for happiness."

"That's just it. Just what I'm trying to say. My in-laws live in the kind of society where matching socks are the *minimum* required for happiness. Denise is always buying Alice little dresses and such."

He and I both watch Alice carry a big rock over to the pile and drop it on top with a look of satisfaction on her face.

"If you leave this daycare after making me take the position of octopus, I will never ever forgive you," I say. "Also, may I just go on the record as saying that other people don't get to run your life, no matter how much they love you or how supposedly nice they are. *You* get to run your life."

He sighs.

I can't sit there anymore. I get up off the blanket, as though I've just noticed that Alice is in dire need of assistance. I need to get away from Jamie, I realize. His feet. Those sandals. Those in-laws who are sure as hell going to take him and Alice away, no matter what he says. He is not a fighter. I get that. I'm not a fighter either. Are we always doomed to be bumped around by people who claim they know what's right for us?

And I've become obsessed with this man quite without my own permission, and now he's going to move away. Sure, I'm helping him, and he likes me, and we have lots of laughs, but this is not real life for either him or for me. I am not his *family*. I'm not really anyone's family, as it turns out. This is not where we're headed. If we were all wearing T-shirts that expressed our true realities, his would say **I'M NOT READY FOR ANYTHING** and mine would say **I'M ENGAGED TO BE MARRIED**.

It shouldn't even matter. I'm just waiting for Ren to get his life in order and for us to get married—and if the spirit guides were being consulted, they would no doubt say that Jamie will end up living in West Hartford with Alice and his very sweet, concerned, heartbroken in-laws and running a company and being loved and supported by people who miss their daughter, and that will be that. He'll be fine. Maybe he'll build bookshelves in his garage in his spare time and that will be enough for him. Who am I to tell him he's got to follow his own heart, when I'm not even on a first-name basis with *my* own heart?

This whole thing between him and me—all these laughs and dinners and relationship-guru stuff—this is just an interlude, the stuff of a temporary friendship, the kind of happy bantering you have with coworkers. Even the gazing into each other's eyes stuff, the private jokes.

Even those moments when we accidentally brush against each other, like when he's come to my apartment to pick up Alice, and we're eating dinner, and then we get up to do the dishes and our eyes meet and our hands touch. I know he feels the same electricity that I do, but it's not going to turn into anything.

I look down at my engagement ring and take a deep breath. I am engaged to be married to a man who loves me very much. He may be in over his head at the moment, but he is getting free, and he loves me, and besides that, I also love him, and by God, I'm not the kind of woman to turn her back on someone who's being a good family man and who is working his way through a whole bunch of life problems just now.

I need to get my head on straight. I'm about to go back over to Jamie and pack up our picnic stuff and get ready to leave, when suddenly I'm stopped in my tracks by such a beautiful, touching family scene taking place.

It's a man and two young women walking, pushing a woman in a wheelchair. They're strolling on the path that leads to the river, with the branches of the elm trees bending down over their heads like a protective canopy. They lean together, smiling, their heads almost touching, and that's when the air begins to tingle, and they swim into focus as they come closer.

Oh my God. I realize with a gut punch that it's Ren and Jenna and Parker, pushing Judith along. I can't take my eyes off them. The three of them are laughing as they bend down toward her, touching her hair. I can hear the lilt of their voices from this distance, moving closer to me—so close that I slide behind a tree. If Ren looked in my direction, he would see me. But he doesn't. He stops and straightens Judith's cardigan, rearranges her legs so very gently. When he stands up again, he plants a kiss on the top of her head. And she looks up at his face and grabs for his hand.

Jenna says something I can't hear, and the three of them laugh, and then Parker hits Jenna in the arm and Jenna acts like she's going to chase her, and Ren has to intervene. I see him laughing and waving his arms at them, and then he says something to Judith and pushes the wheelchair forward.

They're a family. That's what hits me. *They are a complete unit, needing nothing else in the whole world.*

This scene could be in a sappy movie about a family that's been struck by tragedy, and yet here they are—surviving, all four of them. Sadder, wiser, intact, and moving forward, wheeling toward the river while the sun glows orange and purple in the sky. The credits would roll, and the audience would sigh and put away their tissues and go out into the world.

CHAPTER TWENTY

The next day the mail brings a notice from the State, written on its very important letterhead, informing us that the daycare must comply with certain health and safety requirements or face immediate shutdown. We now have only two weeks until the inspection, they say—and you can just tell by the font that they mean business.

I call an emergency daycare meeting to organize a workday.

We gather at Maya and Jerome's house, a little brick apartment crammed with bookshelves and beanbag chairs, posters, and a desk with a manual typewriter in the living room. Black-and-white photos of old political rallies line the walls. Pillows blanket the floor. Clearly it's the home of two intellectuals.

Jamie drives me there, and I sit on a beanbag chair with my charts and lists of jobs and a clipboard, looking at them like I'm the official person we all know an octopus must be. Since I've taken this job, I've discovered the benefits of clipboards and lists.

Things go wrong right from the beginning.

Jerome is, as he puts it, "low-level disgruntled." He's mad that we agreed to do *anything* the State wants. He's in favor of closing down the whole daycare and telling the State, "Okay, you win, we're disbanding," and then secretly restarting somewhere else.

"Hell, we can hold the damned daycare right here. Right, Maya?"

Maya gives him a deadly stare and points out that *no*, this space can't hold a daycare because they have furniture here, and typewriters, and their *lives*. And not nearly enough open space or toys. Then she stops, realizing she's been led into a trap by him, and says, "Why am I saying this? You aren't even serious about the daycare moving here, are you? You're just trying to get everyone riled up because that's what you do so well."

He fingers his beard, as though he's considering this. "Well, okay. So then we'll all take turns. Everybody can have daycare at their house a few times a month. We'll say we're babysitting. The State can't control *babysitting*, can they? We're not in a completely authoritarian state, are we?"

"What the hell is the matter with you?" says Maya. "You're making things way more complicated just for the sake of some self-righteous idea you have. Just let it go, why don't you?"

Katherine leaps into the fray. Nicole and I exchange looks as she says, "No, wait a minute. Jerome riles us up, but that's probably a good thing. He's the one who's been with the daycare the longest, and he's the person we need to listen to. We don't want to just be sheep who do anything the State tells us to do. We know how to take care of our own kids and each other's kids, and we do a damn good job of it." She sits back against the cushions and looks around with her wide blue eyes.

"So it's bad for the State to say we need to cover the electrical outlets?" says Nicole. "It's bad that they think we should make the yard safe?"

"In that vein, I'd like to propose—" I say, but Maya jumps to her feet. She walks over to where Katherine is sitting, and she lowers herself to Katherine's eye level, puts her hands against the back of Katherine's chair, and says in an icy, calm voice, "Look. I know you're in love with my husband. I don't hold that against you, because we can't help who we love."

A jolt runs around the room.

"And I have been kind to you and patient, Katherine, and I have stepped out of the way for you more times than I can count, even when I thought you were being an idiot. Even when you brought fucking *raw clams* for your food week. But if you think for *one second* that I'm going to sit here while you *pander* to him, while you let him believe that he's the king of all knowledge about children and daycare, while you feed his oversized ego when he's just being difficult for the sake of being difficult—then you better watch out. Because I am going to take you on."

Katherine looks like someone let the air out of her. She sinks back against the cushions of her chair and grabs her knitting like it might protect her.

Jerome laughs and starts doing a slow, sarcastic clap. "Very nice, Maya. Very, very nice. Why don't you talk some more about how patient you've been?"

I look around in a kind of panic. Nicole bursts into tears and says she has to go home. Close the damn daycare if you have to, she says, but she can't afford to get this upset now that she has two children to look after. The new baby, whom Joyous is cradling in the rocking chair, wants to nurse forty-five minutes out of every hour, she says through sniffles. And Toby asks every day when the baby is going back in her stomach. And today he threw a truck that narrowly missed the baby's head, and Nicole hasn't had any sleep, and if the daycare closes down, she doesn't know what she'll do.

Then Joyous jumps in and says grimly that a new family came by after hours today, and they're interested in joining. And they have two parents and one child, and they only need part-time care, and this could be the answer to all our scheduling nightmares. But they are certainly not going to want to join an organization that's falling apart like this one will if we don't pass the inspection. And they're not going to be amused at the idea of the daycare taking place in a different house every day.

Jerome sits on his beanbag chair and closes his eyes against such treachery. We all look at him. Finally he says, "Look. The bottom line is I don't want to participate in a daycare that doesn't work right. And this one isn't working right. I've had it with the whole business. Trying to do turns with people who aren't really committed to the movement, negotiating with the landlord about the noise we make. And now there's going to be paperwork? You seriously think that meeting the State's requirements is going to make them go away? Don't you know they'll just think of more things they need to legislate about? But what do you people care? You aren't the kind of people who know how to make a communal project work. You'd be happier in a regular preschool, or a daycare with *teachers* and *administrators*. A corporation that turns kids into robots for the State. So fine. Do that. I don't want to. I don't see the point of continuing."

"Jerome, you don't have the slightest idea what you're talking about," says Maya. "You seriously don't see how *you're* making the problem bigger!"

I look from Maya to Jerome. I squint and wait for all the molecules between them to go gray and start dying off, but that doesn't happen. To my surprise, I see that something else is happening entirely. He's going on and on in his blustery way, and he probably knows he only means about 10 percent of what he's saying, and she knows it, too. The air crackles with their passion. He grins at her. She wags her finger at him. There's something that is dancing between them. Oh my goodness, I see it now: they love each other! They're probably going to go straight to bed after this meeting and have amazing sex. They're each other's painful carbuncle on the heel of love, but it's love, nevertheless. I feel it at the core of me. *They love each other*, and it puts them through hell, but they're in it just the same.

I lose my breath a little. Look down at my hands. Maybe conflict doesn't mean that love is dead. Maybe sometimes it means it's alive.

La Starla wakes up in my head. *Go away*, I say to her. I have a daycare crisis to run. I can't give one more second to thinking about what this new realization might have to do with Ren or Judith, but I know it's something I need to think about.

"Listen," I say, and my voice is a little bit shaky, which I don't really like, but I press on anyway. "You just hired me, and I have to tell you that I'm in love with this job, and I have no intention of letting the whole place go to hell! This is too good to give up on, and we all know it! Sure you're tired! You've all got little kids in your house who are running you ragged, plus you've got jobs and daycare turns and food weeks! But it's ridiculous to let the State shut us down because we don't want to do the things to keep our license. Let's just do them! And keep going! We can have a workday and fix things in one afternoon!" My voice is getting louder, and everything I'm saying is in italics with exclamation points all over the place, and I'm getting so wound up that I realize that I'm waving my arms in the air. "Let's get a sign-up sheet and each take on some jobs! We can fix this so easily! We can get back on track!"

I feel like the corniest person in the whole world, like I'm in one of those Judy Garland movies where all the kids decide to put on a show. But you know what? I don't even care.

They all look at something else, probably embarrassed for me. Katherine is picking lint off her pants. Maya is leaning against the wall now, with her arms folded. Jerome has his eyes closed like he's beyond bored and is shaking his head with a supercilious smile on his face. Nicole has dried her tears and has gone over and retrieved her baby from Joyous's arms because the baby has started to cry and is rooting around for something to suck on. She sinks down on the rug in the middle of the room and hauls out her breast and attaches the baby like a piece of Velcro. Maya goes over to the couch and gets a pillow for Nicole to prop the baby on.

Inspired by that tiny gesture of pillow-providing kindness, I start up again. "Look at all of you. You're a family! A dysfunctional, scrappy family, but you belong to each other. You're so entwined that I bet if you didn't belong to this daycare, you'd still get together five times a week just because you want to. So listen, guys. I've written out a sheet of the jobs that we need to do, and we'll make this fun. And more than that, maybe it's a way for us to all come together again and do something for the good of the whole place. Because I think you're all amazing, and I love your children, and I love this whole space you've made, and . . ." And oh, how I do go on. I'm like a one-woman congressional filibuster.

I tell them the story of a turn a few weeks ago when the kids and I were sitting in the art space all drawing pictures, and Davy was working on some cylindrical object he was coloring pink. And I said to him, "Oh, what's this a picture of?" And he said, without even looking up, "Oh, this is my dad's penis."

"And two minutes later," I tell them, "Michael came to pick him up, and he said, 'Oh, this is so nice. What's this drawing, Davy?' And I couldn't stop laughing. I honestly thought I was going to fall over."

Michael claps his hand to his forehead. "As I recall, you said, 'Nice to see the rest of you.'"

"And there was the day that Sanborn told me that if everybody didn't start being nice to him he was going to 'get very cwanky and do mean stuff to the twucks.' And when Lily said she couldn't eat her tapioca pudding because it was a bowl of eyeballs looking back at her. And when I needed Toby to help me move the plastic chairs, and he said, 'Sorry, Mimi. I'm too new to the world. I can't do it.'"

They're all smiling now. I take advantage of the silence to say, "So we can figure this out. Things that can be fixed with a little bit of paint and soap and water and some raking and weeding aren't really big problems! And sure, maybe a new sandbox that neighborhood cats won't poop in."

Jamie clears his throat. He says we absolutely should do the work-day. He tells everybody they need to step up, sign up for things. Michael mumbles that he knows of someone who's getting rid of an industrial-sized tire, and wouldn't that be great to put in the backyard, for kids to play in and around?

Jamie says, "That would be so great. And now, can we just take a minute here and go around the room and tell why we've got to keep this daycare going, in case some of us have forgotten. I'll start." And he tells them the story of Lauren's death and how, as a man without a wife, the people here taught him everything he knows about how to be a parent.

"I saw your flyer on the bulletin board at the Yale Co-Op, and when I called the number, Emily answered. I broke down on the phone when I was telling her my situation. She just said, 'We can help you. Come and join us. Alice will have lots of brothers and sisters at daycare. You don't have to do this alone.'"

We're all quiet. Nicole, most likely overcome with postpartum hormones, is weeping openly.

Slowly, everybody tells how they discovered the daycare—usually right at a breaking point in their lives. Even Jerome heaves himself up and says that he joined ten years ago when the daycare was first being formed, with his ex-wife, who's now off in California with their son, Dineen. And when he met Maya and they had Gabriela, he knew he wanted to come back.

"But this is not a fucking kumbaya moment," he grouses. "I'm not in love with you people. I'm not sure you're committed to anything beyond your own little selfish selves. I still don't know if this place is worth salvaging."

"Oh, put a sock in it, Jerome," Michael says.

Before we all get up to leave, I say brightly, "So the workday will be on Saturday, one week from tomorrow. I'll write down the items on the State's list, and you can think about what you want to do."

Sure, sure, they all say. They're tired. Write it on the board in the front hall.

They say that they'll be there. If this is what it takes to save daycare, they'll do it. But they're all sighing and groaning. As near as I can tell, I'm the only one bouncing on my toes.

CHAPTER
TWENTY-ONE

Jamie fetches sleeping Alice from Gabriela's bedroom, and we take her out to the car, and Jamie buckles her into her car seat while she snoozes away. Her head flops against the side rest, but miraculously she stays asleep. He tucks a blanket around her and then leans down and kisses her forehead and brushes her dark hair out of her eyes. She makes a little snuffling sleep noise. He stands there for a moment, smiling at her, and then he comes around the car and gets in the driver's seat.

Before he starts the car he looks at me in the passenger's seat. "You were—you were kind of . . . Knute Rockne back there. High five, woman!"

"Was it okay? I felt a little out of control, frankly."

"You're kidding, right? Because it was a tour de force!" he says.

"Well, I don't know about that, but at least we're having a workday, apparently. Do you think anybody will come?" I'm a little bit astonished—almost tipsy with self-congratulations.

"Two," he says. "You and me."

"Yeah. That's what I was thinking."

"Oh, and Michael will show up at some point with a big tire."

"Yeah. And then he'll have to leave again, and you and I will need to figure out what the hell we're going to do with this tire."

He starts the car and pulls away from the parking space. "By the way. Oh my God! Could we talk about the Katherine and Maya moment? What the actual hell was that? I think my eyebrows have permanently moved up into my hair."

I lean over and look at him closely, laughing. "Yeah, you don't have any eyebrows anymore. Apparently it's been going on for a while. That's the word in Nicole's kitchen, at least."

"*Soo*, my main question: How does Maya keep from killing him?"

"I think she loves him."

"But why?"

"Why does she love him? I don't think love is ever explainable, do you?"

"No. I do know that much, relationship guru. But how come *Jerome* thinks it's okay?"

"Because he finds himself irresistibly fascinating? Because he thinks that women need his particular brand of manliness? Because he can? How the hell do I know? You're a guy. You tell me."

"Well, you're the self-proclaimed leader of this place. Aren't you responsible for understanding all the behaviors?"

"Yeah. And who exactly made me proclaim that I was the leader?"

"I couldn't believe you actually did it." He laughs. "When you stood right there and told those State people that you were the director—I thought I was going to bust out laughing. I gotta tell you it's cemented my view of you as the very boldest person I know. Honestly, sometimes I'll be looking at algorithms at work and then I think of you standing there saying you were the director, and I start laughing again."

"I wonder what I would have done if they'd asked me to prove it. I would have run out of there, probably. I would have had to."

"I doubt that. You would have convinced them. I could see that look in your eye. It was the same look as tonight when you gave a speech that made everybody sign up for a workday, and also the look when you talked a certain unsuspecting guy into retrieving a couch in the stairwell—a couch I believe *you* threw down there."

"Seriously, though. Do you think the daycare is going to fall apart?"

"It can't. Otherwise, I really will have to go live with my in-laws. All I've got going for my independent life is this daycare."

Headlights from a car in the other lane briefly light up half of his face. His eyes look like they're shining in the coal mine of the darkness. He stretches his arms against the steering wheel and rotates his shoulders and then turns and looks at me. "Hey, wanna go through the drive-through at McDonald's? There's something about the earnestness of a daycare meeting that always gets me hungry for a Big Mac."

"With secret sauce."

"Oh God. Absolutely. And fries. With ketchup packets. This, I think, may have been a twelve-ketchup-packet meeting."

"Well, what time is it?"

"It's only nine. Ten after actually. Do you have time?"

I hesitate. Ren is coming over. I shouldn't.

"Let's go," I say.

༄

We get burgers that drip all over the place and make a mess of us both. We park under the parking lot light so we can see what we're doing, and what we're doing is getting ketchup and secret sauce all over ourselves. My Coke spills on my pants. Somehow, talking about the craziness of the daycare and the craziness of his in-laws, we can't seem to stop laughing.

Alice, miraculously, stays asleep in the back. I'd give anything for that kind of ability to sleep, I tell him, and he says, "No shit."

He wants to know about my life in New York before I moved here, and I find myself telling him about La Starla and how I would go once a week to get my future foretold.

"Whoa, whoa, time-out! You have a psychic? Like an actual *psychic*?"

"I do. She even has spirit guides from the unknown who tell her stuff."

He loves stories about psychics, he says. He once went to see a psychic at a friend's party in college, and the psychic told him he was going to meet a woman with red hair who had one leg shorter than the other, and he ended up dating a girl for about a year who fit just that description. And then he met Lauren, who had brown hair and both legs matching up perfectly, and he fell in love with her, and when he went back to the psychic for clarification, the psychic said she never meant he'd *marry* the redheaded woman with the leg inequality; she had just said he'd *meet her.*

"Apparently they live in the world of technicalities," he says.

And maybe because I'm warmed up by the french fries or the secret sauce dripping on my chin, or the fact that I've been identified tonight as being brave, I tell him about how, speaking of technicalities, La Starla told me for months that I was going to have this great life, and she seemed to agree that Ren was the love of my life, and that we were going to be happily married—and then once Judith's accident happened, she said, *well,* I still was going to have a pretty great life, but oh yes, some setbacks were coming, and now she's totally noncommittal about whether Ren and I are getting married.

"When I came right out and asked her if he was going to marry me, she said, 'Who cares? You're still going to be happy!'"

"Well, *I* think you two are getting married," he says. "Maybe she hasn't realized that he's now proposed to you three times."

"Oh, the proposals mean nothing to her. She says he could propose a million times, and it still doesn't mean it's going to take place."

"I should get me some spirit guides. Because mine would then challenge her spirit guides to a psychic duel, and mine say you're marrying him," he says.

"Things have kind of gone astray since I lost the magic skirt," I say.

He laughs and makes his eyes bug out. "Oh, please. I was so hoping there was going to be a magic skirt somewhere in this story."

"Are you making fun of me?"

"I am totally not making fun of you. Well, five percent making fun of you until I hear the evidence for the skirt being actually magic."

Despite my misgivings, I tell him all about the skirt's accomplishments in my life, and then when I get to the best work the skirt has done—the most tangible—how little squares of that skirt, placed in the pockets of some disheartened teenagers, managed to bring together an incredible performance of *Guys and Dolls* when all was lost—well, he claps his hands so loudly that he then has to steal a look back to make sure that he didn't awaken Alice. She snuffles in her sleep but doesn't wake up.

"Yeah," I say in a whisper, "but then I got fired on Monday morning, and I somehow didn't realize the skirt was still backstage when I was ushered out of the building—and now the skirt is lost to me forever. It's gone."

"What? Is it still backstage at the school, you think?"

I shrug. "Maybe. I don't know."

"We have to find out," he says. "This is *huge*. Let's pull a caper and go to New York and get that skirt back! I've always wanted to pull a caper, haven't you? And this is the perfect one."

"The Great Magic Skirt Caper?"

"Exactly. Should we plan it all out, or do you think it would be best if we drive there right this minute and break in to the school in the dead of night? Which is more true to the tradition of pulling capers? Chance or organization?"

"Well, we both have to get up early in the morning, so maybe we should plan. Do it another time."

"Okay. But before Saturday. I think it could really assist with the workday."

"It totally would rock the workday."

He shakes his head. He is very close to me, and we're both laughing, and then he does the most extraordinary thing. He reaches over and touches my lips. "There's some secret sauce here," he says. He's looking into my eyes. And then he leans in just a bit closer and kisses me very quickly and softly on the mouth. Both of us are shocked, I think. He draws back and says, "Sorry! Good God in heaven! What am I doing?"

"Yeah, what *are* you doing?" I say lightly.

"The unpardonable sin of kissing an engaged woman—but, if I may say something in my own defense, it was because your psychic's spirit guides came through just then and informed me that you needed a kiss."

I laugh. "Those rascals! They also just told me you needed one!" And I lean over and give him what I'd meant to be a quick kiss but which turns into a little bit more. "Are we drunk? I feel like I'm drunk," I say.

"Goodness," he says. "I'm taking you home before these guys give us any more instructions."

"Yeah. They're known troublemakers," I say.

He's quiet for a bit, and then he says, "But I will say that that kiss is in the category of a harmless, how-funny-are-we kiss. A friendship thing between two people who will never have romance because (a) I'm not remotely ready for anything of this nature and (b) you're engaged. So it was perfectly safe."

"Exactly," I say.

"We probably shouldn't be joking about pulling capers either," he says. "We've got to straighten up our act. It's this kind of behavior that makes my in-laws know I'm not truly competent in the world." He sighs.

"No, you're right. We've got to straighten up and fly right," I say. "That's what my mom used to say. Not that she ever did it. Even once. But she's a story for another time."

"Promise me you'll tell it," he says.

⌒♀⌒

Ren is on my front stoop when we get back. Just sitting there under the porch light, his hands dangling between his knees, waiting. And looking perturbed.

"He's a handsome devil, isn't he?" says Jamie. "He would never have as much secret sauce on his shirt as I do right now."

I laugh. "No, he definitely wouldn't."

"And, um, he looks pretty disgruntled. Pretend the force is with you."

"What force might that be?"

"The magic-skirt force. The daycare-octopus workday force. You figure out which of your many forces are operational. Also, he doesn't get to be part of the caper. If we do it, which we won't."

I get out of the car, close the door, and start up the walkway. "Good-bye!" I call back over my shoulder. "Thanks for the ride! I'll see you tomorrow!"

"Oh, wait!" he calls. He gets out of the car so he doesn't have to yell. "You've got Alice after daycare on Monday, right? I've got a big meeting with my prof!" He makes the throat-cutting signal. "It's . . . yikes time."

"Of course," I say. "Don't worry!"

"It might go late."

"No problem at all!"

"Evening, Ren, how you doing?" he says, as an afterthought.

Ren raises his hand in a lackluster wave, and then sits there watching me silently as I approach. The sound of crickets and the chirping of little frogs fill up the night air.

"Hi," I say when I reach the steps. "Sorry. Been waiting long?"

"Long enough, I guess. I didn't know you had plans. Where were you guys?"

"There was a daycare meeting tonight." I don't know why I do this, but as we go inside and head upstairs, I start talking all excitedly about the workday we're planning, and how I got everybody to agree to come and get the daycare to meet the State regulations. I'm a little breathless and over the top, even to my own ears.

"Well, it doesn't seem that they have much choice if they want to stay open," he says gruffly.

I go through the apartment with him behind me, turning on lamps, getting cheese and grapes for him out of the refrigerator, starting the music. I play the Doors instead of the jazz he prefers. Meanwhile, he sits on the couch, looking at me curiously, the picture of strained patience.

"How's Judith?" I say.

"The same. Sweet-tempered, low-energy," he says. "Now that she's in the downstairs room, I feel a lot better about her safety."

"That was your old room, right?"

He says, "I moved up to the third floor. There's a nice room up there, perfect for me." He crosses and then uncrosses his legs, gives me a fake smile, like he thinks I'm checking up on him and he is going to be perfectly reasonable about it.

I sit down next to him. "I kind of was wondering if you might want to spend the night again. Think you could handle that?"

His face darkens. "Not tonight."

"I thought things went okay when you did that before."

"Mimi. She could stop breathing in her sleep. She could have another stroke. I have to still be there . . ."

"You know, after all these many months, a man in your position *might* consider hiring a night nurse and, I don't know, moving in with his fiancée and simply visiting his ex-wife! You know? You could go there every single day just to check up on things, even if you lived here. Wouldn't that make some sense?"

"It's a nice idea, but it's not going to happen."

"No, that's fine," I say. I get up and turn the record over. I don't love the last few tracks on this side. "I get it. Eventually things will change, only we don't know how or when. It's fine." I smile at him because I'm actually not even mad. I've had a wonderful night of laughing. And . . . that kiss.

"Mimi."

"Forget it," I say. "Really. If you can't, you can't."

"You want more. I get that. I want more, too. But I have to balance the needs of Judith and the girls . . . and if I were here overnight, I'd be worried the whole time. She wakes up. She needs things. She might stop breathing, and what if that happened while I was here sleeping or, worse, *having sex*? Do you think I could forgive myself?"

"Can I ask you something? How would you know? I mean, you're upstairs. How would you know if she stopped breathing?"

He looks for a moment like he might get mad, but then his face relaxes. "I might not know immediately, but at least I wouldn't be somewhere else. I'd be there. On the premises. The girls could alert me."

I stay silent.

"Please, Mimi. For God's sake. I'm doing the best I can! I'm sorry if it's not happening as fast as you think it should. But she needs me. I'm doing absolutely everything, and I can't make things move any faster." He bangs his fist on his lap as he says this last bit.

I take a long, languid sip of wine and then I say, "You know something? I'm sorry, but I have a headache, and I think I'm going to turn in early."

He looks at me with no visible expression on his face. "That's fine. I've got lots of paperwork stuff to do anyway—the lawyers and stuff. I'll just let myself out," he says. "I really should get a key, though, for your door. It's awful to just have to sit out there and wait, you know."

"Of course. Waiting must be so hard for you."

"Think nothing of it," he says coldly. He pecks me on the cheek and heads downstairs, a man disappointed once again by love but grimly trudging on to carry out his adult responsibilities.

As soon as he's out of there, I put on my Donna Summer and Barbra Streisand tape and grab my coatrack as a microphone, and I belt out "No More Tears" at the top of my lungs.

CHAPTER
TWENTY-TWO

Parker calls me on Monday morning as I'm getting ready to go down-stairs to daycare. She wonders if I could come over after I'm done and hang out with Judith for a bit. She and Ren and Jenna have to go see a lawyer to draw up some papers.

Parker has been slowly thawing toward me. Oh sure, she still doesn't include me in conversations that involve Judith, but what would I expect? Judith is her mom, and loyalty, I think, takes many forms, and some of them are hurtful to people on the outside.

"Of course," I say to her, because I always enjoy getting to be Weezy for the afternoon. "Yes, I'll be happy to come. I get finished at daycare at three." I remember that Jamie has a meeting with his professor, and that I'm keeping Alice starting at five.

"We shouldn't be that long," Parker says.

"It's no problem at all," I say.

Faintly I hear the *Mighty Mouse* theme song playing in my head. I will save the day for everyone!

∽∾

I find Judith sitting up in the bed in the downstairs bedroom.

I love this room. Before, when this was Ren's room, when I would come by to drop off meals or to sit with Judith in her upstairs fortress, I would sometimes drift in here and just sit down on his bed, smell his pillow, smooth my hand against the comforter that he slept under. I loved seeing all his things lined up on the sink in the bathroom—all the tangible artifacts of his life, his shaving cream and shaving brush, a razor, his aftershave, his toothbrush, his dental floss, his comb.

There's a way that when someone is almost but not quite in your life that these possessions take on a meaning of their own. The concreteness of them. They almost glow. I liked to touch them, see the damp towel hanging there, the one he'd used in the shower that morning. His bedroom slippers askew by the bed, his folded clothes on the chair, waiting to be put into a drawer. Sometimes I'd open the closet and see the rows of shirts, all on their hangers, awaiting his choosing.

It made me ache in such a good way, waiting for the time when all those things were at a house *we* shared. Today, however, as I'm growing less certain of that happening, I walk around the room with an unsettled feeling in my body, like I have a low-grade virus. I can't quite push the picture out of my head—the Yardleys at the park, smiling, bobbing their heads together like they were a well-oiled machine of a family, the love having been factory-installed. And then there was his behavior with me the other night.

It's like a storm is brewing.

Judith wants to look at photographs.

Even though she's not old—she's only forty-four—she's nothing like the pictures we look at, taken back when she was young and vivacious, a mom with little girls. She once had streaked blonde hair, and her creamy breasts peeked over the top of her bathing suit; her skirts skimmed her round, dimpled knees; and her daughters were cherry-cheeked girls climbing on her, smiling, tugging, laughing into the camera. And there's Ren, young, handsome, smiling at her, holding her, kissing her in the holiday photos, laughing with her on the beach.

And here I am, soaking up aspects of their life together like I'm a vampire. She looks at the pictures silently, smiling, as though we're looking at someone else's life altogether. She traces her finger across a portrait of herself, and she says, "There is no net, Weezy. You know that, right?"

One day, after having seen a picture of her on the mantel, I had asked Ren how he could bear to have left her, a person who looked so lively and bright-eyed. He groaned and said she might have looked great, but she opposed every single thing he ever did. She snapped at him and nagged at the kids, and she served on boards and committees, so she was never home. She mocked his literary plays, she snubbed his creative friends, and she loudly proclaimed to anyone who would listen that he was willing to let her carry the responsibility of being the main breadwinner so he could "dabble" in teaching English.

In their more recent pictures, ones from a decade ago, she's often wearing business suits with long jackets, and she has her hair pinned back, and she's smiling a very corporate, capable, and still loving smile—but he says that he would look across the dinner table at her and not recognize the person she'd turned into, with her jaw set just so. She worried and fretted about every little thing, money most of all, and she wanted him to *make something of himself.*

"Give up the idea of being a playwright," she said; even when one of his plays had gotten good reviews, and he was called "promising" by the critic in the *Village Voice,* she wouldn't come to see it.

When his father died and they inherited money and plenty of it, he told me he thought the constant fear about money would subside, that she would stop working so hard, perhaps, and they could settle down into an easier lifestyle. He could write, and she could quit nagging and belittling him.

But no.

So there you have it; he said that's the way a marriage crumbles, in little slights, arguments, cold stares, distances, hatred.

Anyway, none of that is left in her now.

I watch her face as she looks at the photos.

"Your girls love you so much," I tell her. She's searching my eyes like she wants to talk.

She laughs. "Ah, girls. Do you have girls?"

"No. I don't have any children. I never thought I wanted them."

"No. Me too. I don't have girls. I have . . . pessimisms." And she laughs again.

I stare at her in surprise. "You have . . . pessimisms? Wait. Are *you* pessimistic?"

"Oh, Weezy, you know all that," she says. And then she looks surprised and says, "Wait. That isn't your name, is it?" And she reaches over and squeezes my hand. "Nice," she says. "Thumbs and fingers. So nice."

I can feel her intelligence, her awareness, even though her thoughts come bubbling up through corpuscles and nerve endings and feel as though they've taken a wrong linguistic turn somewhere before getting to her mouth. She told me the other day that the letter *A* is blue, and that *G* and *H* are yellow. She said that chimneys are where we store anything that matters, and that the blender likes her the best of any family member.

And now she's looking at me and calling her daughters pessimisms.

She may be exactly right about that. I think they're pessimisms, too.

I lean over and whisper to her, daringly, "I might marry your ex-husband. Do you mind?"

It feels like I need to know this answer, just to see what she understands.

There's such a long silence. She looks down at her hands, moving her fingers and studying them, as if she didn't hear me at all. I don't know why I even said it. Such a childish thing, to want to stake my claim in the face of all this familial togetherness she has. That's what she has, and I don't.

She just closes her eyes and smiles, like she has a secret.

She moves her mouth, making silent words. I lean down to listen, but she stops.

I hear something. She's started trying to say it again. "My wedding . . . might break your heart," she says, and she laughs.

I stare at my hands for a long moment. These are just strung-together, random words, like the pessimisms. But what does she mean? Does she mean that *my* wedding to her ex would break her heart? Or does she think *he* will break my heart? Or was it the wedding she had with him, the fact that she came first and will always have been first?

Maybe I *am* broken-hearted, and she's seeing something real in my face.

Or maybe this is just what a brain injury sounds like.

After her snack, which is strawberry salad, she says she wants to go back to bed. I help her get to her room and help her back into bed. I feel ashamed of myself, prying into her thoughts. I'm pulling up her covers and walking around to the other side of the bed to straighten them out when I see something that stops me in my tracks: Ren's slippers are on the floor on the other side of the bed, next to the window. And then I see a pair of his pants crumpled up and dropped on the floor. And underwear! His pillow is right here in front of me. I remember his pillow from when I'd visit him in New York: it's a flat, elongated thing, all misshapen. He says it helps his neck.

An electric current goes through me, like being shocked. It's so powerful that I actually draw back, like I've just been zapped.

He sleeps here, next to her.

"Judith," I say, my mouth dry with the words. "Where does Ren sleep?"

She looks sweetly confused and doesn't say anything.

I go and sit on the bed next to her and I take her hand in mine. "Judith, does he sleep here? Next to you?"

She looks down at her hands.

Maybe it's not what I think. Maybe it's just that he didn't quite yet move all his stuff out before he installed her in here. That is not even half-true. There wouldn't be clothing—underwear, yet!

It occurs to me that I can find out. I drop her hand and tell her I'll be right back, and I walk up to the third floor, to the room where he said he was staying. The one with the sloping roof. I can barely breathe, and my fingertips feel swollen and slippery, like they already know the truth.

The third floor is stuffy and dim. I turn on the overhead light and take a deep breath. Sure enough, there's a bed up here, but it's not made up. It's a bare mattress, without sheets. His clothes aren't here. No shoes. No towels.

"Weezy! Weezy!" She's calling me from downstairs, a thin voice from afar.

I go back down, and I think about how loud a heart has to beat before it drowns out everything else.

He sleeps next to her. He sleeps next to her. He sleeps next to her. Of course he does. Why is this such a surprise? I should have figured this out long ago. He's been sleeping next to her the whole time!

She laughs when she sees me come back, a dry husk of a laugh that probably has no remnant of her past laugh. At least I hope she didn't always laugh this way. "Darling, could you move over twenty thousand steps and help me see where the line is?" she says. "Also, I would love water. Cool, cool water."

How can she be able to say one sentence that makes perfect sense, a sentence that follows one that means essentially nothing? Or maybe it means something. Maybe she wants me gone. Twenty thousand steps and I'd be out of here.

All I can see is the intimacy of them next to each other, his hand finding hers in the dark, his breath mingling with hers. The two of them lying on their sides, facing each other. Him watching her eyes close, feeling when she turns over. Do they try to talk at night? Does he hold her hand? He loves her again. That is what I see everywhere I look in this house. This is why he is here. How can he not love her? They have a long history of loving and fighting and pulling and tugging, of family vacations and private jokes, of children's stories, of their own stupid needs, the howlings in the dark, the rampages he describes.

The making up.

I have nothing like that with him. Our relationship is so new that all it consists of now is talking about why we're not together yet, and when that will happen, and what we're waiting for.

"Okay. Twenty thousand steps coming right up, and then I'll hand you a glass of water," I say.

"I love you," she says. She says it the way the daycare kids do, unguarded and true.

"I love you, too," I tell her. She's broken, it's true, but she is the only person I know who isn't striving. And I am so frantic, filled with confusion and betrayal and hurt—a million hurts. My heart is beating too fast.

I am not loved. I am not loved. I am not even seen.

I am in the kitchen getting her a glass of water when I hear the slamming of a car door in the driveway. They're back. I wipe furiously at my eyes, which may have been leaking just a little bit. I look up at the clock: it's 4:45.

The back door opens, and the three of them come filing in, talking and laughing. Jenna and Parker come first, talking about the decor of the lawyer's office, and Ren follows them in, holding a sheaf of papers that he's pretending to swat Jenna with. He's teasing her about a question she asked the attorney, something he says was impertinent.

When he sees me, he looks surprised, like he already forgot I would be there. Parker says, "Where's Mom?" and when I say she's in the bedroom waiting for this glass of water, she starts to hurry off. Before she gets very far, I hand her the glass. "Mind taking this to her?" Jenna floats off somewhere without a word to me.

Then I look squarely at Ren, give him my sweetest smile. "Could we talk for a minute? Outside?"

CHAPTER TWENTY-THREE

We go out onto the deck. I try to take a deep breath, calm myself down a bit. It's like the world has tipped over somehow. I can't believe I'm about to do this. My heart is pounding.

"What a day!" he says. "How was Judith?" He leans against the deck rail, trying to seem casual. He looks tired. He actually yawns, cracks his knuckles, cranes his neck until it clicks. "Those girls—they argued all the way to the lawyer's office. I should have just gone myself." He sees that I'm staring at him.

"I'm breaking up with you," I say.

"What? What are you *talking* about?"

"I'm talking about how it's over between us. I'm done."

"Good heavens. Let's go for a walk," he says in a low voice. He glances over at the sliding door. We can see Parker leaning against the wall, on the phone, wrapping the cord around her fingers. "This isn't a discussion I want to have right here, if you don't mind."

"We don't have to have it at all," I say. "I'm finished."

"Oh, Jesus. Come on," he says. "Let's get out of here." He goes over to the sliding door, opens it, and calls inside: "I'm leaving for a little while. Hold down the fort, will you?" Parker says something I can't quite hear, and he says, "I have to take, um, Mimi here out to dinner. I'll be back later."

"I'm not going out to dinner with you!"

"Just get in the car. Let's go. You owe me this. One dinner and we'll work things out."

"Nothing is going to work this out," I say. "It's over."

"You owe me an explanation. We're engaged. You can't just break it off without a talk." His eyes soften, turn to liquid. "Please. Just grant me this."

We walk down the steps of the deck, and I reluctantly slide into the front seat of his Camaro.

He starts the car grimly. "This is a Hail Mary pass, but I think going out on a real date will make you rethink things." He touches my leg. His voice softens. "I see what's going on here. We need to go out on a date, like normal couples. I've been taking you for granted. And, also, a side benefit: you're not going to want to be screaming at me in public."

I fold my arms. "I really am breaking up with you. I'm really, really, really done."

"I don't think you are. I think you're done with me not paying enough attention to you, which makes total sense. We used to have a nice life in New York, going out and doing things, and now you're feeling ignored. Never mind that I see you most nights each week; you need more. I'm doing everything I can to keep you satisfied, and you're just asking for more."

"You're completely missing the point."

"You can tell me *all* about that during dinner," he says. "And I'll tell you how much I love and adore you and—"

I interrupt him. "You're sleeping with her."

His face contorts. "What is this? Bombshell night?" he says. "Are you just intent on dropping these little bombs on me every time I speak? I am *not* having sex with her. I shouldn't even have to tell you that."

"I didn't say you're having sex. What I said is that you are sleeping in the same bed with her," I say. "I saw your pillow and your slippers right there next to her bed."

He's silent for a moment, staring out through the windshield, calculating how to respond. "All right. You got me. I do sleep next to her! Yes, scream at me all you want. I sleep next to my very, very sick ex-wife who might stop breathing during the night. I make sure she doesn't fall out of bed or wander off because she thinks she can still go do things on her own. I'm there if she has another stroke because one of the risk factors for strokes is having had one before. That is what I do, so sue me. Leave me if you insist. But is it love? No. Do I *want* to be there? No."

"*Yes*, you *do* want to be there."

He bangs on the steering wheel. "I do *not* want to be there. I want her *not* to have ever had a stroke! I want her to be in Chicago at that job she was going to get! I want our lives to go back to exactly the way they were! But I can't have that. What I have instead is the chance to help her stay alive and to nurture my girls through a hard time in their lives—and apparently I have a lover who is trying to make me insane while I'm doing it!"

"You don't even see," I say. "You don't understand that you're back together. You're back in your family again, knitting everything back in its place, and I'm not part of this in any way."

"Oh, for God's sake, would you just listen to yourself? *I* love you! I *love* you! I love *you*! There. Does that mean anything to you at all? And what do you mean, you're not part of this? How could you possibly expect to walk in and be part of this, when it's *my* family?"

"Exactly," I say quietly. "It's your family, and I don't have a place there at all."

He's pulled into the jam-packed parking lot of a seafood restaurant, but neither of us makes a move to get out of the car. I realize I'm now about to cry for real. I hate how every time I'm angry, it comes off as tearful. I so want to hold it together.

"You know what's really going on?" he says. He turns and looks at me. "You're the one who's fallen in love with someone else. That's what's changed here. You found somebody new, and now it's convenient to let yourself off the hook by believing that you'll never be part of my family. But you need to take a good hard look at what's really going on."

"That is not what this is at all."

"I'm afraid, my dear, that's exactly what it is. You're infatuated with that widower guy. But you're making a big mistake, Mimi. You think he's going to be any freer than I am? His wife may be dead, but that guy *lives* in grief. He wallows in it, and he's going to turn out to be a lot sadder than you're expecting. You're trading me away when I'm the one who truly and deeply loves you. I'm the one who protected you at Piedmont! Just remember that. I'm the one who kept you employed there, until I had to leave."

I open the car door and get out. I feel like I might fall over. Am I doing this? Everything feels so crystal clear outside of this car. The breeze lifts my hair. I look around me. I'm in some suburban parking lot banked by cars everywhere and people walking on the sidewalk, talking, living their lives as though everything is completely normal and regular. I see a bus stop right at the corner. People are waiting on a bench. I can go sit next to them and wait, too. The outlines of things are so sharp that it almost hurts.

I start walking, but I can still hear him from inside the car. He rolls down the window and yells to me, "Would you *wait*? I'll drive you home! Get back in the car! Don't be ridiculous! How are you planning to get home? Come on!"

But it's the strangest thing. I feel like I'm floating away, farther and farther from him.

I float all the way over to the bus stop, like I'm not even made of human stuff—I'm a balloon that's gone aloft, escaped its string. The bus comes, I get on, and I ride all the way home, staring out the window.

❧

I find a folded note taped to my front door when I get home.

It says "Are you OK?" written across the top in red marker.

Am I *okay*?

And then I remember. Oh my God. Alice! I was supposed to have Alice. Jamie's meeting! About his capstone project, no less. The professor's concerns. It was important.

Shit, shit, shit. I walk around in circles on the porch, my hand on top of my head. I feel sick. No one should trust me with anything, much less their precious child or their master's degree that will lead them into a career working for their father-in-law's company. I smack myself in the head.

I look at my watch. It's after seven. How had that happened? I had meant to watch Judith from three until five, and then dash back to day-care and get Alice. I had figured—back when I still had my brain—that if Ren wasn't back by four forty-five, I'd simply bring Judith with me in the wheelchair to pick up Alice, and then we'd go back to Judith's house and wait for Ren to come.

And then everything turned upside down.

With my hand shaking, I unfold the note. It says:

M—Thought you were keeping Alice tonite. Have to leave now. Taking A with me. ARE YOU OK??????

It's the red marker saying "Are you OK?" *twice* that kills me.

I call him on the phone, and for the first two hours of dialing, I get only a busy signal. By the time he does answer, at nearly ten o'clock, he's very, very polite about everything. But also mad under the surface. I can tell. Electrically mad. It's practically a current flowing through the telephone.

"Oh my God, I am so, so sorry, but wouldn't Emily or Nicole have kept her?"

"*Well*, Mimi, I didn't call them because I was sure every single second that you were still going to come, until it was too late to call anyone else. So . . . I took her with me to the meeting. Never mind. It's fine."

"It's not fine. I'm sorry."

"Yeah. Well. Let's just say, she was not as charming as some people might think a four-year-old without a nap might be at a meeting that was being held by a professor who was already pissed at me and who doesn't really know anything about children. Or would ever want to, apparently."

"Wow."

"Yeah. Wow. Anyway, I don't want to talk about it. I don't want to be mad at you. This is my own responsibility, not yours."

"But what did she do at the meeting?"

"What did she *do*? You mean, *after* she climbed all over me, and babbled in baby talk the whole time, and interrupted Professor Brain Trust every time he tried to explain to me why things weren't working with the capstone project? Maybe you'd like to hear about when she suddenly sat up and started to explain to him where her mommy is."

"No, no, no," I breathe. "I am so very sorry. Can you just apologize and reschedule, do you think?"

He tells me that his professor is on a plane headed to Spain and won't be available until after the semester starts, four weeks away.

"Yeah. It was pretty important, Mimi," he says. "Like, my whole project is now under water."

It seems I can't apologize enough. Finally he laughs and says, "Okay. Moratorium on apologies from you. It wasn't ever going to go well, even if I didn't have Alice along. Anyway, I can't take any more of this 'sorry' stuff."

"But I'm—"

"Done! No more! Stop!"

"Jamie—"

"Zip it, Perkins!"

"Okay. I zipped it."

"So what happened to you? Are you okay? Please tell me this was just a random bout of ordinary amnesia."

"I'm not going to make this about me. This is me trying to make it up to you."

"You're treading back into the apology territory," he says. "So what gives?"

"Okay. Well, it's no excuse, but I was breaking up with Ren."

He's silent for a long time.

"So . . . that happened," I say.

"For real, or is this just breakup number one?"

"For real."

"Breakup number one most likely," he says. "A warning shot over the bow."

"I don't think so."

"Are you—I mean, are you sad? How are you doing?"

"I'm done," I say. "I don't know what I feel yet. Right now I just feel done with him."

"The adrenaline kicks in and gets you through the first few days," he says. "But then you'll miss him. That's what makes this breakup number one."

"I don't know. I feel pretty certain."

He laughs. "What brought this on, if I may ask?"

"I discovered that he's sleeping with his ex-wife."

"What? Please, please tell me he denied it."

"Of course he didn't deny it. He said that yes, he *was* sleeping in the same bed, but he wasn't having sex with her. Sex is just for me. He sleeps next to her so he can tend to her needs in case she stops breathing or has another stroke."

"Uh-huh. And you didn't buy that?"

"*No.* It doesn't matter. He dresses her and bathes her, Jamie. He holds her at night! He sits up with her, watching her sleep, and he takes complete care of her. Him, not the daughters. Him."

"Well, that sounds . . ."

"Like *love* is how it sounds. It's intimacy. And the main thing is that he lights up when he sees her. Even when he talks about her. He has fallen back in love with her, and he doesn't even know it."

"Ah, Mimi. I'm sorry. And what did he say when you told him this?"

"He acted shocked. He said he doesn't love her, and then he said that the real thing here is that he thinks *I* have someone else."

He lets out a low whistle. "It's always so fascinating what people say right after you've broken up with them, the projections they let slip."

I can't quite bring myself to tell Jamie what Ren really said. About him and me.

"Anyway . . . you going to be all right?" he says.

"So far so good."

"Well, get some sleep. You'll know more in the morning. But if you decide to take him back—well, talk to me first."

"Okay. And . . . once again, I'm so sorry—"

"I thought we covered this. No more *sorries* out of you. I should be the one apologizing to you, actually. I've leaned on you far too much. You've pretty much been taking care of everybody, and I've just piled on with needs. I should have had a backup plan long ago."

"Well, now you don't need one. It looks like there's going to be far less for me to do, now that I'm not taking meals over for Ren and Judith."

"Okay. Well, we'll see what you do. Good night."

"Good night, and again, I'm—"

"Forget it. It was only my stupid capstone project."

⁓

Jamie calls me the next day, early in the morning. I've barely woken up.

"Can I ask you a question?" he says softly.

"Sure."

"Was he your first real love, do you think?"

"Yeah. Why?"

"Nothing really. I just had a thought about the whole thing."

"Please," I say. "Tell me anything you've got."

"Well, I just think that when that first love comes along, it brings with it a huge thunderclap of feeling—something so amazing that we get overwhelmed with it. And that it's tempting to think that it's the only love there ever could be in the world. But then it ends. Most of the time it ends. And then, a long time later, we look back and see that that whole experience of love was just a little kiddie pool we were paddling around in. And that actually a really huge ocean awaits us."

"Wow," I say.

"Yeah. Just something to think about."

"But what if I'm scared of the ocean?" I say.

"Oh, we're all scared of the ocean. Every single one of us. But here's what I think: if you had married this dude, you would have eventually found out about the ocean anyway, and you would have started to hate him for keeping you in that little kiddie pool. I think that when you see bitter people out in the world, people who've been married for forty years and they tell you that love isn't really real, that it never works out, *those* are the people who settled for the kiddie pool, and it dried up, and they never knew what was really out there for them. Saddest thing in the world."

I close my eyes and risk it. "Was Lauren . . . your . . . ?"

"My ocean?" he says. "Yeah. Yes, she was. She wasn't my first love, but she was my ocean, the stars, and all the sea turtles."

CHAPTER
TWENTY-FOUR

The nice thing about breaking up with someone is that it frees up your time. I never knew that would be one of the benefits. I call up Eleanor to tell her of this amazing discovery I've made.

"Uh-huh, right," she says. "But aren't you even a little bit sad?"

"Sad?" I say. "*Sad?* Don't you get it? Now that I'm free of him, I don't have to spend one more second being mad at him. I don't have to try to please his daughters. I couldn't be happier!"

She doesn't believe me. "This is just the adrenaline talking," she says. "You'll miss him. He's too handsome to just give up on."

"I'm sick of looking at him," I tell her.

"Yeah, you'll change your mind about that," she says. "You'll miss sex, for one thing."

"I don't know. It's been a whole day, and all I'm feeling is that I'm now perfectly free to concentrate on getting ready for the daycare workday."

"A whole *day?*" she says sarcastically. "I think it's possible you'll find that workdays aren't really a great substitute for sex."

"Well," I tell her. "So far it's working great."

Two days later, I see Jamie in the morning and tell him I'm panicking about how many things we need to buy to get ready for the workday, and he says, "Sounds like it's time to go to Kmart!"

I look at him blankly. I've heard of Kmarts, of course, but I've never set foot in one. I've never even been in a superstore. Manhattan doesn't have them.

"But do you have time?" I say.

"I can certainly take one evening off. After all, my professor just killed my capstone project and then went to Spain, and besides that, I'm pretty much the vice octopus now."

"Are you? I didn't realize you had a title."

"Self-bestowed. Just like yours." He grins at me. "Anyway, you want to do it?"

"Are we still talking about a trip to Kmart?" I say.

He laughs.

Later he tells me that he's arranged for Emily to watch Alice and feed her dinner. The nearest Kmart is a few towns away, so this will be a genuine field trip for me.

Alice leaves daycare with Emily, waving and telling us all that soon she's getting an antamanda. All day long she's been saying this. The antamanda is coming soon, and it's going to be a great surprise. Whenever we ask what an antamanda is, she just smiles mysteriously. Emily thinks it might be a dinosaur. I'm kind of going with salamander.

I've made a list of everything I can think of to buy: cleaning supplies, mops, brooms, scrubbers. A rake. New sheets for the cribs. New curtains for the nap room. Crayons and markers. Paint for the swing set and the kitchen. Emily wants a new vacuum cleaner. Alice tells me I might need a treat for the antamanda. Jamie has added a plywood board to cover the sandbox. (The State people were horrified by the cat turds they saw there.)

I'm immediately thrown into a spin when we walk inside the Kmart. It's so gigantic, a warehouse filled with people and rows and rows of everything in the whole world, millions of items—everything from screwdrivers to lawn mowers. Light bulbs, tea bags, poker chips, home entertainment centers, bathrobes, TV sets. I keep walking around in dazed amazement, while he steers me through, laughing at my spaciness, putting things in the basket, asking me how is it that they don't have Kmarts on my home planet.

"Did you seriously grow up without blue-light specials?"

"Somehow I managed, yes."

"If you want, we can have dinner in the Kmart Café. They have hot dogs."

I make a face at him.

"Well, okay, maybe not," he says. "We can go out and grab something to eat from one of the fine establishments around here, like Wendy's?" He sees my face and shrugs. "Hey, I can't help it. I love junk food. What can I say? I thought you did, too. You knew about the secret sauce."

"I did, but let me ask you something. Are you seriously raising your daughter on this food?"

"Next you're going to tell me that Pop-Tarts aren't good for her."

"Jamie! This is a cry for help!"

"I didn't get the healthy-cooking gene, I'm afraid. But the way I see it, she has a healthy breakfast and lunch and snacks at daycare, and then two nights a week, you cook both of us a very well-balanced dinner with lots of veggies and protein, and then on the weekends we're with her grandparents, so I think she's fine. Speaking of the grandparents, I've thought of a couple more things I need to get."

"For the grandparents?"

"For my office." He shrugs. "I might as well tell you. Lauren's sister, Mandy, is being sent down to help me through this next little chunk of time while I try in vain to turn my capstone proposal into something my professor might respect. *Soooo* . . . all that aside, I've got to get some decent sheets for the foldout couch."

I stop walking. "Lauren's sister is going to be staying with you? I can't believe you didn't tell me this!"

He nods. "Well, I didn't want to tell you. The in-laws found out that I had to take Alice to the meeting with the professor the other day, and then that got Denise worried, and she told me they're sending Mandy to help me out."

"Oh my God. Oh *nooo*! This is my fault. I'm so sorry—"

"It's not your fault. Please stop. This is just Lauren's family's way of being my well-meaning saviors, which is their favorite role. I'm just glad it's not Denise who's coming."

"But you told them what happened? You actually mentioned that I let you down?"

"Actually, no." He ducks his head. "Could we please not make a big deal of this?"

"But how did they know?"

"Alice told them."

"Alice?"

"Yeah. You and I were talking on the phone, and you know how Alice is. She overheard us talking, and then she told Denise."

"Oh no. And then did she say that Mimi Mommy was supposed to keep her?"

"Bingo."

"Oh God. I think I'm hyperventilating."

"Stop it. If I know psychics, I bet your psychic would say that everything works out for the best, and this will, too."

"She probably wouldn't say that. She's quite realistic."

"Well, whatever. It's done. Relax. You're still one of my favorite people, and I'm going to throw myself into convincing Professor Brain Trust that my project is worthwhile and that I'm the man for the job. That's what my father-in-law recommends, and I think it's a good strategy. And meanwhile, if Mandy comes and cooks some meals here, what's the big deal? I'm resigned to this."

"May I please have permission to apologize one more time?"

"No, but you may atone by helping me pick out some sheets for the foldout couch."

I follow him along to the section of the store—approximately four miles of aisles away—where there are at least a million choices of sheets, pillows, comforters. He's cheerfully baffled by everything he sees, so I end up picking out blue-flowered percale sheets and a foam pillow, a mattress cover, a navy-blue comforter, a rag rug, and four throw pillows.

"Really with the throw pillows?" he says.

"They dress up a room like nothing else. Do you need anything else? Like, how's the bathroom? Most women really care about the bathroom."

"It's clean."

"No offense, but I'm beginning to doubt your domestic skills. Does it have nice towels? A bath mat?"

He frowns, as if he can't quite remember. "Probably not."

"Well, then I think we should buy two fluffy towels and a nice thick bath mat. Do you have a toothbrush holder?"

"I tell you what. Will you come to my house and check out what else I might need to do? Clearly I don't have the slightest idea of what I'm supposed to be doing to prepare for this. I could make us sandwiches for dinner."

"All right," I say. "That would be great."

"You will?" He looks at me and smiles. "Okay. I'm going to the pay phone to call Emily. She invited Alice to sleep over to begin with, but I said no. I'll see if the offer still stands."

"Great! We'll go to your house and redecorate," I say. "I love doing this!"

"First, though, are you quite sure Ren isn't going to be waiting on the steps when I bring you home?"

"Nope," I say. "I haven't had anything to do with him."

"Are you sure? Because sometimes breakups don't stick," he says. "It takes a couple of tries."

I hold out my hand to show him there's no ring. "No more tries needed. I'm done."

He gazes at my hand. Then his eyes travel up to mine and lock there. And *boom*.

What just happened? I think. *Is it possible that the Kmart Corporation has suddenly shut off all the oxygen in the store?*

He runs his hands through his hair and takes a deep breath. I feel all my noticers jumping in to report some things about him. Like the way he's looking vulnerable and pleased and puzzled, all at once, and he has such a serious smile on his face. My brain points out that he's wearing a T-shirt that's the exact shade of blue of his eyes and that his faded jeans are tight and that his longish hair is tousled, and he has probably a day's growth of beard, and an electric current runs through all my nerve endings.

It wouldn't surprise me one bit if there were to be a clap of thunder in the store—or if the lights were suddenly to start flashing, complete with sirens going off. The only thing that happens, though, is that an older woman abruptly veers her cart into me, hard, and I'm knocked over into Jamie, who puts his arm around me to keep me from falling. His nose is pressed up against my hair. I can feel his lips brush against me. He is kissing my hair. In Kmart. I am being kissed in a big-box store that sells approximately one billion random items, and the universe somehow arranged an old woman to show up and push me with her cart in order to make it happen.

"Easy," he whispers. And then, almost to himself, I hear him say, "Here we go."

The first real kiss happens in the car. It would have happened in the checkout line if we had dared to look at each other. But I knew not to meet his eyes. I've never felt so tuned in to another person. We practically run to the car and somehow push all our purchases into the trunk. He's laughing about how much we bought as he slams it shut and smiles at me. I stand shivering beside him, even though the summer night is humid and hot, and all around us are streetlights and car horns and the sounds of traffic, and I am absorbing all of it into every atom of my body. His hand touches mine, and he unlocks the car door on my side, and I slide in, and then we're kissing and kissing, deep, perfect kisses, each one a whole paragraph of meaning.

I realize I've never wanted anybody more.

⌒೨

His place is like him, comfortable and messy, sweet and chaotic—and as we walk inside, I feel like I've gone through a portal that leads me directly into his tender, careful heart. He is gentle and shy, asking me if I need anything. Would I like something to drink? Am I hungry?

"I'm fine," I say. More than fine. We bring the packages inside the living room, and he's talking about how messy the place is, he's going to have to do so much to fix it up before his sister-in-law gets there. His voice seems just the slightest bit trembly, which is fine because it exactly matches my insides. He's saying that maybe it's best if Mandy truly sees how he lives right from the outset, no pretense of neatness or normalcy.

A photograph hangs in the living room—a formal portrait, with baby Alice sitting between her parents. Lauren, her dark hair gleaming and her eyes bright, smiles at the camera through rosebud lips. She had no idea what awaited them. It's almost painful to look at, all that innocent hope. She thought she had forever. She knew she was the ocean, the stars, and the sea turtles.

"Would you like a tour of the house?" he says and winks. "It's okay if you don't."

"I do," I say.

He holds my hand as we go into Alice's room, which has a single bed with a pink gingham bedspread and a dresser and some bookshelves where her toys are all stacked. He built those, he told me, and he made the bed, too, right after . . .

We're silent for a moment. Then I say, "It's beautiful."

"I did her cradle and then a crib, too," he says. "Those are in storage now, of course."

215

I have a fleeting thought: Does he wonder what will happen to those? Does he think he might ever need them again, or will he someday just give them away? I can't meet his eyes.

He clears his throat. "And then the bathroom . . . you can look at it and see if it'll pass muster with a woman who loves to clean things."

It looks fine. Needs a rug, but we bought one of those. The floor is a little bit wet from his shower that morning, and the sink has a blob of toothpaste on it. There's a toy boat in the tub. I give it the thumbs-up.

Next we go into his bedroom, which has a double bed, casually made up with a brown plaid comforter thrown over the pillows. There's an asparagus fern in a basket in the window, and a dresser with stuff on the top of it: a little girl's hairbrush, some beaded bracelets, a clock radio. His nightstand has some books with the spines turned the other way.

He seems like he keeps starting and stopping from saying something. And then suddenly he takes me in his arms and starts kissing me. When I am quite limp from wanting him, we inch our way toward the bed.

"Is this . . . ?" he asks.

"Yes," I tell him, and we sit down, our legs touching.

"I just realized I can't think of anything amusing to say to you," he says. "Our whole thing has been about making each other laugh. And now you're seeing my *house*. And maybe—I don't know—maybe you're expecting even to see my *body*."

"A girl can hope," I say.

"Can I tell you something?" He takes my hand.

"Yes, please."

"Three things, really. I'm starving. I may be losing consciousness. And also, I'm terrified."

"Funny, I'm terrified, too."

"Why?"

"You tell me first why you're terrified, and then I'll say."

"The truth?"

"Please."

"Okay. I'm terrified that I might be making the huge mistake of kind of falling in love with you, and you're then going to tell me that nope, it's that grandstanding blowhard that you really love, and I won't be able to recover. My heart has seen a lot of action, you know."

I blink at him. "Did you actually just say you love me?"

"Wait. Back up here. I believe what I said was that I might be *kind of* falling in love with you. That was not a definitive. Also I believe I qualified it by saying it would be a mistake."

"Right, which, no offense, I resented just a little bit. And what *I'm* terrified of is that you *might* let yourself fall *halfway* in love with me, only your heart isn't mended yet, so you don't have the other half to work with, but I won't realize that and then one day we'll have a disagreement and you'll be like, nope, it's not real, and you'll leave because it will turn out that you've been comparing me to the incomparable Lauren all this time, and I won't measure up, and you'll end up saying you're so sorry but you and Alice have to go live in West Hartford with your in-laws, and you're not ready for anything real with a human other than Lauren, but you'll call me in twenty years *if* you're ready by then, which you probably won't be."

He stares at me, but he doesn't laugh. I had hoped he might laugh. I had hoped he might grab hold of me and kiss me again and again, and then lay me down on the bed and make love to me with all the passion I can see in his eyes. It would be so great. It would be the best thing ever, all this pent-up feeling we both have. My whole body is thrumming. Everywhere his skin is touching mine feels like it's on fire.

Instead he recovers himself and he says, "Come with me to the kitchen. I know how to make a damned good breakfast for dinner. Do you subscribe to the breakfast-for-dinner concept?"

And so that's what we do. He won't let me help because he says he owes me about thirty-five dinners, the way he figures it, and he puts the bread in the toaster and then scrambles eggs and cuts up little pieces of onion and cheese to mix in with the eggs, and he wonders if I'd like him to pour ketchup all over the whole thing, and I ask him what kind of barbarian would do that, and he says only the best people know that ketchup goes on eggs, and I say that is the mark of someone who only eats junk food and thinks fish sticks are a health food, and he comes over and puts his arms around me, and I think, *At last we are going to get down to the kissing once again because I don't think I can go on much longer without kissing him.*

But the toast pops up in the toaster just then, and he pulls away and goes to search for the butter, which is on the countertop, next to the refrigerator but not inside. My shaky hands and I get to work buttering the toast, which is so nice because the butter is soft. Then we put the plates on his little wooden table, which still has some spilled milk on it, probably from this morning, and there's a little booster seat on one of the chairs, and the lump in my throat, seeing that and thinking of Alice, is so big that I can only barely eat.

When we finish eating, we get the bags from the living room, and we take out the new sheets and the comforter, and he shows me the room where Mandy will sleep—his office, which has a couch pushed against the wall, which we fold out. There are bookshelves with novels and his business books, and a desk covered with papers and folders he needs to clear off. He says he'll leave the desk in there and move all the folders and papers to his bedroom, where he guesses he'll need to start working. Or maybe at the table in the kitchen. We say things to each other like how it will be so good for him to have help in the house, someone to cook dinners for him and for Alice. Mandy told him she's bringing Denise's Crock-Pot.

I nod. This means I have to move my head up and down and up and down.

I am held captive by his voice, by the way he moves, how he touches objects so carefully. I think of how he's leaving his fingerprints behind, everywhere he touches, and I could touch those objects, too, and then we would be together somehow. I would have a part of him on me.

We make up the foldout bed together, he smooths out the sheet so carefully, and I am thinking *bed, bed, bed, bed,* but then we move on from that task, and we put down the rug and hang up the curtains. I am as limp with longing as the curtains are, almost unable to speak, which is such a strange, welcome feeling. It occurs to me that Ren never gave me an opportunity to *want him.* He was always just there, two steps ahead of me, unbuttoning, unzipping, removing clothing, breathing his hot breath into my ear. It was sexy most of the time, but now I see there is something holy about longing.

And then, just as I have given up all hope, Jamie strides across the room and takes me in his arms. His kisses this time are at first gentle and then harder and he pulls me tightly to him.

"I'm having trouble resisting you," he says into my ear.

"I don't want you to resist me," I tell him.

"Here's the thing about sex," he says. He pulls back and looks into my eyes. "It can be casual, lighthearted. Like the night we kissed the secret sauce away. If we'd somehow made love that night, it would have been lighthearted and, I'm sure, great. Just between friends. It would have also been wrong, of course, because you were engaged to someone, and I wouldn't have sex with an engaged person—but still. If we take *him* out of the picture, it would have been a great, fun, romping sort of sex with no repercussions."

"Listen to me. This is an intellectualization of sex that I don't think I'm prepared to agree with. Sex is about feeling."

"But you can't deny that I'm making a very excellent point."

"Would you just shut up and kiss me?"

"Hear me out. This is important. Now—now we're something else to each other. We've been to *Kmart* together, for heaven's sake. We've made *purchases.* You've seen my couch! I made you scrambled eggs. And you buttered my toast."

"Jamie—"

"And so now sex would be *important.* It would be noncasual. Like—I don't know—love. And I'm not sure that you—"

There is only one way to stop this stream of nonsense. I put my mouth on his, and while I'm doing that, we walk over to his bedroom and lie down next to each other. He turns on his side to face me and runs his fingers along my arm. He's looking into my eyes, and he's smiling sadly. I am so turned on that I can barely take a breath. And I can see the answer is no.

"You're not ready," I say flatly.

"Actually," he says in a voice that is trembly with feeling, "actually, I've never been *more* ready in my life. But you—you just broke up with a guy. It literally *just* happened."

"Jamie—" I try to kiss him again, but he's closed up the kissing shop.

"Nope. I'm right about this. I'm not going to take advantage of that. I don't want to spoil something that could someday be good. We can wait."

"I can't wait," I say.

He laughs softly. "If I can wait, you can, too."

I stay the night, sleeping beside him. It just kind of happens. We're lying there and talking, his hand slung across my hip, and then the stretches between words get longer and longer, and soon he's breathing so evenly and softly. I lie there, thinking he'll wake up soon, and he'll be startled when he remembers, and say he's got to get me home, he's still got pages and pages of stuff to read, he's so sorry, and maybe this hadn't been the best idea in the world after all. He'll make a joke about how Kmart is a gateway drug to spending the night together.

But he doesn't wake up. I know because I am monitoring his breathing. I am aware of his eyelashes, of his chest moving up and down, at the way he moves ever so slightly. At last I slide out from under his hand and get up and go pee, and I look in the bathroom drawer to see if he has an extra toothbrush, but he doesn't seem to. I use my finger and smear Crest all over my teeth and then rinse my mouth.

As I'm about to turn out the light I notice the bottle of baby shampoo on the edge of the tub. It looks just like the baby shampoo my mother used on me; nothing changed about it at all. Sure enough, I go over and unscrew the top and take a whiff of it—and it smells just the same. I think of how Jamie must kneel down next to the tub and wash Alice's hair while she lies back, closing her eyes against the water that spills over her face in spite of his best intentions. I think I can remember my father washing my hair, putting so much shampoo on that it puffed up into big plumes of lather, and how that made us both laugh, the way he formed my hair into white foamy points.

I want a child. This thought hits me so hard. Oh my God, if working at this daycare has taught me anything about life, it's shown me that I want a baby and the whole catastrophic earthquake of a life filled with messiness and laughter and chaos and kisses. I can't be who I was before. *Bring on the ruckus,* I think. I want it all.

I've somehow never talked to Ren about the possibility of having children. Another thing we didn't get to. I guess somewhere deep down I knew he wouldn't want to start a whole new family. And to be honest, I hadn't realized until just lately how very important it is to me to have a child of my own.

I wipe my mascara off, and I try to comb out my hair with my fingers. And I walk around in circles in the darkness of Jamie's living room. I go back and watch him sleeping, and my heart feels like it's breaking. This man is not ready for love. I can't make him love me. What he meant to say when he was telling me that *I'm* not ready is that he knows I could never be the ocean, the stars, and the sea turtles. He is still in love with his dead wife, and how many ways does he have to tell me that? Joking around is not the same as having deep feelings for me. And while we're asking the hard questions, what the *hell* is wrong with me for seriously doing so badly at this business of picking men?

If I went to a therapist, the first question we could explore could well be: Why do I only pick men who are hung up on other women who are completely unavailable? When can I be confident enough to get a man who is unencumbered, who just wants *me*? Is it too much to ask that I be first in some guy's heart?

Could La Starla and the spirit guides have really meant it when they said I'd have the life I want? I think of her sitting in her kitchen that day so long ago, after Ren had left for New Haven, and she said I'd have to wait. It wasn't going to go smoothly, she said.

But she wanted me to know that my life was on the right track.

I walk over to Jamie's kitchen window and look out at the street-lights and the rooftops and the soft white moon shining down on every-thing. If I start crying right now, if I let myself give in to tears, I'll look like a mess in the morning. So I go back to his bed and crawl in next to him, so softly that he doesn't even stir.

In the morning, he's just as funny as ever. He's apparently the kind of guy who wakes up cheerful. He squeezes my hand, says something about how he can't believe he got so much sleep. Usually Alice comes into his bed around five each morning if not earlier, and often she's sad and missing her mom, and the two of them snuggle together until it's time for him to get them up and going around seven thirty. He says he tells her stories about when she was a baby and how much Lauren loved her, and how the two of them used to make up silly names for her. For a while, they called her the Baked Potato because she was so warm and compact, in her little swaddle thing.

He goes into the kitchen and makes coffee. He's acting natural, like it's not unusual that I'd be there. He wants to know if I'd like Cheerios for breakfast. I can have a red bowl or a blue bowl, he says. He won't fight me.

It is all so delicious and lovely, being here, the buttery light coming through the kitchen window, the cups in the sink, the crumbs on the drainboard, the radio playing classical music from NPR. His jokey voice, his comfort. It scares the hell out of me, how used to this I could get, how much I loved watching him sleep. How I loved seeing Alice's baby shampoo and hearing how he and Lauren called her the Baked Potato.

I feel like an orphan watching through the window. I have this teeny-tiny little opportunity to see this breathtaking view of family life, even with this tattered remnant of a family. Let's face it: Jamie and Alice simply do not have the numbers. Being here, looking around, I just want to join their little team. Where is the sign-up sheet?

But then I remember that Mandy is coming, and I have to build a little fortress for my heart unless I want it squished into a pancake.

CHAPTER
TWENTY-FIVE

The morning of the workday dawns with banner blue skies, some high clouds sailing at the top of the world, and maybe a trifle too much humidity, but who cares about a little humidity? So what that my hair has gone into a frizz that makes me look like an insane person? I *am* insane! I bounce out of bed and throw myself into the day like the fate of the world depends upon it. Yes, I am breathless. I am whistling and happy and organized and engaged with every cell, every breathing molecule.

Forget romance. Forget crazy love. Save the daycare!

I check over my lists once again, looking at the jobs people have signed up for: cleaning, painting, raking—and the jobs that didn't have any takers: planting flowers, putting in some sod, fixing the swing set. Michael told me that he's managed to get some friends to help him bring over the huge tire, and they're going to cement it into the ground, and it will be such a cool structure for kids to climb in and out of. We'll trim the weeds, get new sand for the sandbox, repair the fence.

I've even baked apple cupcakes, and Jamie and I bought some beers and pretzels, and Maya and I plan to make homemade pizzas in my kitchen and then bring them downstairs for the kids and parents.

"Will Jerome come, too, do you think?" I had asked Maya one day last week on her turn.

"Of course he will," she said, "because if there's one thing to know about Jerome, it's that he can't stand not to be part of things."

"Is he going to spend the whole day yelling at us for doing things the State wants?"

She sighed. "I wouldn't be surprised. But I think once he's here, he'll be okay. He's very much a communal kind of guy."

"Also, are you two doing all right?" I said.

"Well," she said. "Some days are better than others. I mean, he's home with me, and he does the dishes, and he plays with Gabriela, and he writes his grouchy letters to the editor for all the newspapers. So we're just *being*."

Everybody comes. *Everybody comes.* Some, including Jamie, arrive later than others, of course. But they all show up, with paintbrushes and hammers and screwdrivers, and children. Joyous brings a kid-sized red plastic table and little chairs for snack time in the yard. Michael and some of his work friends pull up with the gigantic tire on the back of a flatbed truck. They're laughing and whistling as they unload the thing, men calling to each other as they roll the tire down a ramp, across the street, onto the sidewalk, and then through the gate, while the rest of us stand, looking on in surprise. The children jump up and down.

A couple of the neighbors wander over—men mostly, irresistibly drawn to industrial equipment and bags of cement. They all pitch in. One of them leaves for a bit and comes back with a cooler of beer, and the cementers all gather around and discuss things that have to do with cement hardening and tire origins and who knows what all.

The sun blazes hot overhead, an August sun. I make a pitcher of lemonade and bring it out and pour it into plastic cups, and William and Toby take cups to all the parents who are working, walking so carefully and slowly, their eyes wide from the sheer effort of it. It could break your heart watching how careful they are, how hard three-year-olds can try.

I keep getting a ridiculous lump in my throat, seeing how exuberant everyone is as I run around checking out who's where and who needs help. It's like we're a family! I can't quite take it all in. Emily is repairing the cots in the nap room, Joyous is taking apart the stove and cleaning all the little greasy metal bits. Michael and Suki are painting the swing set a brilliant, nonrusty red. Nicole is planting flowers, with her baby strapped to her chest. Some kids are playing chase on the lawn, and I see Jerome herding them over to an area by the fence, where he sits down and plays his guitar. They climb all over him, and he's laughing and groaning as he juggles his guitar and a lapful of children. They're singing the peanut butter song, which is a big hit, especially the part when you yell out in a stage whisper, *"Jelly!"*

At about ten, the daycare phone rings, and I put down my dustrag and my clipboard and go to pick it up. It's Jamie.

"You're not going to believe this," he says in a low voice, "but guess who just arrived as a surprise."

"No."

"Yep."

"Bring her? I guess?"

"*Okayyyy.* I guess."

"There was literally no warning?"

"Literally none."

"Any idea why?"

"She said because Alice and I weren't coming up there this weekend, and Denise and Otto had a golf tournament, so she thought she might as well come and see us . . . just to check things out."

"We'll put her to work."

"Will we, though?" he says. "Also, I have a little surprise for you. I'm bringing a sheet cake big enough for fifty people."

"Fifty people!"

"Yeah, it had to be that big so the whole inscription could fit."

"What does the inscription say?"

"You'll see."

⌒

Around noon, he comes through the gate, laughing his hearty, fake, social laugh, holding aloft a white box containing the gigantic sheet cake, with Alice clinging to his leg like a koala bear. This causes him to traipse along with one stiff leg, moving her up and down as he goes. He's trying to dislodge her while juggling the cake box, and he has the strangest expression on his face, sort of a pained smile. A nice-looking, well-dressed young woman comes up behind him, trying to peel Alice off of him, which is a hopeless task, but she's doggedly working at it. He says something to her, probably apologizing because Alice is not cooperating one bit, clinging even more fiercely to her father's leg, and then the woman gives up and instead takes the box out of his hands, and the three of them make it inside. He locks the gate, and when he turns back, his eyes find mine, and I yell across the yard: "Jamie! Alice! Welcome! So glad you're here! And who's *this*?"

Like I don't know.

Alice jumps down and runs to me, shouting, "I have the antamanda!"

The antamanda!

"Wait. *This* wonderful person is the antamanda you've been talking about?" says Nate. "She's a person? How fun is that!" Antamanda. Aunt Amanda.

Mandy. *Ahhh.* I, of all people, should have known.

"So glad to meet you," I say, striding over to greet her. "I'm Mimi."

"Hi!" she says. "Jamie and Alice were telling me all about you on the way down. You just got the job directing this place, I hear." She looks around like she's a well-meaning lady who's landed in a foreign country and is intent on learning the ways of the natives before she writes her devastating anthropological study on us.

"Welcome," I say. "And how are *you* doing, Alice Dumpling?" And I tousle up her hair just for something to do that doesn't involve looking into Jamie's eyes.

The antamanda is wearing a pink-and-white-checked sundress with a sweet little white leather belt and some white flats. And her dark hair looks like it was just put through a polishing machine, all slicked down in a perfect bob. She looks a lot like the photographs I saw of Lauren.

She starts murmuring things about the importance of early-childhood education—it turns out she has a degree in it!—and how the outdoors has been proven to be *so* important for children's hand-eye coordination! And their oxygen retention! And then she looks at me expectantly, as though I should say something wise about hand-eye coordination or at least *something* having to do with happy child development, and I feel, irrationally, as though I'm at a job interview with a very pleasant but proper person who is probably not going to hire me. I stand up a little straighter and we shake hands. Her hand is cool and well-manicured, and my hand is no doubt sweaty and hot. She's smiling so big and looking around the yard with wide blue eyes like she's never beheld such human endeavor in real life. She actually says, "My, my, my, my! Well, isn't this *something special?*"

"It's so nice of you to come," I say, and she tells me she's glad not to miss it.

"Just *look* at what you're doing here! It's marvelous! Jamie was trying to describe this place to me, but I had *no idea!*"

Jamie, looking dazed, gives me a wide-eyed, pained look behind her back and then retreats to the tire project, as though he were physically sucked in by it. It does seem to have its own magnetic force. Alice bounces off to play in the sandbox with William, and Mandy and I stand regarding each other.

"I've never seen anything like this," I say. "Men around earth-moving equipment! If this was a horror movie, you could see the men being subsumed by the tire. We'd look over just in time to see the last of their ears and toes being vaporized inside."

"Oh dear," she says. "I hope not. Is this a good idea?"

"Very," I say.

She smiles uncertainly at me; possibly she's never seen the kind of horror movies I have. She has that sort of tentative-but-game-for-anything look that could so easily stray into her insisting we call 9-1-1.

I take her with me to put the sheet cake away in the kitchen, which is being scrubbed to a deep shine, and then we go to the nap room, which Emily is dismantling as she sits on the floor alternately singing a Bonnie Raitt song and then lapsing into swearing at the screws that have rusted on the cots.

"Maybe you need WD-40," coos the antamanda, and she happens to know that Jamie has some in the trunk of his car, and when Emily agrees that that's exactly what she needs, the antamanda claps her hands and says it's so good to be useful, and she hurries off to get it.

"Well, that's a bit of awesome," says Emily to me. "Does she have any kids? Can we recruit her to be a member? Who is she, anyway? Besides an angel of industrial lubricants?"

"She's Jamie's sister-in-law, his dead wife's sister," I say, wrinkling my nose because I'm like that. "Turns out she's the antamanda we've been hearing about from Alice. And I think her parents sent her here to help him with his *life*."

"Okay," says Emily, whispering back to me. "But you say that like it's a bad thing."

I whisper, "It's not me who thinks it's a bad thing. He's a little freaked out about her coming. I think he's worried she won't like the daycare and that she'll think we aren't competent enough and that she'll think he should enroll Alice somewhere else. You know, if we're too flaky or something. The way we are. Sometimes. Mostly." I am aware that I'm not explaining this well.

"Hey, we are who we are," she says. "We are flakes of the highest order."

"Exactly. I'm just *saying* that it would be especially helpful to Jamie's cause if Jerome doesn't start in on love being a butterfly today, and if Maya maybe doesn't have to scream at Katherine."

She hasn't taken her eyes away from my face. "Oh my God," she says. "You're in love with him, aren't you?"

"No! No, I just think she's not ready for the full force of the fact that we appreciate a lot of odd behavior. I just hope we don't find ourselves telling poop stories, and that if Davy draws another picture of his dad's personal anatomy, we could say it's a pickle. That's all I'm saying. It would be best if we could be ordinary today."

"You are so in love with him," she whispers.

"Yeah. Okay. I am. Not good, huh?" I wipe my eyes, which have suddenly begun to tear up, for no reason whatsoever that I can explain. How is it that my heart didn't inform *me* of this fact sooner? I've been going along thinking this was all just for fun. And it's *not*.

Emily comes over and puts her arms around me. "Aw, it's good news. Love. He needs somebody to love him."

"But she's going to be *living with him*," I blubber. "And she looks just like his late wife."

"Honey, I don't see that that's going to be a problem," she says and hugs me. "Also, I just want to say: How did we get so lucky to find you?"

As I'm hugging her back I suddenly know the answer to that: I was sent.

La Starla said there would be children. And love. And call me crazy, but *these* are the ones she meant. Not Ren's kids after all. For a moment, the air seems to get a little hazy. I feel a little lightheaded, like everything is going to work out and be absolutely perfect. But who knows how?

⁓

Later, as I'm digging up some weeds, as well as keeping my eye on Jamie, who is helping with the tire, and Mandy, who is watching Jamie, I look up to see Ren coming through the gate.

Ren. Fucking Ren. The air goes out of me, and my backbone stiffens.

Clearly the universe is working overtime on my issues this weekend.

I immediately look down, but not before I notice that he's holding five large pizza boxes—from Sally's Apizza, named the best New Haven pizza, aka the best pizza in the known world, to hear the locals tell it. This is not just *any* pizza. This is statement pizza. You have to wait in long lines to get Sally's pizza. For hours sometimes. And you can't call and order ahead.

What the hell is he trying to prove? It just makes me mad, this kind of gesture.

I hear somebody say, "*Ooooh*, is that Sally's pizza?"

And he looks over at *me*, grinning, as if I'd said that. "Why yes, it sure is!" he says. I look back down at my sod.

"Well," says Nicole, who I now realize is beside me, "guess we don't have to make our homemade pizza after all. Is this who I think it is? The big idiot you just broke up with?"

"The very one. But how did you know I broke up with him?"

"Oh. Word gets around. We're all on your side." She squints at him. "I've also heard that you're in love with Jamie. Although I must say that your ex looks like he's a charmer. Handsome. And he doesn't mind standing in line to buy pizza, which is a good thing in a man. Are you thinking of going back to him?"

"There is a zero percent chance of that. Also, could you not mention anything about the Jamie situation and me? It's very . . ."

"New," she says. "I know. But he loves you, too."

"He does?"

"Of course he does. Is it possible that you two are the only ones who don't already know this?" She pats me on the arm. "One thing that makes me happy is that I'm going to get to watch this whole situation play out. Up close and personal."

"But he loves his dead wife so much, and now her sister is here," I say.

"Don't be crazy," she says. "That kind of thing never works out. Look at literature. But oh my God, what in the hell is your ex doing?"

I'm aware, even without looking up, that Ren is definitely charming the pants off the daycare crowd. I can hear his voice booming over the hubbub. I can't quite hear his words, but I can tell he's praising and complimenting up a storm. A few minutes later, he shows up next to me, with Alice on his shoulders.

"So, hi there," he says. "A nice place you got here."

"Thanks."

"Nice turnout." He looks around, and I'm sure he's smiling his sexy, smoldering smile, trying to be both thoughtful and handsome. As well as over-the-top generous. "I thought I'd bring over some Sally's pizza. Keep the crowd onboard. You know."

"Great," I say, and I keep digging.

"You don't want to risk them leaving because they get hungry."

"No, I suppose not," I say, which is four words more than I had intended to say to him today.

The clock ticks. Possibly the sun goes behind a cloud.

"Well, I'll get out of your way," he says eons later. "Looks like you have a lot of sod there to work with."

Alice, from his shoulders, leans her head down and pulls on Ren's ears. "I told my daddy that I want to be in your wedding. *Aaaaand* I want a dress with nets on it. And with little stars on the nets. And I want the wedding to be right here at daycare."

"Little stars on the nets," Ren repeats. "Fabulous. What do you think about that, Mimi?"

I stab at some roots of the dead grass.

"Yeah, what do *you* think about that, Mimi Mommy?" says Alice.

It kills me, but I pretend I didn't hear Alice either.

He suddenly swings around and puts Alice down on the ground and stoops down next to me. "Mimi, I haven't been able to sleep," he says in a low voice. "I miss you. Can't we . . . work this out? Will you talk to me? I'm sorry if I said anything that offended you. Please."

"Hey! You put me down!" says Alice. "Pick me back up!"

He looks at her helplessly. I think he's trying to figure out if it would help his cause to pick her up, or if he's more likely to get back to having sex every night if he just concentrates on telling me how sorry he is. Neither one of these is going to work.

I stand up, done with this conversation, done with him, done with all of it. "I have to go inside and help clean the stove," I say. "Thanks for the pizzas. But I can't talk to you now. I'm not ready."

I walk away. I shouldn't have said the "not ready" part. That implies that sometime I *will* be ready, and I don't ever want to be ready for another talk about this. It's hopeless. I am really and truly done with him.

I hear the clanking of the gate and realize that I've gotten my wish. He's gone.

Alice tucks her hand in mine and goes with me to the kitchen. "Why you don't want to talk to Ren?" she says.

"I'm just busy," I tell her.

"But why you don't *talk* to him?"

"Are you having a fun day today helping everybody?"

"Why you don't talk to him?"

"I'm just . . . I'm just taking a break. I want to talk to the daycare people. You know?"

"Are you going to marry him?"

"I'm not. No."

She widens her eyes. "You're not going to *marry* him? But you have a ring!"

"No. I gave it back."

"You *did*?" she says.

"Yes. Things have changed."

Why am I having this conversation with a four-year-old?

"Okay," she says and smiles. "That's okay, Mimi Mommy. Did you know that the antamanda is maybe going to live in my house? She said she was. She said she's going to help me and my daddy."

"With what?" I say.

She shrugs. "Maybe she'll draw pictures? I don't really know. Maybe just living. I wanted you to get married at daycare at the new tire."

"Well," I say. "Maybe you'll just have to get married there someday."

❧

By nightfall, there's the most wonderful moment. It almost makes up for Ren and the antamanda and a whole mishmash of uncertainty.

Once the tire is finally cemented in place—though still wet so the kids can't climb on it yet—the men are all milling around looking pleased with themselves. Michael turns toward the children and says, "It's now safe to go inside it! Just don't climb on it or push it!" And they all erupt in cheers, the daycare kids, the neighbor kids, and they all start running over to the tire and running through it again and again, screaming and laughing and jumping.

I feel my eyes stinging. Everybody's hugging and kissing and dancing around. Jerome swings Gabriela up in the air, and Maya grabs his arm and the three of them turn in circles on the grass. Jamie is pumping his fist in the air, and Alice runs around him, her two ponytails flapping around her ears. And even the antamanda looks like she's astonished by all the heraldry going on around her.

We all bring out blankets and little chairs (and one lawn chair for her since she's wearing a dress) and we pass around slices of pizza and open the beers. People are smiling, even though they are all sweaty and tired, and there are mosquitoes needing to be swatted. Someone turns on the outside lights. The neighbors stick around, mostly for pizza and beer, and I hear one of the other men say that he thought this was the craziest place on earth and now, he says with a laugh, he sees that he was right.

"Maybe next we'll build a tree house for you," he says, like that's a hilarious joke.

"And a swimming pool with a diving board," says another one, guffawing.

And they laugh and laugh and laugh. Maybe they're drunk.

I look around at everyone as the darkness slowly descends. Jerome is playing the guitar, and Maya is sitting next to him. Katherine has left with Sanborn, thank goodness. I notice she's been avoiding Jerome all day, for which I'm thankful. Emily is lying on the blanket with her head in Michael's lap, and Davy is curled up next to them. Suki and William are playing a slap game. Jamie and Alice are sitting side by side on a blanket, next to Mandy's chair. He smiles at me in the darkness.

More guitars come out, more beers appear from the cooler, and Jamie goes in and fetches the cake and shows it off. It says, in loopy letters across the top: **THANK YOU TO OUR OCTOPUS.**

My eyes get a little blurry, and I have to swipe at them, which then gets mud across my face, and I end up having to go inside and wash my whole face. I stare at myself in the bathroom mirror. I can't remember feeling so happy.

Nobody wants to call it a night. We sit under the stars and we eat cake and sing all the songs we know by Gordon Lightfoot, Joan Baez, the Beatles, Fleetwood Mac.

Davy calls out, "I don't know these songs! Let's sing 'If You're Happy and You Know It.'"

Right. We're a daycare. So after that we sing our usual playlist, featuring "Little Bunny Foo Foo," "Peanut Butter and Jelly," some foxes and some ducks, "Ten Little Monkeys Jumping on the Bed." The children jump up and dance around, screaming out the lyrics as best they can.

I lie down on my back and look at the starry points of light up so high, feeling full of love and relief and kindness. I belong here.

You did magic today, La Starla's voice says to me in my head. *This is what I've been talking about.*

But then I look over and see Alice plopped on Jamie's lap. He's sitting next to Mandy, who leans down from her chair and says something to him that makes him laugh.

The bubble pops. Just like that.

Don't even go there, says La Starla in my head. *You're fine. You're* more *than fine. Do I have to get on the train and come to New Haven and remind you that you have magic on your side?*

CHAPTER
TWENTY-SIX

"I would say, on a scale of one to ten, that the workday was easily a twenty," says Jamie on Monday when we're working a turn together. "And that's actually with me deducting points because of a certain egocentric blowhard crashing the whole thing, bringing show-off pizza. And as I say that, I realize that I might be way out of line, because for all I know, you *asked* him to bring pizza, and you two are back together and happy, and if that is true, I humbly beg your forgiveness."

"Jamie," I say. "Did we *look* like we were back together?"

"These things are sneaky."

"What *things* would those be?"

"Reunions with people you've broken up with. Nearly everybody goes back one or two times at least."

"I'm not going back to him."

He looks around. There's no one but us in the kitchen, so he comes over and puts his hands on my waist and pulls me toward him and kisses me. I melt against him.

"Why is it okay for us to have kisses, but it's not okay for us to do anything more than that?" I say. "And by the way, thank you for that amazing cake."

"Surely I don't have to explain to you the difference between kissing and sex, emotionwise," he says. "And you're welcome for the cake."

"It just seems that one is a gateway drug to the other, and it's not fair for us not to get to have the whole experience." I can't believe I'm saying these things to him.

He lets me go and smiles. "Promise me one thing, though. If you do go back to him, don't go with him to Sally's. Don't be a Sally's person. Pepe's apizza is the one. And you also gotta give Modern Apizza a try. It's better. Doesn't have the long line that Sally's does, so it can be a little personality test to see if he can handle pizza that doesn't have bragging rights about the line, of all things. Oh, and don't even think of asking why New Haven pizza starts with an *A*. No one knows. But you're supposed to pronounce it *a-beets*. Just so you know."

"Thank you," I say. "I've heard of *abeets,* and I thought it was a vegetable."

"Same here," he says. "Glad I could help you with the natives."

At that moment, I hear a crash and I need to run into the living room to prevent little Gabriela from knocking over a tower that has been painstakingly built by William and Davy and which would possibly result in her being dismantled herself. Meanwhile, Toby is sitting on the floor crying and pushing a spoon into his shoe.

"What's the matter, Tobester?" I say.

"I want the spoon to help me put on my shoe," he says. "Daddy uses a spoon every day, and it works for him."

"I don't think that's a spoon he uses, pal," Jamie says. "It's something called a shoehorn."

"Bring me a spoonhorn!" he says. "I want a spoonhorn!"

Jamie looks at me. "How is it that we forgot to stock spoonhorns when we were buying toys?"

"Beats me. Shall we go back to Kmart?"

He smiles. "I wish."

Later, when we have the kids outside eating their snack of apples and peanut butter on the plastic table in the shade, I say very, very carefully, "So how's it going with the antamanda? Did she love the blue-flowered sheets and the rugs? Is she moving in?"

"Yep. I think it was the throw pillows that really sold it," he says.

"Really?"

"No!" He laughs. "What sold it, I think, is that she really wants to get to know Alice. Plus, her altruistic sense that I am a person in dire distress."

"So when is she coming back?"

"Funny you should ask. She's getting her stuff together now and coming back this afternoon."

"Oh! So . . . shall I bring Alice home with me after daycare today?"

"Nope," he says, and doesn't look at me. "That's all over. You're free from afternoon duty. Mandy's on the scene now. And," he adds with a flourish, "she wants to do turns. That's how much she loved the daycare. And she particularly liked you. She said she's really looking forward to getting to know you."

"Fantastic," I say. The air is fuzzy around us, muddled.

"And she's got a degree in early-childhood education, so she'll be a real asset," he says.

"That's what scares me the most," I say, and he runs his fingers through his hair and says, "I know. Me too, to be honest."

"Maybe—What if this? What if I could just bask in the glory of the daycare workday for a while before we have to call on her for help at daycare?" I say.

"I know, Mimi," he says, "but could you please just try to like her so my life can go one angstrom unit smoother?"

꩜

The next day the antamanda shows up in the morning, bringing Alice. It hits me that now I won't see Jamie at drop-off time anymore. Just another little pinprick in the balloon of my basking.

I look at her and see all the waves of goodwill radiating from her, and I remember that there is not one solid reason for me not to like her. She's a nice person. She wants to help two of my favorite people with their lives. I should not hold it against her that she and Alice are wearing matching sundresses and matching sandals, or that I happen to be in love with her brother-in-law.

"Is there anything I can do to help out?" Mandy says to me. "I have lots of free time, and I'd be delighted to help."

Jerome is on the turn with me. We both look at each other. He growls something about the creeping nature of authoritarianism and the human propensity to give up thinking when independent thought feels too radical, and then he takes himself and exactly two kids to the place where the proletariat can find protection: the backyard.

I smile at her. "This is very nice of you. Would you like to read stories to the kids?"

"Sure," she says, and sets herself up in the reading corner the way Miss Nancy might have done it on *Romper Room*, a show from my childhood. That means she lines the children up in little chairs, and she sits in front of them, also in a little chair, and she holds up the book and tells them the title and the author and the copyright date. She has a big smile. They look at her blankly, as if they're surprised to find themselves on chairs.

She doesn't know that the daycare way of reading stories is that we all lie on the big mattress among the giant pillows, hunkered down together like puppies next to their warm mama—bodies piled on top of squirming bodies, everybody's breath mingled together; everybody's hair, soft as corn silk, brushing against faces. There's the problem of the tangled limbs, of sharpened elbows, the occasional shoving and yelling, and then the drowsy, slowing . . . animalness of it all. Story after story gets read this way. The person reading the actual words has to hold the book very high in the air so that every kid can see the book and not miss anything.

It's very mammalian, you see. It's one of the best parts of my day. Everyone's day, really. You never find a parent who doesn't want to get into a pile of children and read them a story.

⁀੭

The next day she brings in alphabet cards, the kind that feature all the letters written in white against a chalkboard-green background, block style. You see these marching around the walls of elementary school classrooms, and there is absolutely nothing wrong with having the alphabet on display at daycare, so I don't say a thing when she tacks them all up at child's-eye level.

Later in the week she lines the children up outside and teaches them the rules to "Mother, may I," also something that is absolutely fine and innocent and probably good for children. Except that when four of them start crying because they are little and they forgot to say, "Mother, may I?" before taking their turn, she says briskly, "Well, next time you'll remember," and when *that* doesn't go over as well as she expected, she introduces them to the concept of the "time-out chair," where they can go to think about when they might be ready to rejoin polite society.

She explains the concept of "consequences."

"Is that like *sequins?*" says Lily.

And after that, Mandy comes in with reward stickers for good behavior.

She gets a stopwatch to time their turns on the swings so no one gets more than others, which—I don't know—might be a good thing in some universes. However, it does make people cry, but according to Mandy, everything is more fair with timers. It's important that they learn the concept of fairness. Who am I to argue with that? I've been struggling with fairness all my life.

When I really stop and think about it, the main thing that drives me crazy about her is the way she marches around looking officially cheerful. And fake nice. She talks in a high-pitched voice to the kids and totally does not pick up on the laid-back, hippie spirit of the place— how we watch the children while lazily lying on blankets in the shade. How sometimes you have to carry two children, one on each hip, and while you're doing that, you're also calmly explaining to another child that no one should rub peanut butter into someone else's hair. I don't think she would be capable of talking about peanut butter in the hair without also bringing up consequences.

She also worries about the kind of things no one else ever thought of—sunscreen getting into eyes and causing blindness, the possibility of stepping on a bee and dying of anaphylaxis before the ambulance can arrive, and how she once heard about someone losing their eye when it was poked out by a sharp piece of bread crust.

To be fair, she also does some marvelous things. After lunch when everybody is crabby and two kids are crying because they miss their moms, and another is crying because there's a scary thunderstorm outside, and another hates the banana he has for snack because it's broken, Mandy comes up with a brilliant idea. She makes signs for them to wear, expressing their emotions.

I AM SCARED OF THUNDER.
I WANT MY MOMMY.
I DO NOT WANT BROKEN BANANAS.

We pin these on their shirts, and they strut around proudly.

Then Alice says, "I want a sign to say: I do not want my mommy to be in the ground."

"Oh dear," says Mandy. "That's not what I was thinking. I don't think we want to put that on a sign."

But Alice and I make the sign anyway. I kiss her on the cheek. "That's what you want, so you get to have a sign about it," I tell her.

They wear their signs pinned on their shirts for the rest of the day. Alice gets hugged by every single person who comes to the daycare that afternoon.

If I had a sign it would say . . . oh, never mind.

❧

Mandy happens to be on the turn on Friday when the State agents show up for their surprise inspection, making sure we've obeyed our orders.

They come marching up the front walk in their evil, official-looking suits, looking like they're prepared to throw children into the street for the good of God and country. I see them through the front window, pausing to make some last-minute notes on their clipboards, and I mumble a few positive phrases that La Starla taught me.

This will all go perfectly. The daycare will flourish. The workday was a success.

Then there is nothing to be done but to open the front door and usher them inside. I'm just glad Jerome isn't there to lecture them about the military-industrial complex and the Nixon administration. It's far better that I have Mandy on the turn with me, a highly presentable person who still arrives each day wearing a sweet little sundress, and often wearing an apron so that paint doesn't get on her. She even smiles at the inspectors and asks the children to sing a good-morning song to them.

The children don't know a good-morning song, but they give it their best. Mandy, to her credit, is singing at the top of her lungs, with full-throated enthusiasm. She could be Julie Andrews in *The Sound of Music*. I expect the children will be wearing matching uniforms made from curtains if Mandy stays much longer.

Mrs. Hamilton and her sidekick, the guy who clearly belongs in a job at the Secret Service, set to work with their clipboards, moving through the daycare, checking nooks and crannies, shining flashlights into cabinets, looking for God only knows what. When they come into the kitchen, Mrs. Hamilton wants to see the menu for the week, which, as the octopus, I now post on the bulletin board.

"No clams, I see," she says, and actually cracks a smile. "It looks like you've come a long way."

That's when I know we might be all right.

An hour after they arrive, Mrs. Hamilton presents me with the former checklist of our faults—all corrected now and signed off on.

I thank her. It's probably best that it's not until the two inspectors are safely out of the daycare and getting into their cars that

William and Toby launch back into their favorite, hilarious game of "you're-a-weenie-no-you're-a-weenie."

That's a game that Mandy has not been able to vanquish. Silently I applaud these little boys for their dedication.

All in all, there's no way around it: this is a major triumph. When people come in to pick up their kids at the end of the day, they find Mandy and me happily lounging in the backyard, recounting our victory, while the kids run through the tire. Nobody seems to be in a hurry, so we all sit for a while. They all call their partners to come down and join us, and it turns into an impromptu potluck supper on the grass, consisting of peaches, sesame noodles, homemade bread, tomatoes, cheese, crackers, and peanut butter balls. Michael heads down the street and gets a bottle of wine and a six-pack from the liquor store, and I dash upstairs for paper plates and cups and utensils. Emily spreads blankets out on the grass.

The relief in the air is like something you can taste and smell.

"Can't believe we pulled this one off."

"We're set for good now."

"I knew we could do it. Daycare is magic. And the inspectors know we're a force now!"

"Maybe Mimi is magic," a voice says. "She's the one who pulled this together."

I look up to see Jamie coming through the gate, smiling. He's still in his official Yale clothes, looking pleasantly rumpled and hot.

"Wait! How did you know to come here?" asks Mandy, sounding amazed.

"Well, where else would I look for you?" he says. "I drove home from work and hung around the house, and then I figured daycare was a likely place for you. And here you are! And how nice—it looks like dinner is here! And can I ask—is this now a state-certified, licensed daycare that only does good and has no bad intentions whatsoever?"

"Not that anyone can see anyway," says Maya.

He grins and gives me a fist bump on his way over to the blanket with the food, and then Alice jumps up on him and he swings her around and around in circles, and then she insists they run through the tire four times. Nate hands him a beer, which he accepts gratefully.

"Alice, baby, Daddy needs to get some food," he says. She looks a little bit pouty at that, but she comes over and leans against me, watching him.

Mandy starts telling him a whole bunch of domestic stuff: how she went to the grocery store, but she couldn't find the Lactaid milk he wanted, so she bought Lactaid pills, and is that okay? And also her parents called, and they're wondering if they can come down and visit this weekend, and she told them yes. Oh, and they need to pick up the clothes at the Laundromat before it closes at nine.

He nods.

For a moment, I think I can't stand it if he says something domestic back. I look away. They're a fun little team now.

Nicole gives me a knowing look and comes and tucks baby Claire into the crook of my arm as a consolation. The sun goes down, painting the sky pink and purple. People start telling stories from the early days of the daycare. After a while, there is a lot of soft laughter, sleepy children, and the deep, quiet voices of Michael and Jerome and Jamie discussing tire dynamics or something like that. Once the sun sinks into darkness, people get up and start gathering their tired children and their blankets and backpacks, and off they go.

I make sure to be upstairs so I don't have to watch Mandy and Jamie heading off with little Alice Dumpling in between them. I'm just guarding my heart, that's all.

CHAPTER
TWENTY-SEVEN

There is another hard part of life that I'm having to put up with.

Mandy talks about Jamie nearly nonstop. There are days I am limp from all the things I have to hear about him, all the rhapsodizing.

"Being here in New Haven and living with him is like playing house for me," she says in a chirpy voice. "I mean, I didn't think I'd be in charge of a man and his child for at least ten more years! And yet here I am, and it's almost like being a wife: doing laundry, doing the grocery shopping, *cooking*. My mom says she's never seen anybody take to domestic life like I have. Even Lauren didn't enjoy all this stuff."

Did I know, she says conspiratorially, did I have any *idea* that men don't separate their laundry? (I figured.) And how do I feel about dish towels and *underwear* being washed in the same load? (Why is that a problem?) She makes a face. Before she came and explained the disgusting-ingness of that, Jamie didn't see anything wrong with it at all. What, was he raised by wolves?

Also, did I know that he can be lighthearted? Why, sometimes, just for fun, he suggests they jump in the car before Alice goes to bed, and they drive to Hamden to the Dairy Queen and get Dilly bars! He's so spontaneous! He loves to laugh! Who knew he loved to laugh?

Sometimes I, honest to God, have to go outside in the yard and appeal to the universe to make this stop.

One day I say to her, which is probably not very nice of me, but I really do want to know: "Mandy, do you think it's possible that you have a bit of a crush on your sister's husband?"

And she looks at me with her round blue eyes. "Wow, no! That would be so icky, wouldn't it?" she says.

Icky. Yes, it would be completely icky.

She is lost in thought for a few moments and then she says, "I think what I have a crush on is being needed. And organizing a household. Last night I cleaned out the kitchen junk drawer and then, you know what I did? I rounded up all the loose socks I found and I hung them up with clothespins in the basement so we can be on the lookout for their husbands."

"Their *husbands*?" I say.

"Yes, don't you think of socks as husbands and wives? And if you see it that way, then it's like the *wives* have stuck around, and the *husbands* have wandered off and gotten lost, like they do. Maybe they're playing golf like my dad does or something."

I look over in time to see Jerome banging his head against the daycare wall.

"Jerome, do you play golf?" she says sweetly.

"How are you coping?" asks Maya one day when she comes to pick up Gabriela. I'm lounging on the lawn, next to the kiddie pool, while Gabriela and Toby, the last two kids still here, splash around. Mandy has taken Alice and gone home. "And what I mean by 'How are you coping?' is 'How is it that you haven't run into the street screaming or committed a random act of violence?' Jerome has told me a few things."

"Hey, I'm hanging in," I tell her. "It's interesting."

"So are you telling me you've had a lobotomy? Or are you just on drugs?"

"Contemplating both," I say.

"Jerome's theory is that she's secretly a spy left over from the Nixon administration, come to infiltrate the masses and turn the children against us."

"What could he possibly mean? She mentioned one day that she wants to start a helpful little daycare newsletter so all of us can understand children better," I say.

"That's just lovely," she says.

Nicole, cradling Claire in her arms, comes through the gate just then, and Toby gets out of the kiddie pool and runs across the grass and hugs her. "Oh my goodness, what a wet boy!" she says. "And—hmm, now I'm kind of wet, too." She laughs and hands me Claire, which she now knows is expected of her every single time that she and Claire and I are in the same vicinity.

"We're discussing whether Mimi can take much more of this Mandy business, and I'm getting concerned that Mimi might have had a lobotomy without telling us," says Maya.

"Why? She won't say anything bad?"

"Not so far, but I'm working on her."

"Look, guys, I want to try to like her," I say. "She's coming in every single day and working here for free. And she's trying."

"Yeah, she's *very* trying," says Nicole.

"Oh, did you guys hear that Katherine is leaving?" says Maya.

"No!" I say. "When did this happen?"

"Not sure. Jerome told me this morning. He says she's going to Portland, Oregon, to live with an old friend."

"Well, well, well," says Nicole. "That's definitely going to be a switch. You happy, Maya, my love?"

"We'll see if *he* stays happy," says Maya. "I'd almost rather have her here than have him missing her all the damn time."

༄

I live for Monday mornings when Jamie does his turn. Sometimes Mandy doesn't come with him. He and I take the children to the park or we set up the kiddie pool in the backyard and let them run through the sprinkler. It's September, but the days are still hot and hazy. We sit in the shade and eat ice pops we made out of fruit juice. We let the hose water run until we have puddles on the grass and then we squish our toes in them. Mandy would have some thoughts about how that is not a good thing to do. I can't even imagine what those might be—fear of drowning perhaps, if someone were to fall down face-first, or maybe it would have to do with soil microbes getting under toenails. I can't think about it.

"How's it going at home?" I ask him.

He shrugs. "It's fine. She's helping. She makes dinner, and I give Alice her bath and then put her to bed, and then I go back to work."

"How's the project coming? Any news on the capstone situation?"

"Funny you should mention that," he says, and grimaces. "We had a family meeting over the weekend, and it was decided that I need to have a new capstone project rather than try to resurrect this one with Professor Brain Trust."

"This is Otto saying this?"

"Yes. And, happily, he even has one he thinks I should pursue." He has a funny smile on his face. My heart does a dull rollover.

"Doing . . . ?"

"You don't want to know. It's out in left field. The main thing is that it involves me doing a whole bunch of interviews in Hartford and West Hartford. It's kind of centered there instead of here. With Otto's people. Which unfortunately means I'm going to be spending most of my days up in the northern part of the state."

"Wouldn't it just be easier to come up with something else down here?"

"I think my best bet here is to do what Otto thinks will work, because he's friends with Professor Brain Trust. That way, I'm more likely to get it approved."

After lunch, when we've read to the children and I've gotten them down for their naps, I go into the kitchen, where he's finishing up the lunch dishes. He turns away from the sink and I say, "Would you mind just making sure I don't have any taco sauce on my face?"

"Um, I don't believe we had any taco sauce with the lunch," he says.

"Still, I feel there's some sauce there somewhere."

He looks. "Yes," he says softly. "There is definitely some right there. On your lower lip."

And he kisses me. And then he kisses me again.

"I have a bulletin for you," I tell him. "I'm still broken up with Ren."

"Uh-huh." He smiles right into my eyes. "How long has it been now?"

"Long enough that we can say that it took," I say.

He leans in and looks at me closely, lifts up my eyelids to gaze into my eyes, then taps on my forehead, turns me around, and then he frowns and says, "Nope. Still not out of the woods."

"I think you're the one that's not out of the woods," I say. "You're the one who's not ready."

"I told you. I'm more ready than you would believe. I'm just careful with my heart. This is too important to risk plunging in too soon."

But how can things work out if we're both being so careful with our hearts? Seems to me that *somebody's* got to throw their heart into the air and see how it lands.

◦⁹◦

One day Mandy asks me if she can start doing Jamie's turns for him since he's so busy.

"Nope. Sorry. We have a rule about that," I say so very quickly. "Everybody has to do turns. We are against sexism here, and therefore, men can't get out of turns just because they're busy. Everybody's busy, and everybody does turns."

She smiles at me like she knows this is patently ridiculous. "Surely a graduate student—either male or female—who is working extra hard on a new project that requires him to travel to Hartford could find a little leniency, particularly since he's got a stand-in. Me."

"Nope. It's the cornerstone upon which this daycare is built," I say, as though I'm quoting the Constitution. "Everybody does turns. He has to do his. Period."

"I get it," she says. "You don't want it to look like you're playing favorites because you like him. So I'll ask everybody else. Who knows? Maybe they'll go for it."

I feel myself turning colors. "It's not that. I like everybody here!" I say, with just a tad too much heat in my voice.

She puts up a note on the blackboard asking people to vote yes or no on whether Jamie should be allowed to skip his turns for a while. There are only two no votes. I suspect those were mine and Jerome's.

Jamie misses the next three turns. And three weeks of drop-offs and pickups. I hate this.

Sometimes he leaves little notes for me with hearts on them stuck in my mailbox. Once or twice he calls me from West Hartford, from a phone booth near a place he goes for lunch. He says the project he's researching there is borderline interesting. He's still not sure his advisor is going to go for it, but Otto thinks it's a slam dunk. So he has to wait and see.

We sigh a lot on the phone. He says he doesn't want to complain, but at night when he gets home, he finds Alice crying when she doesn't get her way, and now she insists that he do absolutely everything for her. Mandy isn't even allowed to clear her plate off the table or give her a bath or tuck her in at night. He asks how she is at daycare.

"She seems fine," I say. I don't tell him that she sticks to me like she's a little rhesus monkey, and that she talks baby talk now and has stepped up the "Mimi Mommy" business until she's using it in practically every single sentence.

That might seem as if I were pointing out that I'm—well, maybe that I'm the one she wants more than she wants her aunt. No need to rub it in.

Also, I've learned something about kids. All of this behavior could shift overnight, and I'd be the chopped-liver character while Mandy is heralded as the queen of life.

∽

"There's just one teeny-tiny little thing that is bothersome," Mandy says to me one day. "One little fly in the ointment."

"Yes?" I am breathless, both needing to hear this and not wanting to hear this, which is confusing my brain.

"Just between us," she says, "doesn't Jamie baby Alice way too much? All those decisions he leaves up to her: Which pair of socks today? Right or left sock first? Ready to get in the car seat, or do you want to wait? Shampoo hair tonight, or wait until tomorrow? What to wear to daycare? When to go to bed? I think Alice manipulates him. She makes him do everything for her. And honest to God, I heard him ask her about twenty-five questions just before bedtime." She sighs. "I just wonder if nursery school might give Alice a little more *structure*, which could mature her."

"Structure," I say faintly.

"Yeah, I'm a real proponent of structure," she says. "I take after my mother on that one. I'm also a little bit shocked that Jamie's not at all concerned about Alice needing to learn to read. I mean, she's four, and she doesn't know the first thing about phonics. But whenever I bring it up, he just says he has to get back to work. I can't get him to listen."

This is so unhealthy for me, all this news from Jamie's house.

After all, I know what his bed feels like, and how he looks when he's asleep, and exactly what flowers are blooming on her sheets.

∽

One night I dream about Ren.

Yes, it's one of *those* kinds of dreams. We're back together, and we're making love in some public place—a cabana on a beach, I think it might be—and I'm a little worried about it, so I keep pulling the curtains, but Ren is handsome and strong and capable in this dream, and he's also bold and he takes me in his arms and says, "I love you, Mimi. This is the way love looks! No one minds!"

And then things shift, and La Starla is there, too, and she says, "You must remember back to the five most pleasurable moments in your lives, and that's where you have to go whenever you feel afraid."

And Ren says, "Great love can make miracles."

I wake up in the middle of the night, feeling as though I've just been kissed for hours. At first I can't remember if this was real or not. At any rate, I can't fall back to sleep, so I get up and go make a cup of chamomile tea, and I stand at the window looking down at the daycare yard in the moonlight, the way the silvery moon catches the metal swing set, and how the tire looks like a prehistoric animal hovering there.

I let myself realize the thing I've not been allowing in.

I miss sex. I miss the feeling of loving and being held.

And is this crazy? I miss the deliciousness of Ren. The availability. The willingness.

CHAPTER TWENTY-EIGHT

Nicole comes to do her turn one morning, and she's got a stricken look on her face.

She tells me in the kitchen that Nate, who works as a pediatrician at the Yale Health Center, has been lured away to Baltimore. The University of Maryland is offering him a position as chairman of their pediatrics department, and he says they need to go.

As soon as she tells me, she breaks down in tears. "I can't leave this place. How can I go? This is where I learned every single thing about being a parent. And all of you guys are my good friends. And also I don't know a soul in Baltimore, and I'll be stuck at home all fall and winter with two tiny children and I'll lose my mind."

"And who will hold Claire for you?" I say.

"Yes! I can't just trust any random person to hold Claire."

We hug and hug, and between us, the baby squirms in my arms and starts to whimper.

"You know, don't you, Claire?" says Nicole and smushes her face up next to the baby's and gives her a bunch of wet kisses that make Claire laugh. "Laugh all you want. Your daddy is renting a U-Haul truck, he says, and we're packing everything up next weekend and driving out, and your mama is so sad."

As it turns out, the daycare participates in the packing and moving. Somebody gets boxes from a liquor store, and then Maya and Emily and Joyous and I go over in the evenings all week and help Nicole pack up their books and cassette tapes first, then their kitchen stuff, and at last the clothing and bedding. We laugh and cry and drink wine and take turns holding the baby.

By the time moving day comes, Nate picks up the truck, and we all—men and women and children, except for Jamie, who is working—help load it up. It's a chilly day, and one or another of us breaks down in tears at random times and has to stop to be hugged. Jerome, scowling, accuses us of trying to kumbaya ourselves right into the clinical disease he calls *sentimentality*. Maya, wiping her eyes, tells him to put a sock in it, and he goes over and gives her one of those kisses that dips her way down to the ground, and her hair scrapes the pavement. A few of us cheer.

Nicole and Nate and the children sleep at Emily's house in sleeping bags on the floor, and they leave at ten the next morning. We're all out there, waving to them from the curb and cheering them on. Nicole is chronically weeping by then, and I offer to keep the baby for her for the rest of Claire's life, and I'm only half-joking.

Somehow, when we go back on Monday morning, the daycare feels much emptier without them.

It's pointed out at a meeting that we need to start recruiting new families. After all, we're now down three turn-doers: Katherine, Nate, and Nicole. Joyous agrees to freshen up our poster and put it back up at the Yale Co-Op. It's October, and new families have moved into the area. Most of the academic families have probably already solved their daycare problems, but maybe we can still find some.

"Daycare ebbs and flows," says Jerome. "I've seen this before. The numbers go up, and then they go down. And then up again."

"Let's just hope they can go up enough to save us," Suki says. "William and I need this place."

"They always have," he says.

⁓

I know what an octopus should do at a time like this.

I start recruiting families whenever I'm in the park. All it takes is for me to see a toddler for me to head right over to the mom or dad and start talking up the wonders of a cooperative daycare. Sometimes, talking to them, I feel as though we really might save this daycare after all.

Two new families come and look and decide they want to join at the next meeting. Also, one of the neighbors—a man who had come to help with the tire—says their daughter just turned two and they'd like to join as well.

I set up a meeting date and invite the new people to come talk to us so we can officially accept them. Two new three-year-olds and a two-year-old! And *six* parents who can do turns! What could be better? It's like a bonanza, manna from heaven.

The children and I do a conga line around the yard, and then I bring out the kazoos and the bongos and we make as much noise as we possibly can.

"Yay, *daycare!*" I say.

And they cheer right back, "YAY! DAYCARE!" much, much louder than I ever could, because they're so much better than I am at enthusiasm.

⁓

And then on the day we're going to have the meeting to accept the new families, Emily arrives at noon to do her turn. Her face is white. I know this look.

I say, "No, no, no. Please. Do *not*."

"Do not what?"

"Whatever you're going to say, rethink it. Go back outside and come in again, and don't say whatever made your face look like that. If things don't go well at this daycare meeting tonight, I have promised myself a nervous breakdown, and I can't risk having it early with kids around."

"I think I have to tell you."

"Just tell me this. Are you and Michael leaving daycare?"

"No."

"Okay, then. You may tell me any other horrible thing."

"There's a **FOR SALE** sign in the front yard."

"What!"

Everybody goes out and looks at it, and by everybody, I mean Mandy, Emily, the children, and me.

And sure enough: there is a real estate company's **FOR SALE** sign right there in the yard. With no warning.

It's too much.

"Well, we don't know for sure this means we're going to have to move," I say. "Maybe the person who buys the building will want the daycare to stay. Right? I mean, we pay rent—"

"Mostly we do," says Emily.

"Well, we'll try harder," I say. "And we're good tenants. We spruced the place up. And I'm also a good upstairs tenant, and maybe I can stay, too. I haven't thrown any couches since that very first one."

For the rest of the day, every single person who comes to daycare goes into a funk. We can barely function through snack and lunch.

That evening I hear myself trying to explain to the three families at the daycare meeting that we'll probably still have a daycare. I mean, of course we will. We're *established*.

But they're not going for it. The neighbor lady says she wants stability for her two-year-old. She is not starting her sweet daughter at a place and then having to move elsewhere. "I liked it because you were on my street," she says.

One of the moms I'd met in the park says to me, "This *is* a nice space, but I already have enough chaos in my life. Call me when you know where you're going to land."

And the father in the third family shrugs and says, "Uh, I don't know. I heard you had some families leave, so what was that about?"

After the families have all leaked away, gone back to their regular lives, Joyous looks around and says, "So they're just going to leave us here to *die?*"

"Gallows humor," says Suki disapprovingly when we all collapse on the floor, laughing so hard we can't breathe. "Very healing, I suppose. But the next person who leaves this daycare is going to have a lot to answer for. I've had enough."

CHAPTER TWENTY-NINE

We press on.

One rainy day, I'm doing my favorite thing, which is lying on the mattress in a pile of the five children who are left, all of whom are squirming and breathing like puppies, and I'm reading *Mike Mulligan and His Steam Shovel* to them, when I hear loud voices coming from the kitchen.

Mandy and Jerome are both in there, fixing lunch, which is chicken nuggets and macaroni and carrots. This should not be a problem. It shouldn't even take two people to fix it, if you want to know the truth— but when Jerome went in to do it himself, she followed him, with that helpful look on her face that she gets.

And now he's yelling at her.

I turn up the volume on my voice for Mike Mulligan, but it doesn't help.

I hear Jerome say, "You are the antithesis of what a cooperative daycare is all about!" The words *capitalist* and *corporate stooge* may also have been shouted, but I'm concentrating so hard on reading louder and louder that I could have that part wrong.

Then he comes into the living room, where we are, and he pulls down the entire alphabet from the wall. The *LMNOP* section gives him trouble because the tape sticks too well, and he swears at those five letters like they've been put up there personally by Richard Nixon's Watergate burglars.

I start reading louder.

Mandy comes in and stands there staring at him with her hands balled into fists, and then she bursts into tears and calls him a monster, and *then* she unearths Alice from the pile of children, and she stomps out the front door. Alice looks back at us over Mandy's shoulder, and yells, "NO! MIMI MOMMY! MIMI MOMMY! I don't want to go!" I start to squeeze out from underneath the other four children, all of whom also have now started to cry, to go after them, but I think better of it when the wails from the mattress are too pitiful. Also, Jerome is still stomping around the room.

So I stay put. I just keep reading the story, keeping one eye on him, and when I finish and they ask me to read it again, I do just that.

Later, I call Mandy to offer my sympathy, and she says she's thinking she'll stay home with Alice for a while. She's been thinking of taking her to visit her parents for a week since Jamie is so busy, so this seems like a good time.

"You are *not* taking her out of daycare," I say.

"No," she says. "Just a time-out."

Four kids now.

I talk to Jamie on the phone one day while he's on his lunch break. "What's going on?" I ask him, and he says he's not really sure. Alice is hanging out with Mandy and her mom, and the other day they got manicures. Denise is reading her stories from the Easy Reader series and asking her how to spell *cat* and *dog*.

"Please," I say. "I miss her so much. Please make sure she comes back."

"Okay," he says.

"Promise?" I say, and he says, "Yeah, sure, whatever I can do."

A few days later, Jerome posts a note on the board saying he's accepted a job in Washington, DC, at a think tank, and he and Maya and Gabriela will be leaving at the end of the week. He requests that we do not assist his family in leaving. No party is necessary. He will not subject himself or his family to our "tears and sentimental offerings."

 ⌒୨

And then there are three.

I put in another application at Hall-Benedict, for the weekend shift. They give me a look like, *How many times do we have to give you the news that you are not fit to work in our pharmacy, and also, by the way, please don't come in here anymore even to buy Tylenol and lipstick.*

Okay, so they don't look at me like that at all. They hand my application to the pharmacist, who actually smiles at me. But I think it's a pitying smile. He says there are no openings.

 ⌒୨

Later, because I am out of my mind, I tell Eleanor about the daycare troubles, and it's hard not to cry.

"Oh, sweetie," she says, "this daycare just seems like something that is *not* working out. Baby, I told Ira about your situation, and he said that from a business standpoint, it absolutely looks like your daycare is going to close, and I hate to say it, but maybe you'd better make some other plans."

"Thanks," I say in a low voice.

"Maybe your psychic has some ideas."

"You must really be worried about me if you're suggesting I call my psychic," I say.

"Yeah, I'm terrified for you. But, if all else fails, you could . . . come here? Maybe? We really *can* convert the basement office into a bedroom for you. And I bet you could come and work with me at the insurance company."

When I don't answer, she says, "Well, I just don't see what you're going to do, then."

I close my eyes. "What I'm going to do is just limp along with this daycare and keep trying to recruit new families. And maybe whoever buys the building will be amenable to having a daycare on the first floor, and it'll all rise again."

"Maybe," she says.

When I call La Starla, she tells me with a sigh that the guides are not getting themselves into a lather over the daycare troubles, and neither is she. "If you're going to freak out over every little apparent setback in your life, you're not going to enjoy life as much as you could be," she says and actually laughs. "How about you just try to remember that it's all going to work out, and don't sweat the details. Just sit back and be curious, why don't you?"

People come by to look at the building. I do not think anybody has put down a deposit or even come back to look a second time.

We limp onward, even though we're now three families down—with only three children, four on the days that Alice comes—and I have to admit it feels hollow there. I still love sitting on the floor stacking blocks or singing, or holding children in the rocking chair while we wait for sleep to overtake us all at naptime, but to tell you the truth, I miss the chaos of having the whole group of children there.

I loved how we were always on the verge of having things slide into complete anarchy and having to come up with a way of saving things at the last second, reasoning with toddlers. Who would have ever thought that would be something I would love?

Also, the weather is getting colder, and the reading mattress doesn't feel as warm as it once did. Soon, I think, it's not going to be enough to be covered with children, I'm going to need to bring over some blankets as well.

Also, the paychecks, which are based on enrollment, are getting slim.

I double my efforts to recruit. I decide I'll begin with the fact that there's a **FOR SALE** sign in the yard. I'll explain that yes, the building is for sale, but no one has shown the slightest interest in buying it, and besides that, we are going to have daycare *no matter what*. Even if we have to move, we'll find another place. We've been going since the 1970s—and we are not stopping now. No way.

Then one day in early October, I'm in the park after daycare, and I look over and see a young woman talking to a very little boy standing on the top of the sliding board waving his arms in a very dangerous, high-flying kind of way. Another potential daycare client!

She's saying, "Marcus. Go down the slide *now*. Don't just stand there defying gravity. Gravity always wins, and you're making my friend Judith nervous."

This Marcus gets a big grin on his face and then performs an exciting little one-foot dance on the top of the slide and then zooms down to the bottom, where he takes a bow and says, "Ta-*dah*!" This is precisely the kind of boy we need for daycare. I make my way over to his mother—I get my best potential families from the park—and then I'm startled to see that her friend Judith is none other than my own Judith. I feel a sudden pang, seeing her there. I haven't been to see her since I broke up with Ren.

She's sitting on the bench, holding a cane. She's not in a wheelchair anymore. She's looking at the boy with her hand shielding her eyes from the sun, and she's smiling. Judith is smiling! Before I can even think, I call out to her.

She turns and looks in my direction and holds out her arms toward me.

"It's you!" she says. "Weezy!"

She remembers me. Or at least the Weezy version of me. I go over and lean down, and she hugs me. She smells like baby powder and peppermint, and I see that she's chewing gum. She is heavier now, more substantial, and I can see a different light in her eyes, like she's taking in more information. Her hair is longer, and she has it tied back in a bun, which makes her face look younger and more vulnerable. She tells her friend that I was her very favorite of the *optimisms*, and the friend and I smile at each other. I can see that we both love the way she talks.

"You were my favorite optimism, too," I say. "How are you?"

"I am splendid on most days," Judith says. "Some days delirious."

I can't help but smile at her. The friend is lots younger, with dark hair parted in the middle, and she's wearing a long hippie skirt and a peasant blouse. She tells me that her name is Gloria, and that she's a neighbor of Judith's. Then she says, "And you're . . . Weezy?"

"Actually I'm Mimi," I say, and I turn to Judith. "How are the girls?"

"They fight," she says, shrugging. "Nobody ever wants to do the obligatories. Sit down. Can you stay?"

I sit down next to her and she takes my hand.

"You made burritos," she says. "Gloria, she made me food! For so long she made me food. My girls, though, they say they can cook, and they do, but no burritos. Not like Weezy burritos. Chicken curry. Cookies."

For a moment I feel my heart rustling around in my chest. This is Judith in her sweetness, with that look in her eyes that I sometimes would see a glimpse of. I feel so suddenly fond of her that I squeeze her hand.

"Look at you now. You're doing so much better! You look wonderful! Are you feeling well?"

She leans forward. "I gave my brain a name," she says. "I call it Hortense. Isn't that spankingly perfect? Hortense."

She laughs and so do Gloria and I.

"It doesn't deserve to still be Judith," she says. "It acts up. I told it that when it can behave and say good words on time, it can be Judith again."

"Hortense is a nice name, though," I say, wrinkling my nose.

"No," she says and laughs. "It isn't. It doesn't deserve a nice name yet. Someday. We're working on it. Maybe Hortense today and then Florida Crimson by next week, and we'll work back to Judith."

"Florida Crimson," I say. "My, my."

"Not yet," says Judith and puts her finger up to her mouth. "We have to earn it."

Marcus has been going up and down the slide over and over again, and Gloria is keeping an eye on him, biting her lip. So I ask her how old he is, and when she says he's three, I ask whether or not she'd like to come visit our daycare. I tell her all about the philosophy, and every now and then Judith chimes in with a wreath of smiles and she bangs her cane on the ground in front of her. I can't tell if she's completely following the conversation, but she looks like she might be. At one point she says, "Babies and toddlers!" in a loud voice. "I've gone there. With Ren sometimes. On a walk. You have a tire."

"We do," I say. I explain to Gloria about the industrial-size tire.

Gloria says she's a part-time typist for a doctor's office, working from home, but she can only work when Marcus is napping and after he goes to bed at night, and often that's not enough time. She could use part-time daycare, and he needs friends.

"You'll love us," I say. "We're very low-key. And we're fun."

She says she'll come and take a look at the daycare. "It sounds perfect," she says.

"Our building is for sale," I say, "but no one has come to look at it. And even if it sells, we've agreed to continue the daycare in a new location."

"I love when my friends are going lightly," Judith says.

Later, when I get up to leave, she says, "You're not really Weezy, are you? I do know who you are. You're the woman Ren loves."

"Well, not anymore," I say, and I feel embarrassed, in case Gloria will think I was a woman who broke them up. "We're finished."

"Are you?" she says. "I finished with him first." She laughs and leans in like she's telling me a big secret. "How many times can someone finish with a man? Twenty hundred? A million thousand? But you—you still have love for him. I see it."

"No, I really don't," I say. "He doesn't love me. It's you he loves."

"HA!" she says loudly. "Hortense says that is not even a probability! I am finished with that man."

I don't know what to say, and apparently Gloria doesn't either, because we both exchange embarrassed looks.

"Come by and check out the daycare," I tell her. "I'm there every day until three."

❦

"I have to tell you something," Mandy says to me the following Tuesday. After that one week when she took off after the Jerome incident, she's been coming again.

"Is it good or bad? Because I'm kind of all full up with bad news lately," I say. I'm sitting on the floor of the nap room, repairing one of the cots, which broke when William and Davy jumped on it.

"Well, it's good news for Alice and for Jamie, and so that means it's good news for anybody who loves them, but whether or not *you* see it as good news—" She sees my face, which is no doubt crumpling. Or maybe she's reacting to the fact that I have my hands over my ears and I'm chanting, *"Lalalalalala!"*

"Stop! Stop!" she says. I put my hands down. "Aw, Mimi, listen to me. The daycare is falling apart. And it's not going to keep going, so my mother made some calls."

I put my head back into my hands.

She talks fast. "Alice was accepted into the Friends of the Park Nursery School in West Hartford. She was on the waiting list, and yesterday they called my mother to say they have an opening."

I bring my hands down. "Has Jamie agreed to this?"

"Well, he will."

"But he hasn't yet."

"Not technically. We're all going to dinner tomorrow night at my parents' house, and my mom is going to persuade him. My dad thinks he'll agree because most days now, he's already working in West Hartford, and so my dad is going to point out to him that it makes sense for him to give up his apartment in New Haven and save a whole bunch of money by living with my parents, and Alice could go to nursery school, which would really be better for her. I mean, no offense to you or anything, but this daycare is best for kids who are two years old, not four. No offense."

"I beg to differ. I think she's having a delightful year here, and she's learning a lot."

Mandy looks at me with a little smile on her face, a smile I'd like to wipe right off. "Well, but the place isn't going to last, Mimi. It's *for sale*. And people are leaving. Jamie has to think of what's best for Alice. That's what we're going to explain to him."

"I know that," I say, and I can't imagine why I'm arguing with her. She has the institution of family, God, the American Way, and phonics behind her. I just have this tattered little daycare and my belief in psychics and magical thinking to back me up. But I go on anyway: "My main belief is that what Alice needs is a nice, stable, loving place to spend the day a lot more than she needs to read right now. What Alice gets here is worth *a lot*."

"I know, but the other part of this news is that I've been hired there part-time, so I can supervise her transition, if that's what you're worried about."

I'm not sure what expressions must be flitting across my face, but whatever they are, they must not look dangerous, because she comes closer and actually pats me on the arm.

"Aw, you are just the sweetest person," she says. "But really, if Jamie says okay, we can start her in her new class next Monday, so maybe we can have a little good-bye party for her at the end of the week."

I tell you, she's a woman who makes me understand violence.

CHAPTER THIRTY

That night I call Jamie's apartment.

"I need to see you," I say. "Can you meet me?"

"Mimi! So great to hear from you. How about McDonald's?" he says. "I'm in need of a burger."

"Sure," I say. I'm a little out of breath. "And could you—could you not mention to Mandy that you're coming to see me?"

"*Ohhhhkaaaaaay,*" he says. "Really. Um, is there something horrible happening, or is this you trying to get me to certify that you're over that blowhard?"

"I didn't know getting your certification was even a possibility," I say.

"It's always a possibility," he says. "I'll pick you up in fifteen minutes."

⌒

I'm sitting on the porch when he drives up in his VW Rabbit, and when I get into his car, he pretends to peer at me and then he says, "Hard to tell in this lighting whether you're over him or not."

"I don't trust your assessments anyway," I say. "They've always been off, and you know it. And by the way, what happened to your lovely tresses?"

"Corporate haircut," he says, and pats his hair self-consciously. He starts the car and pulls out from the curb. "Also these are corporate bags you see under my eyes." He glances over at me. "Not that I'm not delighted to see you, but you have me scared. What's up?"

"You should be scared. You're about to be ambushed, my friend."

"Ambushed?" He looks amused, like this might be a word I just throw around casually.

"Yep. I was talking to Mandy today, and she told me that she and her parents are going to sit you down tomorrow night at a family meeting, and they're going to tell you the news that they've enrolled Alice in a nursery school in West Hartford. Enrolled her, Jamie. To start next week! All without your permission! And *then* they're going to suggest—"

His face has gone pale. "Wait, they're *what*? She's starting *when*?"

"Next week, according to Mandy. They say that Alice needs more *structure* than our daycare provides, and since you're mostly working in West Hartford now anyway, they're also going to propose that you move back in with them to save money."

He's frowning. "I think I've made it clear I'm not living with them again."

"Yeah, well, they're going to try to talk you into it. I don't know why or how they think they can just control your life this way, going behind your back, but this is what Mandy says is going to happen. Which, by the way, just so you know, Mandy is *not* a fan of our daycare, *and* she and her mom have decided that the time has come for them to get Alice out of there. So they got her into some program, and even though September has come and gone . . . the director said Alice could start anyway . . ."

"Wait. I'm not getting this."

"Well, then I'm glad I'm telling you now, so you won't be totally blindsided. They've really overstepped this time, I'm telling you. Sending Mandy here to live with you was one thing, but *now*—taking Alice away to a whole different school when she's perfectly happy here, and also I've done everything I can to make Mandy feel welcome, and she's not the easiest person to do turns with, I want you to know, and then all along she's working behind the scenes, convincing her mom that the daycare isn't even *right* for Alice? Also, I guess you know she ran off Jerome, almost single-handedly." I am talking way too fast. It occurs to me that I am out of control, and probably coming off just as guilty of overstepping boundaries as his in-laws are.

"Mimi," he says, "maybe when we get to the McDonald's, I would like to recommend that you order a Sprite. I think if you have even one drop of caffeine, you might spontaneously combust."

Overstepping or not, I can't seem to stop myself. "Well, *somebody* needs to combust!" I say. "I trust that this calm exterior you're putting on is just hiding your outrage."

"I'm thinking," he says. He steers the car into the McDonald's drive-through. "What are you having? The usual?"

"Yeah."

"Don't you just love saying 'the usual,' like we do this all the time? We've done it twice, and yet I think of it as a thing we do."

"Big Mac, lots of secret sauce, fries, and twelve ketchups," I say.

"I'll remember that order to my dying day. And what about the Sprite?"

"What the hell is this Sprite talk? I'm getting a chocolate shake."

"That's telling 'em," he says. We drive up to the ordering screen, and he talks to some staticky voice who finally manages to get the order correctly repeated back after three tries. I watch his face, which looks chiseled somehow, with his short hair. I loved his long hair. But now I think I love his short hair, too. I love his fingers resting on the steering wheel. I love his earlobes, his eyelashes. As he rolls the window up and drives forward, he says, "This is going to be interesting, seeing what we get."

"As long as there are plenty of sauce packets, I don't care."

At the pickup window, someone hands him two bags of food and our two milkshakes. He passes them over to me.

"So, what are you thinking?" I say.

"I'm thinking we need a new subject. How's your nondaycare life going?"

"What nondaycare life? I'm trying my best to save its life, which is a full-time job. People keep leaving for various reasons, and I guess you know that the building got put up for sale—so that big-ass FOR SALE sign in the yard is making it nearly impossible to recruit new families. I went to the park several times and talked up the daycare to people I met, and they all decided to join, and then dropped out when they saw we might have to move. They said they didn't need more chaos in their lives."

He chuckles. "Then they certainly might want to reconsider joining a parent co-op," he says.

"Huh. Aren't you the guy I remember saying that the daycare had taught you everything you know about parenting? What about all that appreciation, huh?"

"Mimi, the place was never calm, not even on one day of its life!"

"So what? It may not have been calm, but it was lively and interesting and loving and it was . . . family! It worked."

"Yeah, but—"

I eat a french fry and study him in the overhead light. "But *what*?"

"Organizations have cycles—I've learned this at school—and I hate to say it, but maybe this little social experiment has run its course, and it's time to move on. Cut our losses, admit that it was great, but it's over."

"What the *hell* are you talking about? People still need daycare! We don't have to quit just because the building is getting sold! We can talk to the landlord, Jamie. We can work with whoever buys it and see if the daycare can stay. We had that wonderful workday, and we all came together and fixed the place up . . . and then some people happened to get new jobs and moved away, and suddenly we're just throwing in the towel? People want to join!"

"People are leaving, Mimi," he says. "It's natural. Their lives change."

"And you're one of them, apparently!" I glare at him. "Also, you *said*—you promised that if I took the job as octopus, you wouldn't take Alice out. And now look at you! You're actually considering it, aren't you? You're going to do what your in-laws want you to do." I lean over and look into his eyes, like I can read the answer there. "Oh my God. You are! You believe the lie that daycare is bad and that Alice needs a nursery school, don't you?"

"Look. It's not a question of what I believe. The fact is, I can't save the daycare right now. I'm overwhelmed. I have this capstone project to figure out. And it's not going all that well."

"Why? What's happening with it?"

"I'll tell you if you'll try to bring the temperature of this discussion down about four hundred degrees."

"Okay, look at me. I'm taking deep breaths." I make a big show of breathing slowly. "So tell me. I'm sorry I didn't ask sooner. And—well, I'm sorry for the way I'm acting, too."

"That's okay. I get it." He smiles at me. "This particular project I'm trying to get going is Otto's idea, you know. Not mine, and I'm afraid it's not relevant to anything in life that any sentient being would care about. So I'm experiencing a bit of abject, crushing boredom."

"You can't change it?"

"The fact is, Otto is a friend of my advisor, and so it's likelier that it'll get approved if I do this project."

"Well, what the hell is it that you have to do?"

"I'm talking to business owners about ways to incentivize older workers to mentor younger workers and then to measure the effects on company-wide morale and decide whether the incentives justify the effort required, according to algorithms and self-reported job satisfaction statistics."

"That sounds . . . horrifying."

"So this is why I can't right now figure out how to save our daycare, *and* I also have to admit that I'm not really seeing why Alice going to nursery school is the tragedy you seem to think it is. I mean, it's just a school, right? They're not going to imprison her in the back room and have her making knockoff Gucci bags. They'll teach her to share and sing little songs and play nicely with others, right?"

I stare at him. "Wait. Are you turning out to be a . . . weenie?"

"Did you just call me a weenie?"

"I just *asked* if you are. But if you let them put Alice in that nursery school they already enrolled her in without asking you, then yes. You're definitely a weenie."

"I'm not a weenie, you're a weenie!"

I reach over with both hands and start slapping at him. A slap fight, like we're four years old.

"Oh yeah?" he says. "Are you *coming* for me, weenie?" He shoves aside his hamburger and his fries and his milkshake, practically throws them on the floor, and then he undoes his seat belt and leans over to my side of the car, knocking into the gearshift, and instead of slap-fighting me as I expected, he takes me in his arms and puts his mouth on mine and kisses me until I can't breathe, and oh God, I am so overcome with all the longing for him again. I kiss him back, and we kiss for such a long time, and then he lets me go, and we look into each other's eyes.

"There," he says softly. "I miss you something crazy, and my mind is all tangled up in this fucking capstone project, and I can't do what you want me to do, which is be outraged."

"But why aren't you just furious at the way your in-laws are running your life? This is your life, Jamie! Yours and Alice's."

"Because—I don't know how to tell you this—but this is the price I'm willing to pay for Alice having a family. Which is not to say that they aren't *way* overstepping, and trust me, we *are* going to have to have a conversation about that, and I'm absolutely not going to live in their house again, but nursery school? That's fine with me. I can't do daycare turns anyway."

"But—why even stay in that stupid program you hate? Why not just live in New Haven, build furniture for a living, and let Alice stay where she is? You think they're going to abandon Alice as a family member if you live your own life?"

"Maybe I have to prove to myself that I can stick to something."

"How about you could stick to building custom furniture?" I say. "I've heard rumors from your heart that that's what you really want to do."

"Well, maybe not so much anymore," he says. "I can always do that on the side, after I get my degree."

I am so afraid that I'm going to cry that for a moment, I don't trust myself to speak. But then I say, "What about me? Alice loves me. She calls me Mimi Mommy. We have a relationship."

"I'll bring her down to see you," he says. "I promise." Then he says, "Say, are you going to eat those fries? I seem to have thrown mine on the floor."

"Here. Take them. I'm really, really mad at you."

"Too mad to eat your own fries, but not mad enough to keep me from eating them?"

"That is exactly the level of mad I am. I can just see what's going to happen in your life. You'll get your Yale degree and go to work in Otto's company and live in West Hartford, and you'll eat Sunday dinner over there every week, and Alice will wear little sundresses and white patent leather shoes and go to birthday parties with rich little girls. Maybe your mother-in-law and Mandy and Alice can all get matching dresses together and then they go out for ladies' tea and have their hair done, and then . . ."

He's laughing. "Stop, stop, stop! Or I'm going to have to kiss you again." Then he's quiet. "Listen, I know you think I'm copping out, but I really do like learning this business stuff. I'm actually freakishly good at it somehow, despite all odds. And if Alice has tea with her grandmother . . . isn't that kind of a good thing?"

"All right, dude. Now I have to tell you the worst thing. I heard Mandy tell Alice the other day that girls can't be dinosaurs. Can you believe it's 1982, and girls are hearing that they can't be dinosaurs?"

He looks at me and raises his eyebrows. "*That's* the worst thing? Well, I'll certainly fix *that* as soon as I get home," he says. "I'll wake everybody up and explain that girls *can* be dinosaurs. I promise."

I stare at him so long that I practically bore a hole into his skull with the force of my eyes. "You're making fun of me, but you and I both know that that kind of thinking is exactly what our daycare does *not* do to kids! That kind of limited thinking is how Mandy sees the world. She thinks in terms of girl animals and boy animals. Girls probably have to be bunny rabbits and kittens."

"Jesus, Mimi. I'll make sure Alice knows she can be a dinosaur. I promise."

"Please. Think this over. Alice is happy here. Stay here. Send Mandy home. Let me help you. We had a great thing going. I love Alice. And we can make the daycare work. I promise."

"Don't you get it? I can't! I have to do this capstone project."

"God, if I hear the word *capstone* again in my life, I'm going to scream and run into traffic! Dude! Do a freaking capstone on something *you* care about down here, how would that be? A woodworking capstone? Or a daycare capstone?"

Now he really laughs. "I don't think *capstone* means what you think it means."

"You can find a life that has stuff you actually *like* doing. You can stop letting other people dictate your life for you, even if they are Lauren's sainted parents."

"They're my *family*! They're Alice's family!" he says. "*You* don't really have a family, so you don't know what it's like. You make sacrifices for family. That's what people do."

Is that true, that I don't have a family so I don't know how to sacrifice? Is that what all this is about, why I'm so desperate right now?

What I have, I realize suddenly, is myself. Am I really all alone?

I draw myself up just so I won't start crying. "If family is a bunch of people who get to control you and tell you how to make a living and how to raise your kid and when to eat and when to sleep, then I'm *glad*

I don't have one. I always thought family was supposed to be the people who love you and want the best for *you* because it's what *you* want. If you ask me, by that definition, family is this daycare."

"Was," he says. "It's going away. Face it."

"It's not gone yet. But you know what is gone?"

"What?"

"Us. Your feelings. I now see it. There really never was going to be anything between us, was there?" I say.

He lets out his breath. "Oh my God. What are you talking about?"

"You told me one time that you were *kinda* in love with me, but clearly that didn't turn out to be anywhere near true. You wouldn't even make love when we had the chance . . . Who doesn't do that with somebody he's *kinda* in love with?" I put my face in my hands. "God, this is so humiliating. I can't believe I'm saying all this to you. Please take me home."

"Mimi, Mimi, you were just out of a long relationship. You were vulnerable as hell. It was too—too soon. And now, life is pulling us in a million different directions, but I call you whenever I get a moment. I love talking to you. Alice loves you."

"But do *you* love me?" I put my hands down and look at him.

The air goes out of the car, and he looks at me without saying anything, his eyes blank. He looks down at his hands, starts to say something, and then stops.

Not to put too fine a point on it, but my heart right then takes the first step toward breaking itself into pieces.

"Uh-huh. Okay," I say. "Drive, dude."

"I don't *not* love you. I told you one time that I was terrified. I'm still terrified."

"Please," I say. "Don't even. Start the car."

"You want to know the truth?" he says, but he turns the key in the ignition. "I'm trying to figure out how to give my daughter a future."

"You're grieving your wife, and so you're clinging to her family," I say to him. "You said you were ready, but you're not ready, and you might never be ready. Or maybe I'm just not the right one for you. I don't have a family to give you, as you so kindly pointed out. I don't have what you need. Capstone recommendations! A company you can take over! Lots of money!"

"Mimi, for heaven's sake, stop this. I beg of you. That's not it."

"Don't worry, I'm stopped. I've completely stopped."

After a while, he says, "Look, thank you for telling me about the nursery school thing. I-I don't know what I'm going to do about that. I'll think about everything you said. I will."

We ride in silence the rest of the way. He's chewing on his fingernail while he drives. I'm sodden, sitting there. A lump.

When we get to my house, I walk up the front walk without even once looking back at him.

CHAPTER
THIRTY-ONE

On Friday, which is Alice's last day at daycare, Mandy brings in a little brown cake, the kind made with absolutely no sugar or flour. I honestly cannot tell what it's made of—probably broccoli stems and buckwheat groats, from the taste of it. I'm not even sure what a groat is, but I have no doubt some must have gone into this so-called cake.

Mandy makes a speech in her teachery singsong voice. "Now, *children*, Alice won't be coming here anymore, but she will always think of you as her very *first friends*. Won't you, Alice, honey? And maybe someday she can come and visit again and tell you all about her *new school*!"

Davy wants to know if she'll have a tire at her new school, and Mandy frowns and says she doesn't think so. "But she'll have *bulletin boards*!" she says.

From the silence, I can tell that the children agree with me that it's not a good tradeoff.

Alice has that stunned look on her face that I remember from when I first met her, and she comes over and sits on my lap, and I call her Alice Dumpling and that makes her smile, mostly because Mandy never calls her that. And then she laughs and calls *me* Mimi Mommy at least fourteen times, kissing me on the cheek each time she says it, which might as well be swear words, from the look on Mandy's face, and then I touch her nose, and we also do twenty butterfly kisses for good measure and also because I am now just showing off.

Jamie does not show up.

Mandy says he wanted to come, but his project went haywire, and he had a guy he absolutely needed to see before the end of the day, so he couldn't.

"I'm sure he would have come if he could," she says. "I told him it wasn't really necessary."

I've decided that the silver lining here is that I don't have to try to like her anymore.

By the time late October rolls around, the Realtor has shown the place thirteen whole times, and no one has made an offer, as far as I know. I am always being asked to vacate the premises so that one group or another can look my apartment over as well as the daycare, and often I take a book and go sit in the park, bundled up in sweaters and sweatpants and boots. Now that the weather is cold, I wear a knitted yellow cap with a ball on top that makes me look like a demented elf, and I wrap an orange scarf around my neck, both of those items courtesy of the thrift shop. I sit on a bench and try to read. I see people with children in the park now, but I know better than to go over and try to sign them up for daycare. I have a cold and a cough, as do the three kids who are still in daycare. It would be like Typhoid Mary trying to sign up more families.

On Halloween, which is unseasonably warm, I see Judith again in the park. I recognize the nurse who's with her, Ariceli, whom I've met before at the house. Ariceli is wearing a witch costume, and the two of them are walking together along the path to the river, Judith with only a cane to support her. When they stop and sit down on a bench, I hurry over.

"Hello! Hi!" I say. I feel overwhelmed, seeing her looking so well. "How are you?"

Judith turns and looks at me and smiles. "Ah! Weezy! Come and sit with me."

Ariceli has upsetting green fingernails and a pointy witch hat. "I know I look ridiculous. The agency likes us to make holidays feel festive," she says. "It wasn't my idea. They actually suggested our patients might like to have fun with costumes, but Miss Judith here wasn't having it." She smiles at Judith, who shrugs.

"I am not putting on a witch hat," she says. "For anyone."

"Good for you," I say. "And how are you?"

"I'm much better," she says. "The words. Sometimes they bless me better than before."

"She's doing amazingly well," says Ariceli. "Her recovery has taken such a turn. Hasn't it, Judith, dear? Don't you feel like you've come so far?"

"Well," says Judith. "Sometimes. Hortense is behaving."

"Ah yes," I say. "Your brain Hortense."

She looks at me and smiles. "You know, you gotta marry him," she says. "He's ridiculous sad."

"If we're talking about Ren, I don't think he's sad about me," I tell her.

"He is."

"I think he's sad about how his own life changed. And he's sad about what happened to you."

"That is bullshit," she says, and when I blink in surprise, she laughs and touches my arm. "He is a misser of you. You never had such a misser."

"I don't know," I say. "But let's change the subject. How are the girls?"

She's searching my face with her eyes.

"They are such mad girls. Everything is all complaining. You went to New York with him."

"No. We broke up."

"Unbreak!" she says. "I am sick of him!" And she laughs, and it sounds like a cackle.

Ariceli laughs a little bit. "No filters," she says. "The filters are the last to come back."

"He's in my hair! He's in my room! He's a big fat ghost!" She laughs again, and so I do, too.

"Please," she says. "Take him! Take the girls! Take everything!"

"This is certainly a conversation I didn't expect to be having," I say to Ariceli. "How often are you there now?"

"Three days a week."

"Well, aren't they *together*? She and her husband?"

"They seem to be," she says. "And the girls are nice to her. Everything seems kind of . . . loving? I don't know why she's trying to give her husband to you."

"Do they . . . oh, never mind."

She shrugs. "Every day is like this. She has her opinions. No filters anymore. Part of the healing of the brain, I guess."

"I should go," I say to Judith, and I stand up. "It's so good to see you."

She cups her hands around her mouth. "MARRY HIM!" she yells. And then as I walk away, I can still hear her voice ringing out after me: "WOULD YOU JUST MARRY HIM? MARRY MARRY, MARRY HIM!"

⌒ᵔ

That night I give out candy to about forty little children, so many that I end up staying on the porch next to the bowl of candy bars instead of running repeatedly downstairs to open the door. They come tumbling up onto the stairs, ghosts and witches and princesses and frogs and pirates and firemen, and at around 7:45, when the candy is gone and I'm about to go inside, a car I don't recognize pulls up to the curb, and out from the passenger seat comes a kid with brown, curly hair, and she's dressed in leotards, tights, and leg warmers, and as she comes closer, my heart starts beating faster, because it's Alice. Wearing a wig! And running up the walk, carrying her bag of candy and waving her arms and yelling, "Mimi Mommy! Look at me! I'm Jane Fonda!"

She leaps up the front steps and throws herself on me with such force that I'm pushed back into my chair. We're both laughing, and she's giving me wild smooches on both cheeks, back and forth. There's never been a person more excited to see me, and I hug her as tightly as I possibly can.

"Oh my goodness! You're Alice Dumpling! At first I thought Jane Fonda was coming to my house for candy!" I say.

"You did? You thought I was really Jane Fonda?"

"Of course. Look at you! You look exactly like her!"

"'Member when we did workouts?" says Alice. "Leg lifts, one, two, three. Look, I got some leg warmers finally!"

"Of course I remember," I say. "How could I forget? That's why we're such strong women!"

At that point, I notice that Jamie has gotten out of the car, and he's coming up the walk, looking down.

"Hi," he says, ducking his head and looking a little sheepish. "How are you?"

"I'm good," I say, but I'm afraid I'll start to cry if I look at him too long, so I look at Alice, who has jumped down from my lap and is now lying on my porch demonstrating her workout.

"She's Jane Fonda," says Jamie. "Did she tell you?"

"She did," I say. Then I can't think of anything else to say except "Did you get a new car?" I'm trying to puzzle out how I didn't recognize his car in time to prepare myself mentally for the fact that he and Alice were about to land in my life.

"Oh! No. This one belongs to my mother-in-law. Alice wanted to come trick-or-treating in the old neighborhood, and I needed to pick up a few things from the old place, the last boxes." He has his hands in his jacket pockets, and he smiles awkwardly.

"Oh. Right," I say. So he has moved.

Suddenly he plops down in the chair next to me and peers into the empty bowl. "Big night of trick-or-treaters?"

"Nope. I was hungry," I say. Which isn't even funny. I forget how I used to make him laugh, cannot think of a single light, amusing thing to say.

"Well," he says.

He can't think of anything to say either. We both watch Alice, who is jumping around and running through an approximate Jane Fonda routine, just like the ones she and I used to do. She keeps saying, "Look at me, Mimi Mommy! Look! Am I doing it right?"

"You are!"

"You come do it, too."

"I'm . . . sorry," he says. "For everything I said. And I'm sorry about that night—the Kmart night, that I didn't . . . you know . . . that I stopped us. I shouldn't have done that. I hurt your feelings."

"It's fine. How's the preschool?" I say to him in a low voice.

He shrugs and says softly, so she won't hear, "I think it's okay. She doesn't love, love, *love* it like daycare, but it is what it is."

"Come on! Let's be Jane Fondas together!"

"I can't, sweetheart. I'm not wearing the right clothes," I say. "And your project that shall not be named?" I ask him.

"Eh. Not wonderful. Professor Brain Trust is less than impressed. He says I have to work harder." He flexes his fingers, cracks his knuckles. "Sorry. I can't seem to sugarcoat things. Everything's just kind of rolling along, I guess, always at a slight deficit. Work, school, project. Then meals, bedtime, more work after everybody else is asleep. The basic grind of life, of trying to get everything done. Daycare still going?"

"Three kids still getting excellent care every single day."

Alice stops exercising and comes over and climbs up into my lap, panting and throwing her arms around my neck. "Why you can't be Jane Fonda with me?"

"I'm not dressed for it."

"Can we go upstairs and you could get dressed for it?"

"No sale yet?" he says.

"I guess not. Alice, did you get a lot of candy tonight?" I say.

"Lots and lots," she says. "I miss you. Can I spend the night with you? Pleasepleasepleaseplease?"

"No, sweetie," Jamie says quickly. "It's Sunday night, and we've got to get back. You've got nursery school in the morning."

"Awww," she says. "But I want to stay! I can go to daycare with Mimi!"

"Come on. We talked about this, how we could only see Mimi for a minute."

"But I want to stay! Mimi Mommy, why you don't come to my new school? You could work there!"

"Do you like it there? Is it fun?"

She nestles her face into my neck and starts to cry. "I miss you! I miss you so much!"

"It's okay, Ms. Dumpling," I say. "We'll see each other soon."

"But I *never* see you."

Jamie looks distraught, like he didn't expect this would happen. He cracks his knuckles. "Alice, do you want to get in the car and buckle your own seat belt, or do you want Daddy to do it for you?"

"Neither," she says from my neck.

"Okay, what if I see how fast you can get to the car? I'll count, and if you get there before I get to ten, I'll . . . ah . . . give you a piece of candy."

"No!"

"Okay, *two* pieces of candy."

"No!"

"Jamie," I say. "May I take this one?"

I take Alice's arms from around my neck, and I put my face up close to hers and whisper that we're going to do three butterfly kisses, and then we are going to march *together* to the car, and I am going to buckle her in, and then I am going to kiss her—let's see—thirty-five times on the left knee, and then her daddy will drive her home.

She looks at me and laughs. "Thirty-eleven times," she says.

"Okay, thirty-eleven."

And I scoop her up and we do the butterfly kisses and then we march together in lockstep to the car, and then she climbs in and I buckle everything up, and I make a big show of giving her thirty-six kisses on her left knee. She wants thirty-six on the right knee, too, but I'm too smart for that.

"Thirty-six more next time," I tell her.

And she says, "I love you, Mimi Mommy!" and stretches out her arms.

I tell you, it's almost more than I can bear. But I say, "I love you, too, Alice Dumpling!"

Jamie gives me one of those sad-faced/grateful looks he excels in, and my knees buckle just a little bit, but not enough for him to notice, and I turn and walk very fast back to my porch, before I have to see his red taillights getting smaller and smaller.

CHAPTER THIRTY-TWO

I have what Suki calls "a waif and stray" Thanksgiving, which is really the best kind. We, the unattached, gather in my kitchen—Suki and Joyous and their kids. Me. Arnie, from the junk shop, who told me his wife died last summer. Ariceli, Judith's nurse, shows up; I saw her once again in the park and she told me she would be alone. Emily and Michael stop by for pie—of which we have many.

I cook a turkey that has enough meat on it for everybody to take home practically a full turkey dinner for the next day. We play music. I play "Alice's Restaurant" by Arlo Guthrie because it's the best Thanksgiving story I know.

We dance and laugh and eat, and afterward we all walk Arnie back to his house. He's old and sad, even though we made him laugh for a while. I feel good about that.

The next day, Betty Ann Grabowski, *the* hotshot Realtor in town, shows up at the daycare's front door and tells me that the property is officially sold. "I tell you, in this market, I never expected it to go this fast. It's something of a *tragic miracle* when this happens. That's what I like to call it. What this business has taught me—"

"I knew it would sell," I say wearily, leaning against the doorjamb. "Just tell me. Any chance I can meet with the new owners and negotiate a lease?"

"The new owners don't want the daycare here, or you, so you'll have to have that tire removed." She wrinkles her nose in distaste. "Although why anyone ever wanted it there in the first place is a mystery to me. Such an eyesore. What were people *thinking*?"

"Children like it," I say.

"Yeah, well, children don't buy property," she says, and she turns and walks down the steps.

I say, "Wait. Do I need to move out, too?"

"Of course you do," she says over her shoulder. "Haven't you heard anything I've said?"

I shut the door a little harder than necessary, even before she's made it down the steps, nearly tripping on that rickety bottom step in her high heels. And then I stand there and lean against the door, taking deep breaths. Lily is chasing William with a hairbrush, threatening to give him a ponytail. Luckily they're both laughing.

So it's official, then: the daycare has to move. Or close. And so do I.

Silly me. I guess I'd let myself believe my own story, that any new buyers would opt to keep the daycare, and me, right here. We'd save it. But nope.

I go into the kitchen and tell Suki, who's on the turn with me. She comes over and hugs me. She's a single mom and works full-time as a paralegal, except for her four-hour turn once a week, and I know she absolutely needs daycare. Her ex pays hardly any child support.

"So basically I have thirty days to find a place for William?"

"I believe that is correct. I'm so sorry."

"And you're losing your place to live."

"Yep."

We sit down on the rug and watch the children playing, and I think I see her eyes fill up at one point.

"Where are you going to go, do you think?" she says.

"I don't know. I still can't quite give up on this daycare somehow working out."

"Yeah, you and me both," she says. "But I think we might have to."

Nope, I think. I wish I had a concrete plan. Something will happen: How's that for a belief system?

Later I hear her on the phone, asking her mom if she might know of a babysitter she could hire to come to her house every day, and then she leans against the wall and talks very quietly into the phone, until I hear her say, "No, Mom! What are you *thinking*? I can't afford those prices!"

When she gets off the phone she says mournfully, "It's like we had this amazing dream, and now it's gone."

As people come to pick up kids that day, we tell them the news.

◦⃝

It's hard to be sad around children because they can't ever hold it in their minds that things really aren't okay. Whatever is wrong, they slip back into thinking that life is just grand. Today is no different. They hear us talking about the daycare closing, and yet I hear them in conversation about whether or not the daycare should get a hamster.

"I love hamsters," says Lily. "My friend Annie has one, and it lives in a cage, and she takes it out and plays with it all the time, and it has a little wheel, and that's what I want, too."

"I think we should get an elephant instead," says Davy.

"But it needs to go in a cage," says Lily. "An elephant is too big."

Davy thinks about this for about ten seconds. "Then we'll get a very small, teeny-tiny elephant," he says.

I am going to miss this so much.

◦⃝

That night I call Eleanor and tell her what's happened, and then I listen silently while she tells me that this is perfect timing. She found out they *are* hiring at her company; all I have to do is call her boss, Mr. Meadors, and arrange for a typing test when I arrive. I'll love the girls in the typing pool, she says. Eleanor loves everybody. And Ira is fine with me living in their basement, even though it means giving up his football-watching area.

"Thank you," I say, and I mean it. I write down Mr. Meador's phone number on the back of a cereal box, and then when I hang up, I stare at it for fifteen whole seconds before throwing it away.

✣

Later, I head out to return some of my furniture to the junk shops from which they came. I'm balancing the rolled-up living room rug and a box of cookbooks, which means I have to close the front door with my foot, when out of the corner of my eye, I see Parker sitting on my porch swing. I jump a mile in the air and drop three of the cookbooks on my foot. She's wearing a leopard-print coat and black boots that go up to her knees. Her hair is now fire-engine red and utterly straight.

"You scared the crap out of me," I say. I manage to put down the rest of the books I'm holding and hop on one foot over to the swing. "What are you doing here?" I work on flexing my toes, which, thank God, still work.

"I was just sitting here trying to get up the courage to ring your doorbell."

"It takes courage to ring my doorbell?" For the first time, I realize that she has Ren's eyes.

"It takes courage to say the things I came to say."

"Is your mom okay?"

"Yeah, she's fine. She's the one who sent me."

"Why would she send you? She knows you hate me."

"She wants me to invite you to a going-away party for my dad, because he's going back to New York, *and* she wants me to apologize to you for how badly I treated you."

"Well," I say. "Thank you for that. I mean, if you are indeed apologizing, which I didn't quite catch if you said that part, or if you just meant to."

"So will you come to the party? For God's sake, say you'll come, or my life will be a living hell."

"I don't see why in the world I would want to come."

"I told her that that's what you'd say, and she said I need to be convincing. For once in my life, she said, I have to plead my case."

"Tell her you tried. Also tell her I said hello."

"Could you just listen to my arguments? Please?"

"Okay," I say. "Because I like your mom—and this is the only reason—I will listen to you before I tell you no once and for all."

"So—what's this about?" She points to my cookbooks and rug. "Are you . . . moving out?"

"Yeah. The building got sold. And don't ask me where I'm going, because my life is all in flux right now. But maybe Portland."

"What's in Portland?"

"My friend from college and her pull-out couch."

"I'm sorry you have to move," she says, and I say that I may have to have coffee before I can listen to her telling me lies about her feelings, so she might as well come in and have some, too. When we get upstairs, I remind her of the day when she brought me here, and how disappointed she was when I said I was taking it. And how every single time I brought over food for her family she acted like I was some kind of troublesome, meddling person who had no right to be inflicting nutrition on anyone.

"Well? That's exactly how I felt." She shrugs. "I'm actually sorry. You probably saved us from months of eating SpaghettiOs and Twinkies."

"I wouldn't go that far, but all I wanted was to be part of your family. Which sounds ridiculous now. I don't know what I was thinking."

To my surprise, she puts down her cup of coffee and comes over and reaches out to hug me. I actually jump backward when she approaches and hold my hands out in front of me.

"Look," she says. "I was hideous, horrible, the worst person in the world, along with Jenna—but now I have a deal to offer. If you'll come to my father's party and get my mother off my back, I will drive you and all of this junk to wherever you want me to take it."

I eye her suspiciously. "Exactly how many trips are you willing to make?"

"As many as it takes," she says.

"Tell me one other thing. How is your mom really doing? Except for her obsession with me coming to your dad's party, would you say she's in her right mind again?"

"She's unbelievably in her right mind."

"Except for that one thing."

"Well, yeah."

CHAPTER
THIRTY-THREE

The party is dazzling, the kind of party rich people give. Surely I knew before this that Ren is actually rich—but somehow it never truly sank in.

Walking in, I feel gobsmacked by the full display of elegance. I've been living in the world of daycare parties for a while—potluckish things with everybody bringing some version of tofu sticks and cut-up veggies—and now I seem to have wandered into a party with twinkling lights strung up everywhere and a jazz quartet playing softly in the corner, as well as young people in uniforms gliding about holding trays with shrimp puffs and stuffed mushrooms and elegant-looking red drinks in martini glasses.

I'm a bit late—I lost my keys and spent too much time looking for them—so when I come in, everything is in full swing. People turn to look at me, and Ren strides across the room with both arms outstretched and a big smile on his face. I swallow hard. All around are his pretentious friends from New York, guys with longish scruffy hair who dress like they're auditioning for the role of "hip, young playwright," wearing black turtlenecks and pressed jeans, and they're surrounded by women who have on sparkly tops and black linen pants and boots. These are people I met before when I would accompany Ren to their ghastly opening nights. It seems like a million years ago.

I remember all too well how it felt to sit next to them in smoky jazz clubs late at night, drowsily listening to them talk. No one ever paid me the slightest bit of attention. I'm sure they thought Ren and I weren't going to last.

And, hey, they were right; we didn't.

And now here we are, all together. Ren kisses me on both cheeks. He smells fantastic, like some kind of spicy aftershave I don't remember him wearing before, and his eyes are bright. He whispers, "You look beautiful. Thank you so much for coming. I can't tell you how glad I am to see you." He beckons some uniformed young person over, who hands me a red drink from his tray.

"This looks incredible," I say to him.

"This?"

"This—all of it. The whole party thing you've got going on. It's . . . so . . . celebratory."

"Because I'm celebrating. My ex is now well enough to be kicking me out. She's quite done with me." He's smiling so hard his eyes have become little slits.

"Well," I say, "I don't quite know how to respond to that."

"Say 'Congratulations.' Say 'Job well done, Ren Yardley.' I don't know. Say whatever you please."

We clink our glasses. He's looking at me like he's evaluating me. He reaches over and pushes a strand of hair out of my eyes. "You look nice."

I thank him. I'm suddenly grateful that I didn't wear jeans and a sweater to this wingding. Instead, I wore some actual adult-lady slacks, camel-colored, and a black turtleneck sweater. Not quite up to the level of the sequined ladies, but at least I have on a silver necklace and some hoop earrings.

"Parker may have forgotten to mention that there would be a dress code requiring sparkles," I tell him.

"You look lovelier than anyone here," he says into my ear. "You bring your own sparkles." He leans closer to me again, about to say something, when Parker glides over on her six-inch platform shoes and kisses me on both cheeks. Even Jenna hurries over and tells me I look beautiful. Her eyes, which are normally cold, look almost liquid. She shows me her left hand, where a diamond rests on her ring finger. "Jesse and I are getting married next year sometime," she says. "And I've moved back to DC."

I tell her congratulations, and she hugs me again, as if we're old friends. "Come and see Mom. She's been waiting for you." She starts to drag me away, and Ren gives me a two-finger salute. "Your fan awaits you," he says, and then I can see him change his mind. "Jenna, I just want to tell Mimi one thing first," he says, and he leans into me, whispering in my ear, "I have some news I want to tell you. So come back. I need to tell you before someone else does."

"Is it good or bad?"

"It's *wonderful* news!"

Judith is sitting on the couch, smiling at me, looking serene. She holds out her arms, and I sit down next to her. Her hair is twisted into an updo, and she's wearing a teal-colored, flowered kimono and black leggings. I notice that her nails are polished a deep purple color. She holds them up to show me and says that Parker did this for her.

"They look lovely," I say. "I feel purple is a color that's been overlooked for nails for some time now."

"Parker knows," she says. And then she leans over and puts her mouth up to my ear and says, "No one knows this, but this is my getting-rid-of-Ren party. Look at him pouncing around. You'd think he'd invented get-out-of-town parties. But I thought of it."

I laugh, thinking of Ren *pouncing*.

"And how are you doing?" I say. "You look happy."

"I can't stand hovering," she says. "Is that the right word—*hovering*?"

"It sounds like it might be the right word."

"Hortense is not really certain about words yet."

"She's still around?"

Judith gets a big smile on her face. "She comes around sometimes. To poke at me."

"You said you were going to call your brain Florida Crimson when it got totally better."

"Did I say that? Well, well. Now I just call it Judith. I yell at it sometimes. 'Judith, you can do this! Judith, pay attention.'" She takes my hand. "Parker is going to live with me, and we're staying here. Did you know that?"

"I didn't. That's wonderful, right? It's what you want?"

"Well," she says, "it's not even close to what I *wanted*. You know, my life the way it was. But I'm changing my mind about a lot of things. Things are softer now. Like puffs." Then she pats me. "Have another drink. Drink, drink, drink. You must drink for me and all the others. And then you'll be ready to start your life. Just don't do what I did and get in a car accident on the way to your new life. You might not get back to it."

Someone materializes just then and hands me another glass, and I take it gratefully. This red drink, whatever it is, is actually quite delicious. I catch a glimpse of Ren in the dining room, earnestly talking to a cluster of people I don't recognize. He looks over and waves and blows me a kiss.

Judith's caregiver comes over and helps guide her to the back room—perhaps a bathroom break—and a woman I remember seeing in New York comes over and says she's missed seeing Ren and me. She's so friendly. We talk about her children, and I tell her a little about the daycare, but I'm already a bit tipsy, so I get perhaps a little fervent when I'm describing the pleasures of the reading corner, and I feel myself getting a little embarrassed. She laughs and tells me that reading to children is the absolute best thing in the world.

"It is so good it could cure cancer, put people on the moon," I say.

"And definitely bring about world peace," she says.

"Well, as long as everybody can see the pictures," I say. "Otherwise, there's no peace anywhere."

I have another drink. So does she. A couple of the pretentious playwrights drift over, and one of them tells me that he remembers first meeting me at a teacher conference at Piedmont. His son told him after my departure that I was the wildest teacher there. Which this playwright thinks is the best compliment he's ever heard, and he wonders if I might elaborate on exactly how wild I got. Funny, he doesn't seem so pretentious anymore.

"Oh, the usual," I say. "Magic spells, incantations, love talk about obsessions."

He asks me to dance, and someone changes the music from classical piano to Michael Jackson's *Thriller* album, which was released less than a month ago and has already rocketed through the charts, and he and I start doing dances I remember from the sixties, which no one ever does anymore for some reason, even though they're great. We're out there doing the jerk, the mashed potato, the hully gully, and laughing at the names. I kick off my shoes, or maybe they kick me off.

The playwright is laughing and holds me around the waist. He dips me almost to the floor, and we're breathless when we both come up. He says to me, "I can't believe I'm dancing with the woman who broke Ren's heart." I laugh and push my hands against his chest. I think I like him, but is anyone else dancing? Jenna and Parker are jitterbugging with Ren—an even more ancient dance!—and Ren is watching me and smiling his crinkly smile. He holds up his glass as though he were toasting me. I laugh and hold up my glass, which has somehow found its way back into my hands and has miraculously become full again, and he comes over and takes me in his arms, and the other man melts away into the crowd, and Ren is not romantically taking me in his arms; no, we are dancing, that is what we are doing, moving our feet, and it's wonderful that Ren isn't trying to kiss me or press against me. We're just two people dancing in public. And I am smiling. I wonder briefly where my shoes might have gone, but who cares about that, and I realize that Ren is looking as good as he used to look when we were back at Piedmont, and I find it suddenly so funny thinking of how we used to make out—like teenagers—in closets and anywhere we could find. We were so stupid.

So I say that to him.

"Not stupid, we were in love," he says.

"In stupid love," I say. I look at him and remember the dream I had about him a while back. About sex.

A woman says from somewhere in the room: "Oh my God! Is this Michael Jackson looking *sexy* on the album cover? Wasn't he just a *little boy* the other day?"

"We were all just little boys the other day," says one of the playwrights.

And we all stop dancing to drink to that.

⌒

"And now for my big news," says Ren urgently after he's steered me into an alcove where we're alone. Knowing Ren, I had half expected he was going to try some of his unbuttoning shenanigans, but no, he just wanted to talk. "I wrote a play about us. And it's being produced in New York next spring."

"About *us*?"

"Well, I fictionalized it slightly. It's about a man who's in love and then his ex-wife has a stroke, and his new relationship breaks up when he can't extricate himself."

"*Ohhh*, Ren. It sounds so sad."

"Are you drunk? Of course it's sad. It's the most horrific thing that's ever happened to me."

"*Ohhh* no," I say. I feel my mouth turning downward. It doesn't seem quite connected to the rest of me.

"But here's the thing. He learns something. He learns to love. I think you'll be pleased at how it turns out."

"I don't think I want to see it," I say.

"It's dedicated to you."

⌒

I am drunk. Stunningly, amazingly drunk. Free as a bird, my brain is. Birdbrain: Is that where that came from? I want to ask someone. The red drinks are so sweet, and I have drunk too many of them, and now I get all sloppy when Judith, who has appeared once more, puts her hands on either side of my face and tells me she so appreciates all I've done for their family, and also when Jenna and Parker slow-dance me over to the coat closet and help me find my coat and boots at the end of the party. I've danced and laughed and listened to people's stories and given hugs and kisses, and I'm among the last to leave, and Ren takes me home, and I'm also not perfectly sober for that ride, but I stick my hand out the window into the freezing-cold air, and I'm happy.

"Letting go is the most wonderful feeling," I tell him. I remember that part. I also remember him telling me that that's exactly why he's going back to New York. He's letting go. He's letting go of Judith and his guilt over his marriage, he's letting go of running his daughters' lives, he's letting go of his dream of being the world's best playwright.

"The only thing I'm not letting go of is my love for you." He says that, too. "That, and the fact that I owe you about ten thousand apologies for all I did to you."

We've arrived at my apartment. I may have let him kiss me then. Everyone seems to be apologizing to me lately, I tell him, laughing.

"I have to ask you something," he says. "The widower with the little girl? Are you . . . seeing him?"

"No," I say. "He moved away."

He comes upstairs, and I'm feeling recklessly sentimental, and also under the spell of his handsomeness, which I now remember in full force, and well, it starts to seem okay for us to lie down on the bed together. Then I say we could probably take off our clothes and crawl under the covers. Just this once. He helps me when my head gets stuck in my turtleneck, and he pulls it off and we stand there, practically naked together, shivering, except that when I look more closely at him, I see that he's not naked. He has on all his clothes.

"Take those things off," I say. I remember saying that in the fuzziness.

He smiles at me and gets my robe that's hanging on my door, and then he says that what we really need are glasses of water and hot orange spice tea and also some food, so we go into the kitchen, and he fries us some eggs, and we take the food back and eat it in bed, and then he tells me everything I've needed to hear from him, which mostly is good night and sweet dreams and here are some Advil for your hangover that I know you are going to have in the morning, and yes, I'm staying the night, and I'll be here sleeping right beside you.

"No sex," I say.

"No. No sex," he says.

That's the last thing I remember before I fall asleep.

CHAPTER
THIRTY-FOUR

He's still there in the morning. I turn over and see him smiling at me across the pillow. He reaches over and touches my face so softly.

"You're beautiful," he says.

"Ugh" is the best I can manage.

"No, nothing here is *ugh*," he says. "I am so happy right now being here with you. I was wondering if it's okay with you if I go ahead and start giving you my apologies."

"Really? Seriously? You do know that I have a splitting headache, right?"

He gets out of bed and puts on his clothes. "I'll be right back," he says. "Save my place in the bed."

Sure enough, he's back in a while with coffee, more Advil, and croissants that he says he went out and bought from the shops on Orange Street. In honor of that effort, I manage to get out of bed and take a shower to clear my head.

We sit at my kitchen table, me with my wet-ringletty hair and wearing my bathrobe, and I tell him how ironic it is that the second time *ever* that he spends the night with me, I don't remember more than five minutes of it. "I just hope I wasn't an obnoxious drunk. I hate drinking too much!"

"No. You weren't obnoxious at all. You were rather charming and open and sweet."

"Uh-huh. Sure."

"No, you were. You were a snappy dancer, too."

I groan and put my head in my hands. "Oh God. I do remember being dipped all the way to the floor by your friend, what's-his-name."

"That happened, yes."

"And Judith told me she loved me. Or did I dream that?"

"You both said you loved each other," he says. "And I think you both cried."

"Wow. That was a surprise twist to our little story, wasn't it?"

He's taken his coffee and has gone over to the window, looking out at the daycare yard, which is now bare except for the playground equipment and the tire. The plastic tables and chairs have all been taken home by someone.

"So this daycare—all finished?"

"Yeah. I'm afraid it's gone. I hope it can get revived, but right now I don't see how it's going to happen."

He turns to me. "I think I was too self-absorbed to see how much it meant to you," he says. "That's probably number thirty-five on the list of four hundred things I need to apologize to you for."

"It's all right," I say. "Water under the bridge. It's over. Also, I don't think I even want to hear a bunch of apologies. They'll just make me mad again."

"Well, I do want you to know that I'm more ashamed of myself and also simultaneously more in love with you right now than I ever thought possible."

"Ugh. Please don't say bullshit things about love and feelings," I say.

"I want us to try again. I'm at a turning point in my life right now. And I'm just overwhelmed with all the ways I kept you apart from my life, and I know that I screwed everything up, and I completely would understand if you don't want to see me anymore—but if you can just remember for a moment all the wonderful feelings we had back in New

York and trust me that I know how we can get back to that again, start over, and this time, it can be even better. I love you. I want you in my life more than I ever have wanted anything, and I won't let anything ever get in the way of that again."

He goes on and on like this until I stop him. "Ren," I say. "You're too over the top. Let's go for a walk. This is too much emotion for indoors."

"Okay."

"I'll need sunglasses."

"Let's get them." He goes and finds my purse.

I fumble through and find them.

"May I say more of my list of realizations? While we walk?"

"If you must. But don't make it boring. Or morose."

We walk down the street toward the park. It's cold out, and I shove my hands down into my pockets, but he takes them out and warms them up with his.

"I shouldn't have done any of the things I did, starting with the night I left you in New York when I came to New Haven. If you let me make it up to you, I'll spend the rest of my life putting you first. I promise you that."

"You didn't want me to know your family. You locked me out of everything."

"I did. I know. I was stupid."

"And you were sleeping next to your ex-wife the whole time!"

"I am so sorry, and I will do anything to make this right."

We're walking through the park now, kicking at the leaves under our feet on the path. Here is the spot where last summer I spread out the blanket for Jamie and Alice and me to have a picnic and then saw Ren and his family. I look for Alice's pile of rocks, but everything is covered in leaves. I can almost remember how devastated I was, but it's a feeling that's muffled in cotton somehow. So far away.

Ren says suddenly, "Will you come to New York with me?"

"Will I what?"

"Will you come to New York with me?"

"As what?" I stop walking.

"As *what*?" He laughs. "Well, how about as my fiancée? Or if this is too soon, then as my—I don't know—partner, friend . . . roommate? What do you want to be?"

"Are you crazy? That's what this has been leading to? I can't possibly do that."

"Why not?"

"Because I'm not completely finished with hating you."

"Oh," he says. And then, *"Oh."*

"I saw you once in this park with Judith and the girls—you were right over there, and I was standing *right here*." I can't help it; the hurt is back, and I start to cry. "And you were all looking at Judith like she put up the sun and the moon, and I think it's highly possible she did, in fact—but there you were, loving on her so much, and I just felt like—I just felt at that moment like I was such a fool to have come to New Haven, and it felt like I didn't belong anywhere in the world."

He takes me in his arms. "You belong with me," he says. "Let me take care of you now. Let me pamper you and take you places and spend every day with you, and we'll have a whole life spread out before us in New York, with theater and dinners and people who are interesting."

He kisses me, and I'm leaning against him now, and he's so familiar and gorgeous and he's so sorry, and, heaven help me, I have always been swept away by a sincere apology—from anyone, even in books and movies.

We lean together as we walk back to my apartment, and then we get in bed for real this time, and he makes love to me, and it's the kind of lovemaking that when you're done, all the covers are on the floor, and you can barely catch your breath, and you might just want to sleep for the next fifteen hours because you feel that glorious.

As we lie there he says, "Let's make a life together. Come with me."

"I don't know."

He gets up on one elbow. "Is it the widower dude? Are you still hung up on him?"

I don't say anything.

"You can tell me. I can see where he looked appealing to you—his situation was so sad, and he had that sweet little daughter who obviously adored you. You wanted to save him. I get that."

"No, don't make it sound like a charity case."

"No, not charity. You were in rescue mode. I know all about rescue mode—that's what I was doing too—but what if we both escape rescue mode now and go out and live our brilliant, lovely, luminous lives?"

"I don't know."

"Listen, come with me. We'll have plenty of money. We'll have a great place to live, and we can go places and do things. You couldn't have done that with him, even if he did manage to get over his grief in time to make another life."

"Ren, you don't know him—"

"But I know grief," he says. He puts his hands up. "I wish him well, but you can't save him. No one can. He has to save himself. Also," he says, "I didn't want to tell you this, but I've been talking to Francis X. Flannigan, and he's offered me a spot back in the spring, and don't hate me for this, but I mentioned you, too, and he's open to you coming back as well, as my assistant."

"Are you kidding me? After what Penelope Harrington put me through?"

"Yeah. He seems to think Penelope Harrington was the whole trouble there. He thought you were doing a good job, and that we'd make a good team."

"He certainly didn't interfere to save me before!"

"No. He didn't. He's sorry about that now. But can we move on, do you think? Can you overlook things? Start over with the life you were meant to have?"

"I don't know. Maybe too much time has passed, and we went too far in different directions."

He laughs a low, sexy laugh. "Well, judging from what just went on between us in that bed, *I* certainly don't think we've gone in different directions, do you? I'd say we've still got it for each other. Also, my daughters love you, my ex-wife loves you. Even my friends love you! Come with me and we'll be a family. You'll have the family you've been looking for."

I take a deep breath.

"Let's do it! Let's be bold and dramatic together and throw off all this baggage and unhappiness and go! We can pack up all your stuff and hire a truck driver, and we'll be in our Upper West Side home tomorrow night."

"No," I say. I start to cry. "No, I can't."

CHAPTER
THIRTY-FIVE

And then I do it anyway.

Go figure. It starts to seem possible. He wants to really know me now. He's offering me family. I fall for the look in his eye and the fact that he wrote a play about us, and that his ex and his children now profess to love me.

I fall for family, that old sly seductress.

We pack up in a whirlwind and throw caution to the elements.

The first thing we do as a real, honest-to-god couple in New York is buy a Christmas tree—and in the time-honored way of New Yorkers, we find our tree on a street corner, recently liberated from a box truck. The fragrance of all the New England balsam firs surrounds us, and little, tiny snowflakes land on our eyelashes and on my purple wool coat and Ren's expensive leather one, and I imagine us as two people in a romantic comedy, as Christmas carols play from the tree guy's boom box and people rush past us, talking and laughing, and I can hear the clanging of the Salvation Army guy's bell a storefront away. It's all so beautiful.

I pick out a gigantic tree because I have wanted a big one for my whole life and have never had the space, and as soon as I think of it as gigantic, I'm reminded of the day William made the "bijantic" block tower—and that makes me remember that I left without attending the daycare end-of-an-era party they threw, and it's as though some sharp object just landed near my breastbone.

I couldn't bear going to the party. Saying good-bye.

I'm not sorry I didn't go—I would have been the one crying the hardest, and how ridiculous is that, when I'm not the one strapped for childcare now. I maybe shouldn't have gotten so attached to that daycare and all its chaos. All those personalities! It was probably, as Ren says, always doomed to fail. *Lucky it lasted for as long as it did,* he'd say.

But that's not my problem. I have moved on.

My current problem is simply to stop laughing so hard while Ren and I attempt to drag home the Christmas tree the two blocks to the apartment, dodging other pedestrians, strollers, and dogs, apologizing the whole way, and then we have to somehow shove this humongous piece of the natural world into the elevator. Brice, the doorman, rushes to help us get it inside, and he keeps whistling that this is *some tree.* I tell him we're having a party once we get it all decorated, and he's invited.

When we get in the elevator, Ren says he's found a minister who might agree to marry us. He thinks a big church wedding would be good. What do I think of a winter candlelight service? We could start looking for a dress for me, he says. Possibly something long and frothy with a veil. How do I feel about veils? Long? Short?

I shrug and concentrate on the buttons of the elevator, one, two, three, up to the sixth floor. Lots of girls in my high school got married in long white dresses so lacy and delicate that they looked like they were constructed out of whipped cream. And the bridegrooms lifted the veils from their brides' faces with trembling fingers before the all-important kiss after they were pronounced "man and wife."

I always thought it looked like she was being unwrapped, as if she were simply a package that had just been delivered. That whole image used to make me shiver with delight, but now, not so much.

Later, after we've decorated the tree with the ten boxes of lights and ornaments we bought at Macy's, he turns down the lights in the room and draws me over to the balcony and stands behind me, holding me, while we both look at the glittering city below us. I can feel his breath in my hair and his arms tightening around my waist.

Living here with him still makes me feel like I'm playing house. It's so . . . freaking elegant. All the matching dishes and the glassware sparkling in the breakfront in the dining room! Even waking up each day with him beside me feels like I'm in some kind of theater production, and like I'm the unlikely visitor who still needs to learn where all the light switches are and how to make my presence unobtrusive.

One day I'm looking at the dining room table and marveling that it seats fourteen people when it's expanded to its full size, and I suddenly know what could make me feel at home here. I need my people to come see me. I need a party!

How about a Christmas gathering of our two clans? I say to him. I can't keep the excitement out of my voice. "Let's throw a big party and invite both our families and get all our people together!"

"I was under the impression you didn't *have* much family. Have I missed something?" he says, and his lip curls just a little.

"Well, it's true I don't have a *lot* of people, but I do have my mom, of course, when she's in between cruises. And then Eleanor and Ira would probably come—they'd love to see how settled we are. And some of the daycare families! Oh, and La Starla and her husband, Gary."

"La Starla? Gary? Who might they be? More of your daycare hippies?"

"Actually, La Starla is my psychic, who lives in Brooklyn, and Gary is her husband. They've been like family to me."

"Oh, goodie," he says. "How do I not know that you have a psychic?"

"It was my psychic who knew my skirt was magic, and it was the skirt that led me to you," I say.

He shakes his head, smiling painfully. "Are you always going to come up with new ways to surprise me?"

"Definitely," I say. "I'm the subatomic particle of your bones. That's what subatomic particles do, I believe. Rearrange everything you thought you knew."

"This party," he says. "It sounds like quite a collection, if you ask me. Hippies, psychics, and your mom."

"And your family, too, don't forget."

He makes a squinty face. "I don't believe getting all these people under one roof is quite advisable, my dear."

"But why not?"

"I somehow don't think they all . . . fit together. Like, what would they have to say to each other?"

"But that's the way family gets made," I say. "You mush people all together, and it turns out to be interesting and exciting . . . and sometimes real love and feeling bloom right there in front of you."

"Let's save it for another time," he says. "Could we? It's too soon now. If it's having a party that you're interested in, I'd be more inclined to invite the playwrights over."

Sometimes—and this is one of those times—I have to go onto the balcony and look out at the tall buildings and the lights and take deep breaths so I can remember who I am. So I can remember that he does love me, and that he can't help being who he is, set in his ways and unsure about magic and psychics and such. But this is just what being in a relationship means. Everybody knows this. It takes patience and sacrifice. You feel misunderstood sometimes. You feel alone even when you're with the person who means the most to you.

You just smile, and you go on. It's life. And life has tradeoffs.

CHAPTER THIRTY-SIX

The big task ahead of me, one that I put off each day, is going to Piedmont and sitting down with old Francis X. himself to see officially about getting my job back for the spring semester.

"This is a slam dunk," says Ren. "Just dress nicely and don't talk about the bawdy scenes in Shakespeare, and I think he'll be fine with rehiring you."

I laugh, thinking he must be joking.

"I'm not even kidding," he says. "What *are* you going to wear, by the way?" We go over to my closet and he flips through the hangers, frowning. There's not much there.

"Working at the daycare has weeded out my wardrobe to pretty much jeans and sweatshirts," I say.

"All right, then," he says. "Let's go to Bloomingdale's and get you some outfits. Come on. This'll be fun."

"Can't I just go myself?" I say, but his face falls. He says he really wants to come, too. It'll be so much fun to dress me, he says.

Once there, he steers me right to what I tell him is the Frumpy Matron Department and picks out (and pays for) a navy-blue wool A-line skirt that goes down to my calves and a white angora sweater with a little red plaid scarf to tie around my neck. He's moseying over toward blazers when I stop him.

"No, no, no. I can only barely tolerate the stuffiosity that is this skirt," I tell him. "And I'm definitely not pairing it with a blazer. Franny the X will think I'm there to get a job as the school's legal counsel instead of the drama teacher."

"Franny the X?" he says. He smiles his new smile, which strikes me as being slightly irritated. Like it's more that he's curling his lip at me, the way a dog might do. "Is that what you call him?"

"I'm afraid so."

"Anyway, the important thing is that you look nice. Francis will be impressed that you're Piedmont material now. With all due respect, I think you would do well to dress more like a matron when you're there. You can dress how you want every other moment in your life."

"A matron?" I say. "I'm only thirty-two!"

He sighs. "Just this once, could you follow my advice? Go in and talk nicely to old Francis, and graciously accept whatever terms he has, accept his apologies for how you were treated, and then sign on the dotted line, and we'll become the Yardleys of Piedmont."

"You mean Yardley and Perkins," I say.

"Well, yes. Until we're married."

"Fair warning here: I'm a modern woman, and modern women don't have to take their husbands' names."

He sighs. Put upon. "Whatever you want," he says. "Take it, leave it, hyphenate it, take it out and stomp on it. I just want us to make things official at some point. I want you to belong to me. Get it?"

I trail him out of the store, looking longingly over my shoulder at the flouncy dresses with huge flowers and colors.

⁓

Franny the X is quite talkative on the subject of Ren and me returning to what he laughingly calls "the scene of the crime."

We both laugh at that. I'm being extra bright, I can tell. I have my high-beam eyes on, and I'm wearing makeup and low heels that look very respectful and—yes, I look exactly like a woman who would be welcome at any law firm in the country. I am so excited—thrilled really—to be back, I tell him.

He is equally thrilled. We are thrilled together, F the X and I, and he waxes on and on about how great *Guys and Dolls* was, and he tells me that a few of the students are now considering careers in acting because they loved it so much—but hahaha—"not so sure the *parents* think that's such a great career move," he says. "We aim a little higher than *that* here at Piedmont." He chuckles over that little joke for quite a while. While he chuckles, he makes his fingers into little tents and swivels around and around in his desk chair. His bald head is gleaming from the overhead fluorescent light, which is also making a buzzing sound. He tells me that I was a breath of fresh air at the school, and he did not take it seriously at all that I had a magic skirt! What an idea! That kid saying that—it was just ridiculous.

"But you and Ren are now an official couple, and so we won't be having any . . . of that . . . other stuff," he says, waving his hands. He chuckles. "It was inappropriate, but understandable."

I nod brightly and smile. I'm a daisy in the sun, and Francis X. is putting on quite a show of support and strength. He happily launches into how great the program will be if Ren and I run it again. Of course, being junior faculty, I won't just do drama. I'll be expected to teach English comp and also have lunch duty. Senior faculty, like Ren, don't have to do that.

"Sure," I say. "I love lunch. I try to eat it every day."

"So we're agreed," Fran Man says. "You will teach five classes, and then you'll assist Ren with a spring musical of his choosing—nothing that's going to turn the heads of our board and get us in hot water, heh, heh."

He keeps going on, all about the school's accomplishments, honors, awards. At some point, the daisy in my personality begins to wilt, and I grow tired of all of this.

When it seems he's running down, I clear my throat politely and ask if I might go down to the auditorium. Check things out. Supplies and such. Maybe make some notes.

He blinks a few times. This is out of left field. But then he recovers somewhat and says, "Yes, yes, of course, you'll need to see our setup and how it's changed, and then just stop by the personnel office and sign some papers—your tax forms and whatnot. Make it official that you're coming back next semester."

He walks me to the door. "You know where everything is, so just take yourself along," he says.

School is in session, so I make my way through the empty hallowed halls of Piedmont. I can hear classes going on behind closed doors—there's a man's rumbly voice lecturing in one classroom. I can see him through the frosty pane of glass in the heavy wooden door—and then across the hall, I hear students reciting something in unison. I never thought I'd be back here again. The air smells the way it always did, damp and textbooky. Perhaps a whiff of tweed in the air.

When I get to the auditorium and open the door at the rear, facing the stage, it all comes flooding back to me, along with a big wallop of post-traumatic stress. All I can think of is the night I stood on that stage with the overhead lights shining in my eyes, holding on to my square of the magic skirt, listening to Sky Masterson's out-of-control praise for me, and how crushing it was to be fired the next workday.

And that—I suddenly know—is what I'm here for.

I go up the three steps to the stage, feeling like I'm being somehow led, and then back through the curtain to the left. My footsteps sound loud as I make my way through the backstage area, so I start to walk very softly and slowly. I don't want anyone to stop me. There are ladders and chairs and tables and all kinds of equipment shoved over to the sides. I love backstage areas, the sheer immensity of the space, and also the fact that you never know what you'll find back there. I keep going, filled with suspense now, walking down through the green hallway to the very back, and then down a few stairs into the dressing room. I can hear myself breathing as I walk.

I turn on the switch, flooding the room with dazzling light. The lime-green walls, the worn wooden floor, the little cubicles with mirrors where the actors put on their makeup and have their hair done—all lit up.

The air starts to feel a little funny. Like there are frazzles around the edges of my sight. As if everything isn't quite in focus. I move slowly past the makeup and hair area, careful not to look in the mirror. I think I'd look like a ghost. Or maybe I wouldn't be there at all.

I go to the corner where all the costumes are kept. They're stored in big plastic containers, with generic labels that some industrious stage mom made: RENAISSANCE COSTUMES, WESTERNS, 1920S, DANCE COSTUMES, FORMAL WEAR. And then I see one big bin labeled *Guys and Dolls*.

I open it slowly and touch the fabrics, barely able to breathe. And then I swallow and close my eyes for a second before I start to take out the costumes, one by one: the gangsters' fedoras, the Hot Box Girls' outfits. I take them out slowly and lay them on the ground. Sarah Brown's missionary costume. Adelaide's wedding dress.

The room is so quiet I can hear my heart beating in my ears. Will it be there?

Nothing. I dig through the mishmash of miscellaneous shirts and stockings crammed into the bottom of the container. It's not here. And why would it be? Someone probably just threw it away.

Oh well.

I'm about to replace the lid when I see something blue sticking out from underneath a piece of cardboard at the bottom. A wisp of ribbon.

I push everything aside, barely able to breathe, because there it is! The magic skirt lays crumpled there, wrinkly and soft.

I lift it out quickly and hold it up, appraising it. Is it still okay? Yes, it's intact, except for the bottom ruffle, of course. There are jagged edges from where I cut it up. I put it up to my face, laughing and rubbing it against my cheeks.

It's really as I remember it, just an ordinary skirt, nothing special about it at all. But here it is, mine again.

I think of the night that Jamie suggested we come break in to the school to retrieve it. I wish I could tell him that I have it now. But of course, I have no idea how to reach him anymore. I sit back on my heels and look around this dressing room storage area. And all I can think of is that more than anything in the world, I want to see him.

"Are you still magic?" I say to the skirt. "Don't worry. I'm taking you with me. You don't have to live here in a plastic bin." I place it carefully into my bag and shove it down so nobody will see it, and then I turn off the lights and walk quickly out of the dressing room and back through the backstage area. I know there's an exit door back here leading out into the courtyard. When I find it, I slip outside, closing the door behind me. Thank goodness no one is there. I stand for a minute, blinking in the sunlight, wondering what to do next.

The air seems filled with sparkles. Like the way it feels when you jump up too fast and your head feels light, and you see stars.

I think of La Starla saying to me once, "Everything can change for the better in one instant."

I don't go to the office where there is employment paperwork awaiting me. I don't think I'm going to work here. Junior faculty. Lunch duty.

Instead, I walk quickly to the subway, but then I don't get on the one heading back uptown. Without even thinking, I take the 7 train to Grand Central, and once there, I stand in line and buy a ticket for Metro-North.

Apparently, I am going on a trip.

CHAPTER THIRTY-SEVEN

The train to New Haven is leaving in ten minutes. I walk through the station, listening to Christmas music played by a quartet and reverberating off the ceiling. People are hurrying, threading themselves through the crowd, looking for all the world as though they're going to crash into each other, but somehow they don't. It's magic, is what it is, like it's all been perfectly choreographed.

I find my portal, number 28, and go down into the underground of the train station.

Everything can change in an instant.

I settle into a seat by the window, and the train pulls out of the station, and chugs its way out of the Grand Central tunnel, and then it picks up speed, a metallic bullet flying along the tracks. I look out the window at everything flowing past like a river, all the shopping centers and other train stations and parking lots and highways and traffic lights a blur. I can't stop smiling. People get off and more get on. I think I might be in love with them all. The whole human race with all its foibles and its problems: it hits me how hard people try to make things go right, and how scared they are—*we* are. I beam love over to all of them, tell them that everything is going to be all right, that everything can change for the better in an instant.

In what seems like hardly any time at all, the train pulls into the New Haven station, and I get off.

What next? I hear myself asking inside my head.

A voice comes back: *Just go forward.*

I walk through a corridor that feels like a big metal tube, and then the other passengers and I go up the escalator and are disgorged into the main lobby. I join the flow of humanity out the door into the world, and there are taxicabs all parked in a line, so I go over to one and get in the back seat, and the driver, who's wearing a turban, says, "Where to, miss?"

I give him my old address.

"You got it," he says, and pulls out into the lane in front of the station. He says something into a microphone, but I can't hear what he says because the buzzing is so loud in my ears.

I stick my hand in the bag and feel the fabric of my skirt, just to make sure it's still there.

I need to see the daycare again.

And Jamie. It hits me that I want to see Jamie.

Part of my brain says, *But he lives in West Hartford now . . .* and the other part says, *Shhh, child. Just watch what happens. Look around you. Feel the air.*

It makes no sense.

The cab stops in front of my old building, and I get out, in a daze, and pay the driver. I think of the first time I saw this place, when it had construction-paper flowers taped to the windows, and chairs on the porch, and then the daycare kids spilling out the front door, with Jamie coming outside and down the steps, fighting with the umbrella stroller and looking so harried. Now the windows stare blankly out at the street, and there's no one around. It looks desolate and vacant.

I walk slowly up the sidewalk to the porch. Leaves are piled in the flower bed, which is now filled with dead stalks. The wooden front steps look as though they're being dismantled. The lower step is missing—the one that was always so wobbly—and a brand-new board is propped up against the railing. An electric sander is on the porch, along with a blue thermos. Someone must be working on it.

"Hello?" I say, but no one answers, so I go around the side to the gate.

That's when the world suddenly tilts sideways, like it's slipped off its axis for a moment.

Jamie and Alice are there in the daycare yard.

Jamie and Alice.

It's astonishing. They don't see me. She's climbing on top of the tire, and he's keeping her from falling. His back is to me, and he's telling her to be careful and she's laughing at him and telling him he worries too much and that she's safe.

I can't think. Everything feels fuzzy, like it's going in slow motion.

I feel La Starla saying, *"Child, wake up. Wake up! This is your moment. This is where it all happens."*

I notice with some surprise that he's not dressed in his Yale clothes. He's wearing a black sweatshirt and a watch cap and jeans and work boots. His dark hair pokes out a bit from underneath the cap. I love that hair, a bit longer now than the last time I saw him. And I love his shoulders. His hands against the tire, those fingers.

Alice looks up and sees me and her eyes widen. She yells, "MIMI MOMMY! YOU CAME BACK!"

He turns and sees me, and our eyes lock onto each other's, and I walk toward him, biting my lip and smiling. Alice runs and tackles me, and I lean down and pick her up and she's laughing and ruffling my hair and saying, "I *knew* you would come! I told Daddy you were coming back, and he said you don't live here anymore, and I said I knew that, but you would still come."

"I did, I came back," I say, out of breath. Her eyes are bright, shining like little bing cherries. "I came back."

He comes over to us. Alice is kissing me on both cheeks over and over again and squealing.

"Okay, okay," he says and takes her gently out of my arms and sets her on the ground. "Alice, you're so big now. You're probably crushing Mimi." She howls in protest, but he puts his arm around her and says to me, "What in the world—? How? Why are you here?"

He is not exactly smiling. I'm taken aback at how guarded his eyes are. Oh yes, of course. We had been mad at each other the last time we were together, but I want to tell him that it's all okay now, that I'm pretty certain that some spirit guides have signed off on this.

"I know," I say. "It's crazy." I give him my widest, brightest smile. I am so happy to see him, and soon he'll be happy to see me, too. He *has* to be. "It's amazing that we're *both* here. Because don't you actually live in West Hartford?"

"Not anymore I don't. But you—I heard you moved to New York. Why are you here?"

"I don't know," I say slowly. "I think I must have come to find you."

"Right," he says. "You came from New York, to find *me*? For *what*?"

"I mean, I didn't know you would be *here*, but *something* made me get on the train, and then I got in a cab and came here. I know that sounds ridiculous, but that's what happened. I wanted to tell you that I got the skirt back." I can't stop smiling at him. "Isn't that amazing? I got it back!"

Any second now, he'll stop giving me suspicious looks, and he'll realize that we're meant to be together. "This is too weird," he says.

But not yet, apparently. What did I expect?

"It is weird," I say happily. "It's both weird and amazing that I would get the skirt and then that I'd find you here. Remember when we were joking about breaking in to the school and getting it?"

"Yeah." He looks away. "I remember."

"Well, I got it."

Alice stands there, looking back and forth at us.

He takes off the cap and runs his fingers through his lovely scribble of messed-up hair. He's shaking his head.

"Daddy left his school!" Alice says. "We live here now! We're back!"

"Alice," he says.

"Wait. Really? You . . . left school?"

He nods, looking annoyed.

Alice is jumping from one foot to the other. "Yep! He didn't like it anymore, and anyway we missed it here, and so then he told Grandpa and Grandma that he wanted to quit and that he was going to build furniture in New Haven, and so here we are! And I go to a nursery school, but they don't have a tire!"

I gaze at him.

"It's been an eventful few weeks," he says slowly.

"When did you—"

He looks down. "I quit the program at the end of November. It wasn't working. So a few weeks ago I started my own furniture business. And I'm doing *this*"—he points to the building—"just to help out the landlord and make ends meet while I get established."

"Is this a *new* landlord? Because the building got sold, right?"

"The sale fell through, and so it's still John. He's taking it off the market."

"And you're back in your old place?"

"No!" says Alice. "We live where Daddy works! And we have a teeny-tiny stove and a coffeepot and just our beds."

"Alice, Mimi doesn't need to hear about all of this."

"Yes, I do," I say. "I want to hear all of it. I know the hot-plate life quite well."

He looks at me curiously, and my heart leaps up like the idiot it is. It can't help itself. There's a glimmer there beneath his distrust. He's melting. "So what's really going on with you?" he says. "You're certainly looking like you've got the New York clothing scene down pat. Are you back teaching at the school? And back with what's-his-name?"

I remember then that I look like someone who might be showing up to serve legal papers. "Oh God. I know I look ridiculous in this getup. It's crazy, looking like this. In fact, this whole day is kind of unbelievable. I went to Piedmont for an official interview, you know, to see about getting my job back, but then, while I was there, I went to the drama department and found the magic skirt in one of the costume bins, and then—well, this may sound crazy, but it's the sanest thing I've ever done in my life. I just walked out of the building, and I got on the train, and now I've made up my mind that I'm not going back. I'm here now." I want to add, *And I'm yours*, but I'm not sure if he's ready to hear that part yet.

"So . . . can we see this magic skirt?" he says. Alice jumps up and down.

I pull it out of my bag and hold it up, in all its limp, blue, raggedy glory, and they both look at me like I might not be quite in my right mind to be calling this magic. Even I can see it is nothing but a drab, unremarkable piece of clothing.

"It's magic," I say. "But subtle."

"It passes itself off as very . . . ordinary," he says solemnly. "No offense to ordinary."

"Can I touch it?" says Alice.

"Of course you can."

"It looks a little bit ripped at the bottom." She reaches over and touches it. "But it feels regular."

"It does feel regular," I say. "But it's not."

"Huh," says Jamie. "So now that I've seen it, I guess you're going back to New York?" He's put up the guardrails again. I can hear them clanking into place.

"Well." I take a deep breath. "You see, actually I'm not. And I have a question for you, but I'm a little scared to ask it."

He shrugs. "Is it about the skirt?"

"No, but I think it wants me to ask it." I swallow hard. His eyes are mesmerizing, like a little chip of the sky. "I want to know if you think I could ever be the ocean, too. Like if maybe there's more than one ocean in one lifetime, you know? You don't have to answer now, but I was thinking that maybe she was the Atlantic, and I could be the Pacific. Someday. Maybe."

He doesn't answer for a moment because he's looking down at the ground. I think it's possible that I won't be able to breathe normally ever again after he turns me down.

But then he looks up at me, and his eyes are luminous. "Please don't say this if you don't mean it," he says softly. "I can't—there's not that much left of me at the moment for this sort of thing."

"I do mean it. I want to be the ocean."

Alice says, "What are you *talking* about?"

But neither of us look at her. I am looking into his eyes, where I see everything he feels, and he feels more than I could have hoped for. He glances at Alice and then he takes me into his arms and holds me so close to him that I can hear his heart hammering in his chest. His voice is husky. "I don't see you so much as the Pacific Ocean because you're not all that *pacific*, you know? But you already *are* the ocean. You *know* that. That's why you're here, isn't it?"

"I'm here because I've missed you, and I can't stay away. I have to be near to where you are. And also I came to tell you that I love you," I say, which is very brave of me because he didn't say it first, and all my life I've been waiting for a man to say it first. All this guy ever said was that he was terrified that he *might* love me, and I think he may have even rescinded that at some point in our history. Apparently I'm throwing caution out the window, or to the wind, or wherever it is that people throw caution. I don't seem to have any more boundaries, which might just be the fault of the magic skirt.

It may also be what the magic skirt is good for.

He's not saying anything, but he hasn't let go of me either.

I whisper to him, "And now I also see that what I wanted to come and tell you is that I figured out that you're the one that the psychic meant me to have, and also, just incidentally, if you don't say pretty soon that you love me back, I'm going to fall down on the ground—"

"Do oceans fall on the ground?" he says, and he pulls me back to him, groaning. "Oh my God, Mimi, I love you, too, you know I love you," he says. "You *are* the ocean *and* the seagulls. Also, the sky. And probably the kelp and all the grains of sand, too. I don't know what in the hell is going on with the fabric of the universe, that suddenly you appear right here today when I wasn't even scheduled to be here, and I was pretty sure you weren't coming back ever, but whatever. Is it that skirt? Who knows?"

Alice has lost her mind, dancing around us. "What is going on? What are you both *talking* about?" she says over and over again.

We stop holding each other for a moment and pull her into our hug, which is just where she belongs.

"No more Yale? No more . . . capstone?" I say to him.

"*Shhh.* Don't say that word. Let's get some dinner, shall we, and I'll tell you the whole story, and then when the little magpie here goes to sleep, we can figure things out."

"'Figure things out.' I like the sound of that," I say, even though I think they've already been figured out in some larger perspective.

"Are you staying for a sleepover, Mimi Mommy?"

He's laughing. "Yes, are you staying? I mean, will you? Can you?"

"I'm staying," I say. "I have a phone call to make, of course, and it would be great if we could get me a toothbrush from somewhere. And tomorrow I think I'll put on the magic skirt and call the landlord and see about restarting the daycare."

He links his arm in mine and holds Alice's hand, and we walk to Willow Street to their little loft apartment, where I already know all the good things that are going to happen.

Jamie is grinning at me. "The daycare, huh? How did I know that was coming? Tell the truth. How long have you known you were going to restart it?"

"I'm not really sure. What time is it now?"

CHAPTER THIRTY-EIGHT

When people ask me in the years to come, "How did you meet your husband?" I'll have to tell them about the sofa I threw down the stairwell and a little girl in a tiara who, I think, knew right away that I belonged to them both. I'll mention La Starla and the spirit guides who thought that miracles come about when there is great love. I'll talk about how necessary it is to believe in the power of coincidences. And serendipity.

And of course I'll bring up Kmart.

And maybe also the undiscovered properties of McDonald's secret sauce as a possible gateway to love.

If they're open to it, I'll mention the fact that sometimes objects hold magic, even though we may never understand how a skirt in a thrift shop can call to a person. I'm not going to say that everything happens for a reason, but I will say that there is plenty that we don't understand about life.

The truth, as told by La Starla, is that the path you're on may simply be a little detour that leads you to the *real* path you're supposed to be on, where all your happiness is hanging out, waiting for you.

And, as La Starla says, if you're expecting love to look like it was designed by Hollywood, while meanwhile you're pretzeling yourself into meeting somebody else's expectations, good luck to you. You might just miss what your heart truly yearns for.

And what is it that my heart truly yearned for?

Chaos, upheaval, little children telling me poop jokes, and lying on a mattress surrounded by a bunch of toddlers and their peanut butter breath and their fat little hands holding on to mine, looking seriously into my eyes while serving me a bowl of rocks for lunch.

And Jamie and Alice. Always Jamie and Alice.

᷒

I suppose I should tell you the rest of what happened, since you weren't there.

I went to a phone booth at the gas station and called Ren that same night and told him I couldn't come back to New York after all. I said I couldn't work at Piedmont, I said I couldn't have dinner parties with play-wrights, I couldn't even sleep in a bed with 1,000-thread-count sheets, or eat at a table in my own house that could seat fourteen people with all the plates matching. I couldn't get married in a church wedding with candles. Something rebels in me when faced with that sort of thing, I said.

I told him that I love thrift shops and old paintings and pole lamps and rugs that I have to lug home through the streets. Everything he kind of hates, although I didn't say that part because he would just try to deny it.

I also said he never got over Judith, and that I didn't blame him, but that when we were together, there was a kind of bone-deep lone-liness that permeated my soul and made me ache in a way I couldn't bear. When he snapped at me, "I don't need a postmortem on this," I said that felt exactly like part of the problem. There was never any real talking, never any real depth to us. I wanted to tell him what I learned about first love being the kiddie pool, and how great it felt that I had just climbed out of it and taken the plunge into the ocean.

"We didn't hit the heights you required," he said. "Is that what you're telling me?"

"I'm telling you that my heart was crying out for more," I said. "And I have to go find what it wants. But I also want to say thank you for loving me. And that we're both better off apart." And then I replaced the receiver very quietly. I think he might have already hung up.

I waited a respectful thirty minutes for that relationship to wheel itself out of the picture, for it to say good-bye and sail away. And then I went up to the loft where Jamie was waiting for me in the tiny single bed he had bought when he came back to New Haven.

And there I released all of my doubts and inhibitions and fears, and I loved him and loved him and loved him until the sun came up, which is when Alice came bounding out from the other room and leaped on us in bed.

"Welcome," he said, "to life with Alice."

∽

Later that day, I called up John, the landlord, and very calmly and sanely, we arranged for the daycare to move back into the building and pay rent again. He said we might as well be there since there was a *freaking tire* in the yard that nobody ever removed.

Since then, I have recruited eight families, including Emily and Michael and Davy, Joyous and Lily, Suki and William. The families I met at the park are all members now. And I'm still the octopus.

Alice and Jamie and I fixed up and moved into my former apartment upstairs, and we furnished it from the junk shops once again—some of the same stuff that hadn't been sold to anyone else and was just waiting for me to come back, along with some shelves and dressers that Jamie has made for us.

And I'm saving the best for last.

∽

On a velvety evening the following summer, Jamie and I got married in the daycare backyard. At Alice's insistence, we had four wedding cakes (one of them a Carvel sheet cake with all three of our names on it—that was Jamie's idea), a mariachi band composed of daycare children, a parade of everyone through the tire, and vows that we wrote ourselves and which mentioned oceans and seagulls and grief and new life and the joys of being weird.

All the daycare families came, and so did Eleanor and Ira and Gary and my mother, who managed to fly in from a Mediterranean cruise with husband number eight, I think. (No, I'm kidding; she said he was number six, and maybe the last one.) Jamie's in-laws came—Otto and Denise and Mandy, proving that they still loved him even though he wouldn't ever live with them again.

La Starla was the officiant, and she asked us all to concentrate on magic and the universe and the incredible miracles that wait for us around every corner if we just have the sense to look for them and pay attention. And, lest things get too earnest, she said it was entirely appropriate that this wedding take place right between a teeter-totter and a sliding board.

Jamie read me his vows, which mentioned furniture building and how it was okay to sand the edges of furniture but *never* okay to sand the edges of your personality. Trust me. It was very moving. He said the thing about the oceans and the kelp, which nobody understood but me, I'm sure.

I wore a real wedding dress, one that I found at the junk shop—I mean *antique* shop—with a piece of the magic skirt sewed right into the waist. Alice wore a piece of it, too.

I thought we were done with all sadness and were just sliding along toward happiness while La Starla was pointing out that there is no joy that can even come close to being your weird, strange self and having people love you for just who you are, but then a loud sob erupted from the knot of wedding guests standing behind us.

It was Denise, Jamie's mother-in-law, crumpling into a little ball of sadness.

"Please pause," I said to La Starla.

"Okay," she said. She stood and closed her eyes, like she was communing with the spirit guides.

I went over to Denise, not having the slightest idea what I could say to make this better for her, but then I took her hands in mine, because I understood something I didn't know before—how grief and love can show up in the same moment and be quite comfortable together. I kissed her on both cheeks and then I told her that I promised to love her and Otto if she'd let me, and that I would visit them and help Jamie keep Lauren's memory alive—both for him and for Alice.

"I'm like a pro at being people's second family. It may be my superpower," I whispered. "You'll see."

She squeezed my hand and wiped her eyes, and then I went back to the ceremony, and I said my vows, describing how I fell immediately in love with this man who not only knew how to loosen up a couch from a stairwell but also how to be a father to a heartbroken little girl while his own heart was breaking . . . and also that he was a man who somehow knew how to unearth the real me, which was not easy since I was a woman who spent all of her time trying to be what everyone else wanted her to be.

"I promise to love you and your beautiful little Alice forever and ever," I said.

And that's when I heard: "Wait! Wait *just* a minute! This is not how it was s'posed to be! I object!"

I'd know that voice anywhere. It was Judith. I looked around and saw her standing by the gate, leaning on her cane, with a mortified Parker standing next to her and trying to quiet her.

"How could you *do* this, Weezy?" she yelled. "This is the wrong man!"

I squeezed Jamie's hand. La Starla gave me a look and said, "Okay, sunshine. Shall we take this on, too?"

"Maybe for just one moment," I said. "Another little time-out."

"Are we going to let everybody here make a comment on our marriage? Is that what's happening?" Jamie whispered.

"I think this is the last one," I told him. "Let's definitely think about drawing the line after this one."

"This wedding is breaking my heart!" Judith yelled, and I saw Parker trying to hustle her into exiting back through the gate. But nope. "Stop pushing me, Parker! Weezy, you *know* you were supposed to marry my husband! And now here you are, getting married to the wrong man!"

"I have to go speak to her," I whispered to La Starla. "I'll be right back."

"Hey, it's your wedding," she said. "We can turn it into a committee meeting if you want. Take a vote on whether we should move forward, or if you have to consider other possible grooms." She looked at Jamie. "Don't worry. She's not going to do that. You're her life."

I turned around and walked over to Judith, talking to her as I went. "I know, Judith. You wanted that for him," I said, "but that's not the way it worked out. We broke up. This man here is my husband. He's Jamie. He's the man I love, and it's going to be okay. Ren is fine."

"But you were the optimism," she said. "My favorite optimism."

"Thank you. Let me just finish getting married to this wonderful man here, and then maybe you and I could take a walk, and I'll explain some things to you," I said. "You'll feel better when you hear the story."

"All right," she said.

I went back and took Jamie by the hand. He squeezed mine and smiled into my eyes. "I guess I should have expected marrying you was going to be complicated."

La Starla looked out over the crowd and said, "Whew. I don't believe I'm going to do the part of the ceremony where I ask if anyone has any objection, if you all don't mind."

And everyone laughed.

We were pronounced husband and wife at last—and we pulled Alice up between us and La Starla amended it to "husband and wife and child."

Later, after two of the cakes had been devoured, I took Judith by the hand, and we went for a walk to the park. (I actually have to say that I like the kind of wedding where you can take a break from all that marriage-ing and go off and tend to some unfinished business.) Standing there in the park, near where I'd seen her with Ren and the girls the year before, I told her the truth I know for sure—that Ren will always belong to her in some deep, fundamental way, and that he never belonged to me for even one second. I also said that what he and I had was nothing in comparison to the fireworks display that would always be her marriage to him.

She said, "But we yelled all the time!"

"Yes," I said. "And we never yelled at all. When he looks at you, Judith, or when he even talks about you, it's like Roman candles are going off in his brain. He doesn't even know they're there, but everyone else can see it."

I realized I learned this from watching Maya and Jerome that night at the daycare meeting. Love doesn't always have to look like two hearts melting together as one.

"But I loathe him so much," she said. I'm going to pretend she said "love." That's what she meant.

∾

This is the moment that stays with me forever, that plays again and again in my head.

After the sun goes down, and people are playing guitars and we're all watching the fireflies in the yard, Eleanor tells me that this wedding is more *me* than anything she's ever seen in her whole life. She always knew that I wasn't going to get married in any kind of traditional way.

"I feel like I came to a wedding, and it broke out into a therapy session and then a daycare," she says. "All in all, it took about an hour and a half to have a fifteen-minute wedding."

"It's kinda the way I like it," I say.

My mother tells me that when she has her next wedding, she's going to consider the teeter-totter/sliding board location herself. And then she winks. "I'm very proud of you. You took a long time to come around, but you made it, kid. He's lovely."

Later, Jamie and I hold hands and walk around. We keep having to stop and kiss each other because we haven't gotten in as much kissing as we need.

"What do you think? Should we tell them?" he asks me at one point. We're looking out at the daycare yard, where people are resting on blankets, or sitting in the tire, singing about Little Bunny Foo Foo and cuddling their kids, just like at the daycare workday a whole year ago.

"Let's wait," I say. "They've had enough of us today. We're really hogging all the attention."

But just then, seized by a stray piece of energy now let loose in the world, Alice climbs up on top of the slide and yells out as loud as she can: "HEY, EVERYBODY, I'M NOT S'POSED TO SAY THIS YET, BUT GUESS WHAT WE'RE GOING TO HAVE IN THE WINTER!"

"Hmm, is it a baby?" someone calls out.

She looks at Jamie and makes a shocked face. "I didn't tell them! Daddy, I did *not* tell them!"

ACKNOWLEDGMENTS

I'm convinced that there is no way to be a writer without having writer friends to talk to. I have noticed that a lot—a whole lot—of writing a book requires one to stay at home, wearing mismatched pajamas, eating cornflakes out of the box, and muttering under one's breath. Obviously if you find yourself behaving this way, you need to occasionally discuss these symptoms with others who are possibly doing the same thing.

As weird as daytime is, it's in the middle of the night that a book conducts its real mayhem. Characters you thought you'd lovingly tucked away to bed hours ago awaken you at three in the morning, shouting that you must get up and write. (And no, they say, this can't wait until daylight! Get up. Now. We're rewriting the whole thing!)

I'm so grateful for friends who also experience this. Together, we have decided that there is nothing weird about us at all. Nothing to see here, folks.

I owe unending gratitude to Beth Levine, bless her heart, for being a person who is always willing to answer the phone when I'm in a state of complete paralysis because of some plot point that won't be resolved. She has been known to discuss plot points for hours. Best of all, she's funny and lets me steal some of her best lines.

I also owe deep thanks to Kerry Schafer, who shares my view that we are lucky to be writers together and that there is magic to be found just from sitting down alone in a room and listening to the voices that consent to tell us stories.

There is no thanks big enough for the Ladies in Writing, my writing workshop that has met for several years to offer suggestions, critiques, muffins, tea, and chocolate, including Grace Pauls, Mary Ann Emswiler, Thea Guidone, Nancy Antle, Kim Steffen, Sharon Wise, Marcia Winter, Robin Favello, and Marji Lipshez Shapiro. Thank you so much for all your kindness and willingness to read and give me feedback!

I am constantly inspired by my dearest author friends, including Alice Mattison, Leslie Connor, Marilyn Simon Rothstein, Rochelle Weinstein, Annabel Monaghan, Heather Webb, Kristan Higgins, and Marie Bostwick.

This particular book couldn't exist if I hadn't been a member of a daycare cooperative back when I was a new mom suddenly transplanted to New Haven, Connecticut. The daycare in this book is loosely (very loosely—please don't yell at me!) based on the wonderful, chaotic, delightful, terrifying, and always fascinating days I spent playing with other people's toddlers on Monday afternoons and at evening meetings where we discussed the philosophy of childcare and whether macaroni with orange powder was really food. For several years back there in the '80s, with the women's movement gaining steam, it seemed we were blazing a trail, radically requiring that both men and women do four-hour turns each week. This daycare was where I learned everything I know about how to be a parent. I am still friends with so many of the other parents I met there—people I will love forever. Thank you for all the laughter and love.

My life would be incomplete without my three children who were my guinea pigs in learning—Benjamin, Allison, and Stephanie. Thank you for being exactly who you are! I am so proud of you. And thank you to my husband, Jim, who makes everything possible!

No book would be possible without the talented professionals who aided me every step of the way. My editors at Lake Union, Alicia Clancy and Melissa Valentine, offered wisdom and encouragement and kind, helpful critiques along the way. Jodi Warshaw was the developmental editor extraordinaire who was willing to talk over plot points endlessly! And my agent, Nancy Yost, always believes in me and points me in the right direction. Thank you!

And thank you to the art department that created the cover and the marketing department that figures out how to get this book in the hands of the readers. And thank you to Danielle Martin and the copyeditors and designers and production people who are brilliant at their jobs.

Lastly, I want to thank all the readers over the years who have written me cards and letters, left reviews, and bought my books. You are the reason I love this work—work that I have wanted to do since I was six years old and wrote my first story and sold it to the neighbors so I could buy a Popsicle. You have made my dream career come true and kept me in frozen desserts at the same time.

Thank you, every one of you!

ABOUT THE AUTHOR

Photo © 2018 Dan Mims

Maddie Dawson is the bestselling author of ten novels, including *Snap Out of It*, *The Magic of Found Objects*, *A Happy Catastrophe*, *Matchmaking for Beginners*, *The Survivor's Guide to Family Happiness*, *The Opposite of Maybe*, *The Stuff That Never Happened*, *Kissing Games of the World*, and *A Piece of Normal*. She grew up in the South, born into a family of outrageous storytellers. Her various careers as a substitute English teacher, department-store clerk, medical-records typist, waitress, cat sitter, wedding invitation–company receptionist, nanny, daycare worker, electrocardiogram technician, and Taco Bell taco maker were made bearable by thinking up stories as she worked. Today Maddie lives in Guilford, Connecticut, with her husband. For more information visit maddiedawson.com.